NEVER TRUST THE BOSS

AN ENEMIES TO LOVERS ROMANCE

THE ROSI BROTHERS
BOOK ONE

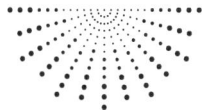

ARIA BLISS

Never Trust the Boss is a work of fiction. Names, places, characters, and incidents are the product of the author's imagination and are used fictitiously. Any resemblance to actual persons, living or dead, events, or locales is entirely coincidental. Contains adult situations and not intended for young audiences.

Copyright © 2023 by Aria Bliss
Written by Aria Bliss
www.ariabliss.com
aria@ariabliss.com

All rights reserved.
No part of this publication may be reproduced, distributed or transmitted in any form or by any means, including photocopying, recording, or any other electronic or mechanical methods, without prior written permission of the publisher, except by a reviewer who may quote brief passages in a review.

Published in the United States by Misadventure Press, Gainesville, FL.
www.misadventurepress.com
info@misadventurepress.com

Book Layout, formatting, typesetting and cover design by
Angelique's Designs, a Misadventure Press Author Service
https://misadventurepress.com/author-services/

Limits of Liability and Disclaimer Warranty
The author shall not be liable for your misuse of this material. This book is strictly for entertainment purposes.

FIRST EDITION
ISBN (Original paperback): 978-1-948169-88-2
ISBN (Special Edition paperback): 978-1-948169-89-9
ISBN (eBook): 978-1-948169-87-5
Printed in the United States of America

BOOKS BY ARIA BLISS

The Mutter Brothers
Truck You: A Hate to Love Small Town Romance
Truck Me: A Grumpy-Sunshine Small Town Romance
Truck Off: An Enemies to Lovers, Mistaken Identity Small Town Romance

The Rosi Brothers
Never Trust the Boss: An Enemies to Lovers Romance

A Drunk Love Contemporary Romance
Not for Me: A Fake Dating Romance
Let Me Stay: A Friends to Lovers, Best Friend's Sister Romance
Lead Me Here: A Grumpy-Sunshine Romance
Aside From Me: A Roommate to Lovers Romance
Make Me Go: An Age Gap Romance

Hearts of Watercress Falls
Healing Hearts: A Second Chance at Love Small Town Romance
Trusting Hearts: A Single Dad Small Town Romance
Falling Hearts: A Secret Marriage Small Town Romance
Laughing Hearts: A Best Friend's Sister Small Town Romance
Forgiving Hearts: A Hate to Love Small Town Romance

Standalone
Good Wine & Bad Decisions: A Sexy Romance

An After-Hours Affair
In Charge: Book 1
One Drink: Book 2

You're Mine: Book 3

Charm Me: Book 4

Stuck Together: Book 5 (A Holiday Romance)

CHAPTER ONE

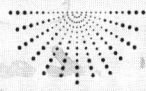

ATTICUS

> **ATTICUS**
> Fuck keeping my enemies close. This is war.

> **ADONIS**
> Let me know if you need help hiding a body.

> **ATTICUS**
> Good to know you have my back.

> **ADONIS**
> Anything for my big brother.

Indigo Simons chose a side, and it wasn't mine. For that, she has to pay.

I don't care if my behavior is childish or that my actions might be a tad bit inappropriate. She should have thought about that before she decided doing her fucking job was beneath her.

I guess that's what happens when the boss hires his daughter to be my assistant and doesn't give me a choice in the matter.

I need an assistant who's competent and capable. One who knows how to use the meeting scheduler in Outlook, can take good notes, and has no problem working a copy machine. Hell, if Indie would at least write my appointments in a day planner, I'd be semi-pleased. But even that seems to be too much effort for her to put into her job.

I suspect she *can* do it. She just doesn't *want* to.

Her apathy toward her job and her dad's company is infuriating. I don't understand why she's even here.

The fact that she hates me doesn't help either.

She didn't even give me a chance. From day one, she's treated me with contempt and has blatantly disregarded all my attempts to create a pleasant work environment between us. It's as if she's out to ruin my career, and I don't know why.

I've put up with it for far too long. I'm done playing nice.

Yesterday's debacle was the last straw. I had an important meeting to which the client arrived three hours early. When I asked Indie about the misunderstanding, she simply smiled and said *oops*.

Fucking oops.

She deliberately told the client the wrong time. Which meant I wasn't prepared. I was still in the copy room, making my own damn copies of the report, because Indie can't be bothered to figure out how to use the damn machine.

Her sabotage made me look unprepared and disorganized, not only to the client but in front of my boss—her father, and the CEO and owner of SimTech Development. I'm probably the most organized person in this entire fucking building.

So, yeah. It's war.

She may be the boss's daughter and the heiress to his multimillion-dollar company, but that doesn't mean I have to accept her sabotage.

It's a little before seven in the morning when I stroll into my office building and hit the call button for an elevator. SimTech shares a building with several other businesses in which we occupy the top three floors, forty-two through forty-four. My office is on the forty-third floor, but I'm working my ass off to earn one of the executive offices on forty-four.

Which is why it would help if my assistant gave a shit about her job.

Most of the employees on my floor don't arrive until closer to nine—Indie included—but I like to get an early start. More like I *need* to get an early start.

It typically takes me about an hour to figure out what meetings have or have not been scheduled. Then I have to sift through all the messages that are piled in a haphazard mess on the corner of Indie's desk. She never gives them to me. I always have to hunt them down and sort through them myself. I should be grateful she knows how to answer the phone and write the messages down. That's something, I guess.

The elevator dings and the doors slide open. The floor is still dark and warm. It isn't until I step into the hallway that the sensors pick up on my movement and the overhead lights flicker on. In another twenty minutes or so, the AC unit will kick in and cool the air. It's always hot first thing in the morning during the summer months.

I make my way down the long outer hallway that leads to my office. I've worked my ass off since graduating with my software engineering degree, and I've done very well for myself, considering I'm only twenty-eight.

Turns out I'm damn good at writing code. I've developed some innovative software that helps financial planners evaluate multiple investment opportunities faster and more holistically. It's what got me my first position with SimTech. Since then, I've developed three more programs that have made the company a lot of money. The success of my software and code writing skills got me to my current level.

I'm one of two senior managers on this floor. I have a corner office on one side of the building with amazing views of Central Park. My competition, Stefon James, occupies the other one.

And yes, he is definitely competition, *not* my coworker. He made that quite clear the first day I met him. We have different skill sets. Where I'm a software engineer, he's in information technology with a specialization in cybersecurity. It's his job to protect the shit I create.

But we're both contenders for a promotion upstairs to the C-suite.

I should be happy with where I'm at. I love my job. I make great money, and I'm well respected. But I want executive-level management. I want one of the offices on the forty-fourth floor that's two times larger than my current office. I want the massive pay raise that comes from being upstairs. It means my family will never have to worry about money again, and my parents can finally retire.

I've had a few setbacks, but with the addition of the forecasting tool I'm working on, I should be a shoo-in for the promotion. That is *if* I could hire an assistant that would help reduce some of my workload rather than create more. Then I'd be set.

I round the corner and walk up to Indie's desk and stuff the stack of messages into my messenger bag. To the right of her desk is a small waiting area, and to the left is a large conference room. The door to my office is directly behind her desk. I can't get in or out without seeing her when she's working.

It's quite the dilemma, considering we can't seem to get along.

I smile when I see her name, Indigo Simons, on the nameplate on the edge of her desk. I pick it up and slide her name out of the holder and dig the *special* nameplates I had made for her out of my bag. Is today a *#1 Daughter* day or a *Princess Simons* day? I look between the two options and smile when I settle on one.

Definitely *Princess Simons*. I've used the *#1 Daughter* nameplate a lot already and *Princess Simons* is new. She'll hate it, and I suspect she has a special place in hell reserved for anyone who calls her that.

I can't hold back a laugh as I slide the replacement nameplate in the holder and put it back on her desk.

"Trying to piss off your assistant again, boss?" I turn to find Leon, my right-hand man, walking up behind me.

I give him a big smile and nod. "You're in early."

He shrugs. "Wanted to get an early start on the next round of testing. It's gonna take at least five hours for the first assessment to run. I'd like to get through two rounds before I head home tonight."

"You don't have to do that. We have a few weeks before we need to finalize everything."

"Yeah, I know. But once this phase is done, we're in the clear."

I squeeze his shoulder because he's not wrong. If this new code comes together like we think it will, both of our careers are set.

"Thanks. I appreciate all your hard work on this. It's nice to know some of my employees take their job seriously."

This drags a sly grin out of Leon. He nods toward the nameplate. "*Princess Simons*. Nice one. I think I like that better than *#1 Daughter*."

"It'll piss her off, and that's all I'm really angling for."

Indie hates being called *#1 Daughter*, but calling her princess is the fastest way to make her face turn red with anger. Her dad calls her Princess Indigo, and she can't stand it.

About once a week, the first thing I do after grabbing my messages is change her nameplate. On those days, I take great satisfaction in the little frustrated growl she lets out when she sees it. She pulls it from the holder, tosses it into my office without a word, and replaces it with another nameplate with her name on it. Then she sits at her desk as if nothing happened.

We've been at it for weeks.

But I'm about to step up my game. If today goes as planned, I'm going to push *Princess Simons* over the edge.

With any luck, she'll finally quit.

Then I can hire an assistant that will do her damn job.

Two hours later, Indie marches into my office and slams the nameplate on my desk. "Must you?"

"I must." I don't bother looking up. I'm in the middle of tweaking code, and I keep my eyes trained on my computer screen as if I'm too busy to be bothered by her.

From the corner of my eye, I can see she's standing in front of my desk with her hands on her hips.

Several moments pass with her staring at me and me ignoring

her. We're in the middle of our version of a standoff. One of these days she's going to learn she can't win with me.

I pause from my work just long enough to fetch a piece of chocolate from the glass canister on my desk. My one and only guilty pleasure.

"Give me *my* nameplate back." She demands.

"No."

I keep typing.

She huffs.

A few more seconds of silence pass before she speaks again.

"Mr. Rosi." I quirk a brow. That's new. She never calls me Mr. Rosi. She rarely calls me anything other than an asshole. "May I please have my nameplate back?" she asks in a rather sickly-sweet voice that gets me to look at her. She gives me the fakest smile I've ever seen.

If I thought for one second that she was the least bit sincere, then I might give in to her.

But she's not.

Indie has made it her life's mission to ruin my career. Therefore, it's my mission to make her life hell.

"And why should I do that?" My eyes roam over her body against my will. It's like they're no longer under my control and have to know what she's wearing today.

Indie may be a pain in my ass, but she's a hot pain in the ass. Petite, with curves in all the right places. She's five-three to my six-two. Even with heels on, the top of her head barely reaches my chin.

Today she's wearing a pale-yellow blouse with a black pencil skirt that falls just past her knees. It cinches in at her waist, accentuating her curvy hips and round ass. An ass I'd love to bite.

The top three buttons of her blouse are undone, showing off her cleavage. Cleavage that I'd also like to bite and lick and suck on until she screams my name.

On one too many occasions, I've imagined what her small, soft frame would feel like pressed against my large, hard frame. Or how her plump lips would taste as I devoured them with mine. But what I really want to know is what she smells like when she comes. Would her usual sweet bakery scent be overpowered by her release? Or does her release smell just as fucking good?

Would she tremble under my touch as my tongue chases my hand as it pushes up her skirt? Would she taste sweet or salty? Would she scream or let out low, soft whimpers when I lick her?

If I gave her an orgasm, would she do her job then?

I silently scold myself for my wicked thoughts. Not only is she my assistant, but she's my boss's daughter. Both facts make her untouchable. Not that I want to touch her. Not really. She irritates me too much.

I'm just fantasizing about the beautiful, sexy woman before me. Nothing more. I blame it on the sugary sweet fragrance that follows her around. She always smells like a damn cinnamon roll. Good enough to fucking eat.

"Are you listening to me?" Her harsh tone cuts through my fantasy.

My eyes snap back to hers. Her brows are raised and there's a hint of a smirk on her face.

Busted.

She caught me staring at her chest.

"No, actually. I wasn't." I sit back in my chair and steeple my fingers before I rest my chin on them.

Her nostrils flare and she stomps her foot. "Give me back my nameplate. That was my last one."

"No."

"Please," she says through gritted teeth.

I lean forward and rest my elbows on my desk. "Earn it."

"What?"

"You heard me. If you want it back. Earn. It." I drag out the last two words. "Try doing your job for a change."

She stares at me for a moment, opens her mouth like she's going to say something, but then shuts it. The fire in her deep green eyes is intense. Like little flames dancing around her pupils, dying to escape and burn me to the ground. The ferocity of her glare is making my dick hard as steel. Thank fuck I'm sitting behind my desk or else she'd see what her feistiness is doing to me.

I shift my hips in an attempt to relieve some of the pressure growing between my legs, but it's pointless. I hate that she has this effect on me.

"Did you have anything else for me this morning?" I ask, keeping my tone firm and demanding.

She gives me a curt smile.

"No, sir," she says with more attitude than a pubescent teenager.

Then she spins around, her long, silky dark hair whipping around her shoulders, and walks back to her desk, leaving me even harder than I was mere seconds ago.

MY PHONE BUZZES AND A TEXT MESSAGE FROM MY BROTHER FLASHES across the screen.

> **ADONIS**
> Time for lunch today?

I check the time, surprised it's already 11:30 am. Between going through emails, yesterday's messages, returning calls I *should have* returned yesterday, tweaking this code, and writing up the report for my next progress update, I didn't realize it was this late.

> **ATTICUS**
> Depends. Where were you thinking?

> **ADONIS**
> I'm right around the corner from you, so you pick.

> **ATTICUS**
> What are you doing near me?

> **ADONIS**
> Tell you when I see you. Can you go or not?

My brow furrows and concern washes over me. Something is

wrong or else he'd just say it in a message. Adonis is the most sensitive of my three younger brothers, but he's also the quietest. He hardly talks about his personal life. Especially since he moved in with his girlfriend six months ago.

ATTICUS
> How about grabbing sandwiches from the deli in my lobby and eating in my office? Busy day, but I can take a break for you.

ADONIS
> That works. What would you like?

ATTICUS
> Turkey club with mustard, no mayo. And a black coffee.

ADONIS
> You got it. See you in twenty.

ADONIS
> And thanks. I know you're busy.

ATTICUS
> Anything for you.

I toss my phone back on my desk and rub my hands over my face. The scruff on my chin scratches at my hands. I typically keep a clean-shaved face, but these past few days have been exhausting and I haven't bothered. It feels a little weird against my skin, but I don't hate it. Maybe I'll keep it. It saves me some time in the shower.

After refocusing my eyes on my computer screen, I determine it will take me about fifteen minutes to finish this report section. I have just enough time before Adonis gets here.

But that plan is immediately interrupted by the sound of my boss at Indie's desk.

"Really, Princess?" James says, his tone laced with disappointment. "Why is something like this being delivered to you at work?"

"Dad, I didn't order this. This has to be a mistake." Indie insists.

I fight to hide my smile. This must mean one of my *gifts* has been delivered. I set up random deliveries of several *gifts* for Indie. I have no clue when or in what order they'll come, but I'm hoping it's enough to chase her out of the office but good.

I snicker and wonder how long it will take her to realize they're from me. Until now, all I've messed with is her nameplate, and that hasn't deterred her.

"Princess," James whispers, but not soft enough that I can't hear him. "I expect more professionalism from you than this. You're twenty-six years old. It's past time you grow up and take this job seriously. If you don't, you'll leave me no choice. Do you understand?"

"Perfectly." She grits through her teeth.

I glance up just in time to see James heading down the hallway toward the elevator. His office is on the forty-fourth floor, but he stops by at least once a day to see Indie.

He doesn't go easy on his daughter, but my assessment is that he loves her very much. I also get the impression he's trying to teach her a life lesson by making her work here. I just wish she could learn that lesson as someone else's assistant.

Indie is standing at her desk with her back to me. My eyes immediately drop to the curve of her ass. Fuck, that ass of hers is very, very nice. I wouldn't mind squeezing it or maybe smacking it. She could use a good spanking.

A loud pop, followed by a scream, drags my eyes up. A smile immediately tugs at my lips.

A plume of hot pink glitter fills the air and surrounds Indie like a fog cloud. The overhead fluorescent lights glint off the glitter, shooting little rays of sparkle in all directions. She's transformed into a bright, glowing haze of hot pink shine.

It's fucking magnificent.

A deep throaty laugh escapes me as I take in my handiwork. I had my doubts about a glitter bomb disguised as office supplies, but now that I've seen it in action, it's the best *gift* I could have sent her. I don't think any of my others will top this.

She slowly turns around and a new cloud of glitter bursts around her. Her lip twitches, and her eyes narrow in on me.

"You!" She points a finger and sends a spray of glitter into my office. I laugh even harder. Several other employees on this floor have gathered in the foyer outside my office and begin snickering at the glowing disaster that is Indigo Simons.

"You did this!" she yells.

She grabs the box the glitter bomb was in and throws it at me. I duck and it hits the window behind me. Thankfully, most of the glitter is on her, her desk, and the floor beside her desk and not much comes out of the box when it hits.

"I don't know what you're talking about," I say through my laughter.

"And this!" She marches into my office, leaving a trail of glitter fluttering around her. When she reaches my desk, she slams an envelope down. "Admit it. I know you did this."

"I hate glitter." I look her up and down like I'm disgusted with what I see. "Why would I do this?"

I pick up the envelope she slammed down and have to pinch my lips between my teeth to keep from laughing. It's a letter from Sad'n Lonely Online Matchmakers. It says her membership has been extended for a year at no charge since, despite her efforts, she's had zero matches.

I look up at her with a straight face. "If you're looking for a date, I've got two single brothers."

"You're an asshole. You know that." The venom in her tone makes it impossible to stop the smile that tugs at my lips.

"Yes, I do. But what does this …" I wave my hand up and down to highlight her current state, "have to do with me being an asshole?"

"Don't play dumb with me. We both know you're smarter than that."

"But are you?" I smirk.

She opens her mouth to retort, but the knock on my door causes her to spin around, flinging glitter all over my desk.

"Am I interrupting?" Adonis asks from the doorway. His brows are raised, and he looks hesitant to come in.

"Not at all," I say. "Indie, I suggest you use your lunch break to go home and change. You're making a mess of my office."

Her nostrils flare and she stomps her foot before she bends at the waist and shakes her head over my desk. Some glitter comes off, covering my papers and keyboard, but most of it remains stuck to her. I can't even bring myself to be upset about it. The anger and frustration on her face are completely worth it.

"You'll pay for this." She grinds out before she turns to leave.

"Please shut the door on your way out, and I am not to be disturbed for the next hour."

She mumbles something that I can't make out before she slams my door shut, leaving me alone with my brother.

"What was that all about?" Adonis asks.

I wave off his question. "That's my useless assistant making a mess, as usual."

I've complained to my brothers plenty about Indie, but I didn't tell them my plans to prank her with ridiculous gifts, hoping to drive her to quit. It's best no one knows I'm responsible for this mess.

His eyes widen and his mouth falls open. "*That* was your assistant?"

"More like pain in my ass."

"You never told us she was hot."

Because if I did, you would razz me endlessly about her.

"Is she? I hadn't noticed through all the insolent behavior and laziness."

Adonis gives me a look that says he knows I'm full of shit. Again, deny everything no matter what. "You know she is."

Choosing to ignore his knowing stare, I stand and brush off the bit of glitter that got on my suit. Undoing my jacket, I slip it off, hang it over the back of my chair, then roll up my shirt sleeves. I point to the table and chairs in the corner. "Let's sit over here and eat."

Once we're seated, Adonis hands me my coffee and sandwich. He's still watching me like he wants to push me further about Indie, but I quickly speak to avoid that discussion. "You gonna tell me what brings you here today?"

He takes a bite of his sandwich and chews slowly, as if he needs time to work up the courage to say what's on his mind. As soon as he swallows, he sits back in his chair and sighs. "Lulu's cheating."

"What?" I manage through a cough. He caught me mid-bite, and I almost choked on my food.

"I came home early to see if she wanted to go out for lunch, but when my cab pulled up, I saw her kissing a man as they were climbing into their own cab. They were all over each other. It was rather indecent. I followed them down here to a fancy restaurant a block away."

"Did you confront her?"

"Not yet. I will tonight. I'm going home after this to pack my shit. I assume my room is still available."

"Of course, man. It's still empty."

We eat in silence for a few minutes. Adonis has always been the quiet one in our family, and he often keeps his feelings bottled up inside him, whereas the rest of us let it out. Something like this will eat at him if we don't get him to open up about it.

"We're going out this weekend. No arguments. Be ready to get shit-faced and talk about it. Okay?"

He looks up at me, and for a second, I think he's going to object. "Only if you talk to us about Indie."

"There's nothing to talk about where she's concerned."

"Bullshit. If you want me to talk, then you talk too."

I huff. "Fine, but there's not much to tell."

"We'll see," is all he says before he takes another bite of his sandwich.

I shake my head and focus on my own sandwich. All I can hope is that Adonis's problems are enough to keep my brothers occupied when we go out.

Not that I want to see my brother in pain, but I can't handle my brothers hounding me about Indie.

Because I'm a shit liar where they're concerned.

One night of interrogation, and I will crack.

CHAPTER TWO

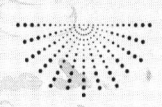

INDIGO

INDIGO

Get bail money ready. I'm going to kill him.

ELON

Should I also call my lawyer?

INDIGO

Yes. And think up a good alibi. I'm going to need it.

ELON

Already on hold with our favorite spa to back date an appointment.

INDIGO

You're the best!

ELON

I know. {Winky face emoji} I've always got your back, darlin'.

Eight more months.
Eight. More. Months.
EIGHT. MORE. MONTHS.

That's all I have to make it through before dad releases my trust fund to me and he can no longer hold it over my head.

Eight more months and I can walk away from my dad and his company forever.

I thought I could handle his demands. All he asked of me was to work for one year at his company, show up on time, work my eight hours every day, then go home.

If I can do that, I get full access to my trust.

No strings. No questions asked.

Then he had to go and assign me to work for his protégé, his golden child, the chosen one.

Atticus Rosi, aka Mr. Ass Kisser.

All that man cares about is making my father happy and brown-nosing his way to the top floor. It makes me sick to see how he bends over backward to appease my father. Either he doesn't care that my father is a Grade A asshole, or he's too blinded by his ambition to notice. Regardless, neither scenario is good for Atticus.

Unfortunately, I'm all too familiar with men who want money or connections from my dad. I've spent my entire life dealing with people just like him. And my patience is worn out.

Every boyfriend I've ever had dated me because they saw me as a path to success, not a girl they really liked. Even my own mother uses me to get to Dad and his hefty bank account.

I've always been treated like a pawn in someone else's game, and I refuse to allow it to happen again. Atticus is no different from all the others. Given the chance, he'd use me too.

Which is why it's a real inconvenience that I find him insanely attractive. My body doesn't seem to understand that we don't like him. Every time I'm near him, a fire ignites inside me, and I tremble with need.

It doesn't help that he's one of the most gorgeous men I've ever met. Tall, dark hair, scruffy beard, and tanned olive skin. According to the rumblings around the office, he's half Greek. Very fitting, considering his name.

He's every bit the sexy Greek god he's named after.

And I swear his piercing brown eyes will be my undoing. He acts like he hates me—and maybe he really does—but sometimes he looks at me like he'd rather press me against the wall and make me his.

If only he didn't work for my father.

I sigh and lift my head to take another look at myself in the mirror.

After leaving Atticus's office, I headed straight to the bathroom. A trail of hot pink glitter followed behind me. I've gotten a lot of it off me, but it's embedded in my hair all the way to my scalp. It's sticking to my skin like glue.

I'm going to be fighting hot pink glitter for days, if not weeks, to come.

There's a light knock on the door before it swings open. The admin supervisor, Mrs. Romano, sticks her head in the bathroom and gives me a tight smile. She's one of the few employees on this floor that's semi-nice to me. As far as I can tell, she doesn't gossip about me behind my back. At least, I haven't caught her gossiping about me like I have all the others.

"Miss Simons," she says in a tentative tone as if she's afraid I'm going to blow up at her. I haven't *blown up* at anyone except Mr. Ass Kisser since I started my prison sentence four months ago. "Your father would like a word. He's waiting for you in his office."

I close my eyes and drop my head back, not bothering to stop the groan that rumbles deep from my chest. Of course he wants to see me *now*. One of the other admins probably rushed to tell him about the glitter bomb the second it went off.

"Thanks, Mrs. Romano. I'll head up after I arrange to have my desk area cleaned up."

"No need." She gives me a gentle smile. "I already called it in. They arrived almost immediately."

"Thank you." My voice cracks.

This might be the first act of kindness an employee has shown me since I started working here. No one welcomed me with open arms when I started. The exact opposite, in fact. It pissed the other admins off that Dad handed me a perfectly good job that I didn't earn. It pisses them off even more that I don't take it seriously.

I take a deep breath and turn to Mrs. Romano. "That was very kind of you. I appreciate it."

"Of course, dear." She nods. "Your father sounds angry. Best not keep him waiting."

∼

My father lets out a disappointed sigh the second I step into his office. I do my best to ignore his reaction as I shut the door behind me and march up to his desk.

With the fakest smile I've ever worn, I take a seat in the chair opposite him.

"You wanted to see me?" I ask.

"Indie." His shoulders sag and he shakes his head. "What on earth are you doing? You look like you belong on stage at a nightclub, not at a professional place of business."

"There must have been a mix-up with the mail. What should have been office supplies was actually a glitter bomb."

"Glitter bomb?" He raises a brow. "How could a *glitter bomb* be mistaken for office supplies?"

"That's an excellent question, Father," I say with enough attitude to fill up this entire office building.

He lets out a low huff, and I know he's irritated with my response. Not only does he hate it when I call him Father, he wants more of an answer from me than that.

But I refuse to give it.

It's not like I know who did it anyway. I suspect it was Atticus. But it could have been any number of employees who dislike me. There's definitely enough of them.

He removes his glasses and rubs the bridge of his nose. "Can we not with the sass today? I have a headache, and this is only making it worse."

"I could leave if you like." I place my hands on the armrests of the chair and push to my feet.

"Sit. Down." He growls.

I plop back down, not caring one bit that I'm acting like a bratty teenager. I even smile at the light dusting of glitter that falls off me. Dad's frown deepens.

"Princess, what do I have to do to get you to take this job seriously?" I inwardly groan at his use of the nickname he insists on calling me.

"Whatever do you mean?" I play dumb.

He doesn't like that either.

"Would you prefer I dissolve your trust fund now and end this torture for both of us? All I asked of you is one year, Indigo. One. Year." He slams his hand on his desk, causing me to jump. "How many warnings are you going to force me to give you before I completely lose my patience?"

Against my will and my better judgment, my temper flies. "Do you think I *want* to be covered in glitter? Or that I'd actually do something this ridiculous to myself *on purpose*? Come on, *Father*. Give me a little credit. I'm not the dimwit you think I am."

"I don't think you're a dimwit. I just want you to take this seriously. Prove to me you can do that for the next eight months, and I'll free you of any further obligation. I need to know my daughter can stand on her own without my money. Is that too much to ask?"

My nostrils flare, and my anger heats even more than it did a moment ago.

I want to argue back.

I want to remind him how absent he's been in my life until a few months ago. That he basically abandoned me with Mom after the divorce and just assumed that I'm just like her.

He's never once asked me what interests me. Or what I want to do with my life. If he did, that answer might shock him.

Instead, he assumes the worst and tosses around demand after demand, bending me to his will.

"Did you need anything else?" I ask through gritted teeth. I need to get out of here soon before I say or do something I really will regret.

He lets out a long sigh. "No, Princess. You can go."

He waves me off as if *he's* dismissing *me*. I don't bother to point out the errors in his actions. It'll just drag this meeting out longer.

"I'll take your warnings under advisement," I say with a curt nod, before I push to my feet and leave before he can detain me any longer.

I march toward the elevator, ignoring all the stares. I'm fully aware that I'm leaving a trail of glitter behind me. Knowing my luck, this shit will still be falling off me for weeks on end.

Once in the elevator, I hit the button for my floor. I don't know how or when, but Atticus Rosi is about to go down.

The sound of my heels clanking on the tile floor echoes off the walls and rings loudly in the otherwise silent hallway. There are several people milling around, and they all pause to look at me as I march past.

I should probably slow down and smile. I'm in charge of this fundraiser, and it's my responsibility to make sure all the volunteers are focused on the tasks at hand.

And happy. I need to keep them happy. We need them to continue to work with us if we want to successfully pull in the kind of donors that will make a real difference.

But I'm running late.

Thanks to that damn glitter bomb, I had to go home and scrub my hair three times and exfoliate my skin until it felt raw. And I still have glitter stuck to me.

I didn't have time for a shower, but there's no way I can be the face of this event covered in that much glitter. Despite how many times I scrubbed it off, it's still there. I'm still going to attract some unwanted questions tonight.

"Indie, there you are." My boss's voice says from behind the registration table.

Lisa McAllister runs one of the most successful charity event planning businesses in the city. If you have a charity and need donors that will make a real difference, then Lisa is the person to help you find them.

She has connections with some of the wealthiest families on the East Coast and even some on the West Coast. Sell her on your charity's needs, and she will guarantee you will reach your goals.

It's why I wanted to work with her. It's why I didn't care that I had to start out as a volunteer and earn myself a paid position. Once I was an official part of her team, it didn't take long until I earned her trust, and she made me the lead event manager.

"I'm sorry I'm late Lisa. I promise it won't happen again." I stash my purse in one of the boxes behind the table, grab my clipboard, and quickly put my nearly invisible headset in my ear. I have fifteen minutes to do what typically takes me forty. If I walk really fast, maybe I'll get it all done.

After a quick perusal of the registration table, I see everything is in order. We have three volunteers who all look nervous. Probably because Lisa was complaining about my absence before I arrived.

Lisa doesn't have a lot of tolerance for tardiness or what she deems as incompetence. To her, there are no excuses, only actions. If you make a mistake, fix it. If you're late, work overtime to correct it.

But no matter what, don't complain to her. She doesn't care. She only cares about results. It's why she's so freaking successful.

I smile at the volunteers. They look ready to impress, dressed in their formal attire. All of our events are black tie, and we expect our volunteers to dress accordingly.

"Do you guys need anything?" I ask with a wide smile.

"No, Miss Simons, we're good," the taller of the three blondes replies. They're all tall. Then again, most people are tall compared to me. I'm only five-three flat footed. Even with heels on, most people tower over me.

I give her a curt nod. "Call me over the headset if anything changes."

I turn to start my rounds, but Lisa is blocking my path. She's staring down at me with furrowed brows because everyone stares down at me. I never minded being petite growing up, but once I entered adulthood, it was like I was surrounded by tall model-types that made me feel even shorter. Lisa is no different.

"Is it your father?" she asks.

I cringe, regretting that I told her about my father's conditions regarding my employment with his company. She knows my father well. Lisa knows all the wealthy families in the city, but they're not exactly friendly.

"Yes." I sigh. "It was a rough day, and I didn't get to leave as early as I'd hoped. But I promise, it won't happen again."

She nods, studying me carefully. It makes me nervous. I don't like being scrutinized to this degree. I'd hoped she wouldn't be too upset with me since I've never been late before. Not once in the three years that I've worked for her have I missed a deadline, been late, or made a mistake.

Being forced to work for Dad's company is a complication I didn't need, nor do I have the time for it. I've got my own career aspirations, and they don't involve my father or his company. But sadly, I do need his money in the form of my trust fund.

I need this job with Lisa too. It's the only way I'll gain the experience and connections I need to start my own foundation. I need her mentorship. If I've just screwed that up by being late, I'll never forgive my father or Atticus. This is his fault for that damn glitter bomb.

"Okay," she finally says, her expression softening. "Get to work. You've got some time to make up."

"Thank you." I sag in relief. "Don't worry, everything will be perfect."

She gives me a gentle smile. "With you in charge, I know it will."

With my clipboard in hand, I disappear into the main ballroom where the event will take place. Closing my eyes, I take in a few deep, calming breaths.

That could have gone very differently. Lisa is a hard but fair boss. I've seen her yell at employees for a lot less than being late to a major event. Hell, she's fired people for less. She doesn't tolerate tardiness, and I can't help but feel like I just dodged a major bullet.

I'm only four months into this year-long contract with my dad. I'm exhausted from working two jobs, keeping up with my volunteer work, and planning for my own business.

At this rate, I will not survive the next eight months.

"Darlin', you look fabulous." Elon takes my hands and holds them out to my side as he looks me up and down, studying my long, black formal gown. It's formfitting, with only one long sleeve. The neckline is lined with rhinestones and cuts from one shoulder in a diagonal across my chest before it wraps around under my other arm. It's a sexy yet modest style.

He spins me on my heel, taking in the low cut in the back. When I meet his gaze again, he raises his brow. "Balmain?"

I mock surprise. "How do you do that?"

"Oh, please." He waves me off as if I'm being silly. "I've always had a better eye for fashion than you. You probably can't even tell me who made my shoes."

He lifts his foot up, and I study them for a moment. They look like all the other shoes he always wears. Stylish. Leather. Expensive. "Um, Burberry?"

"Ugh." He drops his head back and groans. "You're an embarrassment to our social class. They're Jimmy Choos."

"Whatever." I shove his shoulder, making him laugh. We've always bantered like this, and it's a welcome treat after the day I've had.

As soon as the charity event ended, I messaged him, asking if he could meet for a drink. If anyone can cheer me up, it's Elon.

He's been my best friend since we were toddlers. Like me, he also comes from a wealthy family. Elon is the heir to a real estate empire his grandfather created. Unlike me, he's excited about the prospect of one day running the company. As soon as his dad retires, Elon will become *the* real estate mogul of New York City.

Until then, he's enjoying life as it comes.

"Tell me everything," Elon says as he slides a shot of tequila with salt on the rim and a lime wedge on the side toward me.

I pick it up, lick the rim, down the shot, and then pop the lime wedge in my mouth. The sour juices cause my nose to wrinkle.

"Another." I slide the shot glass across the table. "Then I'll talk."

"That good, huh?" Elon chuckles as he raises his hand to flag down our server.

I nod and take a drink of the water he also ordered for me before I arrived.

A few minutes later, the server arrives with another round of shots and a margarita for each of us. I rarely drink hard liquor on work nights, but tonight's an exception.

I down my shot, wincing at the burn from the tequila but loving it all the same. Tequila has always been my drink of choice. I'll take it anyway it's made, but margaritas on the rocks, tequila sunrises, and El Diablos are my favorites.

Elon reaches over and picks at my forehead. His smile grows and his eyes widen in mischief. I don't need him to tell me what he picked off me.

I point at his fingers that are pinched together and scowl. "*That* is why I need bail money and a good alibi."

He leans across the table, studying me more closely. "Darlin', you're dusted with glitter."

"I know!" I say a little too loudly. "And this is after I showered and scrubbed my hair for a good ten minutes."

He pulls his lips between his teeth, attempting to stop his laughter, but his eyes give him away.

"Don't you dare laugh at me. I've been humiliated enough for one day. I don't need it from you too."

He holds his hands up in surrender and forces his face into submission. "Sorry. It's just, the bar lights are hitting it just right. Your scalp is glowing. If that's after ten minutes of washing, I'd hate to see what you looked like before."

"I was covered." I groan. "Every inch of me."

His eyes widen, but this time with an air of seriousness. His teasing demeanor is gone. "What in God's name happened?"

I explained to him how I'd gotten several packages, including the letter with a return address from Sad'n Lonely Online Matchmakers. He chuckles at this, causing my glare to intensify. Maybe one day this will all be funny, but that day is not today.

"It was labeled as office supplies. It was even addressed from the supplier we always order from. I swear I swallowed a pound of glitter when it blew up in my face," I say after I explain the package to him. "I know it was Atticus."

"Are you sure? You've always described him as a serious workaholic. I can't picture the man you've painted as a prankster."

"It has to be him. Who else would've done it?"

He shrugs. "Maybe the admin pool? You've complained about how they all treat you."

"Maybe. But Atticus has been changing out my nameplate for weeks now. Today he used one that said Princess Simons. I wouldn't put anything past him."

Elon snorts. "Princess Simons. That's great."

I reach across the table and playfully slap his arm. "It's not funny."

"Sorry, darlin', but it kind of is. If he's coming up with all of this on his own, I'm impressed."

"You would be." I take a drink of my margarita and sigh. "Anyway, can we stop talking about Atticus and my disastrous work life? Any luck with those contacts?"

"As a matter of fact, yes." Elon smiles and pulls his wallet out of his back pocket to retrieve a small piece of paper. He hands it to me. "Harold Lee Whittington, III. Old money. And I mean lots of money. His great-great-grandfather was an oil tycoon. Harold is the sole heir. He's in investments and is looking for charity opportunities that serve his interests."

I take the paper from him. All that's on it is his name, phone number, and email. "And what are his interests?"

Elon waggles his brows. "He has a son a few years older than Jay with similar social anxieties. He's interested in your foundation. The man is expecting your call."

My eyes widen. "Really?"

Elon's smile is a mile wide. "Yep."

"Oh my God!" I squeal and jump out of my seat, attracting the attention of half the bar. I wrap Elon in a tight hug and fight back the tears. "Thank you for this. I didn't think anything could turn this day around."

"Glad I could help." He chuckles. "Now sit your cute little ass back in that seat so we can come up with a game plan. Harold is a serious man, so you better be ready."

We spend the next thirty minutes discussing the best way to approach a man like Harold. By the time I head home, I'm excited about what the future holds. If I can secure a large donation from a family like the Whittingtons, I can tell my father where to shove his demands.

With a backer like Harold, I won't need my trust fund anymore.

CHAPTER THREE

ATTICUS

EROS
Are you assholes coming or not?

DEMETRIUS
Just waiting for the two old fuckers to get ready.

ADONIS
Who you calling old?

DEMETRIUS
You!

ADONIS
{middle finger emoji}

ATTICUS
Knock it off or I'll take longer.

I stare at myself in the mirror in my bedroom. I look tired, and I feel just as old as my brothers tease me about being. Though I'd never admit that to them. One slip of the tongue, and they'd tease me relentlessly.

I'm not old. Not even close. I'm only twenty-eight. But I feel this weight pressing down on me and it's constant and insistent. It's making me anxious all the fucking time. I keep moving and working and doing new things, hoping that will somehow get me out from under whatever this is that's pushing down on me.

Sometimes it makes it hard to breathe. Like now. I keep staring at myself, taking deep breaths, like that's somehow going to change how I feel. It doesn't.

Is it my need to be the best? Or my fear that my opportunity is slowly being ripped away from me because of circumstances that are out of my control?

I love my job, but my need for more is boarding on obsessive. I want to succeed in ways no one in my family ever thought possible. I'm on track to be the youngest C-suite executive this company has ever had. Just the thought of reaching that level before I'm thirty makes me feel queasy. I'm not sure if that's a good or bad feeling. I haven't decided.

But I know I want it. The goal is within my reach. That's why Indie is driving me to do the crazy things I'm doing. I can't fail because she has some vendetta against her dad.

Then there's the responsibility I feel toward my siblings. I don't need to be the one to take care of them. Not anymore. We're all grown and successful in our own right.

Persephone, our older sister, is married now and expecting her first child. Adonis is about to graduate with his PhD in Pre-Classical Greek Literature. Demetrius is one of the best firefighters in all of New York City, and Eros is finally coming into his own. He's been the slowest to find himself, but he's also the youngest. He's currently a bouncer at the bar we're all meeting at tonight.

By all accounts, I don't need to work this hard for my family anymore. They don't need me to take care of them. *Not anymore.*

We had an odd upbringing. Our parents are kind of like nomads, traveling the country in an RV. We grew up that way. Never living in the same place for more than a month or so. It made for an interesting and challenging childhood.

Our parents still live in the RV, but we're all settled in the city and making lives of our own. But I can't let go of my need to protect and take care of them. The feeling is strong, constantly tugging at my insides, screaming at me to do more, more, more.

Or maybe I'm just an asshole and this weight pressing down on me is the world's way of telling me to be nicer.

It's probably the third option. I *am* an asshole. There's no denying that. Just look at the way I keep treating Indie at work. She deserves to be called out for her bullshit performance, but did I really have to send her a glitter bomb? Several days later and even I'm still picking hot pink glitter out of my hair. I can't imagine how long she's going to be dealing with it.

There's a knock on my door, dragging me out of my thoughts. "Come in."

The door slowly opens, and Adonis steps in, then leans against the wall. "Dem is getting anxious. You about ready?"

I pick up my watch from the top of my dresser and wrap it around my wrist. My Longines Flagship dress watch is the first gift I bought myself when I was named senior manager of my division with SimTech. It's not the most expensive watch I could have purchased, but it still set me back a pretty penny or two.

A nice watch was the one thing I always wanted as a kid. Anytime I watched movies or saw a man in a nice suit, I noticed they wore nice watches. Something simple, yet sophisticated. I wanted that. As silly as it sounds in my head now, the day I bought this watch was the day I finally felt like a success.

"Yeah, just about. Is Dem out there pacing?"

Adonis chuckles. "He's wearing a path on the floor. He keeps checking the time and moaning like he's afraid all the girls will have left the bar by the time we get there."

I shake my head and smile. "We're going to Triple Bs. There are always hot girls there."

"I know that, and you know that, but Dem seems to have momentarily forgotten."

"More reason to make him wait." I pat my brother's shoulder as I pass by him and step into my bathroom.

When we all first moved to the city several years ago, it was a stroke of luck finding this apartment. It's not huge, but we each have our own bedrooms and bathrooms. It's set up to be rented by the room with a shared living and kitchen area. Albeit a very small living and kitchen area.

All four rooms had just been vacated when we looked at this place, and since it's rent controlled, we could afford it. It was a little tight at first, but once we all settled into jobs and started making decent money, things got a lot easier.

Now that I'm climbing the ladder at work, we could afford a bigger place, but we love this apartment. It signifies our first stationary home. It's nice to have one place to come home to every day after growing up in an RV. Besides, we're all young and single, so we don't really need much.

"Did you get all your stuff?" I call through the bathroom door.

Adonis's plan to confront Lulu about her infidelity was delayed a couple of days. The same day he caught her, she had a last-minute, out-of-town trip come up. She said it was to go home to care for a sick relative or some shit like that, but we all know it was a getaway with her secret boyfriend.

The truth came out when Adonis confronted her last night. He'd already packed up most of his stuff. With his schooling, it took him longer than he would have liked.

He runs his hand through his light brown hair and sighs. "Yeah. My room is a mess. With my dissertation defense coming up, it's going to take me forever to get it in order. But at least I got out of my lease."

I snap my eyes to his. "Really?

"Yep. I couldn't believe it. Turns out my landlord is a hopeless romantic. When I explained to her what happened, she cried. Most uncomfortable conversation of my life. But it got me out of my lease. What happens to the other room in that apartment is no longer my problem. Signing separate leases annoyed me at the time but thank God Lulu had insisted on it. Looking back, that should have been a sign that I was making a mistake."

"She had us all fooled, brother." Stepping out of the bathroom, I double check that I have my wallet before we leave. "But don't worry. You'll find someone who is worthy of you. Someone far better than Lulu."

He nods but doesn't meet my gaze. Adonis has always been more interested in finding a girl than the rest of us. Whereas we're all fine keeping things casual and fun, he wants a life partner. He craves that level of companionship and intimacy that the rest of us don't seem to desire.

"What the fuck, you two?" Demetrius barges into my room and crosses his arms over his chest. "Dad gets ready to go faster than you."

I snort. "You say that like Dad struggles to get around. He's more fit than all of us."

"And that's my point. Your office job is making you soft."

I lift my brows in challenge. "Shall we hit the gym tomorrow? I may not have a physical job like you, but I can still bench more than you."

"Ha! In your dreams."

I step closer to Demetrius and smile. "Be ready then. Seven sharp."

"Seven! That's too early."

I chuckle as I walk past him and into the living room. "Careful, little brother. You're the one that's sounding old now."

∼

Triple Bs is as much about entertainment as it is about great drinks. With a cocktail menu focused on unique spins on the classics, it instantly drew a crowd when it opened a year ago.

Thanks to our sister's connection to the family that owns it, Eros was able to get a job with little effort.

It helped that he's a big guy. He's got a good three inches on me, and I'm six-two. He's also as wide as a Mac truck. Add in his intense furrowed brow, and he's the perfect bouncer. One mean look from him, and every man backs down.

The bar is packed with nothing but suits and fancy dresses. I'd call it more business dress than casual. I love the drinks at Triple Bs but the clientele that frequents this bar leaves me feeling uneasy. I feel like an impostor among all the pretty people in expensive suits and dresses that look like they just walked out of a fashion show.

My brothers and I don't fit that mold. Anywhere else, we'd fit right in, but here, we definitely stick out. Especially Demetrius. Being a firefighter, he doesn't have much use for business casual attire. Adonis and I are in dress pants and nice dress shirts with our sleeves rolled up. If we put on a jacket, we'd blend in with the other men.

But not Demetrius. He's in dark jeans, a T-shirt, and a huge smile. That's who he is, and he doesn't care one bit if he's judged for it.

Adonis is the first to see Eros over the crowd. He's not too hard to find, since he's a good head taller than everyone else.

Demetrius leads us to a table in the corner where his best friend and coworker is waiting.

"Took you long enough," Dylan says. "I was beginning to think you stood me up and made me arrange for a night out for nothing."

"Sorry, man." Demetrius plops down in the seat next to Dylan and frowns at me. "This fucker took forever to pick out his outfit."

I ignore his jab and pat Eros on the shoulder. "Busy night tonight. You going to be able to take a few minutes to sit with us?"

He nods with a deep frown as he looks around the bar. He's so imposing that I swear the temperature drops a few degrees when he makes that face. "The boss is here, and he said I could take an hour to hang."

A loud cheer fills the air, and we all look toward the bar. Luke Rockwell, owner of this establishment, is behind the bar putting on a show while he mixes drinks. He takes flare bartending to a whole new level.

Luke can sling bottles and glasses like no one I've ever seen. He takes a glass full of ice, flicks his wrist, and it goes spinning in the air. Most of the ice remains in the glass, but a few pieces fly out above his head. He catches the glass and holds it out, positioning it so the rogue ice falls right back in. He makes it look effortless, but I'm sure it's anything but.

The crowd cheers loudly, just before the other three bartenders join in on the show. All the bartenders that work here can sling drinks like Luke. It's a requirement for employment.

It's also why Triple Bs is so popular.

It makes for a fun night out, but I prefer the atmosphere of the other bar Luke co-owns with his siblings, The Rock Room. It's more casual and they host live bands on the weekends. The crowd isn't as *pretty* there, but it's never lacking for a good time.

We put in our drink orders, all of us opting for whiskey. That's usually our drink of choice when we know the conversation is about to get serious. Adonis still hasn't updated us on exactly what went down with Lulu. Anytime one of us asked, he pushed us off and said not yet.

He's always been the quiet, more reserved of the four of us. Even as a kid, he kept to himself and only got into trouble because we dragged him into it.

As kids, we were hellions. As teenagers, we were headaches to our parents and sister. It was way too much testosterone cooped up in an RV, especially once we hit puberty. Our poor sister didn't have a chance with four horny younger brothers. I cringe when I think about the things we put Persephone through. It's a wonder she's not scarred for life.

Our parents were openly affectionate and never shied from discussions about sex. They also couldn't hide the fact that they had it often. There's no such thing as privacy when you live in an RV with six other people.

Needless to say, we grew up with a healthy acceptance of sex and our sexuality. Our parents taught us to be respectful yet open about our sexual needs. We definitely embraced those needs far more often than we probably should have. But we're all good-looking guys with bad boy tendencies. Turns out that's something women like.

We still get into our fair share of trouble. We're just a tad more mature than we were as teenagers. At least Adonis and I are. Can't say the same for Demetrius and Eros. Those two still pick up women like it's a sport. If I know them, they'll both find a pretty girl to take home with them tonight.

"Alright, Donnie." Demetrius leans on his elbows and stares across the table at Adonis. "No more stalling. Tell us what happened with Lulu and why you moved back in with us."

Donnie picks up his glass and downs the last of his whiskey before he slouches in his chair and sighs. "Lulu's sleeping with a professor in the department. It's been going on for the past eight months."

My hand pauses midway to my mouth, suspending my whiskey between me and the table. Eros stares blankly at our brother, and Demetrius spits the drink he just took across the table.

Demetrius clears his throat and coughs a few times while Dylan slaps him on the back. When he can speak, he says, "But you two just moved in with each other like six months ago."

"No shit," Donnie says before he reaches for his glass, only to find it empty. I hand him mine and he downs that too. I wave down our server to get us another round.

"What kind of sorry ass excuse did she give you?" Eros's furrowed brow deepens and his shoulders tense. He's the fighter of the four of us. He's got a short fuse and growls more than he smiles.

"That I work too much. I didn't pay enough attention to her. So she got it somewhere else."

"But she works the same schedule you do," I say. "She knows the demands of a PhD program. She's living it too."

He shrugs. "That didn't seem to matter to her."

Something crosses over his expression that I can't quite make out. I study him while I wait for him to continue, but he doesn't. He's holding something back. I want to ask him but decide not to in front of the others. I love Demetrius and Eros, but they're not the most sensitive guys.

Demetrius lifts his glass. "You're getting laid tonight."

I close my eyes on a sigh as he immediately proves me right about not pushing.

"Dem, I'm not getting laid tonight. I'm taking a break from women for a while."

Dem's eyes widen like Donnie just said the most ridiculous thing he's ever heard. "Dude, come on. It'll be just like old times. We're all single. Just look around this place." He waves his hand out toward the crowded bar. "So many gorgeous ladies. I guarantee you there's one out there for each of us."

"When are you going to grow up?" Dylan elbows him in the side. "Stop fucking around and settle down."

Dem snorts. "Hell no. I love my single life. The last thing I want is to be tied down like you."

"My wife is awesome." Dylan gives him a pointed stare. "I've never been happier."

"We can't all find keepers like Sydney. That woman is a saint for putting up with your sorry ass."

Dylan's smile grows wide and lights up his entire face. "Don't I know it. I count my blessings every day."

"As you should, motherfucker." Demetrius matches his smile. "But married life isn't for me."

"The day a woman catches your eye, I'm going to enjoy watching you fall," Dylan says just as our server returns with our next round of drinks.

"Enough about Dem's outlook on marriage." Eros takes a respectable sip from his fresh glass of whiskey. He can't drink too much since he has to report back to work soon. "What I want to know is why our oldest brother has pink glitter on his face."

He points across the table toward my temple. When I meet his gaze, all I see is mischief.

"Yeah, Tat." Donnie smiles, using the nickname my brothers gave me after I became obsessed with tattoos. My chest, back, and arms are covered with them.

I snort and rub at the side of my head. "This is nothing. You should see the other guy."

"Or girl." Adonis waggles his brows and I frown.

"What girl?" Dem perks up, suddenly more interested in this conversation.

"Just my assistant." I answer in as neutral a tone as I can manage.

"Oh." Dem deflates slightly.

"What Tat has failed to tell us these past few months is that the devil of an assistant he's always complaining about is a hottie."

I groan and pinch the bridge of my nose. "She's not that hot."

The lie burns coming out more than the whiskey burns going down.

"You'd have to be a blind man not to notice how gorgeous that little spitfire is." Donnie leans on the table and addresses everyone else as if I'm not even here. "Petite, barely over five feet tall, curvy, long brown hair, and a fire in her eyes for our dear brother."

"That's not fire. That's hatred."

Donnie laughs. "Not buying that for a second. You two put on a good show, but that shit is foreplay."

I frown, ready to argue differently when Dylan speaks up. "What does any of this have to do with the pink glitter on your face?"

My frown vanishes, and the smile that replaces it almost hurts. "Well, you see, I sent my lazy ass assistant a package."

I give them a recount of the events from earlier this week, leaving nothing out. I even tell them about her father and how he called her into his office to explain herself.

"I've got a few more gifts planned for her in the coming weeks. With any luck, she'll quit so I can hire an assistant that will actually help me instead of hindering my progress."

"Damn, Tat." Dem's grin matches my own. "I didn't know you had that in you. That's way better than any of the pranks we pulled as kids. I'm impressed."

I lift my glass of whiskey and nod. "Let's just hope it's enough to get rid of her. The day she quits is the day I'll be happy."

As soon as the words are out, a heaviness settles on my chest. It feels weird and foreign, as if my body is rejecting my last statement.

That makes no sense to me. Because I want Indie to quit. I'm beyond ready to have her out of my life and will do whatever it takes to make that happen.

Maybe I should feel bad about the glitter bomb and nameplate and prank letters.

Maybe I should be a little kinder to her.

Maybe kindness would get her to do her fucking job.

And yet I can't help but smile, nor can I find two shits to give. The glitter bomb was just the start. This half Greek, half American asshole has a lot more planned for Princess Simons.

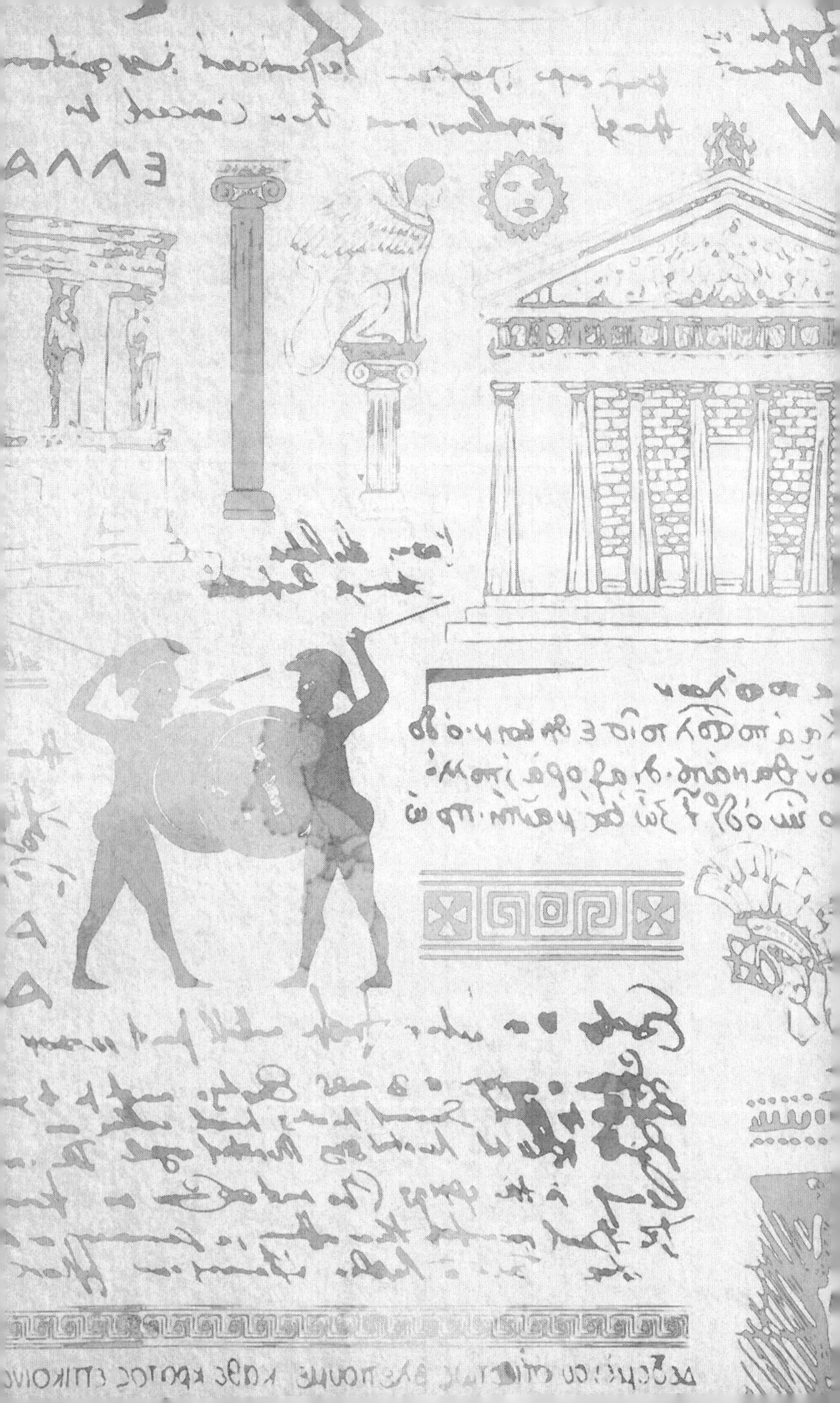

CHAPTER FOUR

INDIGO

> **INDIGO**
> My father hates me.

> **ELON**
> He doesn't hate you. He just doesn't understand you.

> **INDIGO**
> Nope. It's hatred.

> **ELON**
> Maybe you should consider letting him get to know the REAL you.

> **INDIGO**
> Ha! Never.

This has got to be the most boring meeting I've ever been forced to sit through. Normally, I don't have to come to these things, but today, Dad insisted I sit in.

I've no clue why.

I don't need to be here for this. For the past twenty minutes, Dad and Atticus have talked ad nauseam about some stupid code Atticus wrote that is going to change the world for financial planners.

I like to think of myself as an intelligent woman. I graduated

Summa cum laude from Yale, but this meeting is making me feel stupid. I have no idea what they're talking about. I need a key just to understand the acronyms or code or whatever it is Atticus keeps saying. Arrays. Block coding. Loops. Strings. Machine learning. Neural networks. It's all Greek to me.

I don't need to be here for this. Atticus's assistant—whoever the hell it is—doesn't need to hear any of this.

Plus, I don't need to see Dad fawn all over Atticus and his *brilliant* ideas. It's like Atticus is the son he always wanted and didn't get. The pride in his expression makes me want to vomit.

More reason to stay far away from Atticus and make sure our dislike for each other overpowers the attraction. The two of us together are a recipe for disaster. I'd get hurt, used, and tossed aside like I always do, and he'd get his damn promotion.

Nope, not going to happen.

Not that I think Atticus wants me like that. I see how he looks at me though. He may not like me either, but the attraction is there.

While Dad and Atticus continue to talk animatedly about this code Atticus wrote, I use the time to think about how I'm going to present my business plan to the investor Elon found. From the reading I've done, Harold's son struggles with a lot of the same issues as my brother. They're both very smart but have crippling anxiety and sensory issues that make school and classroom interactions challenging for them.

They both need similar types of cognitive behavioral therapy to develop skills and tools that help them have healthier and happier social interactions. It's the same therapy I want my foundation to support and make more readily available to families in need.

We're lucky that money is not an obstacle we have to overcome. Jay gets all the help he needs and then some. But for those less fortunate, insurance doesn't always cover the costs of the therapy these kids need.

I want to change that.

"Indie!" Dad yells and slaps his hand on his desk. My eyes snap up to see he's glaring at me. "Are you even listening?"

"I'm sorry. Did you finally say something I needed to hear?" As soon as the words are out, I regret them. And from the look on my father's face, he's about to let me have it in front of Atticus. The last thing I need is for that man to have more ammunition to use against me.

Dad takes a deep breath and his nostrils flare. "You need to hear everything we're discussing today. Why else would you be here?"

I scoff, digging myself into a deeper hole. "You're discussing arrays and loops and other coding sh … *stuff* I don't understand. I don't need to hear those details."

Dad sighs and drops his head into his hand. "Why did I waste an Ivy League education on you?"

"Waste?" I say a little too loudly. "Need I remind you of my GPA? That was no small feat. Especially from Yale."

"You went to Yale?" Atticus asks from the seat next to me. His tone suggests he's shocked by that tidbit of knowledge. When I glance at him, he's studying me as if he's looking at me for the first time.

"She did." Dad answers for me. "You'd think her education would better prepare her for this job."

"My degree is in business with a nonprofit management specialization and I have a minor in communications. Nothing about that prepared me to speak tech."

Dad waves me off as if what I said means nothing. "That degree is also a waste. You would have been better off with a traditional business management track."

My instinct is to further defend my choices, but I opt to drop it. Nothing I say will ever change my dad's mind about how I want to spend my life.

Instead, I pick up my notepad from my lap and fake being prepared to write. "What did I miss?"

Dad doesn't answer me right away. He opens and closes his mouth several times like he can't decide what to say. Then he sighs and sits back in his chair. "I asked you to contact IT about increasing

Atticus's computing power. It's taking them way too long to test this code. We need to speed this up."

I scribble a few notes down before I look up at my dad. "Got it. Anything else?"

"Yes," Atticus says. "It would be great if you could reach out to Vertigo, the cybersecurity company we're partnering with, and schedule a meeting for early next week. It's critical we meet as soon as possible."

I give him a tight smile. "Sure. Right on top of that."

I make another note below the previous one, knowing damn well I'm not going to do either task. I feel slightly bad about that, but only until I remember the glitter I'm still picking off my scalp.

"Thanks, Princess." I cringe at Dad's use of his nickname for me. It's so degrading and makes me think he'll never see me as the grown woman I am today. I will forever be a toddler in his eyes. "Be sure to give Atticus all the support he needs. He's my best coder and a fantastic manager. I have high hopes for him."

I look up just in time to see Dad smiling at Atticus with nothing but pride. Pride I've never seen in his eyes when he looks at me.

"Is there anything else?" I ask as I quickly push to my feet. I can't sit here and listen to Dad praise Atticus for another second. He's never once said anything remotely close to that nice to me, and I'm his daughter.

Dad stares at me for a moment, a look of surprise on his face. Then his phone buzzes, dragging his attention away from me.

"No, we're done. My next meeting starts in two minutes."

"Great, enjoy the rest of your day." I turn on my heels and hightail it out of there before he can say anything else to detain me. Thankfully, I make it out the door and into the elevator before Atticus leaves Dad's office. The last thing I want to do is share an elevator ride with him.

Needing a break from this place, I hit the button for the ground floor and pull up the Starbucks app on my phone. I order myself a caramel macchiato and a chocolate croissant. I need the caffeine and sugar pick-me-up after that meeting.

~

Twenty minutes later, I step off the elevator to my floor and head toward the break room instead of my desk. While out, I grabbed some fruit and a yogurt parfait for lunch so I won't have to run out and get something. This will give me more time to work on my business proposal for Harold while I eat at my desk.

Just before I reach the door to the break room, I hear a female voice say my name. I stop and listen.

"That position should be mine." Trisha says. She's the only floater on this floor and was in line to be promoted to Atticus's assistant before my dad forced the job on me. I don't blame her for being upset about getting passed over, but I can't help but think she's upset for all the wrong reasons.

"She only took the job to get close to Atticus," Annie, the front desk admin, says. "It's so obvious with the way she fawns all over him."

My mouth drops open at the accusation. I hadn't even met Atticus before taking the job. All the admins except for Mrs. Romano have a serious crush on Atticus. I can't say I blame them, if all they care about is looks. There's no arguing that he's hot, but he's an asshole. They can have him.

"It's so embarrassing to watch her. Especially since I've heard it on good authority that Atticus can't stand her. Stefon is always talking to Atticus about how horrible Indie is at her job," Simone whispers. She's Stefon's assistant and the biggest bitch of them all. And she's lying through her teeth. It didn't take long to figure out that Atticus and Stefon do not get along. Atticus doesn't tell him anything. "I mean, she can't even use the scheduler on her computer. Just goes to show you money breeds stupid."

"And gets you undeserving opportunities," Annie says. "I wish I was a trust fund princess. Then I wouldn't have to work this stupid job."

"Why is she even here anyway?" Trisha asks. "Just to rub her privileged self in our faces?"

At that, I start to barge into the break room to correct her, but a throat clears across from me. When I look up, Mrs. Romano is standing opposite me. Her expression is one of kindness and understanding. She shakes her head to stop me from making a scene and steps into the break room.

"Annie," she says in a scolding tone. "If you're in here gossiping, then who's watching the front desk?"

"I was just taking my break," Annie whines.

"Well, break's over. Get back to work." Mrs. Romano's tone says she's not messing around. Within seconds, Annie, Simone, and Trisha come running out into the hallway and stumble over each other when they see me leaning against the wall.

I plaster a fake smile on my face as they each look at me in horror. They've made it clear that they don't like me, even to my face, but this is the first time they've been busted while gossiping about me.

They scurry away, each heading toward their desks. I've no doubt that this run in will only result in more gossip. I wish I could say I don't care, but it stings. These people don't know me, and they don't care to get to know me.

I don't really blame them. Not really. They're acting on instinct and perceived appearance.

I blame my father. He's clueless to how harmful forcing me into this position really is for me and his employees.

Mrs. Romano steps out of the break room and gives me a sad smile. "Don't listen to them. They're just jealous."

I nod as if I'm agreeing with her. Deep down, I know she's right, but that doesn't make it hurt any less. Being an heiress to a tech empire I don't want doesn't make me immune to pain.

"Thanks," I say and walk past her. "Better put this in the fridge and get back to work myself."

I feel her eyes on me as I open the refrigerator door. A heavy sigh escapes her, but she doesn't say anything else.

When I turn around, she's gone. Relieved I can be done with this interaction, I head back to my desk only to have all the tension return when I see my dad sifting through some mail.

"Dad," I say in a sickly-sweet voice. "Didn't get enough of me earlier?"

His angry eyes flash to mine. Without a word, he tosses the mail down and leaves. He's gone before I can even wrap my head around why he's angry at me now.

Then I look down at the pile of mail. On top is another prank envelope, only this one says it's from The Secret Swingers' Society. In large, italicized font, it says they loved the nude photo I submitted with my application—the detailed and passionate application—that has been accepted.

I drop my head back and groan. This day just keeps getting worse.

~

I WISH I COULD SAY THAT THE PRANK LETTERS STOPPED WITH THAT, BUT that would be a lie. Three more letters came this week. One each day.

One from the Department of Family Services letting me know the paternity test has been confirmed.

Another from Easy Eastern Brides asking why my donations stopped. My kinky online lover misses my chats.

And the last one came from Tiny Jimmy's Condom Company, confirming my one-year subscription. Thankfully, Dad didn't see any of these.

So when today's mail is delivered prank free, I sigh in relief.

Hopefully, this means whatever service Atticus hired to send them has finally run out of prank envelopes. He's never admitted to doing it, but I'm ninety-nine percent sure he's responsible. The smirk he gets on his face every time I confront him is a dead giveaway.

It isn't until shortly after lunch that everything goes to shit, when a delivery man shows up with a large bouquet. It's a gorgeous mix of colorful daisies with a few roses scattered throughout. When I pull the card, I smile.

> *Indie,*
> *May your day be bright and full of surprises.*
> *Elon*

I grab my phone and send him a quick text, thanking him for them. Elon always has a way of knowing when I'm in a shit mood. This isn't the first time he's sent me flowers or chocolates, or even coffee and pastries at the exact time I need it most.

Setting my phone aside, I grab my notebook and open it up to my last page of notes. I stare at the items I was asked to do for Atticus in the meeting we'd had. I still haven't reached out to IT. Nor have I contacted Vertigo about setting up the meeting.

Maybe doing these two things for him won't be so bad. Aside from the prank envelopes, he has backed off some. He's made an effort to be nicer, and he's even left my nameplate alone. It's ridiculous how happy that one little thing has made me this week.

Resolving to call IT to put in the request for a more powerful computer, I reach for my phone. Before I pick it up, something hits me in the nose. It's light and small, but I feel it all the same.

Brushing at it, a tiny ladybug falls to my lap. I frown just as a few more land on my chest.

"What the hell?" I whisper.

A faint buzzing sound fills my ears. At first, I'm not sure I even hear anything, but it's definitely there. I glance around the office to see if I can identify the source, but it seems to come from all directions. At the same time my phone buzzes, a mass of ladybugs swarms out of the vase that was just delivered to me.

When I say a mass, I mean hundreds and hundreds. Ladybugs are tiny, but I don't even know how that many fit inside the vase.

I grab my phone and see it's a message from Elon.

ELON

> Flowers? I didn't send you anything.

Groaning, I slam my phone down on my desk and turn toward Atticus's open door. He's staring at me and doing his best to hide his grin.

"You did this!" I yell, not caring who hears me. "I am so tired of this shit. Why are you doing this to me?"

He raises his brow in confusion. "What is it you think I'm doing?"

"Don't play dumb with me. You did this!" I point toward the vase that seems to spit ladybugs out like it's a factory. "Just like you sent me all those stupid prank letters and keep changing my nameplate."

"I haven't touched your nameplate in over a week," he says, like that somehow absolves him from the other accusations.

I spin around, pull open the drawer where I stashed the prank letters, and grab them. Then I pick up the vase and storm into his office.

"But you sent these." I slam the vase down in the middle of his desk, causing another mass of ladybugs to swarm out of the top. Then I toss the letters at him. "Will you please just leave me alone?"

A maniacal laugh escapes him. The sound of it both infuriates me and causes my stomach to flutter. I really hate this man.

Rather than stand here arguing with him, I turn around to leave. If I've learned anything about Atticus since I started working here, arguing doesn't do any good.

Before I make it out of his office, he calls out, "Maybe if you started doing your job, these pranks would stop. Better yet. *Quit.*"

All humor is gone from his tone when he says the word quit. That one word is laced with anger and threats. It's like throwing down the gauntlet. It's a challenge. And one I don't intend to lose.

I slowly turn around to face him with the sweetest smile I can muster plastered on my face. I step back up to his desk, take the top off the canister of chocolates he has, then pop a piece in my mouth. He tracks the movement with heat in his gaze.

"Oh, there will be no quitting, Mr. Rosi," I say in an equally sickly-sweet tone. "I'm afraid you're stuck with me for eight more months."

I don't wait for his response. After leaving his office, I grab my purse and phone and head straight for the elevator.

I don't care if it gets me in trouble with my dad.

I'm so angry right now, consequences are the last thing on my mind.

This workday is over.

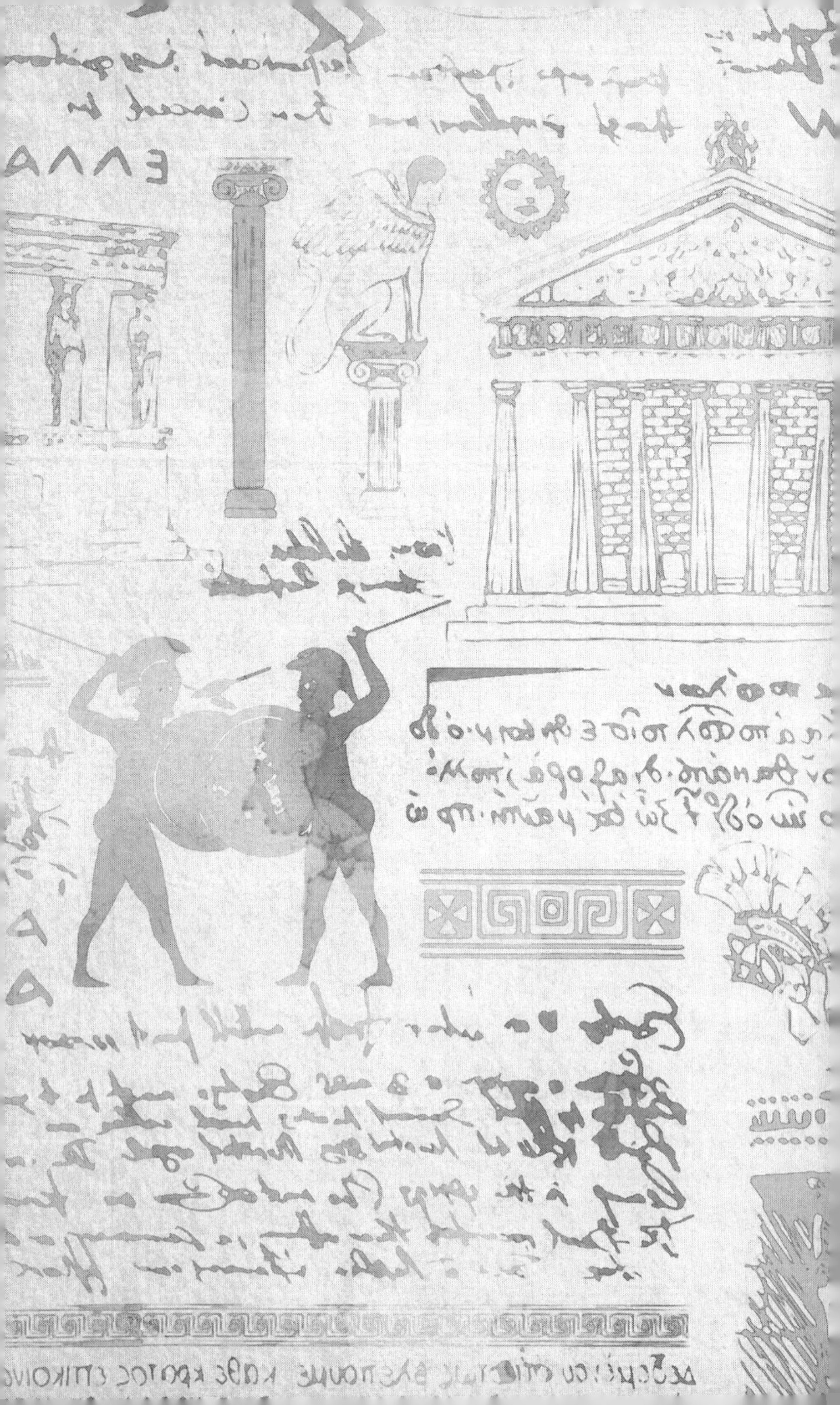

CHAPTER FIVE

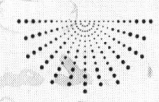

ATTICUS

DEMETRIUS
Where's the video game controller?

ATTICUS
Why the hell would I know?

DEMETRIUS
You're the one that's always putting our shit away. So where did you put it?

ATTICUS
Haven't touched it. Ask Eros.

DEMETRIUS
Eros won't wake up. He's snoring like a bear in hibernation.

ATTICUS
Can't help you, bro. I've got my own battles to fight.

"We're good to go!" Leon says as he rushes into my office with a huge smile on his face. "I just finished the last systems test, and it's running perfectly. We're ready for the next phase. Machine learning, here we come."

I let out a sigh of relief and relax into my seat. "That's great news. How long do you think it will take to run the next sequence of tests?"

"With my current PC, about a week. Maybe longer." He runs his fingers through his hair as he falls back in the chair opposite my desk. "If IT would ever get with me about increasing my computing power, a couple of days."

I furrow my brows. "You still haven't heard from IT?"

He shakes his head.

"Dammit!" I glance past him, ready to yell at Indie, but she's not at her desk. Instead, I pick up my phone and dial the head of IT. He and I have talked a lot over the years about my computing needs. With any luck, he'll be able to rush my request since I'm sure it was never made.

"Hey, Atticus. What can I do for you?"

"Hey, I really need you to rush a request since I suspect my assistant never put in for it last week."

"Whatcha need?"

"Leon needs a computer upgrade, more RAM, and a more powerful processor. Mr. Simons approved it."

"Yeah, I don't see anything in the system."

"That's what I was afraid of," I say, doing my best to hide the fact that I'm seething. Why I trusted her to do that, I'll never know. "Any chance you can rush it? We need to finish our next round of tests within the week. Got an important meeting coming up."

"Let me see." I hear him punching some keys for a few moments before he responds. "Best I can do is in two days."

"I'll take it. Thanks, man."

"Anything for you. Take care."

"You too." I hang up the phone and muffle a groan behind my hand.

"She never made the request," Leon says.

"Nope." I pop the P. "IT will have it ready in two days. We'll have to make that work and hope we can finish before the meeting at the end of next week."

Leon frowns. "What meeting?"

"The one with Vertigo. Indie was …" The words fade off as realization dawns. "Fuck! She never scheduled it, did she?"

I shake my mouse to wake up my computer, then open my calendar. Sure enough, there's no meeting scheduled next week.

I growl, drop my head back on my chair, and stare at the ceiling. "What's the point in having an assistant if she never does her job?"

"I take it the pranks aren't doing a damn thing to make her quit?"

"No," I say in exhaustion. "It's as if she loves the punishment. She acts angry, and even gives me shit about it, but she's not budging. I'm starting to think there's more behind why she's here."

"What do you mean?"

"I don't know." I think back to the meeting we had last week and how harsh James was with her. I can't shake the feeling that there's more going on between them that I don't understand. "James is really hard on her. I've overheard a few conversations that made me think he's forcing her to work here."

"But why would he do that? She clearly doesn't want to be here. If that's true, he's sabotaging his own company."

"I don't know. Maybe I'm wrong, but I'm pretty sure there's more to it than we know. Whatever game those two are playing, I'm the only one that's losing."

Before Leon can respond, there's a knock on my door. When I look past him, I cringe.

"Trisha." My voice is flat and devoid of all emotion. Trisha has made it perfectly clear what she wants from me, and it's something she'll never get. "What do you need?"

"I have a report for you." Her smile widens and her eyes drink me in like she's ready to jump me right here and now with zero regard that Leon is here to witness it.

"You can leave it on Indie's desk." I wave her off and focus my attention on my computer even though there's nothing there I need to see. "She'll make sure I get it."

"Oh, no," she gasps, and I make the mistake of looking up. She presses her hand to her chest and lightly brushes her finger along the collar of her shirt. I inwardly groan in disgust at her attempt to lure me in. "I was told I had to hand it directly to you. We can't let Indie lose this. It's just too important."

She saunters toward me. Instead of stopping in front of my desk, she walks around next to my chair. Then she leans over, making sure her breasts rub against my shoulder as she places the report in front of me.

"Here you go, Mr. Rosi." She drags out the syllables of my name in a seductive tone. Leon snickers and I recoil.

Completely oblivious to my lack of interest, she turns a sultry smile at me before she pulls her bottom lip between her teeth and leans close to my ear. "Let me know if you need anything else. I'm happy to help. And I do mean *anything*."

"Nope, I'm good." I pull away from her, putting as much distance between us as I can with me stuck in this chair.

"If you change your mind, you know where to find me." She runs her finger along the breast of my suit jacket, and I knock it away.

"That will be all, Trisha." I frown at her, and her eyes narrow. She's clearly pissed at my blatant disregard for her pass at me. But she quickly recovers.

"You'll change your mind." Her fake smile returns. "They always do."

She gives me a finger wave as she turns to leave, walking so her hips sway back and forth in an exaggerated motion.

"Damn, she makes me glad I'm married." Leon shivers in his seat with an expression of disgust equal to how I feel inside.

"Something tells me being married wouldn't stop that woman. She's relentless in her advances."

"Look at the bright side. At least you got that report."

"I'd rather deal with Indie." I pick up the report that she insisted she had to deliver to me personally. I have to fight back another groan.

"Even with how bad she is at her job?"

"Yes." I don't hesitate. "Dealing with Indie's inability to deliver my mail or schedule meetings is much preferred to having to see Trisha's fuck-me-eyes and undress-me-smile. That woman is scary. Besides, this is a quarterly financial report. No one told her this had to be personally delivered to me. All of management gets these as a courtesy."

Leon can't stop the laugh that escapes, and it makes me want to throw the damn report at him.

"Don't you have more code to test?" I ask.

He shrugs. "Not until IT gets me that new computer. Until then, I've got some time to spare."

I narrow my eyes at him and point toward the door. "Go bug someone else. I've got a meeting to schedule. Hopefully, it's not too late."

With one last smile, Leon pushes to his feet and leaves. I stare at the report on my desk. Instead of thinking about the scary woman who delivered it, my thoughts wander to Indie.

The fire in her eyes when the ladybug bouquet was delivered the other day has haunted my dreams. That look has been my primary source of spank bank material when I lie awake at night, hard as fucking steel, with no way to relieve myself except to imagine it's her grabbing my cock and not myself.

That little spitfire is the source of every headache I've had for the past few months, and yet she's the only face I see when I jack off.

I think about that woman far too often, and I need it to stop.

˜

A COUPLE OF HOURS LATER, I'M SIFTING THROUGH SOME NOTES AT THE small table in the corner of my office when Indie walks in and shuts the door behind her. I raise a brow as she leans against the closed door with a bag of candy in her hand.

She meets my gaze, and unlike the fuck-me-eyes I got from Trisha this morning, Indie's are fuck-*you*-eyes.

She pulls a piece of candy out of the bag and lifts it to her mouth. At first, I assume it's a gummy worm, but I quickly figure out that I'm wrong. It's a gummy penis.

I follow the movement as her tongue darts out and flicks the tip of the gummy like she would if she were giving head. Then she wraps her lips around it and sucks it into her mouth, moaning as she swallows it down.

It makes my dick twitch in excitement and realize just how big of a mistake I made with this prank. Indie has the upper hand.

"Can I …" My voice cracks, and I clear my throat. "Can I help you?"

A sultry smile lifts her lips and again, unlike when Trisha did this earlier, my body reacts in kind. The way she's looking at me has me so turned on, and my normal level of frustration with her magnifies.

She pushes off the door and takes a step closer to me. "I just thought I'd say thank you for the gift." She pulls another gummy penis from the bag and sucks on it. "Gummy candies are my favorite. How did you know?"

"I … I didn't send those." I haven't confessed to any of these pranks yet, and I'm not about to start. My willpower is strong. I can resist her tempting lips and wet pink tongue. *I think.*

"Your commitment to this farce is remarkable. I'm impressed."

"Farce?" My eyes don't leave her perfectly plump lips once as she slowly saunters toward me. I'm mesmerized by the way they move when she speaks.

Then she slams the bag of candy on the table, snapping me out of my trance. When my eyes meet hers again, they're filled with fire.

Not flames of desire or lust.

No. These are flames of revenge and wrath.

Flames that intend to send me straight to hell.

Where I belong.

For lusting after my assistant who infuriates me on a daily basis, and yet I still desperately want to press against the wall of my office and fuck into submission.

"When are you going to stop sending me this shit?"

"I'm not sending you anything."

"Yes. You. Are." She pokes me in the chest with each word spoken.

I stand and tower over her, but she doesn't seem the least bit intimidated by my size. Her feistiness turns me on even more. "I think a better question is, when are you going to start doing your job?"

"Never." She scoffs.

"Then quit."

"I can't."

"What do you mean, you can't? It's easy. Turn on that fucking computer, open you email app, and type up an email that says I quit. Then send it to me. I'll take care of the rest."

The scowl on her face deepens and she crosses her arms over her chest, pushing her breasts together. It takes every ounce of willpower I possess to keep my eyes on hers.

"I know how to write a letter of resignation. That's not what I mean."

"Then what do you mean?" I growl.

"That's none of your business."

"That's where you're wrong." I charge toward her, causing her to stumble back until she hits the wall. I cage her between the wall and my body. Every instinct in me is screaming at me to press my body against hers and claim that snarky mouth as mine, but I don't let myself touch her. "Everything you do around here is my business. When you don't give me my messages or answer the phone or set up important meetings that I asked you to make, it affects my career. My life. Your very presence in this building makes what you do my fucking business."

"Move." There's nothing but venom in that single word, but she doesn't push me away.

I shake my head, my eyes fixate on her damn lips again. "Not until you tell me why."

"I don't owe you anything."

"Oh, I think you do. Miss Yale Graduate. *Summa cum laude* at that. Tell me how someone who graduates from one of the top Ivy League schools in the nation with a near 4.0 GPA can't figure out how to deliver messages."

She sucks in a breath. "You looked into my records?"

"I have your resume. Never really paid attention until that interesting meeting with your father. What's going on there?"

She shoves at my chest, but I don't budge. "None of your business. Maybe if you'd stop kissing my dad's ass all the time, you wouldn't need an assistant."

"Oh, Princess." I step closer, placing my hands on either side of her head, and lean down to her level. "With each word you speak, all you're doing is showing your ignorance. No one is kissing ass in this office. That's for damn sure."

At the mention of kissing, my eyes drift to her mouth. She's breathing hard. Her lips are slightly parted and the tip of her tongue swipes across her bottom lip. The movement has me leaning in closer until I can feel her breath on my skin.

She lifts her hands and the tips of her fingers brush against the stubble of my short beard. It sends a shock wave of desire through my body and straight to my cock. My need to kiss her, taste those luscious lips, and feel her small frame wrapped up in my large one is so strong, I almost give in. *Almost.*

But right before our lips meet, I push off the wall, spin around, and shove my hands into my hair. *Fuck. Fuck. FUCK.*

My dick aches as it presses against my pants and my heart is pounding so hard, I barely hear her when she speaks.

"Atticus."

I shake my head and rush to the other side of my desk. I need the barrier between us before I do something truly stupid.

"Sorry." I clear my throat. I feel her eyes on me, but I can't bring myself to meet her gaze. "I don't know what came over me. That shouldn't have happened."

In my peripheral vision, I can see she's not moving. She's frozen against the wall as if she's just as stunned as I am by what almost happened. Then she moves toward the door and opens it, but she stops before she exits.

I look up to see her rush back to the table and grab the bag of gummy penises. She looks up and gives me a forced smile. "Gummies really are my favorite. Even in the shape of dicks. Thank you for these."

Then she walks out and quickly takes her seat at her desk, leaving me confused, hard as steel, and wanting so much more from her.

Indigo Simons has officially gotten under my skin in more ways than one. I want her in ways I have no business thinking about. Ways that could put my career and job in jeopardy.

I need that woman to quit now more than I ever did before.

CHAPTER SIX

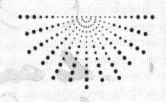

INDIGO

DAD

It's after ten. Why aren't you at your desk?

INDIGO

Because I'm not in the office.

DAD

Why not?

INDIGO

Because I had something else I had to do this morning.

DAD

What could possibly be more important than showing up for work?

INDIGO

I cleared it with Mrs. Romano and informed Atticus. I'll be there in about an hour.

DAD

Next time tell me when you're not going to be here.

INDIGO

Micromanaging the admin staff's time off seems like a task that's beneath the CEO of a multi-million-dollar company, Dad!

"Indie! What do you think of this?" The excited voice of one of the little girls calls from across the room. When I look up, I smile when I see it's Leona. She took the longest to warm up to me, but once she did, she latched onto me like I was a lifeline.

Silencing my phone, I slip it into my purse and vow not to check it again until my shift ends in twenty minutes.

I rarely volunteer in the mornings, but one of the regulars called in sick and they desperately needed help. I couldn't say no. I'll do anything for this clinic, plus, it's hard to say no to pottery on any given day let alone when it's for a good cause.

Two or three afternoons a week and every other Saturday, I volunteer at Play Therapy, a group therapy clinic focused on helping kids with social anxiety develop valuable skills so they can manage their anxiety in group settings, particularly in the classroom. I volunteer as an aide and help execute the logistics of these sessions so the therapists can focus on working one-on-one with the kids. My job is to make sure everyone has the supplies they need to complete each project.

Pottery is one of my favorite activities they do with these kids. Maybe it's because pottery was the first activity that really helped my brother, Jay. Or maybe it's because pottery is just that much fun. Nothing beats getting to help kids while also doing something I love.

"Oh, Leona!" I kneel next to her seat and fawn over her work. "I love the color you used. It matches your dress."

She smiles at me, and her eyes light up as she sways back and forth in front of her workstation, her pink dress swirling around her little legs.

"Pink is my favorite color." She beams.

"I love it too. It reminds me of princesses. And you, my dear," I lightly bop her on the nose, "are definitely a princess."

Her smile grows. "My daddy calls me a princess. He says no matter how old I get, I will always be his little princess."

"As it should be." My smile wanes, but I force back into submission.

There was a time when I felt the same way about my dad calling me princess. He'd beam at me and make me feel like I could conquer the world. Even at the young age of seven, just like Leona must feel.

But everything changed when he and Mom got divorced. I was only ten, but I was old enough to pick up on the change in his behavior. He never treated me the same again and hearing him call me princess didn't make me feel good like it did when I was younger. I get that couples don't always work out, and Lord knows my parents are better off apart than together, but he changed with me too.

My mom isn't the best person. She uses people to get what she wants. With my dad, it was money. I don't think she ever loved him. She loved his status, wealth, and all the luxuries that being married to a millionaire afforded.

Mom was awarded primary custody of me in the divorce, and she got one hell of a settlement. She's never had to work or worry about money again. There have been a few times I thought she might get married again to another wealthy fool who was blinded by her beauty and charm. Mom has more beauty than any one person should be allowed to have. Add in the charm she can turn on whenever it suits her needs, and few men can resist her.

But getting married meant losing her alimony payments from Dad. The only way she'd risk that was if the man she was considering marrying could provide her with more. But those pesky prenups stopped her from ever taking the plunge.

As long as she never remarries, Dad has to pay her a nice chunk of change every month for the rest of his life. Mom's lawyer was better than Dad's, and I swear he takes it out on me.

"This is my favorite part." Leona points at the center of the flower she made from her ball of clay. It's got round pink petals and a big yellow center with a heart drawn in the middle of it.

"I like that part too," I say. "The heart gives it a nice touch that is uniquely you."

"I'm gonna give it to my daddy. He loves my flowers."

"I bet he does." I hold my smile despite how much her words

make my heart hurt. I'm happy she has such a great relationship with her father. It makes me miss what I lost so many years ago.

"Be careful carrying that over to the kiln table, okay? I've got to get started on cleaning up. See you next week?"

She nods, still smiling like she won a prize.

While the kids all transfer their clay art, I get to work putting all the supplies away. I'm at the sink washing up the tools when Shannon, one of the lead therapists, steps up beside me.

"Thank you so much for coming in this morning. Especially on such short notice. I don't know what I would have done without you."

I smile at Shannon, happier than she'll ever know for her words of gratitude. I could work for my father for the rest of my life and I don't think I'd ever get this level of kindness. At Dad's office, I'm treated with contempt and a very heavy dose of dislike.

Here, they love me and treat me like I'm a gift. Being truly appreciated for my contributions makes it so much easier to give myself to this cause. I'm passionate about helping children with debilitating anxiety and would volunteer here no matter what. But their kindness makes it that much more enjoyable.

"It was my pleasure," I say. "I love working with these kids."

"It shows. And they love you just as much." One of the kids cries out, dragging Shannon's attention away from me. "I better go see what that's all about. See you later this week?"

"Yes, I'll be here after work tomorrow."

"Great, see you then." She calls out as she rushes across the room.

I focus my attention on cleaning up so I can get back to the office. While Mrs. Romano said my absence this morning wasn't an issue, I don't want to give my dad or Atticus any more reasons to get onto me.

Especially after that almost kiss in Atticus's office last week. The almost kiss I've been trying really hard to pretend didn't almost happen. I cannot be attracted to Atticus, not like that.

Sure, he's hot. Very hot. Tall, dark, sexy scruffy beard, with tattoos all over his body. Well, I assume they're all over his body.

From the glimpses I've gotten of his arms on the few occasions he's taken his suit jacket off and rolled up his sleeves, I've seen hints of his arm sleeves.

Just because he's nice on the eyes doesn't mean anything can happen between us.

Because it can't.

He's my father's protégé, and therefore, I cannot have anything to do with him. As soon as he gets what he wants from my dad, he'll toss me aside anyway.

I've avoided him as much as possible since then, and he's given me the same courtesy, but that can't go on forever. At some point, we're going to have to interact again.

Until then, I'm going to enjoy the peace it's brought me in the office.

∼

So much for peace.

Waiting on my desk when I finally make it to the office is another prank package. Not a letter. Not a box disguised as office supplies. Nor is it a beautiful bouquet of flowers meant to serve as a delivery mechanism for a swarm of ladybugs.

Ladybugs that we're still finding all over the building.

Nope. This package hides nothing. The box is long and narrow. In big bold red letters are the words Big Ass Dildo on all four sides. To make sure those words stand out even more, the box is white.

I spin around and glare at Atticus. He's not alone. Sitting across from him is the one other person in this building that Atticus might dislike more than me. Stefon James.

Stefon manages the other half of this floor. Where Atticus develops the software and code for my dad, Stefon protects it from cyber theft. At least, that's how I understand the difference between their jobs.

Stefon is maybe ten years older than Atticus and has been working for my father twice as long. Rumor has it they're both being considered for a promotion upstairs and Stefon is pissed about it.

I'm not the only person the admin staff gossip about around here, and I've become very adept at eavesdropping on their conversations.

Victor Dumas, a longtime friend of my dad's, and someone I call Uncle Vic, is retiring later this year. My dad doesn't have any siblings and Uncle Vic has been more like a brother to my dad than a friend. They're both from money and grew up together in New York's high society. He's always been nice to me, and in many ways, I like him better than my dad.

Uncle Vic helped Dad start this company when the tech industry boomed in the late 1990s. SimTech's success is largely attributed to Dad seeing the direction the market was going and getting ahead of this industry. Uncle Vic serves as the chief information officer for the company, a role that either Atticus or Stefon should be equally qualified to fill.

Turns out Stefon thinks the position should be his without question simply because he's worked here longer. But according to the rumor mill, my dad likes Atticus more. If this new code Atticus has been working on is as successful as everyone says it will be, the job is likely his.

Stefon knows this and has been out for blood almost since the day Atticus started working here.

But none of that means a damn thing to me. I couldn't care less who gets the promotion. I don't plan on being here for the long haul, no matter what Dad tries to force on me. As soon as my year is up, I'm out of here.

In the meantime, I want the prank gifts to stop coming.

With no regard for the meeting taking place, I barge into Atticus's office and slam the box on top of his desk, scattering little foil-wrapped chocolates across his desk and onto the floor.

"This has to stop," I say through seething teeth, glancing around at the mess I made. Atticus must have gotten a new type of chocolate because I haven't seen those before.

Atticus's eyes shift from Stefon to the box to the chocolates scattered across his office to me and back to the box before a sly grin lifts his lips. His sexy, pink lips look so soft between the stubble of his beard. Lips that I want to know what they feel like against mine. I want to taste them, lick them, maybe even bite them until he's growling at me to stop.

I hate myself just a little bit for noticing and having such lustful thoughts.

"What's this?" Atticus picks up the box and studies it before he lifts a heated gaze to mine. The look in his eyes has me stumbling back a couple of steps. "Ordering *toys* on the job?"

"You know damn well I didn't order that." I point a shaky finger at the box. I'm not sure if my body is trembling from anger or need. Maybe a little of both. "When will this end, *Mr. Rosi?*" I say his name with all the sass I can muster beneath this blanket of anger. "I can't take it anymore."

Something close to sympathy crosses his expression, but it's gone almost as quickly as it appeared. Our eyes lock and the unspoken emotions passing between us are far more complicated than I have time to digest. There's dislike there, but also something much more primal and needy. *Desire.*

That desire floods my senses like a gentle whisper in my ear. I swallow back a groan, fighting these feelings like my life depended on it.

"I think I'm going to go," Stefon says as he pushes to his feet. "We can finish discussing your security needs when you're not …" He waves his hand in the air at me, then looks down at the box I slammed down on Atticus's desk. "Hell, I don't know what this is, and I don't want to know."

"No." I hold my hand up to stop Stefon. "You stay. I'm leaving. And by leaving, I mean the building."

"But you just got here." Atticus's deep rumbling voice causes my insides to shiver. *I hate him. I hate him. I hate him,* I chant to myself as I fight to get my body under control. One almost-kiss doesn't change anything between us. Why can't my stupid body understand that?

Stefon ignores my comment, slips past me, and out the door. I give Atticus a closed lip smile that I hope expresses my disgust toward him and not this annoying attraction building between us. "And now I'm leaving. I'll see you tomorrow."

"Indigo!" He calls out my name with so much authority and power that my legs nearly give out under me. "I *need* you to do your job."

"Then stop sending me this shit!" I pick up the box and toss it at him. It hits him square in the chest. He bats it away as if it didn't even phase him. Then I pick up a handful of the foil wrapped chocolates and throw those at him too. They hit him in the face, but he doesn't even flinch.

"You weren't doing your job before these started coming." He points at the box. "Why should I expect anything to change if they stop?"

"I guess you'll never know." I spin around and head to my desk.

He calls out to me before I pass through the door. "Just quit and make both of our lives easier."

I turn around to face him. The look of desperation in his eyes makes me think he's just as exhausted with our dynamic as I am. My shoulders sag as I reply, "I can't."

Without another word, I grab my purse and head for the elevator. I can't take another moment of this day.

Atticus has made it clear he's not going to stop or own up to these pranks. Maybe it's time for me to come up with one of my own.

I don't know when or how, but I will get Atticus back when he least expects it.

~

"Thank God you're here!" Francesca, or Frannie, my dad's second wife, pulls me into a hug. She's in tears and looks like she's ready to collapse in a puddle. "He's finally calmed down, but he won't talk to me. He just wants you."

I return her hug and give her a kiss on the cheek. I've always loved Frannie. She's a kind woman with a gentle heart. Dad married her about four years after he and Mom divorced. I later found out they got married because Frannie was pregnant. They love each other, even though I struggle to see what Frannie sees in my dad, but I can't help but wonder if they would've gotten married had she not gotten pregnant.

Regardless, I got a great stepmom and brother out of it, even if Dad can't see the good in Jay.

"I'll talk to him." I squeeze her arm before I release her from our embrace. "I take it Dad's not home yet."

I glance around the modern and sleek penthouse that takes up the entire top floor of this building. It's got panoramic views of Manhattan and more open space than anyone needs. Especially with the private rooftop garden they have as well. The kitchen is huge with appliances that rival most restaurants. The living space is devoid of much furniture. There's one long sofa and two chairs on either side that face the floor-to-ceiling windows. There's no TV or any other signs that people actually live here. I find the space utterly depressing.

She shakes her head. "He's still at the office. He's been working long hours lately. With Vic retiring and some new product launches they're working, it's been like this for a while."

"Story of Dad's life," I say under my breath, but not quiet enough that Frannie doesn't hear me.

"That's not fair, Indie, and you know it. He doesn't always work this much."

I shrug. "I guess I've never seen him any other way. And now that he's making me work for him, I see it firsthand."

Frannie sighs before she leads the way down the hallway toward Jay's bedroom. "You should tell James what you've been up to. If you explained your plans to him, he'd go easier on you."

"Nope, not his business."

She looks over her shoulder at me and gives me a motherly stare. The kind that says I'm disappointed in your decisions, but I'll support you because I love you. I ignore the feelings of guilt it evokes in me.

Frannie and Elon have both been on my case about telling Dad about my plans for a foundation. It would certainly make my life easier if I could convince Dad I'm not a gold digger like my mom, who has zero ambition beyond mooching off him. But I've tried that before, and he didn't listen.

That's what led to me being stuck working for him for a year. He thinks my plans are dumb and pointless. He called me a bleeding heart with no real vision.

The hard truth is that Dad doesn't care to understand me or my dreams. He just wants me to take over his company because he doesn't think Jay will ever be emotionally stable enough to do it.

It's my life's mission to help kids with social anxiety like Jay to learn to manage their anxiety so they can take over multi-million-dollar companies should they choose to. I refuse to give up on that dream simply because Dad can't see the value in it.

Or, more like, refuses to see it. It's easier for him to ignore the hard truths concerning Jay than it is to learn how to work with him so they can both come out on the other side as better people.

When we reach Jay's bedroom, Frannie lightly knocks before pushing the door open. "Jay. Indie's here."

He immediately jumps up from where he's sitting on his bed and rushes toward me.

"Hey, buddy." I give him a tight hug. "How's it going?"

He shrugs and stares at the floor. "I had another meltdown today."

"Do you want to talk about it?" I learned a long time ago that he responds better if I ask him if he wants to talk rather than asking him to tell me what happened. Leaving it up to him typically gets him to open up faster.

"Not really."

"Okay. You don't have to." I lift his chin so he has to look at me. "Just tell me you're okay."

He sighs and his little shoulders sag even more. It's hard enough being an eleven-year-old kid without this anxiety on top of it. It breaks my heart to see him struggle this much.

"I don't know. Everyone thinks I'm being dramatic—like I'm doing this on purpose—but I'm not. If I could control it, I would."

"Hey, don't be so hard on yourself. You'll get better at it with time. Those therapy sessions have been helping, right?"

"I guess." He drags his feet as he walks back to his bed and drops on it as if the weight of the world is pressing down on him. "It's just slow. I wish I could learn faster."

"I know, buddy." I sit next to him and wrap him in a hug. He willingly hugs me back. Not everyone gets hugs like this from Jay, and it makes me smile every time I get one. His sensory issues often hold him back. "I wish I could make it better faster too. Unfortunately, these things take time. But I promise, if you keep working, then so will I. Before you know it, you'll be the king of your emotions, and no one will be able to stop you from achieving all your dreams."

He looks up at me with hopeful eyes. "You think so?"

"I know so." I smile at him, meaning that with every ounce of my being. I will not stop until he's received the best help known to man.

And no one, not even Dad, will stop me from making that a reality.

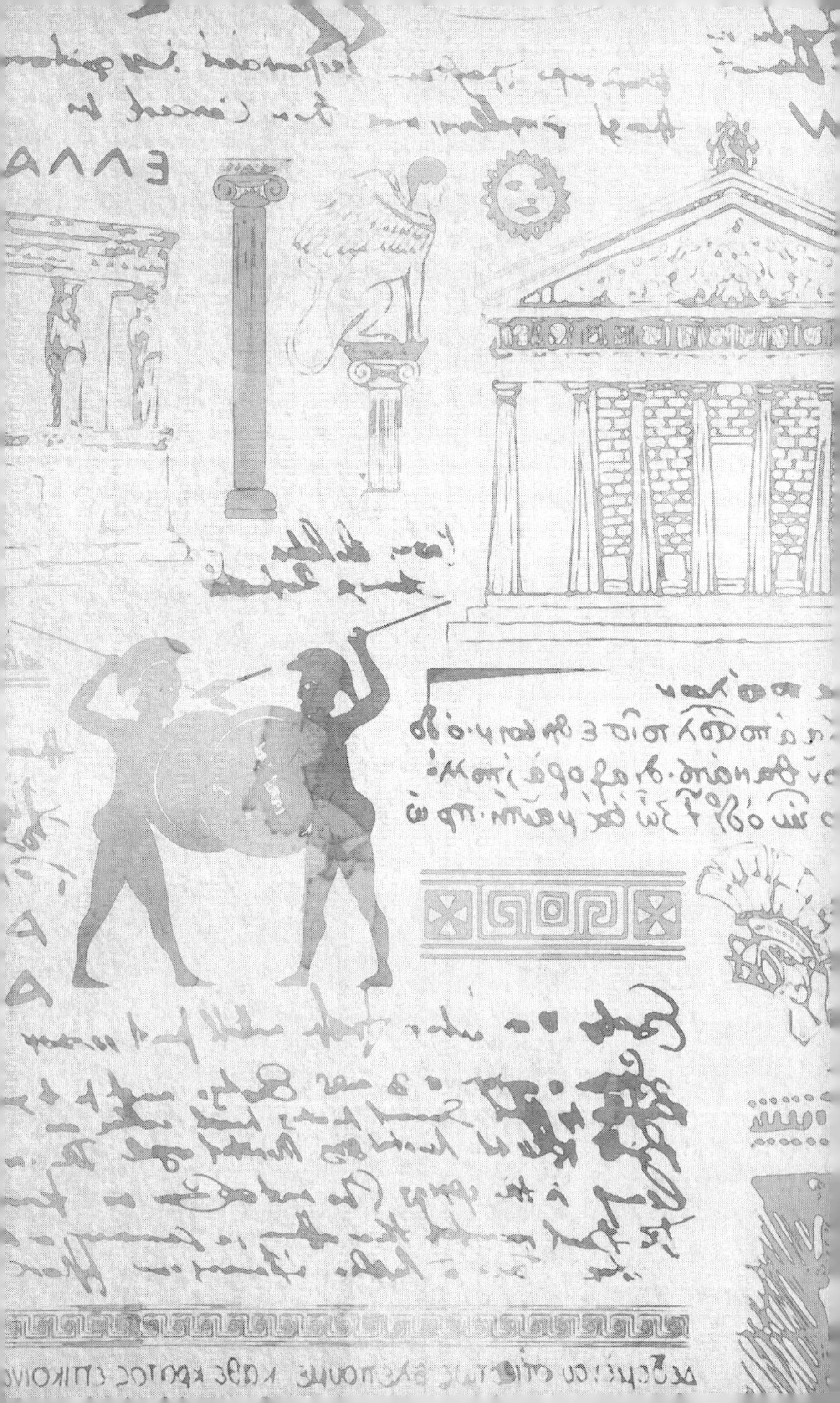

CHAPTER SEVEN

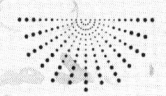

ATTICUS

LEON

Dude, this new computer is kick ass.

ATTICUS

I take it that means it's processing much faster than before.

LEON

You have no idea. I just wish we'd had it sooner.

ATTICUS

As long as we get the tests done before the meeting, we'll be fine.

LEON

Oh, don't you worry. I got you!

I pocket my phone and grab my notebook before I exit my office. It's been a quiet morning so far. Ever since I almost kissed Indie, we've avoided each other. The longest conversation we've had since then was when she threw the dildo box at me.

There wasn't really a dildo in it. It was stuffed with shredded paper and a letter congratulating the receiver on their embarrassment. I don't think embarrassed is the right word to describe Indie's reaction. Pissed. Infuriated. Murderous. Those are all better descriptors.

She's not at her desk as I leave my office. I pause as I'm walking by. My brows furrow when my eyes catch on a brochure on top of her calendar. I pick it up and frown—cognitive behavioral therapy. Flipping through it, it's clearly meant to help kids struggling with anxiety, depression, and other social interactions.

Why does Indie have something like this? She's only twenty-six. She's never said anything about kids, and she's too young to have a kid old enough to need this kind of therapy.

After the meeting where she mentioned her education, I couldn't stop myself from looking into her employment files more closely. Her Yale transcript is impressive, with her near perfect GPA, only earning herself one A- during her time there. That's no small feat at any university, let alone from an Ivy League college.

She lives modestly in a small, one-bedroom apartment in Chelsea, not too far from where my brothers and I live. With her wealth, she could afford something much bigger and nicer. Not that where she lives is bad. It's just surprising considering I've been to her father's penthouse for parties and there's nothing modest about how he lives.

With every small piece of insight I gain about her, it only makes me want to know more.

Indigo Simons is a mystery that I want to solve. There's so much more to her than she lets on. My interest goes beyond wanting my assistant to do her job. My interest is in *her*, and that's a dangerous avenue to pursue.

She's off limits. She's the boss's daughter and my assistant. That's a recipe for disaster if I ever saw one.

But hearing her defend her education and intelligence to her father the other day triggered something in me that I can't explain. It made me want to know more about the petite spitfire of a woman insistent on making my life hell.

There's more to her story, and I want to know what it is. This damn brochure is only making her more intriguing. I don't have the time to be intrigued by my assistant.

Putting the brochure back where I found it, I make my way down the hallway toward the elevator. I have a meeting with James to discuss my future with SimTech. It's a last-minute meeting that he called me personally about yesterday afternoon. I may be on a first name basis with James, but his assistant always sets up his meetings. James never does them himself.

This has to be a good sign. I'm ahead of schedule on code development. The machine learning tests that Leon started are producing great results. The report summarizing the findings could be further along, but I'll get that done. I should probably rely on staff to help with it, but I'm holding that close.

The last time I trusted someone with sensitive details, they stole my work and pawned it off as their own. The shitty part was that the thief was my supervisor. Since I was fresh out of college, the higher-ups didn't believe me. My boss got a promotion from my work, and I was out of a job. I couldn't continue to work for a company that supported that level of intellectual theft.

Three months later, I started with SimTech and have worked my way up the ladder fast. That's largely because I keep a lot of my work to myself. The only person I trust is Leon, and even then, I don't share everything with him.

Getting burned like that makes it hard to fully trust your colleagues, and it's not something that's easy to get over. But if I want to make it to the top floor, I'm going to have to learn to let go more. I can't micromanage everything I do and still climb the management ladder.

"Atticus!" I cringe at the sound of my name coming from Trisha. She's standing at the front desk, most likely gossiping with Annie.

With my head down, I make a beeline for the bank of elevators, pretending like I didn't hear her. That doesn't seem to make any difference to her as she steps in my path, effectively blocking my escape.

"What do you need, Trisha?" I ask, my tone laced with annoyance.

She steps closer to me and lightly runs her fingertip over the lapel of my jacket. I take a step back, and her hand drops. Seemingly undeterred, her lips turn up in a seductive smile. I step around her and press the button to call an elevator, hoping she takes the hint.

No such luck.

She leans against the wall next to the button and looks me up and down. "I just wanted to remind you that I'm here and available if you need any assistance."

"Thanks, but I have an assistant," I say coldly.

She pushes off the wall and leans close to my ear. "We all know that Indie barely does any work. I hate thinking about how hard that must be for you. I'm here for you, Atticus." She pauses and presses her hand to my chest. "For whatever you need."

The elevator dings, and the door slides open, saving me from this nightmare of an exchange. I push past her and step inside, pushing the button for the top floor. I look up at her and say, "No thank you. I'm good."

I see her smile drop just before the doors slide closed. I sigh, drop against the back wall, and focus on regaining my composure before I reach James's office. The last thing I need is to be annoyed with the admin staff before a meeting to discuss my future with the company. Hopefully, a future that will put an entire floor between me and Trisha and any other admin that gets crazy ideas about me.

I'm greeted with a professional smile from Sloane, James's assistant, the moment I step out of the elevator.

"Good morning, Mr. Rosi," she says. I nod and smile. This is how an assistant should greet me. There are no uncomfortable grins or looks that make me think she's undressing me. "Mr. Simons is ready for you. Go right in."

"Thanks, Sloane." I nod and walk past her toward the closed door of his office. I give it a knock and wait until I hear James call for me to enter.

I poke my head around the door, and a broad smile spreads

across his face when he sees me. His warm greetings always make me feel on top of the world. His smile tells me he's pleased with my performance and I'm on the path to success.

"Atticus. So glad you could meet with me on such short notice."

"Of course. I've always got time for the boss."

He waves off my flattery and points toward one of the chairs opposite his desk. "Please sit. We've got a lot to discuss."

I take a seat, adjusting my tie before I get comfortable. James is easy-going for someone in his position. He's never made me feel inferior because I don't come from money. I wasn't born with opportunities handed to me. The only way I've gained anything in this world is by working my ass off to get it.

No matter how many times I tell myself I deserve to be here, sitting in his office always makes me nervous. I don't know if it's him that intimidates me or the grandeur of this office. It's large, probably half the size of my entire apartment, with a million-dollar view of Central Park.

His ornate mahogany desk probably cost more than I make in a year. The walls are lined with dark wood bookcases, a wet bar, and art to rival that in the nicest galleries in the city. He's got a closet with a full wardrobe, a full-sized bathroom, and a lounge area bigger than my living room and kitchen combined.

So yeah, this office is intimidating for someone who grew up with minimalist parents in a modest RV with not much other than the clothes on his back.

If I get this promotion, I'll earn the office down the hall that's similar in grandeur. It's smaller. The lounge area is half the size of James's office, but it has a private bathroom and the same million-dollar view.

I want it all.

"Tell me how Indie is doing," James says. "Is she doing a good job for you?"

His question catches me off guard and he sees my hesitation. A slow smile lifts his lips as I answer. "Um, she's doing okay."

The laughter that escapes him fills the entire room. "That doesn't sound very convincing."

I shrug, not wanting to throw Indie under the bus. There's something more going on between them. I just know it. As much as I want an assistant that does her job and does it well, I don't want to make things worse for her. It's an odd turn of events that just now hits me.

Besides, I can't exactly tell James that his daughter infuriates me or that she hates me. I can't imagine that will give me a leg up with this promotion. He doesn't need to know about the office war we wage against each other or the inconvenient attraction building between us.

I didn't know it was possible to desire and lust after someone that frustrates me this much until I met her.

Before I can respond, there's a light knock on the door before it opens. When I turn around, I'm surprised to see Indie standing in the doorway.

"I'm sorry. I thought we had a meeting. I'll come back another time." She steps back, but James lifts his hand to wave her in.

"No, you're not interrupting. I wanted to see you both."

Indie meets my confused gaze. She looks worried, maybe even a little surprised by this impromptu meeting.

I furrow my brows and turn my gaze back to James. He told me he wanted to discuss my future with the company. What does that have to do with Indie?

"What do you need with both of us?" I ask, my confusion and concern coming out with every word.

"Indie, please have a seat." James points at the chair next to me without answering my question.

Indie sighs and steps into the room. Whatever worry I saw in her expression a moment ago is gone and replaced with irritation.

"What was so important that you had to drag me away from my desk?" Her words are laced with sass and sarcasm. "I mean, I have so much work to do, answering the phones and setting meetings. Those things don't get done by themselves, you know?"

"Could have fooled me," I mumble.

Her eyes snap to mine and her irritation flares.

"What was that?" James asks.

"Nothing." I wave it off like it was no big deal. "Just telling her it can all wait."

His eyes narrow as he studies me for an uncomfortable beat. Then he shakes his head and smiles.

"I called you both here today to discuss your futures with the company. I've made it clear to both of you that Atticus is in line for a promotion. I couldn't be more pleased with your performance. The productivity of your department is the highest in the company. You managed to do that while maintaining the respect and loyalty of those beneath you. That's a sign of a great leader."

"Thank you, sir." I can't stop the smile that lifts my lips. "That means a lot to hear you say that."

"You're an asset to this company, Atticus. I'm grateful to have you leading that team. However, with Victor's retirement upon us, his departure will leave a huge hole in upper management. Vic has been with me since the start. He helped me build this company into what is today, and I'd love nothing more than to have my daughter step in and fill the void he'll leave."

"What?" Indie and I both say at the same time, the surprise evident in our tone.

James holds up his hands as if to calm us. "I'm not saying that's what I intend to do. I'm just putting it on record that I want my daughter involved in executive leadership. I'm not going to be around forever, and she is my only heir."

Indie grunts. "What about your son?"

James sighs as if exhausted before this conversation even gets started. "James Jr. will never be able to lead a company."

"You don't know that." I can feel the animosity radiating off Indie's words, making me instinctively recoil. "Give him a chance and recognize him as your heir too. He's a smart kid."

"I didn't ask you here today to discuss Jay's mental state. Even if he were stable, you're still my firstborn."

"If you would acknowledge his needs and support his treatment, his mental state would be fine. You talk about him like he's a lost cause, and he's not!" Indie shoots up out of the chair and glares down at her father. I can almost smell the smoke from her eyes, something new and unfamiliar. And for once, it isn't directed at me. Her body is tense, and she looks like she's ready to go to war for her brother.

It's the hottest thing I've ever seen, and I can't take my eyes off her.

"This is not the time for this conversation. Sit down!" James's commanding voice booms through the room, causing me to flinch. Indie, however, doesn't budge.

"I can't do this, Dad. Whatever it is you want from me, I can't."

"Yes, you can. Stop acting like your mother. It's time you grow up and take life seriously. I want you to lead this company when I'm gone."

"I take life very seriously. You just refuse to see *me*. Just because I don't want to be like you doesn't mean I don't have dreams and ambition."

"Sit down." James slams his hand on top of his desk so hard it shakes his monitor. I've never seen him this angry or emotional since I started working for him. Indie takes a step back. When her legs hit the chair, she falls to a seated position.

"You might be able to bully me into working here for the rest of this year, but you can't make me run your company. I don't want it."

"I want you to mentor under Atticus," James says, completely ignoring every word Indie just said. "Learn from him. He knows this company inside and out. He's been training to step up since the day he joined us. I trust him to teach you what you need to know to take over. Put that business degree of yours to good use."

"No!" she yells. "That wasn't the deal. You said one year. One. Year. Working as an assistant, not training to run the damn place. We signed a contract."

"I know what we signed, but I'm altering the arrangement."

"Sir, if I may," I interject. "I'm not sure what you're proposing is such a good idea. I want that promotion, and I'm not afraid to tell you that. If you're asking me to train Indie so she can step into that position instead of me, I don't think I can do that."

James shakes his head before I even finish. "That's not what I'm suggesting. I know you want the promotion. Prove to me that you've got what it takes by working more closely with Indie, not as your assistant, but as *your* protégée. Teach her the ropes. Show her what it means to be a leader in this company. Help her to be able to step into my role one day."

"You can't be serious?" Indie cries out next to me. Her entire body is shaking, and her eyes are wet with unshed tears. I have a strong urge to comfort her.

"I'm completely serious," James says, his tone devoid of all emotion.

"But we had a deal." She pleads.

"And I'm making an amendment to that deal. You still have to give me a year. I will accept whatever you decide at the end of that year, but you have to give this a fair shot, or you will not get your trust. Am I clear?"

My eyes dart between them, and for the first time since Indie started working here, it's clear there's a lot I don't know about why she's here or her relationship with her dad.

"Dad. Please, don't do this." Her voice cracks. There's something close to desperation, or maybe even anguish in her words, that has me aching to reach for her. To hold her close and hug her. Whisper in her ear that everything will be okay.

"It's done. I expect more from you, Indie. I expect the best."

Indie's eyes are fixed on the floor. A lone tear breaks free and runs down her cheek. I have to fight to keep my hands to myself and not wipe it away. I hate seeing her like this. She may drive me crazy, but I like her fire and spunk. She's strong and independent and never takes any shit. Seeing her look hopeless nearly breaks me.

She's clearly stunned by this turn of events. I know I am. When James called me to his office to talk about my future with the company, this was not what I expected.

It's bad enough that Indie is my assistant. But protégée? She barely does the job he hired her to do, and now he expects me to train her to take over the company.

He didn't say as much, but I suspect that if I fail, he won't promote me.

This fucking sucks. My life is already complicated enough. I don't need this too.

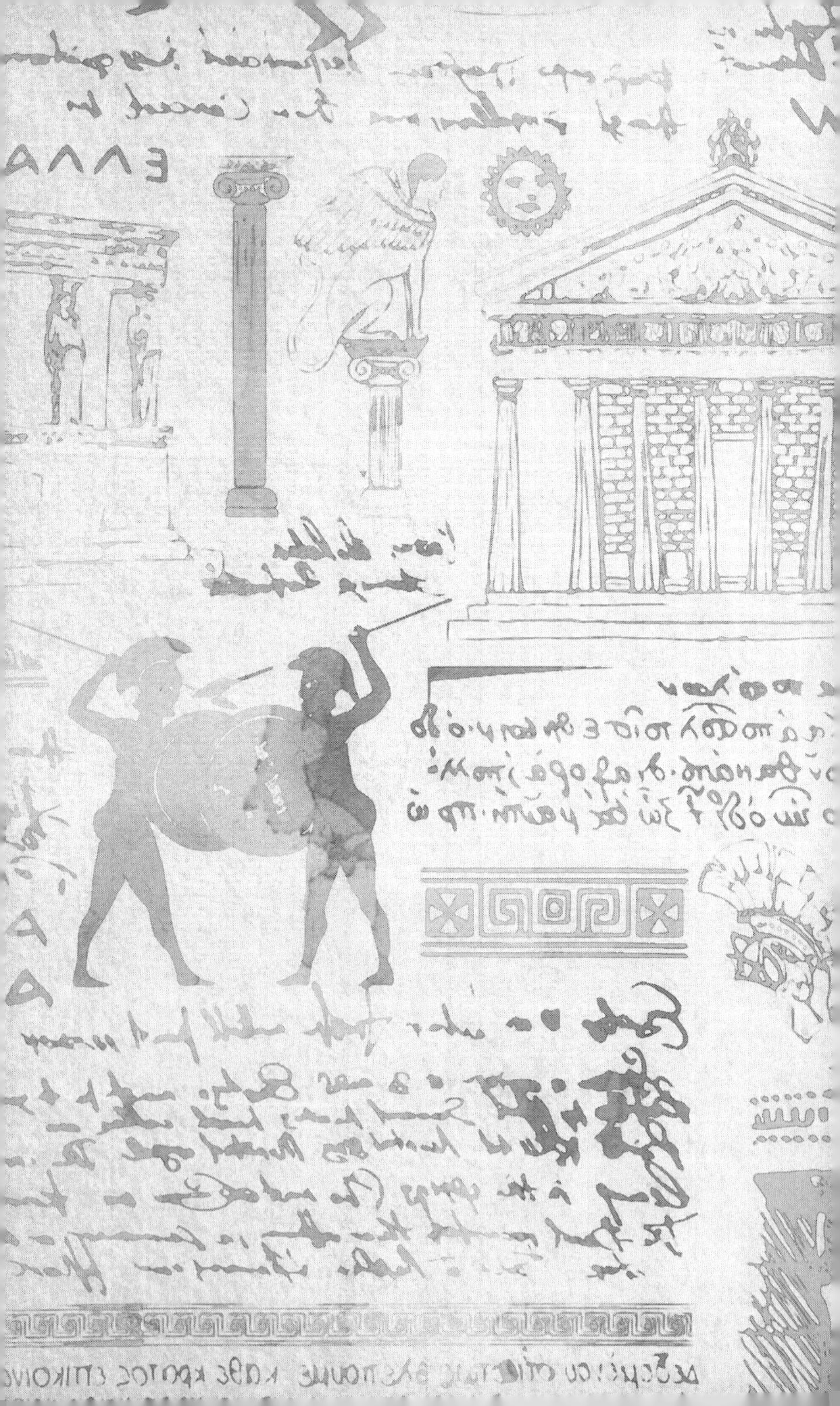

CHAPTER EIGHT

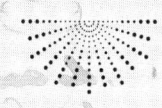

INDIGO

INDIGO
My dad is a bigger asshole than I thought possible.

ELON
Uh oh …

INDIGO
Yeah … uh oh is right. He's making me a mentor under Atticus.

ELON
Mentor?

INDIGO
Learn the ropes so to speak so I can take over the company.

ELON
Is Atticus hot?

INDIGO
{angry face emoji} What do his looks have to do with anything?

ELON
Well, if you have to get under the man, hot is better.

INDIGO
Don't be an ass.

"Atticus, will you please give me a few minutes alone with Indie?" My dad says, as if the conversation we're having is perfectly normal and something we discuss every day.

"Of course." Atticus stands and looks down at me. I quickly swipe at my face to wipe away the tears.

Our eyes meet and I don't like what I see. I see compassion and understanding. Maybe even acceptance. I don't want Atticus's compassion. I don't want anything from him or my dad. I just want my life back.

Atticus leaves without another word, and the silence that fills the void between Dad and me is heavy with tension.

"I can't do this." I plead, hating the desperation in my voice. I've always rolled over and done whatever Dad asks of me. Doing what he asks is easier than fighting against him, but he's never asked me for anything this huge, this life altering.

"You can and you will." Dad's voice is calm and resolute, and that only makes me angrier.

"How can you ask this of me? Even if I wanted to run your company, I'm not qualified. I know nothing about the tech industry."

"You don't need to know everything. That's what experts like Atticus are for. You just need to know enough to lead." Dad sighs and stares at me. I know that look, and I hate that look. He's about to dive into a lecture I don't want to hear.

"Princess, do you think I know everything about the tech industry? Half the time, I don't even understand some of the things Atticus says when he talks about his codes. I can't tell you what machine learning is to save my life. I don't *need* to understand. I just *need* to trust *him*. Same goes for Stefon and Victor and every other employee that walks through these doors. Build trust in your employees, earn their respect, and then all you have to do is lead. Atticus has done that. Every person who works under him is loyal to *him*, not me. He's not only a brilliant software engineer, but he's a leader people want to follow. Learn from him. I know you can do this."

"I don't want to learn from him!" I cry.

Dad's eyes harden, but his tone remains calm and even. "Atticus takes his career and position in this company very seriously. You take nothing seriously. Who better to learn from?"

"Isn't it bad enough that you're forcing me to be his assistant? That was the deal. One year as his assistant. If I had known you were going to change the game, I never would have stepped into the arena."

Dad studies me for several beats. Several uncomfortable and agonizingly painful beats. I know this look too, and I hate it when he gets like this. He's not going to change his mind. I either do this or lose everything.

"Dad, please." Tears well up in my eyes again, and I hate myself for it. I never show weakness around Dad, and I'm about to completely fall apart. "Don't do this to me."

"I'm not doing this *to* you. I'm doing it *for* you." His eyes shift to his desk. He picks up a pen and makes a note on the pad in front of him before he continues. "Clearly, you're not learning anything as his assistant. You treat that job as a joke. Do you know how many people would kill for that position? I've taken a lot of heat for giving that job to you."

"*You* have?" I yell. "Do you have any idea how *I'm* treated? The way people talk about me? It's not good. None of it. Your employees don't even want me here. All they see when they look at me is daddy's little spoiled princess. *You* did that. Not me."

"Then change their minds about you. That's part of what I want you to learn. Prove to them that you're not just my daughter. Prove to them that you're worthy of their respect and you'll get it. But it has to start with you taking your job seriously."

The sigh that leaves Dad is one of complete exhaustion. He tosses his pen across his desk and rubs his hands over his face before he starts on me again. "You've treated this opportunity like a joke from the day you walked through those doors. Those packages you have sent here? Those need to stop. Now!"

"I didn't send those!"

"But you somehow caused it to happen. Fix it. Change whatever you have to change to make sure it stops. You will do what I ask. You will learn from Atticus, or I will follow through with my plans to cut you off permanently. Once I do that, there's no going back."

"Dad!"

"You have one month to turn this around or your trust fund is gone. And I mean every single penny. Am I clear?"

I stare at him, my eyes pleading with him not to do this. His eyes are hard, and I see the finality of his demands. Nothing I say or do will change his mind.

"Crystal," I say as I push to my feet. I walk out the door without another glance, word, or even breath exchanged between us.

I'm stuck, and there's nothing I can do about it. Unless…

I take a deep breath as I approach the bank of elevators. I don't look around me or even dare to make eye contact with anyone on this floor. With the way I was yelling, they probably heard every word of our fight.

Thankfully, an elevator comes quickly. I step inside, hit the button for my floor, more determined than ever to win over Harold Whittington's support for my foundation. His donation is the only thing that will save me from this hell.

∼

Before heading to my desk, I make a detour to the bathroom. My emotions got the best of me in that meeting, and I need a few minutes to regain my composure before I get back to work.

Thankfully, it's empty and I have a few minutes to myself. Dabbing my face with a wet paper towel, I slowly wipe away any evidence of the emotional outburst that just drained me.

Leaning against the counter with my head down, I take a few deep breaths. I can't believe my dad is making me do this. He's always been demanding of my time and how I spend it. Even as a kid, he would make me come to the office with him for what he called mentoring days. He started doing it when I turned eleven, almost exactly one year after he and Mom got divorced.

He said I was never too young to learn how to run a successful business. He droned on and on about business metrics, how to treat employees, financial management strategies, and even some of the newest tech trends that he was ahead of.

Dad is very good at his job, and he makes a lot of money doing it. He clearly loves it, and I've never faulted him for that.

But it's not something that ever interested me. Not even back them. When I complained about his mentoring sessions, he got angry and accused me of being just like Mom.

All I wanted was to go back to being daddy's princess. The little girl he took to the zoo or out for ice cream. He used to take me shopping and let me go crazy with trying on dresses and shoes. He'd take me to get my hair done. It didn't matter that I was just going to go home and mess it up. I was his little girl, and he wanted to give me the world.

We used to be so close. But all that changed after the divorce. It only got worse when I rejected his company.

He eventually stopped making me come on those work outings, but he never really forgave me for my lack of interest in his company. As time went on, I saw less and less of him. During my scheduled weeks with him, I spent them with Frannie while he worked. We rarely spoke.

He left me alone for years, never really interfering with my life choices until he forced me to work for him for one year or I'd lose my trust fund. I thought I could do it. There's so much at stake if I lose my trust. I need that money to support the foundation. Especially if I can't win over the right donors. Harold is a great option, but there's no guarantee he'll support me.

Lifting my head, I stare at myself in the mirror. The redness on my face is gone, and I almost look normal again.

My immediate reaction is to take my new predicament out on

Atticus. But this isn't his fault. He looked and sounded just as shocked as me at my dad's demands.

Maybe being at odds with Atticus isn't the right approach. Not anymore, at least. Maybe if he and I work together, he'll get what he wants out of this—a promotion to upstairs—and I'll get what I want —my trust fund and freedom from my father.

Taking a deep breath, I spin around and head for Atticus's office. He's leaning against his desk with his arms crossed over his chest and his head turned down. He looks deep in thought, and I think twice about barging in. But I'm a woman on a mission, and dive in headfirst before I chicken out.

"Let's call a truce." I blurt out. "If you stop with all those damn pranks, I'll start doing my job. Like I'll actually answer the phone, take messages, and enter appointments on your calendar. I won't make you dig for them on my desk anymore. And I'll actually help with things like copies and mail and whatever else I should be doing as your assistant. All I ask in return is that you don't do what my father is asking. I do not want to run this company. Like, ever."

He stares at me for several beats too long. His eyes are wide as if this outburst from me is the last thing he expected. Then his eyes shift over my shoulder toward the corner of his office. When I turn around, I find he's not alone.

A gorgeous, curvy woman with long dark hair and warm brown eyes is smiling at me. She's a few inches taller than me, but then again, most people are. She's got an air of elegance and sophistication to her that makes her seem completely out of place in Atticus's office. But what strikes me most is how she's rubbing her very pregnant stomach.

"Oh, I'm sorry. I didn't know you had a visitor. We can discuss this later." I start to leave, but Atticus calls after me.

"It's fine. Stay." I turn to meet his gaze and it's softer, friendlier than I've ever seen it before. Then he points toward the woman. "This is my sister, Penny Love. She stopped by unexpectedly."

I turn to the woman and hold out my hand. She takes it in a firm handshake. "It's nice to meet you. I'm Indigo, but you can call me Indie. Did he say your name is Penny Love?"

She laughs, tossing her head back as if she's used to this question. "It's actually Persephone. My middle name is Love and my brothers think it's funny to use. Most people just call me Penny."

"Oh, Persephone Love." My grin grows. "I like that. Persephone is a great name. Much better than Indigo, a deep blue dye from a plant."

"Indigo is a cool name, and blue is one of my favorite colors," she says.

"Thanks." I pause and look over my shoulder at Atticus. "Do your parents have an obsession with Greek gods or something?"

"Something like that." Atticus smiles, and it's the first genuine smile I've seen that wasn't dragged out of him in a moment of torment. It does weird things to my insides. My belly feels light and a buzz of energy rushes through me.

"Our dad is Greek, and our mom is American. They're obsessed with Greek mythology and *love*," Penny says as she puts extra emphasis on the word love. "Atticus's middle name is Αγάπη which is Greek for love."

Nothing can stop the laughter that rolls out of me. "Are you serious? Your name is Atticus Αγάπη? No wonder you're always walking around like you have something to prove. With a name like that, did you get picked on a lot as a kid?" I tease.

His smile is gone and replaced with the scowl I'm all too familiar with. It makes me laugh harder.

I turn my attention back to Penny. "I didn't know Atticus had a sister. It must have been hell growing up with a man as immature as him."

Penny laughs even harder, this time to the point of tears. It feels good to smile and tease like this, especially after the meeting I just had with Dad.

"You have no idea," she says as she wipes under her eyes. "And to think, there are three more just like him. It was hell. Especially since we grew up in an RV. Eighteen couldn't come fast enough."

"Wait, what?" All humor drops from my face as my eyes dart between them. "Did you say you grew up in an RV?"

Penny gives me a confused look. "Has Atticus never told you anything about him? Unlike me, he loved all the traveling we did as kids."

"That doesn't mean it's something I talk about at *work*." He gives Penny a pointed stare. It makes her smile grow.

"Oh, I could tell you some stories." Penny ignores her brother. With one hand on her belly, she loops the other through my arm and leans in close like she's about to divulge all his secrets. "My brothers turned tormenting me into a sport. And this one here," she points at Atticus, "was the ringleader. Our brothers would follow his lead like he really was a god."

"Is he the oldest?" I ask.

She shakes her head. "I am. He's the second oldest. But he thinks he's older than me. Always trying to protect me like I can't take care of myself. He likes to act all tough, but he's really a softy. Don't let his hard exterior or bad attitude fool you."

"Alright, that's enough." Atticus interjects. He reaches for Penny's hand and pulls her to his side. "Let's go get that lunch. I have a busy afternoon." He turns his dark brown eyes to me. "We'll discuss this morning's meeting later."

I nod. "Sure, sounds good."

"It was so nice to meet you." Penny rests her hand on my arm and gives it a squeeze. It's a nice, friendly gesture that makes me feel welcomed and liked. It's a feeling that I wish I'd get from the people who work here.

"You too." I smile. "Enjoy your lunch."

They step out of the door before me and head down the hallway that leads to the elevators. Before I take my seat, I hear Penny say, "I like her. You should ask her out."

My eyes snap up just in time to see Atticus look over his shoulder to meet my gaze before they disappear around the corner. I don't hear his response.

It doesn't matter anyway. Atticus doesn't like me. He's made that very clear over the past few months. Which is good. Because I don't like him either.

That thought makes my stomach turn. Atticus and I may have gotten off on the wrong foot, but I don't dislike him quite as much today as I did yesterday. Or the day before that.

Atticus Αγάπη Rosi is growing on me, and I'm not so sure that's a good thing.

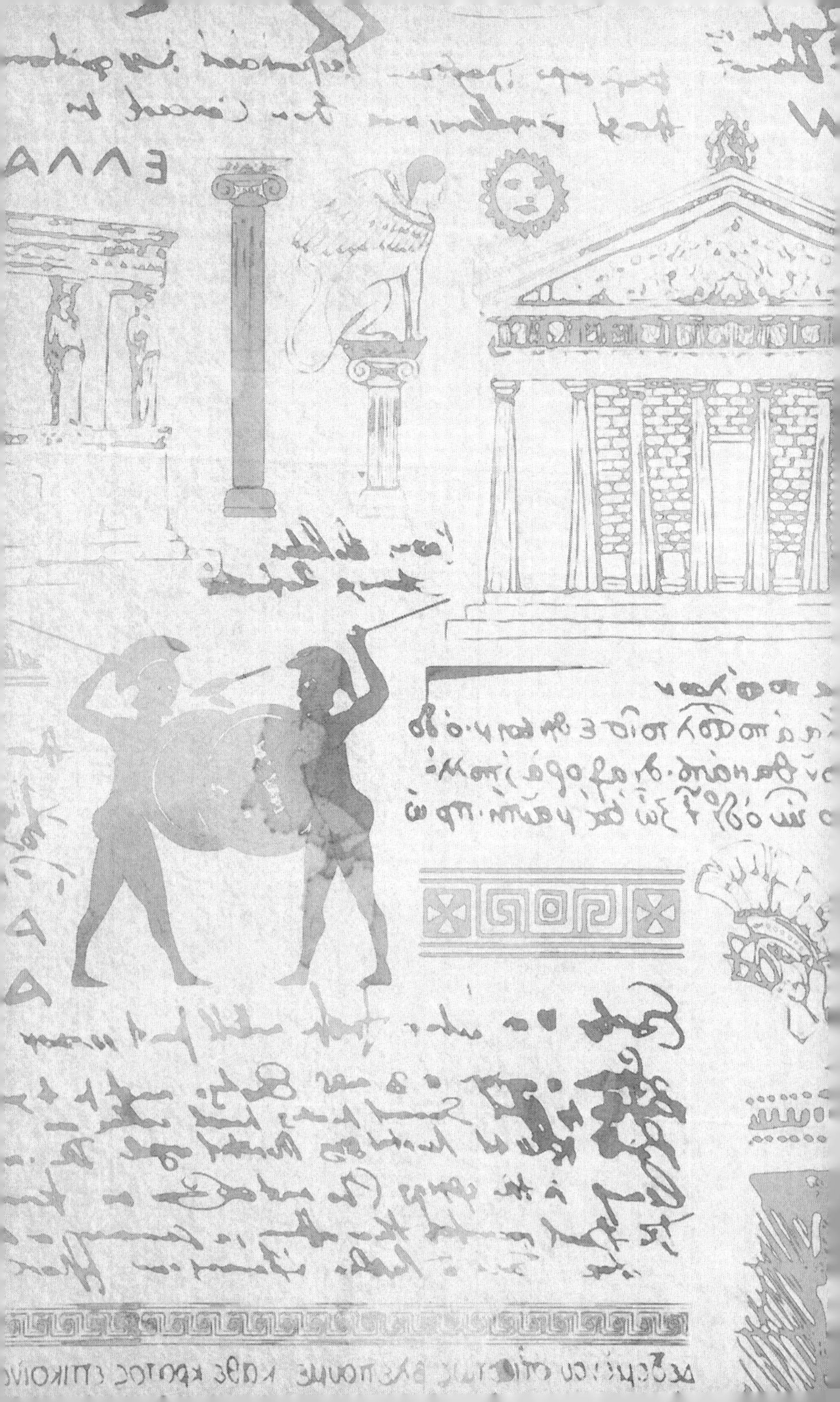

CHAPTER NINE

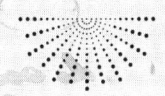

ATTICUS

PENNY LOVE
Invite Indie to dinner this week.

ATTICUS
Why in the fuck would I do that?

PENNY LOVE
Because I like her, and so do you.

ATTICUS
I do NOT like her.

PENNY LOVE
Sure you don't. {laughing emoji} INVITE HER!!!

ATTICUS
NO.

I've never been more tempted to skip family dinner night than I am tonight. And I love family dinner nights. It's my favorite night of the week.

But tonight, I'm hesitant to join them. Now that Penny's met Indie, I know they're all going to gang up on me about dating her.

Growing up, our parents always made a big deal out of eating dinner together every night. It was the one thing they'd insisted we do as a family. No exceptions. It didn't matter what any of us had going on or wanted to do outside the family, we ate together. Either we had to adjust the time of our outings, or we adjusted the time we ate.

Family dinner is a tradition that we've held onto now that we've all moved out on our own. We don't eat together every night, not even my brothers though we live in the same apartment, but we get together once a week, almost without fail.

We used to host dinner at our apartment before Penny married Trent. Their apartment is much nicer and bigger than ours. Unlike them, we don't have the space for a dining table. Nor is our kitchen big enough to hold more than two people at a time, and even then, it's cramped.

I clutch a bottle of Penny's favorite wine in one hand and knock with the other. My sister opens the door, and her wide smile fades when she sees me. She sticks her head out and looks down the hallway.

"You didn't bring her?" she asks, her voice sounding a little dejected.

"I told you I wasn't." I shove the wine toward her and push my way past her. "Don't let your husband drink that. It's for after the baby's born."

"And risk losing a limb?" Trent calls from the kitchen. "I'm not *that* stupid."

"You sure about that?" Eros growls from where he's standing next to the island. He's watching Trent's every move like we're still scrutinizing him.

Penny may be the oldest, but that never stopped us from acting as her protector. We didn't care much for Trent when they first started dating. It wasn't really him. We could tell he was a good guy from the moment we met him. We just didn't like anyone that dated our sister.

With the exception of Eros, we've all accepted Trent as our brother and stopped giving him shit. Eros still insists on acting like

Penny needs protecting from him. I suspect it's more for show than anything. He likes acting all tough and imposing.

"Down boy," I say as I pat Eros's shoulder. He stiffens slightly before he meets my gaze. Then he relaxes when he sees my smile. "They've been married for close to three years now, and they're expecting their first child. I think it's safe to say we're keeping Trent."

Eros grunts, and then turns toward the living room, where he takes a seat on the lavender couch next to Demetrius.

Trent and Penny's apartment is nice and spacious. The living, dining, and kitchen area are one large open room. All the furniture was Trent's and here when Penny moved in. Trent's tastes are eclectic and a little on the feminine side. He's also into fashion and is a popular food critic. He dresses nicer than most women and always looks perfectly put together.

Penny met him through mutual friends—gay friends, I might add —and had thought he was gay as well. She moved into his apartment under false pretenses as his roommate. When we found out the truth, it pissed us off because we thought he had purposefully deceived her just to get her to agree to move in. But it was all one hilarious misunderstanding. They started out as roommates and their relationship grew from there.

Everyone except Eros has let the misunderstanding go.

"Thanks, man." Trent hands me a beer as I step up next to him. "I thought you were bringing a date tonight?"

I groan. "Not you too."

"Date?" Dem calls from the couch. "Since when are you dating someone?"

"He's not." Adonis answers for me. He's sitting at the dining table with Trent's brother Toby and his husband Owen, with their little girl Tabitha on his lap. "But he wishes he were."

"Right!" Penny says with way too much excitement in her voice. "I just loved her. She has great energy, and she's so pretty."

"You met her?" Donnie asks with a raised brow. I groan and drop my head into my hand. This is going to be a long night.

"I did. I stopped by his office before we went to lunch the other day." Penny continues. "I sensed a lot of tension between them, if you know what I mean."

"That was dislike." I bark out in response. "We can't stand each other."

"She really that pretty?" Dem asks. They completely ignore my comment and talk as if I'm not even here.

"So gorgeous." Penny says with way too much emphasis. "Petite, long dark hair, a smile that melts your heart, and she was so pleasant. I think she's perfect for Tattie."

"She's not perfect for me." I say in protest. "She's a fucking harpy."

"Language!" Owen scolds me, and points at Tabitha. She looks at me and giggles. I can't help but smile back at her. She's an adorable three-year-old whose smile lights up any dark mood.

"Dating her would be like multitasking, if you think about it," Donnie says. "Tat's always complaining that he works too much to date. Dating his assistant solves that problem."

"Didn't work out so well for you now, did it?" I say, but he doesn't even look at me.

"I'd date someone I work with," Dem says. "A romp at the office sounds sexy as fu—" He stops and looks over at Tabitha, who's still sitting on Donnie's lap. He's so good with her. He's always wanted a wife and kids. It's a shame things didn't work out with Lulu. "Sorry kid. Cool. It sounds cool."

Tabitha giggles again and squirms. By the way she squeals, I assume Donnie's tickling her.

"I just want to see all of you as happy as me," Penny says with a far-off gleam in her eyes as she rubs her pregnant belly. "Love really is a wonderful thing. Our parents were onto something when they gave us our middle names."

We all groan in unison. None of us like our middle names, which all mean love in different languages. We're Persephone Love, Atticus Αγάπη, Adonis Amour, Demetrius Liebe, and Eros Aşk. To say our names get attention is an understatement.

"Just because you're happy in love, doesn't mean we want that too," I say. Again, no one even bothers to look in my direction. "Am I talking to myself over here?"

"Do we need to intervene?" Dem asks, directing the question to Penny. The gleam in his eyes makes my stomach coil. Nothing good ever comes from my siblings ganging up on me. "I've got two days off next week. I can go by his office and do a little recon. Maybe talk him up to this girl."

"No one is coming to my office!" I yell.

"What you should have done is invite her to dinner yourself," Eros says to Penny, finally joining the conversation.

"I know." Penny's shoulders sag, disappointment written all over her face. "I didn't think about it until after I left. I guess I could always stop by again. Do you think I should give it a week or two? Give them some time to accept their attraction first."

"There is no attraction!" I call out, but I might as well be in a room alone with how they're ignoring me.

"Here." Trent nudges my arm. When I look over at him, his hand is outstretched, with a glass of whiskey in it. "You're going to need something stronger if you want to survive this night."

I sigh, take the glass, and toss it back in one gulp. "More."

He laughs as he picks up the bottle of whiskey and refills my glass. "You don't stand a chance, man. Your sister has been planning this conversation ever since she got home from lunch with you. Your assistant made quite the impression on her."

"How? They only talked for like five minutes."

Trent shrugs. "Don't know, but she saw something in you, and now she's determined to see you with that woman."

I snort. "Dislike. Irritation. Annoyance. That's what she saw."

"Attraction and lust." Penny's voice cuts through me like a sugary sweet knife. "That's what I saw. You want her. Admit it."

I shake my head and sigh. "Now you acknowledge that I'm talking? Drop it, Penny Love. I don't want her."

I toss back my whiskey, reveling in how it burns going down. It's almost enough to burn away the lie I just told.

Indie infuriates me in ways no woman ever has, but my body

doesn't seem to care. Penny is right in that I'm attracted to her. It's almost primal. Like I don't have a choice in the matter. I can fight it all I want, but that doesn't change the way she makes me feel.

I want her, but I can't have her.

Anything more than a working relationship is a recipe for disaster. *She's* my boss's daughter, and *I'm* her boss. I'd do well to remember that.

∽

Not wanting to go home and listen to my brothers continue to nag me about Indie, I head to the office. It's a warm summer night, and I opt to walk part of the way before I hop on the subway. I need to clear my head.

I still have a lot of work to do before our next team meeting, and I can't afford to be distracted by inappropriate thoughts of Indie. Plus, I've spent more time answering emails and scheduling appointments than I have on actual work.

I should probably delegate some of the report writing, but I can't seem to let that task go. The last time I did that, my ideas were stolen.

I trust Leon, and he writes up the sections related to the testing he does, but he doesn't have time for much else. The modeling and coding he does sucks up most of his time.

James's praise of how pleased he is with my leadership skills has bugged me ever since I left that meeting. I know my team respects me. They all work hard, but aside from Leon, I don't let any of them help with my sensitive projects. I keep those close and private.

Maybe I should bring Jen in to help more. She's a brilliant software engineer, and she's been working for us for two years now. She manages a lot of our top clients in the applications division and has written some pretty savvy code herself. I'm ninety-nine percent positive I can trust her. But that one percent holds me back.

Before I know it, I'm standing in the lobby of my building. I sigh as the elevator doors open and I step inside. Punching the button for my floor, I lean against the wall.

My body sags, and all I want to do is slide to the floor and forget about this day and every day before it. My exhaustion is getting to me. I need a good night's sleep, and maybe a good fuck. I can't even remember the last time I got laid. Six months? A year? *Shit*. I think it's been longer.

There was a time when getting laid was a regular occurrence. My brothers and I would go out almost every weekend and have our fair share of fun. Demetrius and Eros still do, but Adonis and I have settled down these past couple of years. Is this what getting older and more mature means? I no longer get laid on the regular. It fucking sucks.

The elevator comes to a stop and dings when the doors open. I expect to be greeted by darkness, but the hallway lights are already on. I pause and listen. Not hearing anything, I make my way down the hallway toward my office.

I don't make it but a few steps when I hear the loud yip of a dog followed by the scurry of little feet. I see the little dog running for me before I hear Indie's voice.

"Beatrix, stop!"

But the little dog keeps running and barking like she's on a mission to protect her mistress. I smile and drop to my knees, ready to greet the little dog, when Indie yells out again.

"Don't. She doesn't like strangers and she bites."

As soon as the dog reaches me, she stops and wags her little tail before she jumps into my arms and tries to lick my rough beard.

Despite the shitty day I've had, I can't stop the smile that spreads across my face. The dog is small with marbled light gray, white, and black fir. She's got the palest blue eyes I've ever seen on a dog with a black tipped nose.

"What a pretty girl," I say. "And sweet."

Pushing to my feet, I sweep the little dog into my arms and continue walking toward Indie. She's standing next to her desk, looking at me in complete shock while her dog snuggles against my chest.

Against my will, my eyes fall down her body, and I take in her appearance. She's changed into casual clothes—jeans and a light pink short-sleeved sweater that fits snugly around her chest. It's low cut and her cleavage is on full display. Indie may be petite, but her chest is not.

"Huh," Indie says, dragging my eyes back to hers. Her jaw drops slightly, and her bottom lip almost looks like a pout. The sudden urge to bite it is strong. "She doesn't like anyone. Especially not assholes."

I tilt my head and glare at her. "Maybe because I'm not the asshole you make me out to be."

Her dog licks my face again, leaving a trail of doggy slobbers in my beard. I snuggle her closer and let out a deep chuckle. "If this is how she acts with strangers, she's not a very good guard dog."

Indie crosses her arms over her chest, pushing her cleavage up higher. I have to swallow a groan. She tries to look angry, but it doesn't work. She's intrigued with me right now and can't hide it. "She never acts like this with strangers."

"What did you say her name was?" I rub her dog's belly, causing her to stretch out in my arms like a baby.

"Beatrix."

"Beatrix?" I furrow my brow. "As in Beatrix Lestrange, the second worst villain in Harry Potter?"

She shakes her head. "That's Bellatrix."

"Oh, right." I nod as I search my memories. It's been a long time since I read those books. "It sounds similar though."

When I look up, Indie's watching me curiously. "You've read Harry Potter? Or did you watch the movies?"

"Both." She raises both brows. "What? I know how to read, Indie. And yes, I occasionally watch movies for fun."

"Just surprised is all. I didn't take you for a Potter fan. Or a fan of anything really."

"Maybe that's because you don't really know anything about me."

We stare at each other for several beats. The air between us thickens and feels heavy as the tension builds. My reaction to her confuses me on so many levels. I can't decide if I want to yell at her or pull her close so I can breathe in her sweet scent.

Then she pulls her bottom lip between her teeth and my cock becomes instantly hard. I want that lip between my teeth, and I'm starting to not care about the damn consequences. This attraction I have toward her is starting to win out over reason and logic.

Then her dog barks in my arms, dragging my eyes away from Indie. My hand had stopped moving, and her dog nuzzles into it as if to insist I pet her more.

"Why Beatrix?" I ask, hoping that eliminates the sexual tension between us.

She holds my stare for a moment longer before she shifts her gaze back toward her desk. She moves several papers around as if she's trying to do the same thing. It doesn't work. The pull I feel toward her is strong, and I take a few steps closer.

Her eyes snap back to mine as if in warning, but it only makes my cock harder. "She's named after my favorite heroine."

When she doesn't continue, I probe for more. "Which is?"

She lets out a deep sigh, never breaking eye contact. "Beatrix Kiddo from *Kill Bill*."

My eyes widen. "You're a *Kill Bill* fan?"

"I'm a fan of all things Quentin Tarantino."

"You're a Quentin Tarantino fan?"

"Are you going to repeat everything I say with a question?" Her eyes narrow as if she's frustrated with my line of questioning, but nothing she does can hide the heat behind her stare.

I have to fight the urge to step into her personal space. We're already too close. I want to be irritated with her, not turned on.

Why is my attraction for this woman growing? It makes no sense. Maybe it's because she's shared something about herself that we have in common. Quentin Tarantino is one of my favorite directors and screenwriters. The fact that she loves his movies too is hot.

Needing to squash the intense heat building inside me, I change the subject. "Why are you here? With your poor work ethic, you're the last person I'd expect to see in the office."

Thanks to my insult, the heat in her eyes vanishes, and her angry mask is back. *Thank fuck!* If she's angry with me, I'll keep my distance.

"I forgot something."

"It couldn't wait until tomorrow?" I ask as I push past her, still holding her dog in my arms.

"Obviously," she says with nothing but sass, causing my cock to strain against the zipper of my pants. It's not fair what her sassy mouth does to me. I want to whip around, press her against the wall, and fuck that sass right out of her.

"Why are *you* here?" She calls out as she follows me into my office. "You're still in your suit from earlier. Do you sleep in it or something?"

I put her dog down at my feet just before I reach my desk.

When I turn around to look at her, she's close enough that I can touch her. Her eyes are roaming down my body and all I see is appreciation.

My heart rate kicks up several notches, and my chest feels tight. "I have work to get done. My assistant prefers to play incompetent rather than doing her job, and now I have to mentor my boss's ungrateful daughter for a position I've been working my ass off to earn. So no, I don't sleep in my suit. I've just got more important things to do than go home and change."

She sucks in a deep breath, something close to an apology written on her face. "I don't want that job. I'll *never* take that job. Besides, my dad has no intention of replacing you with me."

"Sure sounded like it to me," I mumble and turn back to my desk.

"Why?" she asks, her voice sharp and forceful.

"Why what?" I take a seat and wake up my computer. I need a distraction. Anything. I have to stop looking at her before I do something truly stupid.

"Why do you want that job? Why my dad's company?"

Sighing, I lean back in my chair and rub the bridge of my nose.

"Because your dad treats me like an equal. He has since the day I joined the company. I've never once been treated like my ideas or contributions to this company aren't valued or necessary for the company's success and continued growth. He's never looked down on me because I don't come from money or have the right name. He sees *me*. The person I am inside and the skills and knowledge I bring to the team. I don't expect you to understand, being as you're a trust fund baby who's never had to work for anything a day in her life."

Her eyes narrow into little slits, and I swear laser beams are about to shoot out and destroy me. "Can we *not* with the jabs? Maybe even admit that we don't really know that much about each other? We're stuck together for the next eight ..." She glances toward the ceiling like she's tallying something in her head. "Seven months, and I'd rather not spend it fighting."

"Or you could just quit." I add.

She crosses her arms over her chest and the action pushes her breasts up. Her cleavage peeks out of the top of her sweater again and I bite back a groan. "I can't."

"Why?" I force my eyes to stay on hers. That last thing I need is for her to catch me staring at her chest.

"I have my reasons."

"Fine." I tear my eyes from hers and focus on my computer screen. "Do you think you could at least not take me down with you, then? I don't know what game you're playing here, but I need this job. It's important to me. It would be so much easier to do that if my assistant gave a shit."

She's silent, and I don't bother looking up at her to see her reaction to my request. I don't trust myself to look at her right now. My body is way too keyed up to risk it. She may infuriate me and push all my buttons, but that doesn't change the fact that I want her.

"Okay," she whispers. "I'll try. Just don't expect me to like it."

"I don't care if you despise this place. I just need your help," I say without looking up at her. It pained me to admit that last part. As much as I would like to think I can do this all on my own, I can't. I need a good assistant, and for now, she's it. That means I need her.

"Truce?" she asks.

I nod, still focused on my computer screen. After typing in my login information for the third time, my screen finally lights up the room. It's then that I realize I never turned on my office light.

"Atticus. Will you please look at me?"

I close my eyes and sigh, then rub my hands over my face. I can do this. I'm an adult with control of my carnal urges.

With one last deep breath, I lift my eyes to hers. Her hand is outstretched, and her eyes plead with me to accept her olive branch.

Lifting my hand to hers, I shake it and say, "Truce."

Her hand is soft and warm and sends a zap of electricity from my head to my toes, waking up every part of me in between.

I want to pull her over my desk and into my lap.

I want to feel her legs straddling me so my hard, throbbing cock can feel her warm, wet center.

I want to bury myself deep inside her and feel her body tightening around me.

I want to taste those pouty lips and devour every inch of her.

My mind is so overwhelmed with all the things I want that I almost give into the urge and drag her to me. But I don't. Instead, I release her hand and pull my eyes away from hers.

"Good night, Indie." The words come out clipped and cold. I can see her body stiffen at the tone, and I prepare myself for a sassy retort.

But it doesn't come. She spins around, her dog on her heels, and leaves. She lingers at her desk for a moment longer before she practically runs down the hallway as if she can't get away from me fast enough.

Once I hear the elevator doors shut behind her, I slam my fist down on my desk.

I'm angry, frustrated, and more turned on than I've ever been in my life. I'm not sure I can survive seven more months of Indie. At least not without touching her.

Touching her is not an option. Not if I want to keep my job and earn that promotion.

I sigh, knowing I'm completely screwed. Because no matter what I keep telling myself, I'm only so strong.

That woman gets to me in ways no woman ever has. And when I slip my hand under my desk and grab my aching cock, and I know without a doubt that I'll claim her as mine the next time she looks at me with the same need and desire in her eyes that I feel burning deep inside me.

CHAPTER TEN

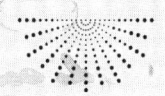

INDIGO

ATTICUS
I can't find my messages on your desk.

INDIGO
That's because you don't have any messages on my desk.

ATTICUS
Did no one call me yesterday?

INDIGO
You got calls.

ATTICUS
Then where are my messages?

INDIGO
Check your calendar. You know, the one on your computer.

For the first time in weeks, I'm smiling. Despite still being under my dad's thumb, I finally feel like my life is settling into a workable and bearable routine.

Ever since Atticus and I called a truce, it's been more pleasant in the office. Turns out actually doing work makes for a more enjoyable day. It's less boring. The monotony of doing nothing, even if it was deliberate, is gone.

The admin staff still gossips behind my back and sneers at me every time I pass, but I'm finding it doesn't bother me as much as it did before. Nothing I do will ever change how they feel about me, and I'm okay with that. They're the ones that are miserable. I'm only miserable if I let them get to me.

Now that Atticus and I aren't fighting every day, I can actually say he's not so bad. He's still demanding and bossy, but he at least stopped changing out my nameplate. No more *Princess Simons* or *#1 Daughter*. And for that, I am grateful.

It's also why I'm smiling and have a bounce in my step as I make my way down the sidewalk to meet my mother for our monthly lunch, with Beatrix on her leash next to me.

My mom isn't the most pleasant person. She's needy, self-centered, greedy, and narcissistic. She's super critical of me and acts like everything I do is one giant disappointment. She also despises my dad and talks shit about him every chance she gets.

I never look forward to our lunches. They're tolerable at best. Once I moved out of her home, I've limited our interactions as much as possible. Except for a few holidays a year, these monthly lunches are the only times I see her.

Mom has only ever seen me as a tool to use against my dad, not her only daughter or her pride and joy. I don't even think she ever wanted kids. I was only ever a means to an end for her.

Mom never loved my dad, though he loved her in the beginning. She sought him out, made sure he took notice of her, and she told him whatever he needed to hear to make him fall in love with her. She married him for his money while he married her for love. She allowed herself to get pregnant with me as a way to keep him and get more of his money. Not because she wanted kids or had an ounce of motherly instincts.

To say I grew up with parental issues is an understatement. All my parents did was fight, and those fights tended to center around me. I felt responsible for their divorce, as if I was somehow to blame for their decisions.

Had it not been for Elon and our friendship, I would have lost myself to depression and self-loathing. Thanks to my parents, I've never felt like I was good enough or worthy of another person's love. No matter how hard I tried, or how perfect I did in school, it never felt like enough.

Eventually, I stopped trying. Aside from my monthly lunches with Mom, I can mostly avoid her. Though she uses these lunches to tell me all the things that are wrong with me.

Until recently, I didn't see much of Dad. Now I have both of my parents up my ass. Between Dad forcing me to mentor under Atticus and Mom constantly probing me to get more money out of Dad, it's a wonder I can smile at all.

When I reach the restaurant, I bypass the front door and cut around through the alley to the back patio. When the weather is nice, we always eat outside so I can bring Beatrix with me. It's one of my conditions for keeping these monthly lunches.

Beatrix isn't just a pet or companion. She's like my child, an emotional support animal. She calms me when my surroundings get too tense. All I have to do is hug her close and I instantly feel better. She helps me get through these lunches with Mom while maintaining my sanity.

Mom is already seated at a table when I pass through the gate. The server waves me over, all too familiar with our monthly ritual. While I want to come here for the patio, Mom loves the food. Don't get me wrong, the food is good, but I want to have my dog with me.

Since Mom is also a creature of habit, we eat here every month. When the weather is nice like today, we eat outside. When it's not, we're seated inside at a table away from the other patrons so Beatrix isn't a bother.

To say the staff is all too familiar with our brand of crazy is an understatement.

As soon as my eyes meet my mom's gaze, my smile fades. She's in a mood, and it's written all over her fake as shit smile. I pull my phone out of my pocket and shoot Elon a quick text.

> INDIGO
>
> She's got crazy eyes. Be ready to rescue me in fifteen.
>
> ELON
>
> Darlin' already on my way. I'll be there in five.

"This is why I love you," I whisper to myself as I slide my phone back in my purse.

"What was that dear?" Mom gives me a pointed stare as I take my seat.

"Oh, nothing." I wave off her question. "Just telling Beatrix to be good."

She scoffs as if my dog is a bother to her. "I don't know why you insist on taking the mutt with you everywhere you go. Dogs should be left at home. Or better yet, at the pound."

"She's not a mutt, Mom. She's a Pembroke Welsh corgi. A cardigan blue merle corgi, to be exact. It's a rare breed coloration, and I *love* her."

Mom waves her hand at me as if this conversation bores her. Thankfully, the server comes over to take my drink order before she can insult my dog again. I really am in a good mood, and I'd prefer to keep it.

But that's wishful thinking. As soon as the server leaves, Mom starts in on Dad.

"Have you managed to get your father to increase the amount of your trust fund in exchange for that horrid work-study thingy he's forcing you to do?"

And there it is, ladies and gentlemen. My mother, Margarette Simons, first class gold digger, never misses a chance to suggest ways to get money out of my father.

"There's plenty of money in my trust, Mom. I don't want more of his money. The balance of my trust is more than enough."

"Nonsense. There's no such thing as more than enough money.

You need to make him pay for this charade. I mean, it's ridiculous of him to think you, of all people, could ever run that company. That requires someone with a different kind of intelligence than you."

"Thanks for the vote of confidence, Mom." I give her a tight smile. At least she didn't insinuate I was stupid like Dad always does. Mom at least celebrated my Yale graduation and achievements. She even threw me a party and bragged to all her friends about how well I did. Granted, she did it to make herself look better, but still.

"You know what I mean, dear. You are not suited for that life. It's time to settle down. Find a husband to take care of you. I bet if you did that, your father would forget all about that work thingy."

"Stop calling it a work thingy. It's a professional job, and I can handle it just fine. I don't need your advice."

"I beg to differ." She presses her hand to her chest as if I've truly offended her. "Have you even bothered to look in the mirror? Those dark circles under your eyes are not attractive. You'll never find a husband if you don't start taking better care of yourself."

"And you would know all about that, now wouldn't you Margie?" Elon smiles down at my frowning mother before he turns his smile to me. He loves calling her Margie because of how much she hates it. She insists everyone call her Margarette. Leaning down, he kisses my forehead. "Hey gorgeous."

"Hey you!" I return his smile as he takes the seat between us. Beatrix lets out a low yelp before she lifts her paws onto his leg. Elon picks her up and nuzzles his nose in her neck.

"Who's a good girl? Did my little Beatrix miss me?"

I laugh at his antics, mostly because I know he's putting on a show for my mom. One we both know will only serve to piss her off. Sure enough, she scoffs and hides her frown behind her drink.

"Elon." Mom looks over the rim of her glass and glares. "Good to see you, as always."

"Now, Margie." Mom flinches at the use of the nickname she hates, and Elon's smile grows. "No need to lie. We both know you'd prefer it if you never saw me again."

"That's not true." Mom mocks horror by pressing a hand to her chest. "You and your family mean so much to mine. I just love having you around."

"More like you love the connections we afford you. *You* do not love *me*."

"Don't be absurd. I think you're a—"

"Can I get you a drink, sir?" The server interrupts before Mom can finish her false flattery. I immediately pick up the margarita he set in front of me and take a huge gulp.

Elon points to my drink. "I'll have the same as her."

"Go ahead and bring me another." I add. "I'm going to need it."

"Of course, ma'am." He nods and turns to Mom. "Shall I bring you another martini?"

"Please. And make it a double this time." Mom points at us and asks, "Are you ready to order? I'm starving."

"You two go ahead," Elon says as he flips open the menu. "I'll decide in a second."

We place our orders, and thankfully, Mom behaves for the rest of lunch. She may not like Elon, but she won't give him a reason to defend me. She never has. She saves all her insults for those times when we're alone.

∽

TWO HOURS LATER, ELON IS DRAGGING ME THROUGH THE DOORS OF MY favorite spa. He scheduled a mani-pedi knowing I'd never treat myself, even though it's one of my favorite things. Ever since Dad froze my trust fund, I've stopped spoiling myself with things like this. I don't trust Dad or the outcome at the end of my one-year sentence. Instead of spending my salary on myself, I'm saving every penny I make in case I need it for my foundation.

"You really didn't have to do this." I glance over at Elon in the seat next to me. We're both relaxed with our feet soaking in a warm salt bath. Our hands are lathered in an intensive moisturizer, then wrapped in foil. Even Beatrix is getting a spa treatment. This spa caters to pets as well as humans. It's one of the reasons it's my favorite place.

"Yes, I did." He looks at me out of the side of his eyes. "You deserve to be treated like a queen. One of these days, you'll find a man to do this for you. Until then, you've got me."

"What if you find a man before I do? Don't you think he'd be jealous of you spoiling me?"

"Psh." He shakes his head. "If he is, then he's not the man for me. Besides, I'm not looking for anyone. I like my freedom."

"Famous last words." I chuckle.

"Oh, yeah." He rotates in his seat so he's facing me. "So, tell me how things are going with Atticus."

I narrow my eyes, and he grins. I know he's fishing for information, but I refuse to give it to him. "There's not much to tell, really. We've called a truce, and so far, so good. No more pranks and work has been ... Better."

"Darlin', I'm not talking about your working conditions. I want to know more about the man behind all your drama. When do I get to meet this Greek god?"

I roll my eyes and do my best to put on a show of annoyance. "Will you stop talking about him like that?"

He presses his foil wrapped hand to his chest and scoffs. "Whatever do you mean?"

"Who said anything about him being a god?"

"His name is Atticus. That's literally the name of a Greek god."

"So." I shrug. "That doesn't mean he's a god."

He raises his brows in challenge, and I hold his gaze. But when a slow smile lifts his lips, I know I'm screwed. Elon knows me too well, and he can read every single one of my expressions like I'm an open book.

"You like him." He teases.

I scoff. "No, I don't. I *loathe* him."

"Let me rephrase. You want to fuck him."

"Don't be crude."

"Don't be evasive."

"I'm not being evasive. There's nothing going on between Atticus and me, so don't try to turn it into something it's not."

He holds his gaze on me for a few more beats before he turns his attention to one of the attendants. "We've changed our minds. We'll have that champagne now."

"Elon!" I reach over and shove his shoulder. "I had enough to drink at lunch. I don't need more."

He waves me off. "You're fine. Besides, I need you to talk and you're more apt to do that with a drink in your hand."

"There's nothing to talk about." I insist, knowing damn well he's not going to let this go.

Elon rests his elbow on the armrest of his chair and grins at me. "Is he cute?"

I roll my eyes. "What does that have to do with anything?"

"He is." He waggles his brows. "I need to pay you a visit at the office so I can see for myself."

"Don't you dare." I point at him even though he can't see my finger since it's wrapped up like a sandwich. "We're finally getting along, and I don't need you showing up and making things awkward."

"Awkward because you have the hots for him?"

"I do not." I quickly turn away, hoping he can't see the lie on my face. My cheeks warm, and I'm sure they've turned a bright shade of pink.

"Then why are your lips twitching?" He teases. "They only twitch when you're lying."

"Will you stop!" I slap his arm, not caring if I mess up the moisturizing wrap. "I thought this was supposed to be relaxing. I can't relax if you're interrogating me about Atticus."

"Okay, fine." Elon tosses his foil wrapped hands up in surrender. "I'll stop on one condition."

"And what is that?"

"Just tell me he's hot."

I drop my head back and groan. "Fine."

I close my eyes and picture him a little disheveled like he was that night he showed up in the office after hours. He was still in his suit. His jacket was undone. He'd ditched the tie, and the top few buttons of his dress shirt were undone showing off a hint of his chest hair and tattoos. Thoughts of running my fingers through that hair kept me up late into the night.

When I look over at Elon, he's staring at me with a knowing grin. "He's so, so hot. Like it should be illegal for a man to be that freaking hot."

"I knew it!" Elon jumps in excitement, splashing water out of his foot bath. The attendant frowns at him. "Sorry," he whispers. "Just tell me when I can meet him. I need to see this Greek god for myself."

"Sorry, Elon. There will be no meeting. You are not allowed to get attached to him. In less than a year, I'm outta there, and I will leave him behind. I don't want any attachments to Dad's company."

"Spoil sport." He sticks his tongue out at me like we're still five years old. It makes me laugh.

Normally the days I see my mom are hard and leave me feeling sad and depressed. But today, I'm happy. The good mood I started with wasn't lost to her insults and poor parenting skills.

"Thanks for this." I reach over to squeeze his hand and remember I can't. We're both wrapped up in foil.

Sensing my struggle. He holds his hand up, and we do our best version of a fist bump. "Anything for you, darlin'."

No one has ever spoken truer words to me. No matter where our lives take us, we will always have each other's backs. Ride or die.

CHAPTER ELEVEN

ATTICUS

PENNY LOVE
Tat, have you asked her yet?

ATTICUS
Asked who what?

ADONIS
Don't play dumb. It's unbecoming.

ATTICUS
Since when do you use words like unbecoming? Is this what a fucking PhD gets us?

ADONIS
{middle finger emoji}

DEMETRIUS
Maybe it's old age and Tat's memory is slipping.

EROS
He did lose his phone the other day. It ended up being in his pocket.

ATTICUS
Fuck you guys.

TRENT
Don't text that shit to my wife.

ATTICUS

> She started it.

This meeting is dragging on thanks to Stefon James. He's been going on and on about his latest security update like it's groundbreaking news. It's not. It's the same shit he tells us at every staff meeting. But today, he's particularly chatty.

The man doesn't know when to shut up. He's shit at reading facial cues and he's ignored every single one of James's attempts at steering the conversation in a different direction. We still have three more projects to update with less than ten minutes left in our meeting.

How in the hell is this man a contender for the C-suite promotion? He's dry, monotone, and while he may do a good job at managing his department, he has no clue how to inspire or motivate his staff to do more, be more. He does just enough to be successful but not enough to be exceptional.

I'm by no means perfect in my management style—especially when it comes to my personal projects—but I work hard to give my staff the freedom to succeed without inference. That also means I've given them the freedom to fuck up. But that's how we learn and grow and become better. We fuck up, and then we do better next time.

Stefon's a fucking micromanager. No one likes a micromanager. He needs to give his team leaders a chance to present their work for a change rather than doing it all himself. Like how I let Jen discuss the progress in applications development since that's her expertise. I stepped in to discuss my personal project updates within systems development. But I let Leon discuss the progress with code debugging. No one knows more about debugging. Not even me.

Letting our team leaders give updates boosts morale and employee confidence. Stefon doesn't get that, which is why we're still listening to him talk after thirty minutes of droning on and on about the new firewall.

I can't believe he's my competition.

"As you can see, this is why last-minute requests for new systems is a drain on our security resources." Stefon's eyes shift to mine, confirming that is a dig at me. He was pissed when I informed him Leon was issued a new processor to speed up our testing efforts. It meant his team had to rush the implementation of the security protocols. "We really need more time to prepare for that level of protection."

"And yet your team did an excellent job for us recently, despite the rush." I shift my gaze to the man sitting next to him. Greg is the one who does all the security installs for my team, and he does a damn good at his job. Fast too. "I really appreciate all of Greg's hard work for my team. Thanks, man."

Greg sits up a little straighter and smiles for the first time since the meeting started. "Just happy to help."

I feel Stefon's eyes narrow. When I shift my gaze from Greg to him, my smile only grows wider. Stefon is shooting ice daggers at me. I love pissing that man off.

"While that may be so, I'd prefer more advanced notice."

"I can appreciate that," I say. "But sometimes we can't always control the demands of the job. Being flexible is just as important as good planning."

"Are you saying I'm not flexible?"

While his frown deepens, my smile grows. "Not at all. Just trying to express my gratitude."

From the look on his face, he knows my praises are nothing more than insincere platitudes. This is the game we've played since the day I joined SimTech. He's just pissed that I play it better.

"I, for one, am extremely grateful for your efforts to accommodate Atticus's needs." James cuts in. Unlike mine, his praise is genuine. "His project is a top priority. It means a lot to all of us when you make quick adjustments."

Stefon's gaze shifts from James to me and back again. I know him well enough to see that he is not happy that James basically said the same thing as me. Stefon wants to reprimand me, not cooperate with me. But James just made that next to impossible.

Before Stefon has time to come up with a retort, there's a knock on the conference room door. All heads whip toward the door in surprise. No one ever interrupts our team meetings.

An unfamiliar face peaks around the door as it's slowly pushed open.

"Can I help you?" James asks. I can see the irritation in his expression, but it doesn't come out in his tone.

"Uh, yeah," the guy says. Though he looks more like a kid. Based on his pimpled face, I'd say he's barely out of high school. "I have a delivery."

James's brows furrow. "You can leave that at the front desk."

The kid shakes his head. "I have to deliver this directly to the person it's addressed to. Can't leave it with anyone else."

James lets out a low huff. "Who's it for?"

The kid looks at the address label and says, "An Atticus Rosi."

Now it's my turn to frown. I raise my hand and the delivery kid's eyes instantly shift to mine. "That's me."

The kid nods his head in my direction and smiles. "Cool. Just need you to sign for it."

"Okay." I shake my head, more than a little confused. "Why couldn't you leave this with my assistant? She signs for me all the time."

"Dunno." He shrugs. "I just do what I'm told."

He hands me a clipboard and points toward the open space next to my name. I sign it and hand it back. His smile grows. It even turns a little mischievous as he hands me the box.

"Enjoy." He chuckles and rushes out of the conference room before I even look at it.

I stare after him until the door clicks shut. Only then do I divert my eyes to the package in my hands. There's a small envelope taped to the top. Peeling it off, I rear my head back at the words written on the box beneath it. "What the ..."

Ripping the envelope open, I pull the card out. My frown grows when I read who it's from. My eyes fly to James's confused gaze.

"Who's it from?" he asks.

"It says it's from you." I toss the box down on the table so he can read it.

"But I didn't send you anything." He shifts his eyes from mine, and they widen when he sees the top of the box. "Is this some kind of sick joke?"

"That's what I'd like to know." I growl. "Who did this?"

"It wasn't me!" James shoves the box across the table, and it hits Stefon's elbow.

He looks down and laughs. "Piece of shit? That's priceless."

"Did you do this?" I grind out through gritted teeth. "Because so help me God, I'll—"

"It wasn't me." He manages through his laughter.

Leon reaches across the table and pulls it toward him. He's trying hard not to laugh, but there isn't anything he can do about the way his lips tug up. He lifts the lid and his control breaks. His laughter fills the room.

"What is it?" I ask, getting more pissed by the minute.

"It's small pieces of chocolate in the shape of piles of shit." He wipes his eyes, and everyone else snickers. Everyone except James and me. James looks just as irritated by this prank as I am.

"Glad you all think this is funny." I reach across the table and gather up the box. "If you'll excuse me."

I don't wait to see if James protests my sudden departure. Our meeting was coming to a close soon, anyway. But even if he doesn't follow me now, he'll definitely have a few choice words to share with me once he gathers his thoughts.

Until then, I need to deal with the person who sent this.

And I'm pretty sure I know exactly who's to blame.

∽

WITH THE BOX CLUTCHED TO MY CHEST, I BARGE DOWN THE HALLWAY toward my office. Indie is sitting at her desk with her eyes focused on her computer screen.

She doesn't even see me coming.

When I reach her side, I lean down and whisper-shout in her ear. "My. Office. Now!"

She jumps in her seat and a small yelp escapes her. She presses her hand to her chest and stares at me with wide eyes. Our faces are close, and I can feel her breath tickle the hairs of my beard. It makes my cock twitch, and I hate my body for how it reacts to her.

"What's wrong?" She sounds breathless and more than a little stunned.

Straightening my back, I point to my office. "We need to talk."

"O-okay." Her eyes never leave mine as she pushes to her feet. I can only imagine how I must look. Angry and pissed beyond reason. Considering all the pranks I've pulled these past several weeks, I have no right to be this mad at her, but I thought we called a truce.

As soon as she's in my office, I step in behind her and shut the door. She spins around to face me, worry etching her expression. "Atticus. What happened?"

"This is what fucking happened." I shove the box at her as I move past her. She fumbles for it but manages to grab hold of it before it falls to the floor. I continue past her until I reach the window and stare at the city beyond.

"Shit," she whispers.

"Shit is right." I spin around to face her. Her expression is pained and full of regret. My anger wanes but only slightly.

"Atticus. I'm sorry." She takes a step toward me, but I hold up my hand. She stops. "I forgot about this. I scheduled this before we called a truce. I didn't even know when it would arrive. The element of surprise was part of the package deal."

"They delivered it to the conference room during our team meeting." She winces as her eyes fall closed. "Your father was there. He saw the whole thing." I run my fingers through my hair and tug at the ends. "Fuck, Indie! How could you?"

"Seriously?" She charges toward me and shoves me back against the glass. "You sent me a fucking glitter bomb disguised as office supplies. I'm still picking glitter out of my scalp. And don't get me started on the ladybugs. The entire building is dealing with that one."

"I didn't do it in front of your father." I push back against her, forcing her to step back. "Your father—*my boss*—is fucking pissed. Do you have any comprehension whatsoever about how important this job is to me? Do you even give a fuck about anyone but yourself?"

"Oh, that's rich. I could ask you the same thing." She throws the box of chocolate at me. The lid pops off when it hits me in the chest and little piles of brown shit-shaped chocolate flies across the room. "You've been nothing but an asshole to me since the day I walked through those doors."

"Not true." I yell and take another step in her direction. She slowly steps back like she's the prey and about to be eaten alive by the angry predator. "I tried to welcome you to the team. I might have been the only person here that did. Everyone else was too busy being pissed that daddy's little girl was getting a handout—a free ride—while the rest of us had to work our asses off to get here. Then you had to sabotage everything I did. For months, you've refused to do the job daddy gave you. That's the only reason I took action. I thought maybe you'd ..."

I pause and take a deep breath as I realize I've backed her up against the door. Blinking several times, I'm unclear as to how I got here. In my outburst, I must have walked her backward and pinned her between my arms.

Her eyes are hot with anger and something else I shouldn't dare acknowledge.

Lust. Desire. Need.

My chest heaves as the same emotions flood me. I'm so pissed at this woman, and yet I want her. My body craves to feel hers against mine.

"What did you think would happen?" She spits out the words and I swear her pouty lips get fuller the angrier she gets. I stare at her mouth, desperate to taste her lips. I'm mesmerized by the deep pink color and the way they part just slightly as she breathes.

"Atticus!" she yells my name. My eyes snap back to hers. "What did you think would happen?"

I take a deep breath and get a whiff of her sugary sweet scent. I dip my head, bringing my mouth closer to hers. She sucks in a breath and her breasts press against my chest. I groan, wishing there was nothing between us and we were skin-to-skin.

"That you'd quit," I whisper.

"Oh." A little more of her anger fades. Her hands slide up between us and her fingers wrap around the lapel of my jacket. "I can't quit."

"Why?" I ask, even though at this point I don't give a shit. All I can think about is eliminating the rest of the distance between us and claiming her mouth.

"Dad is making me do it. For one year. If I don't, I'll lose everything I've worked for."

"And what is that?" I inch even closer. Our lips are mere millimeters apart.

"You haven't earned that story yet."

Then she pulls me the rest of the way down and presses her lips to mine.

Hot. Wet. And an odd mix of soft and hard. That's how Indie's lips feel. I've studied these damn lips often over the past several weeks, imagining how they'd feel and taste. Their plumpness taunted me as did every single sound that came out of them. Every breath. Every gasp. And every single groan of frustration.

My imagination didn't do them justice.

She tastes sweeter than the fucking bakery she always smells like. Sugar. Cinnamon. Caramel. She's a fucking piece of caramel candy that I want to devour until she's one with me.

Those taunting lips part and her tongue brushes against mine. I growl and she lets out the softest, sexiest little gasp.

Whatever self-control I had left, snaps. My hands slide down her sides, hips, and then under her round ass. Lifting her into me, her tight pencil skirt rides up her thighs and bunches around her waist. She spreads her legs and wraps them around me.

It's a fucking invitation to take her, feel her, make her mine.

And I waste no time fitting myself between her legs. I press her small frame into the door and grind my aching cock into her center.

Inhaling deeply, I swallow her moans, reveling in how well she fits against me. How perfectly her lips meld with mine. Even through all these layers of clothes, I can feel how hot and welcoming her center is against my cock.

Her hands slide up my chest, around my neck, and into my hair. She fists the strands and tugs hard in a punishing grip. It only makes me plunder and take more from her.

"Atticus." The desperate way my name sounds on her lips causes my blood to simmer. My body roars to life with something I've never quite felt before. A need so strong and fierce it feels like it's going to rip me to shreds.

With every breath, every lick, every press of my body to hers, we devour each other. I don't know where I end and she begins. All I know is I need to be inside her hot, wet center. Her body is calling to mine like it's the missing piece it needs to survive.

When her hand reaches for my belt, a deep, feral growl escapes me. She wants this just as much as I do.

She. Wants. Me.

And that fact makes my agonizingly hard cock ache even more. She can fight with me, refuse to do her job, insist that she can't stand me, but her body doesn't lie. And I'm going to take everything she's willing to give me.

Moving quickly, she unbuckles my belt, undoes my pants and has my hard as steel cock in her delicate soft hands in a matter of seconds. My body sings. No hand has ever felt better wrapped around my length. She tugs gently, almost tentatively, like she's testing how I'll react.

But I don't get a chance to react because a loud knock on my door interrupts us, and we both freeze.

"Atticus?" James's harsh voice calls out. "Are you in there?"

I meet Indie's panicked eyes. Her hand releases my cock like it's on fire and is about to burn her hand. Her legs loosen from around my waist, and I slowly put her down. When her feet hit the floor, I back away.

There's another knock on my door, and this time we spring into action. She quickly rights her skirt while I tuck my hard cock back in my pants and zip them up.

Turning to my desk, I walk around it and fall into my chair. More to hide my raging erection than anything else. With the way my morning has gone, the last thing I need is for my boss to see the evidence of what I was about to do to his daughter against the very door he's still knocking on.

Indie steps forward just as the door handle turns. She crosses her arms over her chest and takes a deep breath. James steps in and looks between us, then he glances around the room. His eyes land on the chocolate pieces of shit scattered around the floor.

"Everything okay in here?" he asks, but everything about the way he says it suggests he knows we're anything but okay.

"Yep." Indie says with emphasis on the P. "Everything is great."

James stares at his daughter. His expression suggests he's about to dive into a lecture about her behavior. One I suspect she's heard a lot over the years. But instead, he sighs. He looks at the chocolate and then at me. And I swear he knows. He knows exactly what I was about to do to his precious princess.

"Whatever is going on between you two, get it under control." He points at the chocolate before his eyes land on Indie. "And no more stunts like this. This is a professional place of business. I expect you to treat it as such."

"Sir, this isn't entirely her—"

"Don't defend her." He snaps, cutting me off. It's the first time he's ever raised his voice with me and spoke to me like I'm being reprimanded. I fucking hate it.

Then he turns his steely gaze to Indie. "Do you understand me, Indigo?"

All the heat and lust that was raging through both of us is gone. Her eyes turn hard and cold as she looks at her father. "Understood."

That one word cuts through me like a sharp blade. She doesn't look at me as she walks out the door, bypasses her desk, and vanishes down the long hallway.

I broke through her resolve, and she gave me a glimpse of what it would be like between us. And I want more. So much more than this little taste.

But her wall of anger and resentment is firmly back in place, and I'd bet my paycheck, it will be even harder to break through it again.

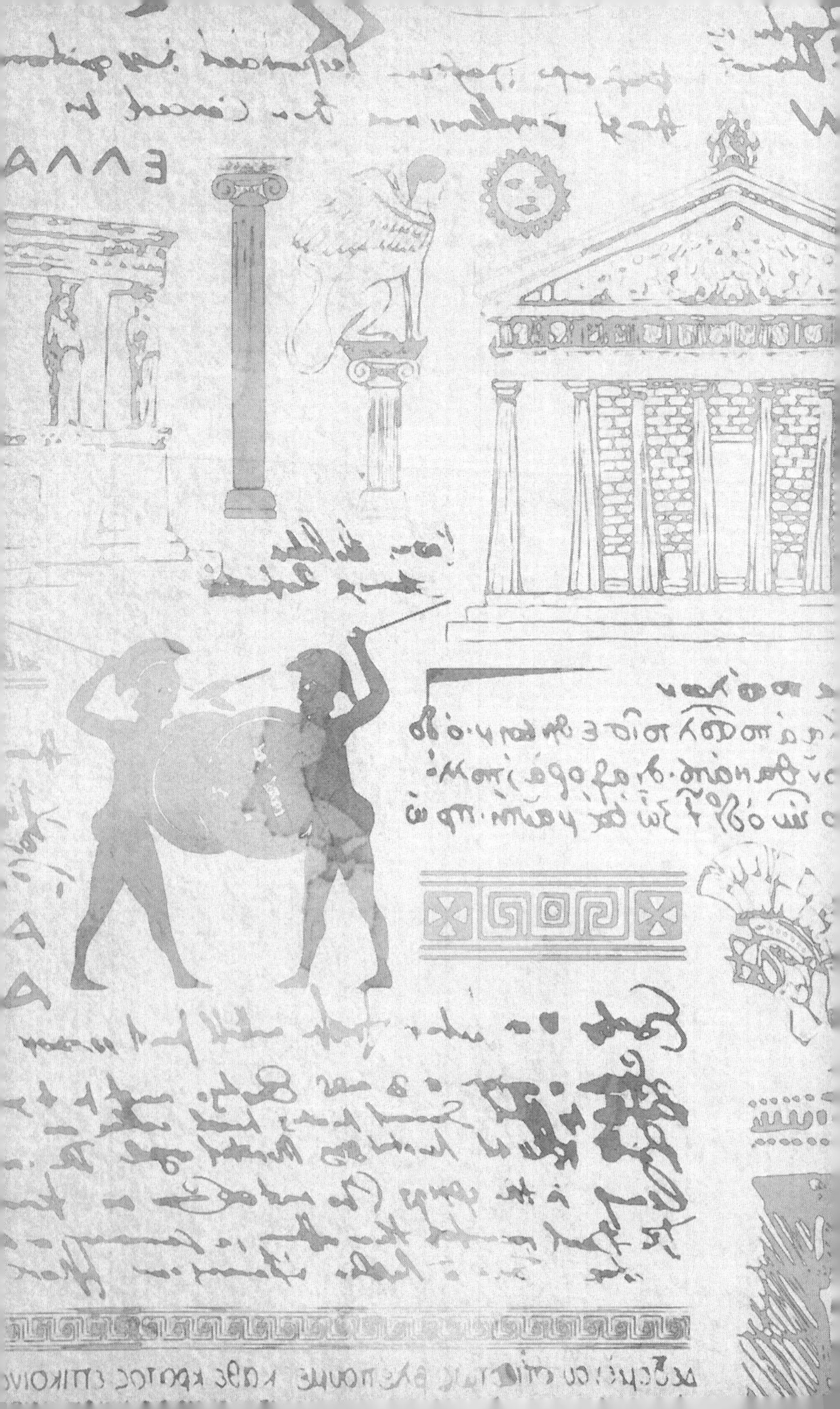

CHAPTER TWELVE

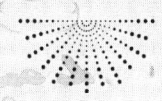

INDIGO

INDIGO
I'm a bad person.

ELON
No, you're not. But, for the sake of argument, what did you do that makes you think you are?

INDIGO
I sent Atticus a box of chocolate shaped like little piles of shit and addressed it from my dad.

ELON
Oh, well ... After all his pranks, that's not so bad.

INDIGO
It was labeled Piece of Shit.

ELON
Lol, that's actually funny.

INDIGO
My dad was in the team meeting with him when it was delivered.

ELON
Oh, boy.

INDIGO
And ...

> **ELON**
> And what?

> **INDIGO**
> ...
>
> Afterward, we fought. In his office. With the door closed. Things got heated.
>
> I kissed him and grabbed his you know what. There's seriously something wrong with me.

> **ELON**
> Whoa ... I'm gonna need you to be more specific.
>
> Don't ignore me. Give me all the deets.
>
> Darlin', answer me.
>
> Based on your silence, I'm gonna assume you grabbed his man stick?

After running away from Atticus and my father like I was on fire and needed to be doused, I headed straight for the bathroom and locked myself into a stall until I could breathe normally again.

Even now, two hours later, I can't catch my breath. I also can't get myself to go back to the office.

No one—or anything, for that matter—has ever made me feel like that. It makes no sense. Atticus and I hate each other. How can we argue and fight like we're ready to rip each other's heads off and then kiss? *Like that.*

That wasn't just any kiss. My entire body felt like a live wire, ready to zap anything and everything in its path. I was so alive with energy that I'm surprised Atticus didn't combust into flames.

And I grabbed his penis. What in the hell is wrong with me?

I drop my head and rub my hands down my face. I've been hiding out in the coffee shop down the block from the office. A few people have given me funny looks because of the sounds I keep making.

Every time I think about how he felt in my hand, I groan. He's so hard and thick and silky soft. His erection laid heavy against my palm, and the way he flexed when I wrapped my fist around him is still making me wet.

I cross my legs and clench my thighs—*again*—attempting to stop the need pulsing through me. Two hours away from him has done nothing to ease the ache between my legs. I still want him just as much as I did when he had me pressed against his office door.

The door my father banged on just as I was about to drag Atticus's cock to my center and show him exactly what I needed. And wanted.

Oh gawd. I wanted him to fuck me. I never needed a man so much before in all my life than how I had needed him in that moment. Maybe I need to call my doctor. Get a full check up and make sure I don't have a tumor or some mental illness that's affecting my judgment.

My phone buzzes from where I turned it down on the table so I couldn't see the screen. Dad, Atticus, and Elon keep texting me, and I have no clue what to say to any of them. So I've been ignoring them instead.

I pick it up, and this time it's from my dad.

DAD

> Princess, where are you? Atticus said you didn't come back from lunch. Care to explain to me what happened in his office?

Darkening the screen, I ignore it. It's not like I have any idea what to tell him. *Sorry, Dad. I groped your protégé and was ready to fuck him before you interrupted us.*

Yeah, that'll go over well.

I pick up my coffee cup only to find it's empty. Based on how much my hands are shaking, I've had enough caffeine for the day, but that doesn't stop me from getting up and heading to the counter.

One more cup, and maybe a pastry, and then I'll head back to the office. I can't stay here forever. As much as I'd like to hide from Atticus, I can't. I still have time left on my prison sentence, and that sentence includes working for him.

When the barista asks for my order, I give her mine, plus I add a black coffee for Atticus. I even order two chocolate croissants. He's never told me how he drinks his coffee, but I know he likes it black.

I also know he loves chocolate. So I assume a chocolate croissant is a good choice.

At the last minute, I pause before handing the barista my credit card. "Can I add a few more coffees and add a dozen more pastries to the mix?"

She looks at me like I'm crazy, but then nods. I give her coffee orders for the other admins on my floor. Again, I shouldn't know how they drink their coffee, but I do. I've eavesdropped on them enough over the past few months that I've picked up on a few details I didn't realize I'd stored in my memory bank.

Since it's late afternoon, I don't have to wait long for my order. I grab the cardboard drink tray and balance it on top of the box of pastries. Per my request, the two croissants for Atticus and me are each in separate bags.

I probably shouldn't be doing this, but I have to do something. I won't survive the rest of this year working under such hostile conditions. Maybe if *I* make an effort with the admin, they'll be nicer. Or at least stop talking about me behind my back.

And maybe Atticus will see this as a peace offering, and I can convince him to forget about that kiss and my hand on his dick.

I'm a woman full of nothing but hope with coffee and pastries. It's not much, but it's all I've got. With the way my luck always goes, that probably means I'm screwed.

∼

As soon as I step off the elevator, Annie raises her brow and smirks at me. I swear it's a look that says she knows exactly what happened behind Atticus's closed door this morning. She and all the other admins watched me storm off after my dad interrupted us. I'm sure the gossip started the second I was out of earshot.

I step up to the front desk and smile. Lifting the coffee I had made for her, I set it on the desk. "This is for you. I also bought some pasties. They'll be in the breakroom, but if you want one, you better act fast. I only got a dozen."

Her wide doe eyes stare at me in disbelief as I walk away. It's not a great look on her and it makes me chuckle. I swing by the break room and leave the pastries on one of the tables. The staff will find them quickly enough.

Then I drop off the other coffees. Simone looks at me with suspicion and sniffs her coffee before she takes a tentative sip. Trisha just turns her nose up at hers and pushes it to the edge of her desk as if it will bite her if it gets too close.

But Mrs. Romano smiles and graciously accepts the cup I hand her. "This is so nice of you, Indie. Thank you."

"You're welcome. And there are some pastries in the breakroom. If you hurry, I bet you can get first pick."

I wink as I quickly make my way down the hallway that loops around the floor and comes up to my desk from the opposite side. From this angle, I can see into Atticus's office, but he can't see me. He's at his desk typing just like he would be any other day. If I didn't know any better, I'd say nothing happened between us.

He removed his suit jacket and rolled up his shirtsleeves, revealing his strong tattoo covered arms. Can we say arm porn? So sexy. So hot.

Taking a deep breath, I step up to his door. As soon as he catches sight of me, he pushes to his feet.

"Indie." He pushes his shirtsleeves higher up his arms before he steps around his desk. I struggle to keep my breathing even as I swoon over his sexy arms. "Are you okay?"

"I'm fine." The words rush out of me, suggesting I am anything but fine. I grab his coffee and shove it at him. "Here. I got you a coffee."

He stares at it for a moment as if he has no clue what it is. Then he blinks and shakes his head. "You didn't have to bring me coffee."

I shove it in his hand and force him to take it before I hand him one of the small bags. "I got you this too."

Lifting his hand slowly, he takes the bag and opens it. His eyes soften when he sees what it is. "This is my favorite."

"I know," I say as I take a step back and turn around. "Anyway, I better get to work."

"Indie." He calls out, but I wave him off.

"I'm sure I have a ton of messages since I've hardly been at my desk all day. Might take me the rest of the day just to listen to all of them."

I rush out of his office and take my seat. The message light on my phone is blinking, so at least that part of my excuse is true.

He steps out next to me and looks down at me. His gaze is pleading with an underlying hint of heat.

"Can we talk?" he whispers.

I look up at him and give him a huge smile. It's so fake it makes my face hurt. "Not now."

He opens his mouth like he's going to argue with me, but then stops. He nods and lets out a deep breath.

"Okay. Later?" It comes out as a question, or maybe a plea. Either way, I don't ever want to talk about what happened.

I shrug and pick up my desk phone. Moving quickly, I punch in my passcode to retrieve my messages. He stands next to my desk for far too long before he finally heads back into his office. I have to listen to the first message three times before I actually hear the words that the caller said.

I'm distracted and antsy and turned on in ways I shouldn't be.

The coffee and the croissant were a bad idea. I've shown a card I never intended to let him see. He knows I've paid attention to the things he likes.

I drop my head into my hands and shove my fingers through my hair.

I can do this.

I can be professional and forget how his mouth feels against mine. Or how sexy that damn beard of his is as it brushes across my sensitive skin. And I definitely can forget how big and hard and silky soft his cock feels in my hand.

Yep. I can completely put him out of my mind.
Liar.

～

For the first time since I started working as Atticus's assistant, he's not at his desk when I arrive at work the next morning. His office is dark and there are no signs of life.

He's always the first one in. I wouldn't know firsthand because I don't come in until nine most mornings, but according to the rumor mill, he's in every day by seven. His absence is notable, and I'm sure it has everything to do with me.

His office remains dark the entire day.

I hate that it's because of me.

And I hate how disappointed it makes me feel even more.

～

When I arrive at the office the next day, his door is shut. He rarely shuts his door. Seeing it closed now is a direct hit to my ego. Especially since he never came in yesterday.

I received no calls or emails from him letting me know he wasn't coming into the office today. But I'd heard through my eavesdropping that he called in sick.

That was a first and had everyone speculating. In all the time he's worked at SimTech, he's never missed a day of work. Not once. I wouldn't be surprised if it was the first time he'd missed work in his adult life.

He's a workaholic, and nothing keeps him away from his desk. Apparently, he got sick a year ago with a severe case of bronchitis. He was coughing up a lung, barely able to breathe, let alone talk, and he still refused to go home.

Sick my ass.

He's avoiding me.

That should make me happy. Avoiding him is for the best. Now that I know how he feels and tastes, I don't trust myself to be close to him.

Rather than knock on his door and confront him, I sit at my desk and stare at my nameplate. I pick it up and study the letters of my name. Indigo Simons. Not *Princess Simons* or *#1 Daughter*. Just Indigo Simons. Boring. Plain. Humorless.

As much as they annoyed me, I miss his pranks. It's been weeks since he changed my nameplate to one of his prank names. I know I asked him to stop, but I didn't think he'd actually listen.

"This is for the best," I whisper to myself.

Turning on my computer, I'm determined to get Atticus Rosi and his hard, thick penis out of my head. I log in and open my email to see if there's anything I need to address. Several new emails hit my inbox, but only one catches my eye.

It's from him. He rarely ever emails me. He can just walk right up to me and tell me what he needs. Is he that ashamed or embarrassed by what happened? Do I disgust him so much that he can't even talk to me, and he has to email me instead?

I click on it and brace myself for whatever he has to say. But there's only one sentence, and it makes me more nervous than seeing his name in my inbox.

Please come into my office as soon as you get in.

I stare at it for several minutes, debating on ignoring the request. But if I do that, things will become more awkward between us. I have no choice but to work with him for the foreseeable future. Hell, my dad wants me to work more closely with him. That's not going to be easy.

Talk about awkward. Awkward will only make my time here worse.

Taking a deep breath, I push to my feet and face his door. I smooth out my skirt and adjust the collar of my blouse. Then I step forward and knock.

"Come in," he calls out.

His eyes are on me the second the door is open. Even from across the room, I can see the heat and want in his deep brown gaze. I straighten my shoulders and step inside. I will not let his looks get to me.

"You wanted to see me?"

"Please shut the door and have a seat." His voice is calm and for some reason that makes me angry. I want him to be distraught with need and desire. I want him to be panicking and freaking out. It's the least he can do, considering the effect he has on me.

Ignoring his request to shut the door, I leave it open and take a seat opposite his desk.

He sighs, pushes to his feet, and walks the twenty feet to the door and closes it. As soon as it latches shut, I close my eyes.

"Indie." His voice is low and gravelly and way too close. "We need to talk about the other day."

I'm shaking my head before he even finishes talking. "Nope. There's nothing to talk about."

He huffs. Or maybe it's a snort. I can't tell because I refuse to look at him. If I look at him, I might do something truly stupid. Like jump him and take his dick out of his pants again.

"But there is." I hear his footsteps and he walks up behind the chair. He places his hands on the back, and his fingertips brush across my shoulders. "We kissed. I can't ignore that."

I jump from the chair and take several steps back. "Well, I can. So forget it ever happened."

His hands curl into fists at his sides. Then I make a critical mistake. I look him in the eyes. The same need and desire I saw when I kissed him is still there. Begging to be unleashed. "I can't forget it. I don't want to forget it. I want to do—"

"Too bad." I cut him off, not wanting to hear the rest of that sentence. "I will do my time and meet Dad's demands without making your life difficult. You have my word."

"That's not enough." He pleads.

"That's all I can offer you." My voice cracks, and it's all the invitation he needs to charge toward me.

He cups my cheeks and lifts my face to his. My body instantly heats from his touch. My face feels warm and a tingling sensation rushes over me like tiny little flames licking my skin.

"Please, Indie. I know you feel this. I see it in your eyes. Talk to me."

Squeezing my eyes closed, I push against his chest. His hands fall away as he moves backward, taking all the heat his touch brought with them.

I don't look at him as I push past him and head toward his office door.

"Indie." He calls out my name.

I pause, take a deep breath and say, "We will not be revisiting that kiss. Ever."

Then I walk out of his office, shutting the door behind me.

Hot tears prick at the corner of my eyes. I hate how much I want him. And I hate even more how dejected my rejection made him look. I've never felt so miserable in all my life.

Did I just make a huge mistake? One far worse than kissing him in the first place.

This is going to be a long, long year.

He's unhappy. I'm unhappy. No one is fucking happy.

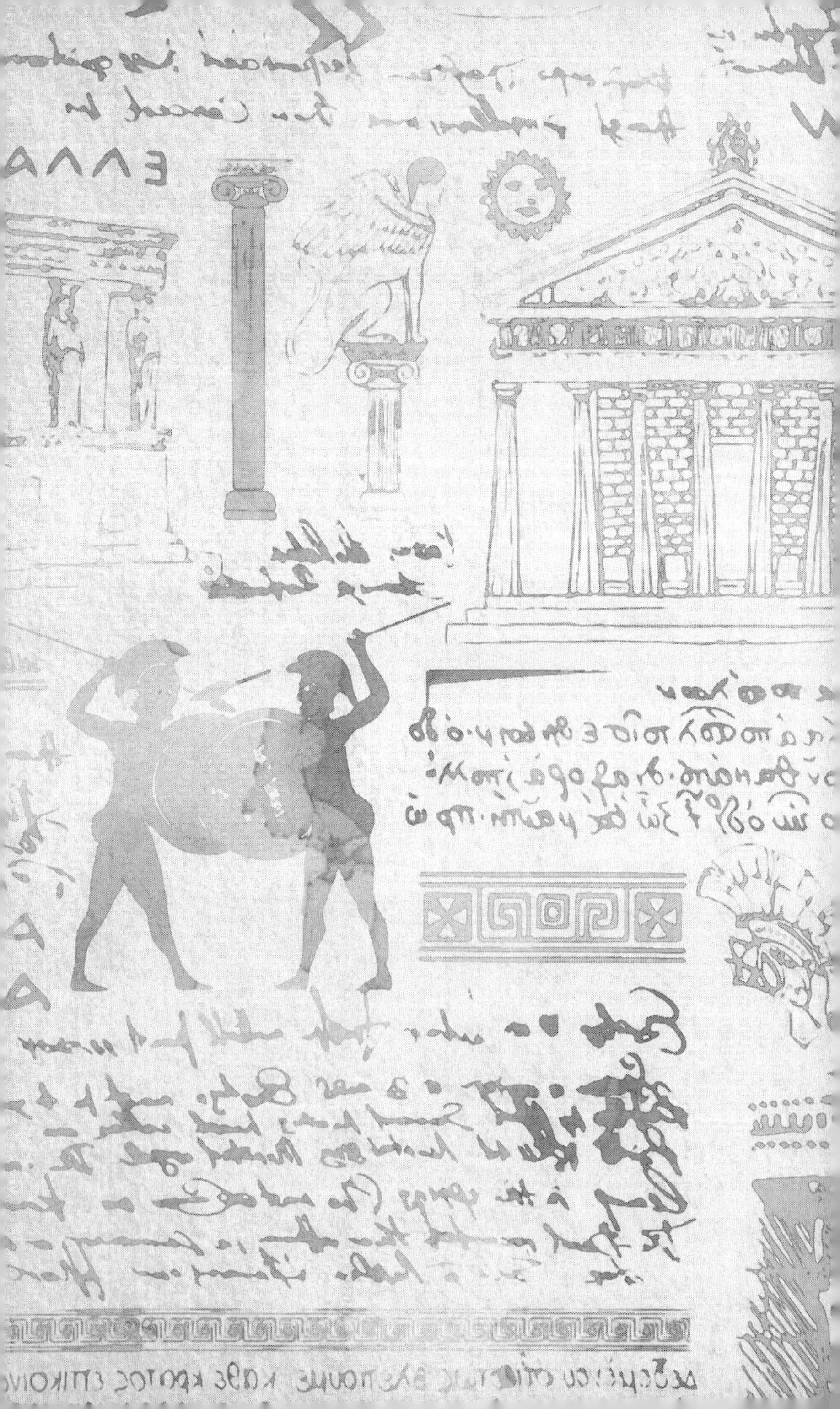

CHAPTER THIRTEEN

ATTICUS

ADONIS

I passed my defense. I'm officially Dr. Adonis Amour Rosi.

DEMETRIUS

Fuck yeah! Let's celebrate.

EROS

Congrats bro!

PENNY LOVE

Celebratory dinner next week. I'll make all your favorites.

GIF of a woman jumping up and down in excitement.

GIF of balloons with the words congratulations in big bold pink letters.

ATTICUS

I'm so proud of you. We're taking you out on Saturday.

DEMETRIUS

Yes!!!! Party at The Rock Room!

EROS

I have to work on Saturday. {frowning face emoji} Come to Triple Bs instead.

ADONIS

You know The Rock Room is more my style.

DEMETRIUS

We'll celebrate with you at Penny Love's house.

EROS

Assholes.

This week is shit.

I didn't think things could get worse at work than what they've been for the past few months, but I was wrong. So very, very wrong.

Indie Fucking Simons kissed me and completely turned my world upside down.

Her mouth. Her hands. Her small soft frame pressed against my large hard one is a feeling I'll never forget.

And she's been ignoring me like I'm the fucking plague ever since.

I may have been the one to press her up against the door, but she kissed me. She undid my pants and pulled out my hard cock. She wanted that just as much as I did.

If her dad hadn't knocked on my door, she would've been the one to guide me to her warm, wet center. She had all the control, and I was powerless to her lure.

"Dude! Snap out of it." Demetrius punches me in the arm, causing me to stumble backward. I grab at the barstool in front of me to keep from falling over.

"What the fuck?" I frown at him and lift my fist, ready to punch him back.

"What. Do. You. Want. To. Drink?" He says slowly like I can't hear or understand English. My hands ball into tight fists as my urge to punch him magnifies.

But then Dylan, Demetrius's best friend and coworker, comes up behind me and slings his arm over my shoulder with a huge smile on his face. "This guy giving you shit?"

I relax my fists, and my expression softens. I need to calm down and have a good time. Tonight is about Adonis, not my shitty week.

The fact that we exited the cab and walked into the bar without it registering is a sign I've got problems. I love coming to The Rock Room. It's one of my favorite bars. Especially on nights when live bands play, and tonight should be a good one. This is exactly what I need to relax.

"Always," I say, then I turn back to the bar. "I'll have a whiskey on the rocks. Bartender's choice."

"You got it, man." The bartender knocks his knuckles on the bar and turns to grab a bottle of Jack Daniels.

The Rock Room is owned by some good friends of Penny's husband. They're actually a group of siblings, the Rockwells. One of the owners, Luke Rockwell, also owns Triple Bs where Eros works. Triple Bs isn't really my thing. I prefer the laid-back vibe of this place over the noise and entertainment Triple Bs provides. Give me great music and the occasional football game any day over bartenders tossing drinks in the air.

"Where's the graduate?" Sydney asks as she slides up next to Dylan. They've been married for years—long before we met them—and are the only married couple among our small group of friends.

"Bathroom." Demetrius says as he picks up the shot he ordered for himself. He tosses it back without even flinching. "Give us a round of these," he calls out to the bartender.

"No shots for me," Sydney says. "We have to pick up Kat tonight."

Kat, short for Katrina, is their baby girl and the reason Sydney rarely goes out with us anymore.

Dem scoffs. "It's one shot, Syd. I think you can handle it. For Donnie."

"Come on, babe." Dylan pulls her close to his side and kisses her cheek. I'm instantly jealous and angry and worked up in ways that make no sense. It makes me think of Indie, and she's the last person I want to think about tonight. "Just have some fun. I'll take it easy on the drinks."

Sydney smiles and melts into his side. I have to look away from the show of affection. "Fine. Just don't complain when she cries because I'm too drunk to nurse her."

As if it were an invitation, all our eyes drop to Sydney's breasts. They're much fuller than they were pre-baby. She always had a nice rack, but now they're hot as fuck.

Dylan's fist flies up and punches Dem's shoulder. "No staring at my wife's tits."

"Sorry, man." He chuckles and grabs his drink from the bar just as the bartender lines up five shot glasses. "Can't help it. But don't worry." He pushes past us and playfully slaps Dylan's arm. "I'll never touch your wife. I got all the hot single women I need to flirt with right here."

He scans the bar with a huge predatory grin on his face.

"You're a pig." Sydney rolls her eyes.

"Nah." Dem smirks. "I'm single. Ain't nothing wrong with having a little fun while I'm young. Come on. Grab your drinks and let's get a table."

"The problem is you have too much fun," Sydney retorts.

"Are you going to nag me all night?"

"Just enough to annoy you." She teases.

"Listen, Syd. My sister's at home. If I wanted to hear a lecture about my behavior, I'd go visit her."

"Then you shouldn't have become best friends with my husband."

"Alright, you two. Stop bickering." Dylan takes his wife's hand and grabs two shots with the other before leading our group to an open table near the back.

Adonis appears just as we all sit down.

"There he is!" Sydney shoots up and pulls Donnie in for a hug. "Congrats!"

"Thanks." His smile is a little shy and uncomfortable. Unlike Demetrius and Eros, he's never liked being the center of attention.

Dylan holds his hand out, and Donnie takes it. "Congratulations. So what's next now that you're Dr. Rosi?"

"Well." Donnie smiles as he slides into the seat next to me. "I might have a job teaching at NYU. There are a few retirees, and they've asked me to apply."

"What?" I say, my eyes wide. "Why didn't you tell us this?"

"Relax, bro." He chuckles. "I just found out yesterday. Besides, I have to finish up the edits on my dissertation first. And the job may be contingent on the grant I applied for. It's not easy getting grants in my area of expertise. Not many care about pre-classical Greek literature."

"Who would've thought our parents naming us after Greek gods would turn one of us into an obsessive ..." Dem turns to Donnie and with a raised brow. "What did you call it?"

"Pre-classical Greek literature."

"Yeah, that."

"Regardless," I pick up my shot and motion for everyone to pick up theirs, "this is still a reason to celebrate. Not just the degree, but the request for an application. That's a tremendous achievement too. We're proud of you."

"Here, here!" Everyone cheers before we toss back our shots and then slam the empty glasses on the able.

"Come on, man." Dem nudges Donnie's arm. "Let's go pick up some chicks and get you laid."

"No way." Donnie waves him off like he's crazy. "I'm still licking my wounds after Lulu. No chicks for me for a while."

"I'm not suggesting you date any of them. Just have some fun."

"When are you going to grow up, D." Sydney starts on him again.

But Demetrius just shrugs. "Don't know. I'm only twenty-five. I've got plenty of time to have fun before I have to grow up."

"We're also twenty-five." Sydney points between her and Dylan. "And we have a baby. That's plenty old enough to be a grownup."

"Yeah, but that works for you two. I'm not ready." Dem tosses back the rest of his drink and waves at the server. "I like my irresponsible single life."

"I'm going to enjoy the day when a woman catches your eye for real," I say. "You won't know what hit you."

"You take that back, asshole." He glares at me, and everyone laughs. "Can't be caught if I'm not looking or making myself available."

"You do know that's not how it works, right?" Sydney asks.

"All I know is if I don't open my heart to a woman, then she can't catch me. And that's how I intend to keep it for a long time to come. Why settle for one when I can have many?"

"Yeah, but that gets old," I say before I think better of it.

Dem snorts. "Speak for yourself, Grandpa."

Before I can respond, the hairs on the back of my neck stand on end and an awareness I've become all too familiar with these past few weeks rushes through me. I glance over my shoulder and suck in a deep breath when I see her.

Indie is walking toward our table, laughing with a man who looks to be about the same age as her and an older man closer to her father's age. She's deep in conversation and doesn't notice me watching.

They walk past us and take one of the empty tables a few feet away. Indie's back is toward me as the young man with her steps around her and pulls out a chair opposite us. I hear her tell him thank you just before she sits.

She's facing me, giving me a clear view of the huge smile she's wearing. I seethe.

Is she on a fucking date?

The older man takes a seat opposite her and sits with his back to me. But the younger man takes the seat next to her.

He puts his arm around her chair and leans in close to whisper something in her ear that makes her laugh. I've never seen this man before, but I fucking hate him. I want to be the one making her laugh like that, putting a smile on her face, and wrapping my arm around her chair.

The man next to her looks in my direction and meets my angry glare. His smile drops and he tilts his head to the side like he's studying me. No doubt he's trying to assess how we know each other, but that's a fruitless effort. We've never met before.

Then he leans close to Indie again and whispers in her ear. My hand tightens on my rock glass to the point my hand hurts. Indie's eyes flash to mine and widen in surprise. She says something to the man next to her and he raises his brows in understanding before he tosses his head back and laughs.

"Is that your assistant?" Adonis asks from next to me as he points toward Indie.

Everyone at the table whips their heads around to look at her. Indie's eyes dart around our group before they come back to me. She no longer looks happy. She looks ... *Irritated*.

"The assistant Penny Love was giving you shit about?" Dem asks. "Damn. She's fine."

I growl and they all look back at me with raised brows. Dem is the first to laugh.

"Bro, you should see your face." He slaps the table as if I'm the funniest thing he's ever seen. "You look like you're about to murder someone."

"She's really pretty," Sydney says. "But she doesn't look happy to see you."

"Well, I'm not happy to see her either," I mumble under my breath. Lifting my glass, I take a large gulp of my whiskey, relishing the way it burns going down.

"No, you look downright territorial." Dem teases. "Who's the boyfriend?"

I slam my glass down hard, causing some of the ice to pop out and bounce across the table.

"Something happened? Didn't it?" Donnie asks.

"Nothing happened." I snap. The lie comes out of me so fast, they see right through it. That only makes them laugh harder.

"Bullshit." Dem leans across the table and stares me down. "I can see it in your eyes. You may not have fucked her. *Yet*. But something *did* happen."

I hold my brother's stare and it takes every ounce of my strength to keep my ass in my seat. I'm torn between dragging my brother outside and shutting him up or marching out of this bar and forgetting that I just caught Indie out with another man. Either way, I have the strong urge to hit something.

"Gentlemen," a deep, masculine voice says from next to me.

When I look up, I see the young man that was with Indie standing next to me. I look him up and down, taking in his appearance. He's dressed in expensive designer clothes. He's wearing a blue and pink silk paisley shirt, shiny black dress pants that shimmer in the light, and brown leather shoes that look like they cost more than I make in a month. It's clear he comes from money.

Is this what Indie's into? I suddenly feel very inadequate and wrong for her in every way.

"Can I help you?" I ask. My voice is rough, and the question comes out more like a growl than actual human words.

His smile grows and humor lights up his eyes.

He pulls his gaze from me and glances around the table. When he sees Sydney, his smile drops and he holds out his hand to her. She gladly takes it. "My apologies. I didn't realize there was a lady among you."

He leans down and kisses the back of her hand. I wait for Dylan to shove him away, but he just smiles like he's amused by this entire interaction. In fact, everyone at our table is smiling except me.

"Who are you?" I bark out.

His eyes dart back to mine and his smile returns, but he doesn't answer me right away. Instead, he pulls up a chair and sits down.

"I'm a good friend of Indie's. I believe you know her well." He holds his hand out for a shake, but I ignore it. "Name's Elon Ruppert."

He raises his brow in challenge. Almost as if he's daring me to not take his offered hand. I've heard Indie mention his name often. He's the friend she's always conversing with. I slowly lift my hand and squeeze his harder than is socially acceptable. It only makes him laugh.

"I see why Indie is frustrated with you," he says before he gives me a friendly slap on the back.

"Wait!" Sydney snaps her fingers. "Elon Ruppert as in the heir to the real estate empire, Ruppert Properties?"

The damn man's smile grows. "The one and only."

"Ruppert Properties owns the building I work in," I say.

Elon nods. "My dad cut Indie's dad a deal when he was starting up SimTech. That kind of thing happens with lifelong friends."

I furrow my brow. "So you and Indie …" I look past him and find her watching us curiously. "You two aren't together. Like that."

He laughs. "You mean, are we dating?" I give a single nod. "No. She's not my type." Then his eyes peruse my body. "But you'll do."

Demetrius snorts, and I can see Adonis fighting a laugh in my peripheral vision. "Excuse me?"

Elon rolls his eyes in an exaggerated motion that looks forced. Then he looks at my brothers. "Is he always this dense? It's not an attractive look."

"Oh, honey." Sydney answers for them. "They all are. They're men. They can't help it."

It feels like they're talking in code and my brain can't unscramble their words to make sense of it because of how close Indie is. All I can think about is that kiss and her hand on my cock.

"What are you talking about?" I ask, hoping someone will get to the point.

"Bro, he's gay." Dem says in a tone that suggests I really am that dense.

I turn to Elon and study his expression. Realization dawns, and now I can see it. "Oh, you're not dating Indie."

He squeezes my shoulder and nods. "Nope. I've known girls aren't my type since I was old enough to have my first crush. And Indie," he nods his head in her direction, "is as single as single gets."

I glance over at her and she's deep in conversation with the older man that arrived with them. Her eyes dart to me every few seconds, but she's doing her best to pretend I'm not here. I want to get up and go to her. Beg her to revisit that kiss and all the tension pulling us together.

"Let her finish her meeting first." Elon says, clearly reading my mind. "Shouldn't take long. Then you can drag her off to a dark corner and kiss some sense into her."

Donnie spits the drink that he just took from his mouth, and Dem slaps the table again, then calls out, "I knew it!"

"She really is pretty," Sydney reiterates. "And she has kind eyes. She looks nice."

"Shut up." I whisper behind my glass. I toss back the last of my whiskey, wondering if the server is ever going to come to our table.

"Hey. Don't talk to my wife like that." Dylan points a finger at me and frowns, but there's humor in his eyes. "She's a great judge of character."

Dem snorts. "Hardly. She married you, didn't she?"

"I didn't say she had great taste." He retorts.

They continue their banter, and Elon joins in as if he's always been a member of our group. I try to pay attention to the conversation, but I'm too distracted by the petite brunette bombshell sitting a few feet away.

She smiles a lot, and I take that as a sign that her meeting is going well. I like seeing her smile. Her entire face lights up and she looks so happy. I've never seen her look like that at work. And I decide right then that I'm going to change that.

I don't want to see her scowls and frowns anymore.

I only want her smiles.

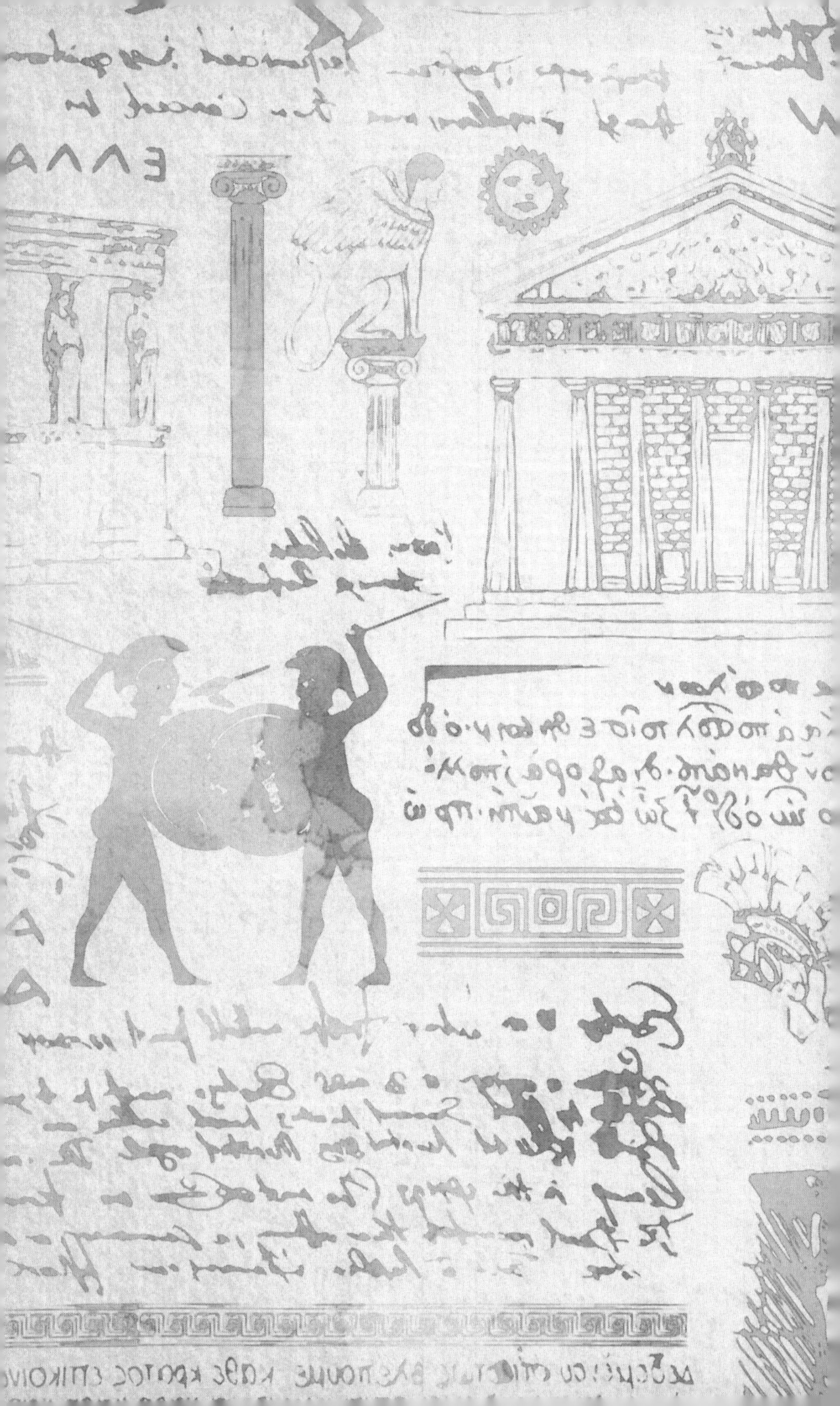

CHAPTER FOURTEEN

INDIGO

INDIGO

What are you doing?

ELON

Relax. Nothing to worry about over here.

INDIGO

Then why does he keep scowling at me?

ELON

Darlin' that's not scowling. That look means he wants to rip your clothes off and make you his.

INDIGO

{angry face emoji}

ELON

Actually, I think he already sees you as his. He just needs to make it official.

INDIGO

I AM NOT HIS.

ELON

We'll see. {winky face emoji}

Atticus is the most frustrating and irritatingly distracting man I've ever met. I think I hate him more now than I did before.

I also hate my best friend.

Traitor.

While I'm sitting here trying to remain focused on an important business meeting—a meeting that could give me the freedom to walk away from my dad—Elon is across from me, rubbing elbows with Atticus. They're laughing and generally look like they're having a good time.

Elon is supposed to be on my side. If I hate Atticus, he has to hate him too. That's like in the top ten list of best friend rules. Maybe even the top five.

"This all sounds great," Harold says as he tosses back the last of his drink. "If your business proposal is as good as this pitch, I'm in."

I peel my eyes away from Atticus and *the traitor* and force myself to smile. "I'm so happy to hear that. As soon as the business plan is finalized, I'll send you a copy. In the meantime, please reach out if you have any other questions or concerns."

"I will." He reaches across the table and shakes my hand. "It was a pleasure talking with you, Miss Simons."

"You too, Mr. Whittington." I stand with him as he slips on his suit jacket. "Thank you for your time."

"It's me that's thankful. I wish more people had your heart and vision. Your father must be very proud."

He gives me one last nod before he turns around and heads toward the door. As soon as he's outside, my smile falls.

I stare after him, trying like hell not to let his last comment drag me down. Not after how well this meeting went.

Proud? My father isn't proud of me. He doesn't even know me. All he wants to do is turn me into his version of what he thinks his child should be. What I want for my life is irrelevant. My dreams and aspirations mean nothing to him.

"Indie." The deep, gravelly voice causes me to close my eyes. A warm tingling sensation runs through me, and my breath gets caught in my throat. "Are you okay? You look upset."

My eyes snap open, and I look up at the man towering over me. The concern etched on his face only serves to anger me more.

"I'm fine." I reach across the table and grab my clutch. Then I push past Atticus and pause next to Elon. Leaning close to his ear so only he can hear, I whisper, "Thanks for setting up the meeting, but I really hate you right now."

He chuckles. "No, you don't, darlin'. Go talk to your man. I like him."

"He's *not* my man," I say through gritted teeth.

Elon winks at me. His teasing smile only serves to feed my frustration more. "We'll see."

I narrow my eyes and growl. "Will you stop saying that?"

His smile grows. "Only when you admit you *like* him."

"I don't like him." I grind out.

"Sure you don't."

I roll my eyes so hard they almost pop out of my head. "I'm going home. Have fun with your new friends."

I straighten my back and glance around the table. Everyone is staring at me in amusement. Shaking my head, I spin around and head toward the door. Maybe if I walk fast enough, I'll escape before Atticus catches up to me. It's a lie I tell myself because that's all I've got. If Atticus wants to talk to me, he'll catch me. His legs are twice as long as mine.

I don't bother looking back. I don't need to look to know Atticus is hot on my trail. Ever since that damn kiss, his presence is like a beacon. When he's near, I feel it. My body comes alive, and I'm instantly drawn to his position.

I felt him the moment I stepped inside The Rock Room tonight. I didn't see him, but I knew he was there. With every step I took toward the table, I felt him getting closer and closer. His presence was so intense—so overpowering—that I refused to look around the bar for fear of what would happen if our eyes locked.

Of course we sat at a table directly across from him. And, of course, I sat in the chair that gave me a perfect view of his handsome face and gorgeous body. He's hot in his suit and tie but seeing him in relaxed jeans and a casual button-down with the sleeves rolled up is mouthwatering.

His arms are solid and strong. Every time he flexes his muscles, he causes his tattoos to dance across his skin. No wonder he was able to pick me up and pin me to his door as if I weighed nothing.

"Indie, where are you going?" He grabs my arm and spins me around.

"Anywhere but here," I bark in reply.

He stares down at me. His eyes are intense and full of want and need and longing. Elon is right. He's not scowling at me. He wants me, and that scares the shit out of me.

He steps closer, resting his hands on my shoulders. Then he slides them down my arms, leaving a trail of red-hot flames in their wake. I tremble from his touch, and it makes me want to run and put as much distance between us as possible.

I can't fall for a man that works for my father. I can't allow myself to be attached to anyone that's close to Dad. It would give Dad control he doesn't deserve.

Atticus is too ingrained in SimTech. He's on a career path that will make him closer to Dad than he already is.

And if he's like everyone else in my past, he'll end up using me to get what he wants. I'll be discarded like yesterday's garbage as soon as he doesn't need me anymore.

The next thing I know, I'm being shuffled into the back of a cab and Atticus slides in next to me. He leans forward and gives instructions to the driver before he sits back and stares at me.

He takes my hand, lifts it to his lips, and gently kisses the back. I snatch it away and clutch it close to my chest.

"Don't be nice to me," I say. The words come out all breathy and weak.

He furrows his brow as he brushes a strand of my hair behind my ear. "Why not?"

"Because," I say a little too loudly. I open my mouth to give him all my reasons why I don't want him to be nice to me, but nothing comes out. He has me all twisted up inside and I can't think straight.

"I like it better when you act like you hate me." I blurt out before I say something truly stupid that ends with me on his lap with my hands tangled in his hair and my tongue down his throat. "Better yet, just go back to hating me for real."

He tugs me closer until my body is flush against his. Then he cups my cheek. His fiery gaze lights me up like fireworks on the Fourth of July. My brain is telling me to pull away, but my body refuses to listen.

"There's no going back," he says as he brushes a featherlight kiss to my nose. "Not anymore. Not ever."

"Atticus." My voice cracks. I rest my hand on his chest with the intention of pushing him away, but the opposite happens. I lean in closer and breathe in his woodsy scent. "This thing between us—whatever it is—can't happen."

"I hate to break it to you, Princess. It's already happening. There isn't anything either of us can do to stop it."

The cab comes to an abrupt stop and the driver turns around and says, "We're here."

"Here where?" I ask.

Atticus doesn't answer me. He pays the driver before he opens the door. Then he takes my hand and pulls me out next to him. He tugs me into his arms and holds me close to his chest. All the stress and worry regarding my confusing feelings for Atticus fade into the background and I suddenly feel safe.

I'm not sure anyone has ever made me feel safe like this before. Other than maybe Elon, but that's different. He's just a friend.

I look up and meet Atticus's gaze. There's so much emotion and want in his eyes, but there's something else there too. Something I've never seen when a man looks at me and it has me trembling in my shoes.

"Indie," he whispers as he leans down, moving his lips closer to mine. "I'm going to kiss you now, and then we're going upstairs."

"Upstairs?" I ask on a breath.

He nods. "My apartment."

"Oh, no." I take several steps back like that's somehow going to protect me from his lure. "That's such a bad idea," I say the words, but there's zero conviction in them.

He charges toward me, wrapping his arm around my waist. His strong arm lifts me off the ground so my chest is pressed tight against him. We're both breathing hard. Our mouths slowly inching closer to each other.

"Princess, we're not done. Not by a long shot. Tonight, we're going to settle this tension between us once and for all."

His lips crash down on mine with so much force I feel like I leave my body. He holds me so close, it's almost as if we become one. His tongue dives in, parts my lips, and he devours me.

Just as quickly, he sets me down and steps away, leaving me panting. *Fucking panting.* I've never panted for a man in my life.

I don't know how long I stand there, struggling to get my lungs to work again, before I finally open my eyes. Atticus is no longer next to me. He's standing at his building entrance with the door held open. He's watching me with a raised brow. If his expression were put into words, he's asking me if I'm coming.

He brought me here, but he's still leaving it up to me whether or not I follow him.

I should go home.

I should turn around and flag down a cab and put as much distance between Atticus and me as physically possible.

Every logical part of my being is telling me this is a really bad idea. Getting attached to someone like Atticus will not end well for me. It never does.

But God help me, I can't stop myself from taking a step toward him. I enter his building willingly and eagerly.

When he steps in behind me and places his hand on my lower back as he guides me toward the elevator, I tremble with need.

His touch sets me on fire, and I want more. I want everything he has to give me. Even if it's just for tonight.

When the elevator doors slide closed, we crash together. He lifts me off the ground and backs me up against the wall so fast it knocks all the air out of me. It's all I can do to take a deep breath before his mouth is on mine.

The kiss is deep, and his lips are strong and demanding. Accepting his tongue is not a choice. He devours me, tasting me like I'm the best piece of chocolate he's ever had.

I wrap my legs around his waist, locking our body together—my core pressed against his hard cock. He groans when I rotate my hips, creating friction right where we both need it most.

The elevator dings and the doors slide open, dragging us both out of our lust induced lip lock. Slowly releasing me, his hand shoots out to stop the doors right before they close on us again.

"Fuck, Princess," he mumbles as he buries his face in my neck and breathes in deep. "Your lips taste so damn good. I can't wait to taste the rest of you."

My legs tremble as my feet hit the floor. I have to brace myself against the wall to keep from falling. Atticus chuckles, then takes my hand. Bringing it to his lips again, he places a light kiss on my knuckles.

I swoon.

And then I scold myself for allowing him to affect me like this. I can't be swooning over my boss—my dad's protégé. It's too much, too risky. I need to keep this in perspective. It's just a fun night of sex. We're exploring this tension between us, just like Atticus said. Nothing more.

With our hands laced together, he leads me down the hallway in silence. When he reaches his apartment door, a burst of anxiety washes over me. What in the hell am I doing? I don't do one-night stands, and this can never be anything more than that.

And how can I have a one-night stand with someone I have to see again? Isn't this something that's reserved for strangers? Not coworkers. Or worse, my dad's golden child.

"I can hear you overthinking this." Atticus says as he swings the door open. Then he tugs me close and places a soft kiss on my lips. It's sweet and confuses me even more. "Relax. Let me take care of you."

I absently nod and let him lead me inside, even though my insides are tied up in knots. I want this, but at the same time, I'm terrified at what it means.

His apartment is small, but it's homey and clean. There's a welcoming vibe to it that I never get when I visit my father's massive sterile penthouse or the overly ornate showroom my mom lives in. The living room is just big enough for a couch and TV. He doesn't have a dining room or the space for a table. The kitchen is a small galley style with a bar separating it from the living room.

Despite how limited the space is, it's nice. For some reason, that surprises me.

"Do you live alone?" I ask.

He shakes his head, runs his hand around his neck, and squeezes as if he's nervous. "I live with my three brothers. It isn't much, but we each have our rooms. That was more important than a large area for entertaining."

"And your brothers?" I look up at him in question. "Are they who you were with tonight?"

I recognized the man who had visited Atticus at his office a few weeks ago, but I'd never seen the others before tonight.

"Yeah." He turns to me and reaches for my hand. "They won't be home for a while. So ..." He steps closer to me. The heat of his body and his woodsy scent are intoxicating, making me feel a little drunk on him. "We have the place to ourselves."

He doesn't give me a chance to respond, which is probably a good thing since I overthink every decision I make.

And I undoubtedly think doing this with Atticus is a mistake.

If he leaves me to my own thoughts for too long, I will leave before anything happens.

He sweeps me up into him, sliding his hands under my ass. Just like in the elevator, my legs wrap around his waist, and I squeeze tight.

Suddenly, I no longer care about mistakes or consequences or potentially awkward future work environments. All I care about is how it feels to be wrapped up in his arms. Or how hard I moan when his impressive cock flexes against my center.

"Fuck," he whispers against my lips. "I love hearing those sounds come from you. Gives me all kinds of ideas of things I'd love to do to you."

"Oh, yeah?" I ask as my fingers slide into his hair, gripping the back of his head. "Like what?"

He growls, then turns around and carries me down the narrow hallway. "For starters, stripping you out of this dress and spreading you across my bed completely bare."

"Then what?" I brush my lips across his in the lightest of kisses. He nips at my bottom lip and then sucks it into his mouth.

He growls and then tosses me onto the bed. "Take that dress off and find out."

Pulling my legs under me, I spin so I'm sitting up on my knees. Obeying, I grab the hem of my dress and pull it off.

Atticus's gaze lingers down my body. All I see in his heated stare is appreciation and need. He lifts his hands and starts to unbutton his shirt, but I knock them away.

"Let me," I say as I scoot closer to the edge of the bed so I can reach him better. His hands immediately fall to my hips, and he tugs me flush against him.

His grip is warm and firm. Heat instantly pools between my legs.

I groan in appreciation as I take in his inked chest, shoulders, and arms. Every hidden inch of this man is covered in tattoos. I run my finger over the edge of the ink and down his chest. The shadows of the dark room make it hard to make out the details, but something tells me his ink is a work of art and meaningful to him.

His hands slide up my back, stopping when he reaches the clasp of my bra. He deftly unhooks it, and the straps slip off my shoulders.

He buries his face in my neck and breathes me in the same way he did in the elevator.

"Why do you always smell like a fucking sugary sweet dessert?" His lips nibble at the sensitive spot below my ear, and my ability to speak is momentarily lost. Between the softness of lips and the scratchiness of his beard, I'm in heaven.

"Atticus." I don't know how, but I manage to say his name.

"Hmm?" He moans right before he sucks my earlobe between his teeth.

"Wait." I press a hand to his chest, and he pulls back. My bra falls the rest of the way off, exposing my breasts.

His eyes drop to my hardened nipples and the sound he makes is otherworldly. This handsome god of a man is looking at me like I'm the most desirable and beautiful goddess he's ever seen. It takes my breath away.

Before I regain my ability to speak, his mouth is on me, and he sucks one of my nipples between his teeth. My moans only serve to increase the intensity of his affection for my breasts. My back arches into him as he nibbles and bites and pushes me closer to the edge.

I want more. *Need more*. But I need to get my head on straight long enough to set some boundaries.

Leaning into me, he slowly pushes me back onto the bed, his mouth never leaving my chest. He continues to lick and suck and tease my nipples. Then he presses his long, thick erection into my center, sending my head into a tailspin. I'm barely able to breathe, let alone think.

Digging my hands into his hair, I clench my fingers into fists and tug his head up, forcing him to look at me. He looks dejected.

"What's wrong?" he asks. Worry etches the corner of his eyes.

"This is just for the night." I breathe out quickly.

He furrows his brows and stares at me like he doesn't know what to do with me. "Atticus. Tell me you understand that this is a one-time thing."

He takes my hands and lifts them over my head. Wrapping one of his hands around both my wrists, he presses his hips into mine. He secures me against the mattress, making it so I can't move. "We'll see."

He runs his other hand down the side of my body, causing my breath to catch. The things this man's touch does to me are so unfair. Why did the first man to get me this worked up in God only knows how long have to work for my father? The one person I'd do just about anything to avoid for the rest of my life.

"Why does everyone keep saying that to me?" I ask through a rugged breath.

"Maybe because you're stubborn and difficult and need to be taught a lesson," he whispers into my ear. There's something dangerous and sexy and unfairly alluring about the way he says those words.

"I am not," I protest, but there's zero conviction behind my words.

Atticus hovers over me, his eyes dark and piercing and needy for me. His breathing is heavy. He looks equal parts turned on and pissed.

"Princess," he growls. "I don't want to argue this point with you. Are you going to be a good girl and spread those legs wide so I can claim what's mine?"

My mouth falls open and I stare up at him in shock. No one has ever spoken to me like that before, and I can't decide how I feel about it. The heat pooling at my core suggests I like it. A lot. But the rational part of my brain is telling me I should be pissed. He can't claim me because no one owns me. I'm my own person, dammit.

He lifts a brow in challenge, and my breath hitches. His hand slips between my legs and his fingers make a slow, swirling motion over the wet spot on my panties. It feels way too good, and I involuntarily arch into his touch. This man is going to be my ruin.

"So fucking wet, Princess." His fingers make their way around my panties and slide beneath them, nudging at my entrance. The tension in my legs loosens and my knees fall to the side. His lips hover just above mine, and I feel them turn up in a grin. "Good girl."

"Oh God." I moan. "You're so confusing."

"How so?" he whispers as he plants soft, reverent kisses down my neck.

"You hate me. And yet ..." He sucks one of my nipples into his mouth and bites down. It's not exactly hard, but it stings all the same. I cry out, surprised by how much I like it.

He shakes his head as he licks and kisses where he bit me. "You infuriate me. There's a difference."

"But you—" He bites my other nipple and slams two fingers inside me, cutting me off before I can finish. My head falls back on the bed. I dig my hands into his hair and pull hard. It only serves to make him bite me harder.

"Are you done yet?" He almost sounds angry, but the way he's fingering me and rubbing his thumb over my clit suggests otherwise.

"Done ... Done with what?" I ask between pants.

"Trying to talk yourself out of letting me fuck you."

I pull at his hair again until he looks up at me. "You looked so pissed when I showed up at the bar. And now look at us. What am I supposed to think?"

"I was pissed." His expression is hard, and the heat blazing in his eyes burns right through me. "Because another man had his hands on you."

"Elon?" I whisper. "He's just a friend."

"I know that now."

"Were you jealous?"

He growls and crawls up my body until his lips are close to mine. "Princess, if you don't stop talking, I'm going to stuff my cock in your mouth just to shut you up."

My eyes widen at the crudeness of his words, but my body tightens around his fingers that are still pumping inside me. "You wouldn't dare."

A sinister grin spreads across his face. "Try me."

I open my mouth to argue, but I stop myself when he arches a brow.

When I don't speak, he leans down close to my ear and whispers. "Be a good girl, Princess, and I'll lick and suck on your sensitive little clit until you're screaming my name so loud everyone in this damn city hears you. I'll have you begging for my cock by the time I'm done."

"Don't make promises you can't keep," I say all breathy and needy.

His hand leaves my center and he has me flipped over and on my stomach before my brain can even register what he's doing. Then he smacks my ass. Hard. I cry out from the pain and my core clenches in excitement.

"Goddammit, Indie." His throaty growl sends a shiver down my spine. "You can sass me at work all you want, but not in the bedroom." He leans over me, rubbing my ass where he spanked me. His heat blankets me and the bulge in his jeans presses against my thigh. Then his voice drops to a raspy whisper in my ear. "Unless you want to be punished."

His hand continues rubbing circles over my ass before he slides it between my legs again. I eagerly lean into his touch as his fingers slowly push back inside me. My breathy moan has him chuckling.

"That's what I thought, Princess."

He makes his way down my body, peppering light, open-mouthed kisses down my back. His hand pumps inside me as he lifts off me, and I immediately miss his warmth. But when he wraps his arm around my waist and jerks me up on my knees, I cry out. His fingers thrust forward, hitting that glorious spot deep inside me.

My body trembles and the pressure building between my legs has me gasping for air. I'm so close, and he's relentless with his fingers. He thrusts his cock against the back of his hand, pushing his fingers deeper and harder inside me. Over and over again until I can't take another minute of this torture.

But it's when his thumb circles around my clit that I lose it. I come hard. My core clenches around his fingers and I scream his name so loud my own ears ring.

I'm still on my orgasm high when he flips me over, spreads my legs wide, and buries his face between my thighs. He sucks my clit between his lips at the same time he thrusts his fingers back inside me.

It's intense and painful and somehow still agonizingly good. Every nerve ending in my body is overly sensitive and aches for him to stop and keep going at the same time.

"I don't ... Can't take anymore ... Please." I gasp and pant and beg for him to stop. I just need a break.

"Yes, you can." He groans right before he pinches my clit between his teeth. Then he replaces his fingers with his tongue. My hips buck off the bed, causing him to tighten his hold on me.

"I refuse to stop until you come in my mouth." He thrusts his tongue inside me while his finger slides further down and teases my other hole. I suck in a sharp breath. "Whatever it takes, baby. This is happening two more times."

"Oh God." I moan as he relentlessly works me over, switching from sucking on my clit to fucking me with his tongue. All while teasing the tight little hole on my backside.

I detonate. My entire body spasms. My mouth falls open, but no sounds come out. At least not at first.

But then he rides out my orgasm, licking and sucking and nibbling on me until I'm crying for him to stop.

He pushes to a standing position and undoes his jeans while my body falls limp. I'm exhausted and more sated than I've ever been in my entire life.

I finally manage to catch my breath long enough to focus on Atticus. He's standing at the edge of the bed, naked and stroking his very hard erection. *His very thick and long erection.* I recall all too well how impressive his equipment is from the brief moment I had my hand wrapped about it.

He reaches into the top drawer of his nightstand and pulls out a strip of condoms. He clenches his teeth on the edge of one and rips it from the strip, tossing the rest of them on the bed.

"You ready for me, Princess?" He strokes his cock again before he starts to tear open the condom wrapper.

I shake my head and find the strength to sit up. "Not yet. I need a break."

I swat his hand away from his cock and take it in my own. I give it a squeeze before I open my mouth and suck him down my throat.

"Fuck!" He bucks forward, and I wrap my hands around his ass and pull him down on top of me. He scoots with me until I'm flat on my back and he's straddling my face.

"Dammit, Princess. Warn a guy."

He falls forward and rests on his hands until he's on all fours over me. I eagerly lick and suck on him until he's groaning just as much as I was a moment ago. His hips thrust forward, pushing his cock deeper into my mouth. When his tip nudges the back of my throat and I gag, the erotic sounds that escape him have me determined to suck my way through this.

But he has other ideas. He pulls himself out of my mouth with a pop and sits back on his heels. "Baby, that just earned you at least two more orgasms before this night is over."

"Oh God. I don't think I can handle one more, let alone two." I groan, and he chuckles.

"Yes, you can, baby." He quickly rolls the condom on and positions himself between my legs. His tip nudges at my entrance, but he doesn't push inside. He hovers and looks down at me with so much heat and lust I think I'll combust into a plume of ash. "Starting. Right. Now."

He pushes inside me in a fast, hard thrust, filling me completely. I cry out from the sting of his thick cock stretching me open. Atticus must also feel the tightness of his fit because he stills and drops his forehead to mine.

"Baby, you okay?" he asks through a ragged breath.

"Yeah." I wrap my arms around his shoulders and cling to him. "Give me a minute."

"I'll give you all the time you need." He presses a light kiss to my lips. "Just tell me when you're ready for me to move."

He brushes my hair away from my face, then rests his elbows on either side of me. Cupping his arms around my head, he kisses my forehead, my right cheek and then the left, before he kisses my lips again. The gentle sweetness he's showing me now is in complete contrast to the dominating sex god that spanked my ass earlier.

Both versions of him have me swooning. If I don't get my fluttering heart under control, I'm going to do something really stupid, like fall for this man.

Needing his sweet side to take a back seat to the dominating sex god, I nudge him to move. "Go ahead. I'm ready."

It stings when he pulls out, but I bite back the pain in favor of squashing the emotions swarming around in my chest.

He moves slowly at first, but once my body adjusts to his size, it sings and dances every time he pushes all the way inside me. He's the perfect size to hit that spot deep inside me every single time.

"Baby, I need to move faster," he says through clenched teeth. "Please tell me you can handle it."

"Yes. Do it."

He doesn't hesitate and I'm grateful for it. Mr. Sweetness is gone. He fucks me hard and fast and without abandon.

I don't know how it's possible, but he has me coming again in no time. I'm crying out his name as his thrusts increase, dragging out my release until he's coming with me.

He thrusts a few more times before he collapses on top of me, gasping for air the same as me.

We remain like that for several beats before he pushes up on his hands and stares down at me. "Fuck, Princess. That's the best sex I've ever had."

Then he kisses me long and hard. And I can't help but think the same thing.

No one has ever made me come like this. It's a shame it can never happen again.

CHAPTER FIFTEEN

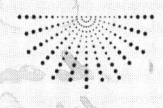

ATTICUS

> **ATTICUS**
> Mind telling me why I woke up alone in my bed?
>
> Indie …
>
> Don't ignore me.
>
> INDIE.
>
> …
>
> You can't hide from me forever. I know where you work.

Needy, hard, and irritated as fuck, I toss the covers back and sit up in bed. I woke up about an hour ago, ready to pull Indie under me and give her another orgasm.

But she's not here.

I don't know when she left, but it had to be late. Or really early, depending on how you look at it.

After we both downed some water, it took about thirty minutes before I was ready to go again. Turns out my little spit fire is a very responsive, good girl in bed. As promised, I gave her another orgasm. It didn't take much to make her go off like a rocket again, desperate to break the stratosphere.

Despite my irritation about waking up alone, I smile, knowing my body could give her exactly what she needed. More than once.

Being buried deep inside her while her tight walls clench around my aching cock might be my favorite place to be. And I'm pissed that I'm not balls deep inside her right now.

Grabbing my jeans from last night, I pull them on and head out to the kitchen. It's still early. Considering it's Sunday, I have no reason to be up yet.

If it had been a weekday, I could understand Indie wanting to leave early so she had time to go home, shower, and change for work. But she doesn't.

Instead, she left without so much as a goodbye. She snuck out like a thief in the night.

That shit doesn't work for me.

When I open my bedroom door, I'm immediately hit with the scent of coffee. The kitchen light is on and Adonis is standing at the counter eating a bowl of cereal.

"You're up early," I say as I grab a mug from the cabinet.

He nods around a spoon full of cereal. After he swallows it down, he says, "The office should be empty today and I want to get an early start on my edits. The sooner I get the final draft done, the sooner I can get the hell out of there and away from Lulu."

I cringe at the thought of having to see the woman I thought I loved every day after catching her cheating on me. "I take it she's making no effort to stay away from you."

"Not in the least." He drops his head back and groans while I pour myself a cup of coffee. "The bitch thinks we can be friends. She's fucking crazy."

"She does get how fucked up what she did is, right?"

Leaning against the counter, I cross my feet at the ankles and take a sip from my mug. It makes me feel marginally better about the fact that I woke up alone.

Donnie stares at the space in front of him for a moment before he answers me. "You know, I don't think she does. The woman sees the world very differently than me. There's no black and white for her. No rules. All she sees is gray. I don't know how I missed it."

"There's nothing wrong with living a little in the gray. Not everything is cut and dry."

"True. But not in my love life. When a woman is with me, it's very cut and dry. No fucking gray whatsoever. Me and her. That's it."

I raise a brow and watch my brother carefully, picking up on what he's not saying. "I take it Lulu doesn't agree. She wants you *and* her side piece."

He snorts. "Yeah. She doesn't understand why I moved out. And she also doesn't understand why she can't have both of us. She actually suggested the three of us enter into a relationship. A throuple. Can you believe that shit?"

I'm mid-drink and almost choke on my coffee before I manage to swallow it down. "Wow. I didn't see that coming."

Donnie turns around and leans on the counter so he's facing me. "I mean, to each their own. Everyone is free to live their lives how they see fit, but I am not that guy. I don't share my woman with anyone."

I lift my coffee mug and nod. "Don't disagree with you on that one. I couldn't do it either. Guess Lulu underestimated the Rosi possessiveness."

"Yeah, well." He scrubs his hands down his face and groans. "I should have known better than to date someone I work with. That's always a recipe for disaster. I just have to make it through the next few weeks, then I can wash my hands of her."

My gaze shifts to the floor as my mind fixates on his words. Did Indie and I make things worse between us instead of better? It sure as hell felt better last night. If she doesn't feel the same way, things are going to be awkward at work.

Now that I know what she feels and tastes like, seeing her every day at the office without touching her is going to be hard. Maybe even impossible.

"Oh shit," Donnie says. "Just because my experience blew up in my face doesn't mean yours will."

I shake my head and wave him off. "Things with Indie aren't serious. We're not moving in with each other."

"Ain't that the damn truth?" Dem chuckles as he stops next to me and pours himself a cup of coffee.

"What the fuck is that supposed to mean?" I glare at him.

His smile grows. "Caught your girl sneaking out in the middle of the night. No way it's serious if she's leaving without so much as a goodbye."

"What makes you think she didn't say goodbye?" I growl.

He breaks out into a full bellied laugh. "For one, the angry scowl on your face. You're clearly pissed. And two, I caught her coming out of your room. You were passed out on your stomach, and she looked guilty as fuck."

I push off the counter and straighten my back. "What's that got to do with anything?"

"Can't be too serious if she doesn't bother to stay for breakfast. Or maybe ..." He cocks his head to the side and wrinkles his brow like he's thinking. "Was the sex terrible? Maybe you need some pointers on how to satisfy a woman."

My chest puffs out, and my fist tightens around my coffee mug. "I don't need pointers. She left plenty satisfied. Besides, I don't see a woman joining you for breakfast."

He shrugs, and his grin returns. "Didn't find anyone interesting at the bar."

"More like you got cocked blocked by your best friend's wife all night," Donnie says under his breath.

Dem shrugs. "No joke. Syd is a pain in my ass. Next time we go out, she's not invited. Then maybe I can get laid like grandpa here."

He pats me on the shoulder before he walks around the bar and sits down on one of the stools. I flip him off and turn to the fridge to hunt down some breakfast.

"In all seriousness," Donnie says. "You like this girl."

"I brought her home with me last night, didn't I?" I say with my head stuck in the fridge. I grab the eggs from the shelf and then dig around in the drawer for the cheese and ham, deciding to make myself an omelet.

He crosses his arms over his chest and stares at me like I'm an idiot. I ignore him in favor of making my breakfast.

Donnie shakes his head. "You know that's not what I mean. You've been complaining about her for weeks now. Going on and on about how much she drives you crazy. But that's all bullshit. She's gotten under your skin in a way that has nothing to do with the job."

"Here, here!" Dem says as he lifts his coffee mug in the air. "What he said."

I glare at Dem. "Don't act like you know a damn thing about liking a girl for more than just a good time."

"See." Donnie points at me. "I'm right. She means more to you than you're willing to admit."

I sigh, knowing he's right. "It's not that simple."

"It never is. But pretending like it's nothing won't do either of you any favors."

I pause, considering his words. "There's a lot at stake if things don't work out between us. Seeing her could have serious consequences for my career. Plus, her relationship is shaky with her father, aka my boss."

Donnie puts a hand on my shoulder. "I get it. Look at my current situation. But you won't know if it's worth it unless you take the risk. Sometimes you win, and sometimes you lose. If I can say that after what Lulu did to me, then you can explore whatever this is you've got going on with your assistant."

I nod, grateful for his support and advice. It's a much healthier outlook than I'd expect from him, considering how raw his breakup with Lulu still is.

To my surprise, I don't need to think about it. I'm willing to take the risk and explore something more with Indie. But I'm not the problem in this equation.

Considering how she left without so much as a goodbye, in the middle of the night, after receiving what I know were the best orgasms of her life, I'm not so sure she and I are on the same page.

One thing is certain. I'm going to fight like hell come Monday morning to change that.

∼

My mood didn't improve on Sunday. If anything, it got worse as the day waned on.

I messaged Indie more times than what is socially acceptable, but I can't bring myself to give two shits about that. That's what happens when one person ignores the other. Today she'll answer for her silence.

I arrive at the office at my usual hour of seven. Also, as usual, I'm greeted with a dark and silent floor.

It matches my mood.

The lights flicker on as soon as I step out of the elevator, and I make my way down the long hallway toward my office. I stop at Indie's desk and stare down at the clean surface.

There are no piles of messages waiting for me to sift through from the previous workday. As promised, she's been doing her job and doing it well. Aside from the chocolate shit incident, things between us have been good. Everything about Saturday night suggested our relationship was heading in a new direction.

Now I'm not so sure.

And I have no clue how to feel about it.

Pissed comes to mind. Maybe even a little hurt. That's a feeling I'd rather erase from the catalog of emotions to choose from. I've got a lot of experience with being pissed off, but not so much in the hurt department.

I don't like it.

I step inside my office and flip the lights on. I've got much more important things to worry about than how Indie makes me feel.

Plopping down in my chair, I fire up my computer and focus my energy on the report I need to finish for this project. Leon has done his part. Now it's time for me to do mine.

Unfortunately, that includes most of the report writing, including a summary of all the financials. I haven't even started the cost benefits analysis I need to include. The proposed software will require an annual subscription, and I need to prove its value.

Pulling up some of the research I completed a few weeks ago, I decide to tackle the cost benefit analysis first. The sooner that piece is complete, the closer we are to rolling out this product.

I lose myself in my work, completely tuned out to the rest of the office slowly coming alive as my coworkers arrive for work. When I finally look up from my computer screen, I'm surprised to see Indie sitting at her desk. I didn't hear her arrive.

I'm even more surprised when I see it's almost ten. Saving my work, I decide this is as good a time as any to take a break and deal with her. Rather than yelling out for her to come into my office, I pick up my phone and dial her extension.

I watch as her shoulders tense when her phone rings and she sees my name pop up on the caller ID. She glances over her shoulder and looks at me as if to question why I'm calling. I raise my brows in answer.

Instead of answering her phone, she stands. Her shoulders rise and fall as if she's taking a fortifying breath before turning around and stepping inside my office.

I hang up the phone. "Shut the door, please."

For once, she doesn't argue with me. She shuts the door, steps up to my desk, and stares down at me. Her face is devoid of emotion. Either Saturday night really didn't mean a damn thing to her or else she's a fantastic actress.

"Listen," she starts, before I get a chance to speak. "I'm sorry I didn't get back to you yesterday, but I was busy."

It's not the response I was hoping for, but at least it's something. That she came in here and immediately talked says she knows she's in the wrong. It still leaves me feeling hurt and frustrated.

"You left without saying goodbye." My voice is surprisingly calm and composed. Lord knows there's nothing about me that feels calm and composed right now.

"You were asleep. What was I supposed to do, wake you up?"

"Yes," I say curtly. "That's exactly what you should have done."

She lets out a low huff as if she's already tired of this conversation. Little does she know we're just getting started.

I push to my feet and walk around my desk so we're standing next to each other. When she looks up at me, I don't like what I see in her eyes. *Fear.*

"Why did you leave like that?"

Her nostrils flare, and her expression hardens. "Why are you making a big deal out of this? I told you it was a one-time thing. It's done. We're not doing it again."

I take a step closer to her, crowding her space. "I never agreed to that."

"I don't care what you did or did not agree to. We cannot do that again."

"Why the hell not?"

"Because!" She presses her hand to my chest and pushes against me, but I don't budge. I clasp my hand over hers and hold it close to my pounding heart. Her eyes widen and her breath hitches. "Atticus. Stop."

"Or what?" I tug her closer until I can feel her breath against my cheek. "Afraid you'll find yourself in my bed again?"

She shakes her head and her body tenses. I fucking hate it. "That was a mistake. I was thrown off guard by running into you while I was out with friends. I wasn't thinking straight."

I let out an incredulous laugh. "A mistake. That's what you're going with?"

"Well ... t's true," she says, but there's no conviction behind her words.

"Really." I lean down close to her ear, dropping my voice to a whisper. "Was it a mistake when my face was buried between your thighs?" I rub my nose down the length of her neck and relish the way she shivers. "Or how about when your plump lips were wrapped around my cock? Was that also a mistake?" Pressing my nose into the crook of her neck, I breathe in her sweet sugary scent. Her skin pebbles with goosebumps and I love it. "What about when my dick was buried so deep inside you, and you were screaming my name loud enough for the entire city to hear? Was that a mistake? Cause let me tell you, Princess, I felt the way your body responded to mine, and it sure as hell didn't feel like a fucking mistake."

She tugs at her hand, but I don't release her. I keep it pinned close to my chest.

"Atticus, please." She pleads. "You know we can't do this. It's too complicated and … And I—"

"What? Tell me what you really think."

"We'd never work. We come from different worlds, and you work—"

"I'm not good enough for you? Is that what you think?"

"No, that's not what I meant."

"I get it." I growl through clenched teeth. "It's not the first time a rich, spoiled *princess* snubbed me after a tumble in the sheets. I'm good enough for a fuck, but nothing more."

"You know that's not true."

"Do I?" I release her and take several steps back. Staring at her, I don't know how I missed it. Of course she wouldn't be interested in anything more with someone like me. Like she said, we're from two different worlds, and I'm not good enough to be a part of hers.

Stepping around my desk, I sit back down and wake up my computer. "I think we're done here."

"Atticus." Her voice cracks. "Don't be like this."

I snap my eyes to hers, and the moisture in her troubled gaze almost breaks me. If she fucking cries, I'm a goner. I need to put an end to this conversation, and fast.

"Close the door on your way out," I say in a cold, detached tone. "I am not to be disturbed for the rest of the day."

Turning my attention back to my computer screen, I do my best to pretend she's already gone. I refuse to look at her.

She hesitates for a moment before she releases a heavy sigh and turns around to leave. When my door closes on a soft click, I exhale just as deeply.

Dropping my head to my desk, I bang it a few times like that will knock some sense into me. It doesn't.

Then I pick up the small glass canister of chocolate I keep on my desk and throw it against the wall. It shatters and sends the chocolate in all directions.

I still don't feel better. If anything, I feel worse because now I've lost all the chocolate I love so much.

I'm better off without her.

It was just one night. She's right. It meant nothing.

We have to work together. Plus, she's my boss's daughter. That's a recipe for disaster.

I spend the next several minutes telling myself lie after lie, hoping I'll believe them.

Spoiler alert—it doesn't work.

ΕΛΛΑΔΑ

CHAPTER SIXTEEN

INDIGO

INDIGO
Why did you let me drink that much?

ELON
I'm never drinking again.

INDIGO
The shots were your idea.

ELON
I'm literally sweating tequila.

INDIGO
I need bacon and eggs. And pancakes with strawberries. And maybe some French fries. Oh, and a cheeseburger. A cheeseburger sounds really good. Is it too early for a cheeseburger?

ELON
Darlin' it's eight in the morning.

INDIGO
Don't care. I want.

ELON
Afraid you're on your own. Currently in the fetal position, begging for death.

> **INDIGO**
> So …
>
> Are we going out again tonight to drink away my anxiety so I can forget all about the dominating sex god and his magical penis?
>
> **ELON**
> Hell yeah we are.

After eating my weight in pancakes and bacon and downing a gallon of coffee, I feel marginally better after my binge drinking night out with Elon.

And by marginal, I mean I no longer feel like I'm going to hurl every time I stand up. I still feel like shit and would rather crawl back into bed and sleep until my prison sentence ends instead of going in to work.

Over the past four or five months, I've seen Atticus pissed plenty of times. My behavior and actions have been a great source of frustration for him since the day I walked through the doors of SimTech.

But nothing—and I mean *nothing*—has ever made him look like he did yesterday. He wasn't just mad or pissed or ready to seek retribution.

He was hurt.

And I did that to him.

I saw the pain in his expression the moment I got to the office. He was absorbed in his work, but he no longer possessed the energy that feeds his drive and determination. I'd debated on interrupting him—getting the hard conversation over with sooner rather than later—then decided against it.

I put that vacant look on his face, and I hated myself for it.

I did nothing to reverse the damage I'd done. Instead, I sat at my desk and tried to focus on anything except him and his stupid mouth and stupid hands and stupid magical penis.

It didn't work.

It felt like an eternity of agony and torture before my phone finally rang. When his name popped up on the caller ID, my heart skipped several beats and fluttered back into its normal rhythm.

Holding my ground and telling him those lies was the hardest thing I've ever done. But I had to do it. It would never work between us. Not with how close he is to my father.

Before heading to the office, I make a detour to the coffee shop. Despite how much coffee I've already consumed this morning, I get another one. But it's the pastries I really need.

After a night of too much tequila, a constant supply of junk food to nibble on is a must. They'll at least get me through to lunch when I can finally get that cheeseburger I want. Turns out, no one offers cheeseburgers this early in the morning.

Since the last round of coffees and pastries I bought for the office, the gossip about me has been less. At least I haven't walked into any more not-so-secret meetings with the other admins while they're talking shit about me. If a few coffees and pastries are all it takes to make the rest of my time there bearable, then it's well worth the investment.

With coffees for each of my counterparts in hand, plus one for my boss, and enough pastries to feed a small army, I head to the office.

Annie is already at the front desk when I step off the elevator. She immediately eyes me with suspicion. I ignore her look and plaster a smile on my face.

"This is for you," I say as I hand her a coffee.

Her eyes shift between mine and the coffee in my hand. She tentatively reaches for it like she's afraid it might bite her if she gets too close.

Once it's in her hand, she lifts the lid and smells it. Her eyes dart back to mine and narrow. "What is this?"

I force my smile into submission. "It's a mocha cappuccino. Just the way you like it."

Her eyes roll back so far into her head all I see is white. "I know that. I mean, why are you buying us coffee and pastries? It's not going to make us like you."

"Here's the thing, Annie." I lean on the counter and smile broadly. "It's not about making you like me. I'm doing this for myself. You can be mean and hateful and say all the horrible things you want behind my back, and there's nothing I can do about it. How you and the other admins choose to behave is on you. But I'm choosing kindness. So, enjoy the free coffee or not. Up to you."

With a wiggle of my fingers, I push off the counter and head down the hallway to the break room. Despite the sour feeling in my stomach from drinking way too much tequila last night, there's a pep in my step that wasn't there before.

Who knew taking the high road would be so freeing? I sure as hell didn't.

I round the corner and the break room entrance comes into view. That pep comes to a screeching halt.

Atticus is leaning against the wall next to the coffeemaker with Trisha pressed up against him. Her lips are dangerously close to his ear, and every territorial instinct inside of me comes to life. I can't see his face because his head is turned in the opposite direction, but Trisha is wearing a huge smile.

I want to wipe that smile right off her pretty face.

Her hand rises and her finger runs down the length of his arm and all I see is red. My first instinct is to barge in there and push her away from him. She has no right to touch him because *he's mine*.

How dare she think she has the right to put her hands on him? She's nothing more than ... *Wait*.

I shake my head and snap myself out of my jealousy induced rage.

Atticus is not mine. I made sure of that when I rejected him by telling him we come from two different worlds. Yeah, that unintentional insult went over really well.

Neither of them have seen me yet, which is probably why Trisha is coming on so strong. To his credit, Atticus's body language suggests he's not interested in whatever it is she's offering. His arms are tucked in close to his sides and his hands are balled into fists. If I could see his face, he's probably frowning.

Trisha presses up on her tiptoes so she's closer to his ear. I wish I could hear what she says because it finally gets him to react. He grabs her by the arms and pushes her backward.

It took him long enough.

I'm both equal parts pissed and elated. I'm pissed that he let her get that close to him and elated that he's rejecting her. At least I hope that's what this means.

Doing my best to maintain my stony expression, I step into the break room and drop the box of pastries onto the closest table with a thud. Trisha and Atticus both jump in surprise.

Once Trisha regains her composure, she gives me a seductive grin as if to suggest she and Atticus were doing exactly what it looked like.

Atticus, on the other hand, looks terrified.

"This isn't what it looks like." The words rush out of him as he takes a step toward me.

Trisha reaches out and presses her hand on his chest, effectively stopping him. Seeing her hand on him like that sets off something inside me I would prefer to pretend doesn't exist. It's primal and fierce and ready to fight for what's rightfully mine.

"Atticus, it's okay. Indie doesn't care about us," she says in a sickly seductive tone.

He knocks her hand away and frowns at her. "There is no us. There will never be an us."

Holding my hand up and slowly backing out of the room, I say, "Hey. It's none of my business. You two do what you want. I'm just dropping off some pastries."

I turn to leave when Atticus calls out. "Indie. Wait."

There's so much desperation in his tone that I cringe. Pausing, I look down at the drink holder in my other hand. Distracted by seeing them in what looked like an intimate embrace, I'd completely forgotten about their coffees.

Spinning around, I give them a fake smile. "I almost forgot. I got you each a coffee too."

Setting the drink holder down, I quickly pull theirs out and set them on the table next to the pastries. "Your names are on the cups."

Grabbing the remaining drinks, I dart out of the room before either of them can say anything else. That whole interaction was awkward enough, and it'll only get worse if I stick around.

Once I reach the turn in the hallway, I glance over my shoulder and sigh in relief when I see Atticus isn't following me. As soon as I'm around the corner, I fall against the wall. My heart is beating way too fast, and my hands are shaking.

But worst of all, the jealous woman inside me is screaming *he's mine* at a decibel so loud my ears are ringing.

∽

BY THE TIME I MAKE IT TO MY DESK, ATTICUS IS ALREADY IN HIS OFFICE and he's not alone. My father is sitting in a chair across from his desk.

I inwardly groan as I pull out my chair and sit. The last person I want to see this morning is my father. Knowing him, he'll smell the remnants of last night's binge drinking fest with Elon and use it as another excuse to control my life.

I pull my blouse out from my body and sniff. I frown.

Even I can smell the tequila seeping out of my pores.

Maybe I should've gone with a floral scented body spray over my usual vanilla bean. The floral fragrances are stronger and better at covering the evidence of bad decisions.

Booting up my computer, I note the time. It's a little before nine. Despite my hangover and detour to get coffee and pastries, I'm at my desk earlier than usual. It's typically closer to nine-thirty by the time I make it in.

I don't let myself dwell on the fact that I woke up early because I had a sex dream last night that had me moaning so loud, I woke myself. I also refuse to let myself acknowledge that said dream may have included the demanding sex god sitting in his office behind me.

The man has ruined sex for me forever.

Heat pools at my core at the memory of how he commanded my body and gave me more orgasms in a single night than I thought humanly possible. Hell, I always considered myself lucky if I had one orgasm during sex. Before Atticus, I would have argued that multiple orgasms in a single night were a myth.

The man proved me wrong.

I clench my thighs together and drop my head onto my desk. As realization dawns, I bang my head a few times to really drive home the point.

I'm an idiot for pushing him away.

"Indie, Princess." I freeze mid-bang when I feel my dad's hand on my back. I sit up and his frown deepens when he sees my face. "Are you feeling okay?"

My answering nod is too quick, earning me a furrowed brow to accompany his frown. "Why wouldn't I be?"

He moves his hand to my chin and lifts my face to his. Then he sniffs the air. I cringe. "Are you sick?"

"No." I relax, but only slightly. "Just tired."

He takes another deep breath and eyes me curiously. I can't tell if he can smell the evidence of last night on me or not. "Maybe you shouldn't stay out so late on nights when you have to work the next day."

Busted.

"I wasn't out *that* late." I scoff. "Besides, what I do on my own time is none of your business."

"It's my business when it affects my company."

I wave my arms out to my side, making a show of my presence. "I'm here, aren't I? And early, I might add. The only thing interfering with my work right now is *you*."

Dad drops his head and rubs the bridge of his nose. "Princess, when are you going to grow up?"

I huff in disdain. "When are you going to open your eyes and realize I grew up a long time ago?"

"Don't get mouthy with me. I'm not in the mood."

"Then don't stop by my desk and accuse me of bringing down your company when I've done nothing wrong."

I don't know how it's possible, but his face hardens even more. He opens his mouth to say more but is cut off by Atticus.

"Indie, have you finished the projection reports I ask you to summarize?"

We both look behind me to find Atticus standing in his doorway. I meet his stare. He raises his brows like he's waiting for my answer, but we both know he never asked me to do anything involving projection reports. *Is he attempting to save me from my dad's morning berating?*

"Um, not yet." My voice is hesitant when I respond. "But it's the first thing on my morning to-do list."

"Thanks." He knocks his knuckles on the door frame and takes a step back. "As long as I have it by the end of the day, you're good."

He spins around and heads back to his desk.

"You'll have it by lunchtime," I call out, my words much more confident.

"Even better," he replies as he takes his seat.

When I turn back to Dad, he's staring at me like he's seeing me for the first time. I hold his gaze with a challenging stare, waiting for him to say more. But he doesn't.

Instead, he nods and turns to leave. I breathe out a sigh of relief the moment he disappears down the hallway.

With my elbows propped up on my desk, I drop my head and run my fingers through my hair. That could have ended differently if Atticus hadn't stepped in and kept me from drowning. He literally tossed me a life preserver and saved me, even though I didn't deserve it.

Pushing to my feet, I take a deep breath before I turn and head into his office. He looks up at me with a slight smirk that says I owe him. I'm torn between kissing that smirk off his face or giving him hell.

I opt for a thank you instead.

"That was nice of you to get my dad off my back. I appreciate it."

He stands, walks around his desk, and stops next to me. "It was the least I could do, considering what you saw in the break room. It wasn't what it looked like."

"It's none of my business." The words are out before I even think about what I'm saying.

His stare hardens, and he takes a step closer to me. "Are you saying you're fine with me dating someone else?"

"You're not dating Trisha." I huff out through an incredulous laugh.

"I know that." He takes another step toward me. "But what I don't understand is why you looked like you were ready to strangle her when she laid her hands on me. Yesterday, you were determined to convince both of us that we were a mistake. You can imagine how your reaction surprised me."

I close my eyes and take a deep breath. When I open them again, his expression is feral. It sends a jolt of electricity right to my core.

"I should get back to work," I say before I move past him and head to the door.

But I don't make it.

He reaches around me, shuts the door, and pins my chest against it. He presses his front against me, and with our height difference, I feel his hardening cock dig into my lower back.

"We're not done," he growls. "In fact, I reject every argument you've made." His voice drops to a low, raspy timbre. "My claim on you has only just begun, Princess."

"Atticus." I suck in a breath and try like hell to pretend my entire body didn't just light up with excitement at his claim on me.

He leans down and whispers in my ear. "Tell me how you felt when you saw Trisha's hands on me."

"I ... It was nothing." The words rush out of me. My head is a fog of need and the lingering effects of my hangover.

He clicks his tongue and I feel the shake of his head as his strong hand wraps around my throat, tilting my head to the side. His grip is firm, demanding, and has my pulse racing like a high-speed train.

"Don't lie to me, Princess. You should know by now that I'm not above punishing you."

His other hand brushes my hair to the side, exposing my neck to him. He leans closer, dragging his nose down the curve of my neck before the stiff bristles of his beard tickle the sensitive skin just below my ear. I suck in a breath as my entire body burns in excitement.

"I'm going to ask you one more time. How did it make you feel?"

"Jealous," I say in a rush.

His lips wrap around the lobe of my ear, and I groan. "And why were you jealous?"

"B-Because …" I'm panting and it's making it hard to formulate words. But I squeeze my eyes closed and force myself to speak the truth. "Because you're mine."

If I thought the look on his face was feral, that's nothing compared to the sound that comes out of him at my admission.

His warm breath rolls over my skin like a blanket before his soft lips press against my neck and cause me to quiver. My knees buckle and I feel like I'm going to fall. But his hand around my neck tightens, securing me close to his chest.

"Atticus." I breathe out his name as my hands fly up and clench around his fingers. His hold on me is strong and leaves no question about who's in control. I'm terrified and excited.

He must sense the war going on inside me because he loosens his hold on my neck and whispers in my ear. "It's okay, Princess. I'm not going to hurt you. I'll never hurt you." His words trail off just as his teeth bear down on my shoulder, causing me to moan. "I promise you will enjoy every single thing I do to you. You will beg me for more, same as you did the other night. This is just the beginning. Do you understand?"

With his free hand, he locks the door, and then slowly walks me back.

"I've already claimed you, Princess. Now I'm going to mark your body so you never forget who you belong to."

It isn't until he's bending me over the table in the corner of his office that I come to my senses. I press my hands on the table and push back. That proves to be a mistake because his very hard cock presses into my core.

"We can't do this. Not here." I whisper-yell.

He chuckles and rubs his hand over my ass, slowly tugging at the material of my skirt. "Are we going to have this argument every time I'm about to fuck you?"

I snap my head around and glare at him over my shoulder. "We're at work. Someone might hear us."

"Then I guess you better be quiet."

His hand is back around my neck, pulling my lips toward his. His mouth covers mine in a searing kiss that leaves no question about who he thinks I belong to. And as much as I feel the need to argue otherwise, it would be a moot point.

I may feel differently about it later, but right now, I'm his and he's mine.

His lips leave mine, but only for as long as it takes him to retrieve his wallet from his back pocket and fish out a condom. He rips the foil wrapper open with his teeth before his lips crash to mine.

His grip around my neck tightens as I feel him remove his cock from his pants. With the way he's pressed against my back, I can't see what he's doing. I can only feel. And when his hand slips between my legs and tugs my panties to the side, I gasp.

His fingers tease my slit, swiping from my entrance to my clit. "Fuck, you're so wet, Princess. Such a good girl. You're ready for me, and I barely have to work for it."

"Atticus, please." I beg. It's a good thing I'm pressed against the table because my legs tremble with need.

The tip of his cock nudges my entrance.

"Is this what you want?" he growls.

"Yes," I breathe.

The word is barely out of me before he slams inside me, filling me completely. I let out a loud whimper and his hand around my neck tightens.

"Quiet, baby," he says between thrusts. "If you cry out again, I'm going to spank you. Is that what you want?"

I glance over my shoulder. My breath catches at the fire dancing around in those deep brown pools of lust and need. It's primal, and I feel every bit like the prey about to be devoured.

I can't stop the smile that lifts my lips from knowing that I do this to him.

He leans down and presses a quick kiss to my lips. "Fuck, I love it when you smile like that."

"I love it when you look at me like you want to eat me alive."

"I did enjoy having my face buried between your thighs. But we'll have to save that for later." He smirks as he slowly pulls out of me before slamming back in. "Brace yourself, baby. I'm going to fuck you hard."

With one hand over my mouth—because being quiet is impossible—and the other gripping my hip, he fucks me from behind.

It vaguely registers in my brain what he's doing when he buries his face in my neck and sucks on the curve right above my shoulder. The harder he fucks me. The harder he sucks on my neck.

I know he's leaving his mark on me, just like he said he would. But at this moment, I can't bring myself to care. At least my hair will hide it.

And when I come around his cock, all I feel is pleasure and pure bliss.

And all I can think about is when we can do it again.

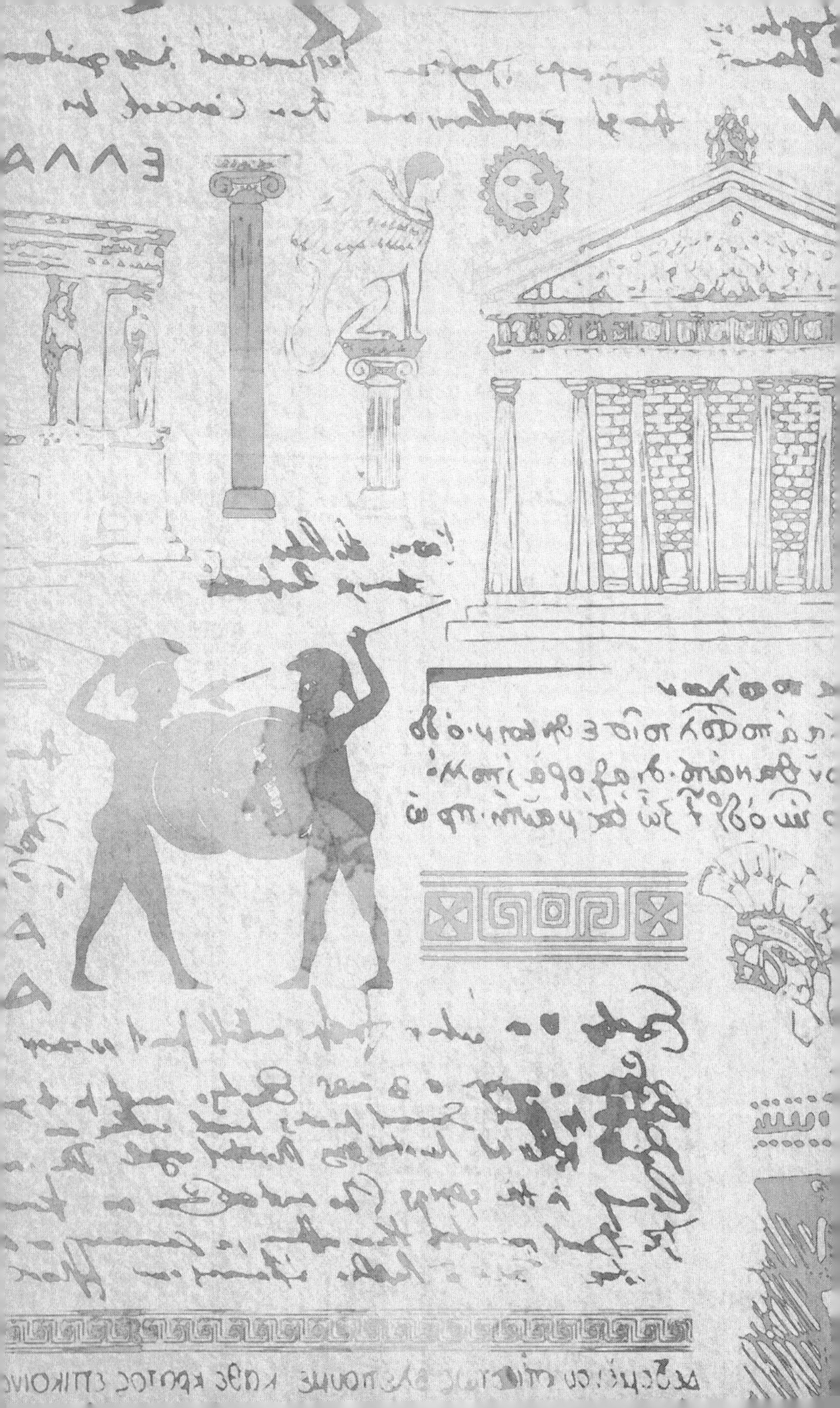

CHAPTER SEVENTEEN

ATTICUS

INDIGO
Maybe this isn't such a good idea.

ATTICUS
Why do you do this?

INDIGO
Do what?

ATTICUS
Doubt our relationship unless my dick is inside you.

INDIGO
Is that what we're calling this? A relationship?

ATTICUS
Yes!

With groceries in hand, I hit the button for Indie's floor. She thinks I'm on my way over to take her out to dinner when really, I plan to surprise her with dinner in.

I learned a long time ago that women love a man who can cook. Hopefully, Indie is no different.

Lord knows I could use a break. That woman is not making this easy on me. She's determined to put roadblock after roadblock in front of us. Tonight, I hope to abolish a few of them.

I get her concern. An office romance isn't ideal. Nor is the fact that her father is my boss and I'm hers. But if she's being honest with me, she won't be working for me for long. Our situation is temporary.

She still hasn't told me the reasons she's working for her dad. She's been secretive about the whole thing. That's something else I hope to get an answer to tonight.

Where Indie is concerned, I need all the advantages I can get. I hope a romantic dinner in will give me exactly that.

The high-pitched bark from her dog immediately follows my knock. It brings a smile to my face. I haven't seen Beatrix since that night at the office, but winning over her dog is another point I plan to use in my favor.

Beatrix scratches at the door. Then I hear Indie call out that she'll be there in a minute. I'm earlier than I said I'd be. I wanted to give myself extra time to cook, so I hope she doesn't mind.

As soon as she opens the door, Beatrix rushes out and jumps around my feet. She looks excited to see me. I lean down and scratch behind her ears. She licks my arm and pants.

"Hey there, girl." She nuzzles into my touch, and I can't stop the smile that spreads across my face.

"I still can't believe how much she likes you," Indie says. When I look up at her, I have to fight my inner beast. Her hair hangs in soft curls around her shoulders and her makeup is done to perfection. But she's wearing a short satin robe that barely covers her ass.

"You're early." She raises a brow like she's about to let me have it for my transgression.

I push to my feet, then pull her into my arms. Pressing a kiss to her forehead, I step past her and glance around her apartment.

"Change in plans," I say when my eyes locate her kitchen.

Her apartment is modest, and not at all what I expected from James Simons's daughter.

It's an open concept and not much bigger than my place. The main difference is she has room for a dining table. Her kitchen is slightly larger, but not by much. It's modern with an industrial feel with slick white cabinets, black countertops, and stainless-steel appliances. It's definitely been remodeled recently.

"What do you mean by change in plans?" She shuts her door, then turns to me with her arms crossed over her chest.

"We're staying in and I'm cooking you dinner." I don't wait for her to answer. I set the grocery bag on the counter and start unloading it.

"You cook?" She cocks a brow as if she doesn't believe that's possible.

"I do." I rest my hands on the island counter and stare at her. My dick thickens at the thought that she might be naked under that robe. "The way I see it is, you have two choices right now. Go finish getting dressed while I start on dinner, or take that robe off and I'll eat you instead."

Her eyes flare with excitement, and for a moment, I really hope she chooses option B. "I'm starving. I'll get dressed while you cook."

I nod and watch in appreciation as her ass sways as she walks down the short hallway and disappears through a door that I assume is her bedroom. It clicks shut, and I swallow a groan at the thought of her peeling that robe off and revealing her naked body. It takes all my strength to stay put and start on dinner.

I did a lot of the prep work in advance, so it would go faster once I was here. I'm making her one of my favorite Mediterranean meals. It's not fancy, but it's delicious.

Seasoned grilled chicken with a cilantro yogurt sauce on fresh pitas. I made the pita dough at home so it would have plenty of time to rise before I roll it out and fry it up. I even marinated the chicken in advance. The only thing I didn't do before arriving was make up the yogurt sauce and dice up the cucumber. Those are best made at the last minute.

When she finally exits her bedroom, I've got the chicken in the oven and am halfway through making the pitas. She stops at the edge of the kitchen. Her eyes are wide, and her mouth falls open like she can't believe what she's seeing. It makes me chuckle.

"Never seen a man cook before?"

My eyes meet hers and heat flares in her green irises before her gaze rakes down my body. I follow her path. I took off my jacket and rolled up my shirt sleeves. I'm also wearing an apron so I don't get flour on my dark blue shirt.

She lets out a ragged breath, and I raise a brow. "Everything okay?"

"Yeah," she croaks. "It's just … You look really, really good in the kitchen."

My smile grows. "Thanks. You look pretty damn delectable yourself." I take a moment to appreciate the soft pink dress she's wearing that hugs her curves and flows in layers around her thighs. She's wearing matching high-heeled shoes that I want to see pressed against my shoulders later tonight while my cock is deep inside her.

"I need to take Beatrix for a walk." She points over her shoulder toward the door. "How long do I have?"

"Why don't you give me ten minutes, and I'll go with you. I just need to finish the last of these pitas."

Her eyes dart toward the counter where I've rolled out several pitas waiting to be fried. "You're making pitas from scratch?"

Her voice sounds disbelieving, and it makes me laugh. "Yeah."

I turn back to the stove and remove the one currently in the skillet and add the next one. When I glance over my shoulder, she's staring at me like she's never seen a man cook before. In fact, she's staring at me like she's never seen a man like me before and it has me puffing my chest out.

I clear my throat and turn the pita in the skillet before it burns. These don't take long to fry. "I brought some wine. Do you mind opening it and pouring us each a glass?"

"Uh, yeah." She shakes her head and jumps into action. Her hands shake as she reaches for the bottle, and it makes me smile. I love seeing her flustered, and I love it even more that I'm the one doing this to her.

I feel her hand on the small of my back and it sends a jolt of need straight to my dick. When I look over my shoulder, she's holding a glass of wine out for me.

"Thank you." I take it from her and then toss back a sip. It's a red I drink often. It's not exactly the best pairing for the meal I have planned, but I don't care. It's good, and I wanted to share it with her.

She's still staring at me like she's confused by what she sees. I subconsciously run my hand over my short beard like there might be something on my face.

"What's wrong?" I ask.

"Nothing." She shakes her head like she's snapping herself out of a daze. "It's just ... You're not who I thought you were."

A slow smile lifts my lips. I scoot the skillet off the burner and turn to face her. Pulling her into my arms, I press a light kiss to her lips. "Right back at you, Princess."

Then I kiss her again, only this time it's hard and deep. The kiss leaves her breathless and me hard. As much as I want to bend her over the counter and fuck her from behind, I resist. There will be plenty of time for that later.

∽

"Tell me more about what it was like growing up with so many siblings," she asks as she hops up on the island counter behind me.

I can't help but stare at how relaxed she looks. She's leaning on one hand while the other twirls her wine glass. Her petite, shapely legs are crossed at the knees, causing the skirt of her dress to ride up her thighs. My hands itch to grab those thighs, spread them wide, and make her come on my tongue.

But that'll have to wait. Kitchen cleanup first, then I'll give my princess more orgasms.

She offered to clean up since I cooked. Normally, I'd accept the offer, but I refused her help. Tonight is about spoiling her and showing her I'm worth the risk.

That *we're* worth the risk.

"Noisy, crowded, and sometimes crazy." I toss her a smile. "But we had fun. Especially with all the traveling we got to do."

"Did you really grow up in an RV?" she asks, her tone a little disbelieving.

"I did. My parents met on the road and have never stopped traveling. Five kids, and we were all born in different states. We were always on the move. The longest we ever stayed in one place was a year, I think. Not that it really mattered. We were all homeschooled."

"That sounds expensive to travel that much with five kids. What did your parents do for work?"

"My parents do well for themselves. Plus, we lived simply. My dad is an engineer and does contract work. He's able to work from anywhere. Mom is a traveling nurse. Most people don't realize how in demand traveling nurses are. Neither of them have ever struggled for work. Since they live a minimalist lifestyle, I imagine they have a lot more money saved than the average person."

"I can't imagine a life like that. It sounds wonderful." She swirls her wine glass, staring at it with a longing in her eyes that I don't like. She looks sad. "My parents never traveled with me. Mom traveled. Dad worked. And I was left with nannies or sent off to boarding school."

I put the last of the dishes in the dishwasher and dry my hands. Then I turn toward her, spread her legs, and step between them. "I'm sorry. They hurt you, didn't they?"

She nods but doesn't elaborate.

I cup her cheek and lightly kiss the tip of her nose. "Will you tell me why you're working for your dad? Please tell me I've finally earned that story."

She holds my gaze and all I see is hesitance. Her shoulders sag and she looks down at where my body is pressed against hers. "You really know how to kill a mood."

Disappointment washes over me. "You don't have to tell me if you don't want to talk about it. I get that it's hard to trust others."

Her eyes snap back to mine. "It's not about trust. I trust you. It just makes me mad to think about, and we're having such a great time."

Rubbing my thumb along her bottom lip, I smile. "What if I

promise to make it all better with orgasms and dirty talk? Will you tell me then?"

She lifts a brow. "Something tells me I'll get orgasms and dirty talk no matter what I tell you."

I shrug. "Maybe. Maybe not. There's only one way to find out."

A smile tugs at her lips and I know I've won. With a light kiss, I pull her in for a hug. "Why is your dad making you work for him?"

She sighs, sits her wineglass down and wraps her arms around me too. She rests her cheek against me, and my chest tightens. The urge to keep her close like this is a strong, forever feeling.

"Because he thinks I'm just like my mother." Her voice is low, almost a whisper. "A good for nothing, gold digger who would rather live off someone else's money than make a life for herself."

I pull back, place my fingers under her chin, and lift her face to look at me. "Please tell me that's not true."

She shrugs and gives me a sad smile. "Unfortunately, I can't. It doesn't matter what I do to prove myself, all Dad sees when he looks at me, is my mother. I sympathize with him to a degree. My mother is not a good person, and she used him for money. I exist because she figured a kid would earn her more money in a settlement. She couldn't care less about me as a person."

"God, Indie." My hold around her tightens. I want to kiss and love on her until she knows exactly how special and amazing she really is. "No kid should grow up without parents that are fully invested in them. I'm sorry you had to grow up like that."

"It wasn't all bad. Dad eventually got remarried. My stepmom is cool, and I'd do anything for my half-brother. He's the only reason I agreed to Dad's terms."

"What do you mean?"

"I'm sure you picked up on the fact that Dad doesn't think Jay or James Jr., that's my eleven-year-old brother, will ever be capable of running the company. He struggles with social anxiety on a crippling level. With treatment and therapy, he's getting better. But Dad doesn't see it. He refuses to. The cognitive behavior therapy he needs isn't cheap. Neither is the diagnosis and testing process. Most insurance doesn't cover a fraction of the costs. Since earning my degree, I've been working tirelessly to start a foundation to help lower-income families with kids like Jay. That's why I work a second job and do so much volunteer work. I need the experience and connections if I want this to work."

"Wait, you're working a second job? Why didn't I know that?"

She nods. "I'm the events coordinator for one of the best charity event planning businesses in the city. Plus, I volunteer for a center called Play Therapy that helps kids just like Jay. That's my passion. But Dad doesn't recognize what I do as a job. He thinks I'm a bleeding heart that will burn through her trust fund and come out the other end with nothing to show for it. So, he demanded I work for him for one year or else he'd dissolve my trust and leave me with nothing. He's forcing me to do this or else I lose everything I've worked so hard to get. Without my trust fund, I don't have the money to start the foundation."

"That's why you can't quit," I say, finally understanding.

"Yep. Believe me, I'd love nothing more than to turn in my resignation and walk away from my dad forever, but he has the upper hand. I might have a solid investor that will make it possible without my trust, but it's not a done deal yet. Until then, I'm stuck."

Running my finger along the edge of her jaw, I lean down and hover just above her lips. "I'm sorry he can't see the amazing woman you are. But maybe we can make the rest of your time at the company a little more enjoyable despite him."

I feel her smile before it reaches her eyes. "And how do you propose to do that?"

"Orgasms. Lots and lots of orgasms." I crush my mouth to hers and kiss her hard and deep.

Then I not so gently push her back until she's spread out on the counter like an offering. Grabbing her thighs, I tug her forward until her ass is at the edge of the counter.

"I've been dying to get my mouth on you since I walked through that door. Teasing me with your sugary sweet scent and this pretty pink dress." I growl as I run my nose down her body, starting at her neck and stopping only when I reach her delicious, alluring center.

I press my nose and mouth into her, loving how wet her panties already are. "So ready for me, Princess. Let's see how hard I can make you come tonight."

Looping my fingers around her panties, I rip them off her in one quick jerk of my hands. Then I drop to my knees and feast on her. I push my tongue inside her before I lick her and suck her tight little clit between my teeth. Her hips jolt from the action and I can tell it won't take much to bring her to orgasm.

"Not so fast, Princess. Let's enjoy this for a little longer."

"Atticus." She breathes and pants my name like a prayer. It drags a smile out of me and has my heart doing weird flutters in my chest. This woman is going to be my end.

Pulling back, I blow on her clit before I put my tongue on her again. This time I'm rougher, more forceful with my mouth. I feast on her like she's the best meal I've ever had. Licking and sucking and fucking her with my tongue until she's begging me to make her come.

Right before I feel her body tense beneath me, I back off, blowing a light burst of air over her clit again. She cries out, but not in ecstasy. This is a cry of frustration, and it makes me chuckle.

I replace my mouth with my finger, lightly teasing her entrance with the tip before I run it up her center and around her clit. She sucks in a breath.

"Atticus. Please." She throws her head back and runs her fingers through her hair in frustration. Maybe it makes me a dick, but I love seeing her like this. Writhing. Begging. So close to her release and completely at my mercy.

"Look at me." I order. And to my great pleasure, she obeys instantly. Pressing up on her elbows, she stares down at me and meets my gaze. She looks so disheveled and desperate. This look on her does something to me that I can't quite explain. It's primal and instinctive and makes me want to never leave this spot.

I shift my gaze to her spread legs and groan as I slowly press two fingers inside her tight, pulsing center. "Fuck, Princess. You're so fucking pretty. I could watch you take my fingers all day and night."

I can't help myself when I press a gentle kiss to her clit, causing her to gasp at the sensation. There's a war going on inside me right now. One part of me wants to devour her like a wild beast, claiming her, marking her, so the world knows she's mine. The other part of me wants to cherish her like the amazing woman she is so she knows she's worth so much more than a good fuck.

Indigo Simons is about to be my undoing, and I can't even bring myself to worry about what that really means.

I slowly move my fingers in and out of her before I run them down her center and over her tight little hole. I put a little pressure there while I replace my fingers with my tongue.

She gasps and when I look up, she's staring at me in both panic and excitement.

"Has anyone ever taken you back here?" I ask, my voice a low grumble.

She shakes her head. And that pleases me far more than it should. Never breaking eye contact with her, I put a little more pressure there. The tip of my finger breaks the barrier, and her eyes widen.

"Tell me to stop if you don't like it."

She nods, and I continue. With my tongue inside her, I run my teeth over her clit and press my finger a little further in. She lets out a low whimper of pleasure.

"You like this, don't you?" I grin at how responsive and willing she is to let me explore every inch of her. "You're such a good girl, Princess."

"Yes," she moans as I lick up her center and suck her clit between my lips. At the same time, I push my finger deeper inside her ass. She cries out just as her body succumbs to me. It's an otherworldly experience feeling her come this hard, this deeply.

A wetness unlike anything I've ever experienced before fills my hand and mouth. I continue to suck and lick and devour every drop of her release like a starving man.

Her hips buck and her head falls back as she cries out my name.

She wraps her pretty legs around my head and squeezes like her life depends on keeping my mouth right where it is.

"Oh my God. What did you just do to me?" she asks when she's finally able to catch her breath.

I wipe my mouth on my shirtsleeve and kiss my way up her body, biting at her pebbled nipples through her dress as I do. "Baby, you came so hard, you squirted."

Wrapping my arms around her waist, I pull her to a seated position so I can lift her dress off her. She's limp in my arms, and the sated expression on her face has me smiling.

"Really?" she rasps out through ragged breaths.

"Yeah, really." I chuckle.

She pants as my lips glide down her neck and chest before I pull her bra down and suck her dusty-rose nipple into my mouth. Her hand reaches for my cock and squeezes it hard, causing my body to jerk in response.

"My turn," she breathes, but I shake my head and remove her hand from my aching erection. As much as I'd love to have her plump lips wrapped around my cock again, tonight is about her.

"Not tonight, baby. You can suck my cock another time." I undo my pants and quickly dig a condom out of my wallet. My hands work quickly to rip it open and sheath my erection. "Tonight is just for you."

I slam inside her, filling her completely. We both moan at my sudden invasion. Her head falls back, and she's still so weak from the orgasm I just gave her that she's struggling to sit up.

My hands glide down her sides, savoring every curve with reverence like I've never felt something so amazingly beautiful before. Probably because I haven't.

Once her back is on the counter, I grip her hips and thrust into her hard and fast. In no time, her body is clenching around my cock like she's trying to suck the life force out of me. She feels so good. My head spins.

"You were made for me, Princess. Swear to fucking God. So perfect. So good."

I'm barely breathing as her body unleashes again. Her cries are animalistic, and her body convulses. Seeing her come so completely undone is all it takes to push me over the edge. I tumble into my own bottomless pit of pleasure.

My body stills inside her as I revel in her. We may have gotten off on the wrong foot when she first started working for me. But that's all changed. She's right where she belongs—in my arms.

We fall apart together, and I can't think of anywhere else I'd rather be than right here with her.

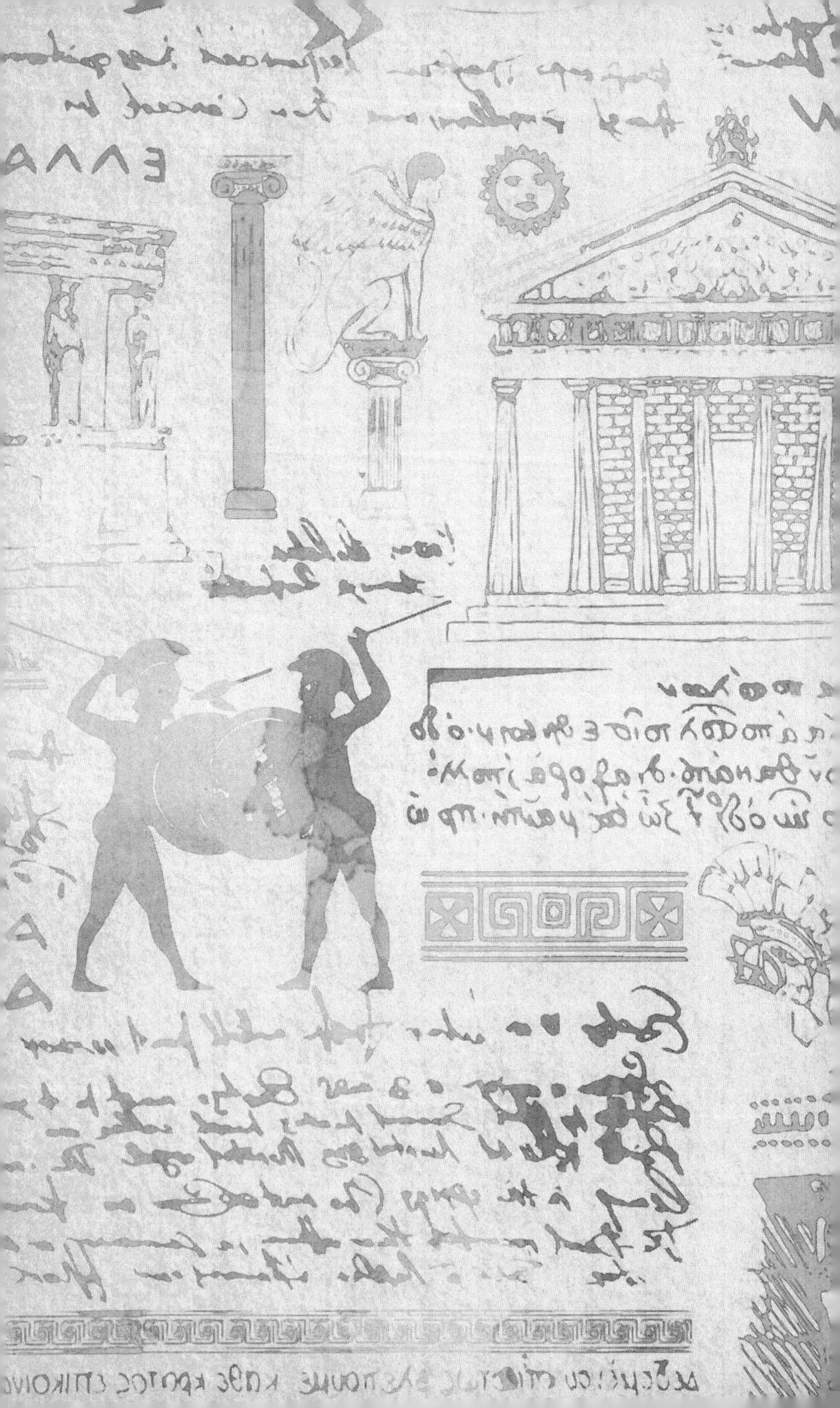

CHAPTER EIGHTEEN

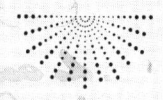

INDIGO

INDIGO
Is it possible to die from orgasms?

ELON
Um, darlin' I'm going to need ALL the deets.
Like NOW!

INDIGO
He's so freaking good. Like too good. This can't be real.

ELON
More magical penis action?

INDIGO
The man is not human. Now I have to add magical hands and mouth to the mix. I'm officially ruined.

ELON
I am so jealous.

Snuggling up next to Atticus after he so expertly demanded multiple mind-blowing orgasms from my body is quite the juxtaposition. Tonight, I've seen two very different sides of this man. He's gone from sweet, generous, and thoughtful to demanding, rough, and still generous to back to being sweet.

I never would have pegged him as a cuddler. But here we are, tangled together between my sheets with his arms around me, his fingers playing with my hair, and our legs tied in knots. This feels nice—better than nice—and it's something I could get used to.

And that makes this entire scenario dangerous.

I probably shouldn't let myself get used to being in Atticus's arms. No matter how good he makes me feel, that doesn't change who he works for. Dating Atticus puts me too close to Dad, and I'm not sure I can handle that long term.

Why couldn't Dad assign me to work for someone like Uncle Vic? Or someone with zero personality like Stefon. But no, Dad had to force me to work with the demanding Greek sex god who's trying really hard to steal my heart.

Atticus's arms tighten around me before he kisses the top of my head. "I swear I can hear you thinking. Talk to me, Princess."

Stifling a groan, I look up at him. He cups my chin in a gentle embrace before brushing his lips across mine. It's so sweet and loving I can't help but swoon.

In an attempt to break this spell he's slowly casting on me, I swing my leg over his middle and straddle him. Then I lean down and rest my arms on his chest.

He chuckles. "Baby, you're going to have to give me a little more time if you want another round. Still in recovery here."

I shake my head. "I just want to talk."

His smile fades, and his expression turns to one of concern. He lifts his hand to brush a strand of my hair out of my face and behind my ear. Then he cups the back of my neck and pulls my mouth to his. His lips find mine in a firm, reverent kiss. It's not dirty or claiming, or nearly as feverish as our other kisses have been. This one is full of meaning and heart and something I don't even want to let myself think about yet.

When he breaks the kiss and pulls back, his eyes are closed and his lips are turned up in a smile. It's a relaxed, satisfied look that I like seeing on his face.

"If you're going to question our relationship status again, don't," he says before I regain my wits. Then his eyes open and pin me with one of the most serious stares I've ever seen on the man. His expressive chocolate-brown eyes are dark and smoldering. There's so much emotion I don't know how to process the meaning behind this look. "You and me? We're happening."

I sigh, trying not to let the squealing little girl inside me get too excited. Attempting to force myself to relax, I cross my arms over his chest and rest my chin on them. "Define *happening*."

"Dating, a couple, boyfriend and girlfriend, *exclusive*." He says exclusive with so much finality, there's no questioning what he wants from me. "Pick whichever one of those makes you feel best. Just note that you're mine, and I'm yours. No one else touches you."

My heart flutters in my chest and my stomach feels like a swarm of butterflies just took flight. I nod. My throat tightens and I have to take a moment to calm my body down before I can speak. This man is stirring feelings inside me that I'm not prepared to process right now.

I clear my throat and take a deep breath, deciding a change in subject is in order. "Why is this promotion at work so important to you? You're great at your job and you seem to love getting your hands dirty, so to speak. Wouldn't this promotion remove you from getting into the weeds of coding?"

His eyes narrow as he stares at me, then he drops his head back and stares up at the ceiling like he's deep in thought. He takes a few moments before he finally answers me.

"Yeah, it will. That happens with any advancement. I used to do a lot more before I was promoted to senior manager. Accepting a promotion upstairs will remove me even further from the day-to-day tasks I love. I'd still oversee all the projects and give input. I'd have to trust my replacement to do the job just as well as I did. That'll be a struggle for me, but I'll adjust."

"I've noticed you don't pass off a lot of tasks to your staff that you probably should. Except for Leon, you don't let anyone else get close to your projects."

He shakes his head and lets out a soft chuckle that rumbles in his chest. I feel that rumble all the way to my toes. "You noticed that, huh?"

"Kinda hard to miss. You trust Jen with applications because that's not your strength or passion. But when it comes to software development and coding, especially when it's your baby, you micromanage. Why?"

He raises a brow as if to say he's shocked I noticed any of that. It's my turn to chuckle.

"I only pretend I'm a brainless twit," I say. "I pay attention."

He lets out a deep sigh and wraps his arms around me, hugging me closer to his chest. "I've been burned before. Had ideas stolen. So yeah, I don't trust easily. I'm working on it though. If I get this promotion, I won't have a choice."

"Why not just stay where you're at for now? You're young. You have plenty of time for C-suite level promotions. Enjoy the work you love while you still can."

"Because it'll be a huge pay raise." He doesn't hesitate with his answer. "It would ensure that my family never has to worry about money again. I didn't grow up with wealth and stability and the things I'm sure you take for granted. Not that it's your fault. You didn't ask to be born to a millionaire any more than I asked to be born to nomad hippies."

"I thought you said you loved your childhood."

"I did. But because I love my family, not the lifestyle. Living in an RV like my parents is not my idea of life. When my brothers and I first moved to the city, it was rough. Penny Love moved here after she graduated, and we followed her. We couldn't stand the idea of her alone in a huge city like this."

"Protective younger brothers?" I can't help but smile at the image of Atticus going all caveman on some guy Penny dated. It probably drove her mad.

His relaxed smile makes him look even younger. There's a boyish charm hidden underneath all Atticus's bossy and demanding tendencies. "Over the top. And Penny Love had the worst taste in men. She kept dating all these losers. Thank God she found Trent and we don't have to worry about her anymore."

"But you still worry about your brothers?" I ask as I trace my fingers along the lines of his tattoos covering his chest.

"Yeah." His sigh is deep and full of worry. "None of us had a plan. We took the first jobs we could find and got lucky as hell in the apartment we live in. Rent control really is a godsend. But money was tight while we all figured out career paths. My brother Adonis is doing great. He's the one who visited me at the office. He just finished his PhD and may have a full-time job teaching at NYU. But until my other two brothers get it together, I'm not going to be able to relax."

"What do they do that makes you so worried?"

"What don't they do is more like it." His hand traces lazy circles on my back as we both relax more and more into each other's embrace. "Eros, my youngest brother, he's still floundering. Works as a bouncer at a bar. Money's not great and the hours suck. Demetrius has a great job as a firefighter, but he still refuses to grow up. I worry he's going to fuck up his job because he still parties too hard."

"They're young. Isn't fucking up a rite of passage into adulthood?"

"Yeah, I suppose. But we don't have trust funds or parents with money to bail us out if that happens." I wince at his statement. He didn't say it in a harsh or accusatory tone, but it stung all the same.

He places his finger under my chin and forces me to look at him. "I didn't mean that as a dig at you. You asked me to explain my drive. Right or wrong, I've taken on the responsibility of making sure I can take care of my family. No matter what they need."

Leaning forward, I press my lips to his. There are way too many emotions swimming around in my head right now to put into words. I could never fault Atticus for putting his family above his own needs. It's noble and makes him even sexier in my eyes.

His life choices are not unlike my own. With each minute I spend with him, it's becoming clearer that he's not the man I thought he was. He's so much more.

The man he really is scares me. And not because he's all wrong for me.

But because he's all kinds of right.

~

Shifting the papers scattered around my desk, I search for my notepad. I can't seem to find it, even though I swear it was just here. I sigh and sit back in my chair. I need about twenty hours of solid sleep to catch up and feel rested.

Days are starting to run into weeks and suddenly I feel like there aren't enough hours to get all my shit done, let alone get a good night's rest. Not that Atticus allows for much sleep when we're together. And we've spent almost every night together this past week. He's taking this exclusive boyfriend-girlfriend thing seriously.

I can't say I mind all that much. I'm enjoying his company and all the orgasms that come along with it.

But my work life is becoming too much. Something has to give. And soon.

Between helping Atticus prepare for the product launch, my second job, and trying to land investors for my startup, I'm exhausted. I've been so busy I had to cancel my volunteer work twice. I hate leaving the center hanging and shorthanded, but it's the kids I worry about the most. The thought of disappointing the kids I've grown so attached to makes me feel physically ill, but I didn't have a choice. There's only so much of me to go around.

I'm burning the candle at both ends and if something doesn't give soon, I'm going to crash and burn.

Now that I'm doing my job instead of sitting around stewing over how much I hate my dad for making me do this in the first place, I see just how busy Atticus is. No wonder my behavior pissed him off so much. He needs help like I need oxygen to survive.

When I think about him doing all this alone for nearly four months, it makes me feel like the worst person on this planet. It's not his fault my dad is an asshole to me. I shouldn't have taken my frustration and anger out on him. I'd sit here for hours on end, picking at my nails just to defy Dad, and I didn't once consider how that might affect Atticus.

Rather than taking the time to get to know him and give him the benefit of the doubt, I lumped him into the same class as my father. I shouldn't have done that.

I could spend the rest of my prison sentence working here, trying to make it up to him, and it wouldn't be enough.

Resting my elbows on my desk, I drop my head into my hands and rub my forehead. I take a few deep breaths and attempt to clear my mind of all my stress. Worrying about every detail and all the ways I feel like I'm failing right now won't do me any good.

"Are you alright, dear?" I look up to see Mrs. Romano standing in front of my desk, holding my notebook.

"Oh my God. Where was that?" I reach for it like getting it in my hands will somehow save my life.

She chuckles as I take it and hold it close to my chest.

"Found it in the copy room. You must have left it there when you were making copies for your boss earlier."

"Thank you. I don't even remember taking it in there with me. I've been frantically looking for it on this mess of a desk for the past twenty minutes."

"No problem." She smiles and turns to leave but stops before she makes it very far. She turns back to me with a hint of mischief in her eyes. "It's good to see you finally finding your footing around here. And to see you and Atticus getting along so well. I'm glad you decided to give that man a chance. He may be a little rough around the edges sometimes, but he's one of the good ones."

My mouth falls open, and her smile grows. I shake my head and frantically try to find the right words. "I ... But ... But there's nothing—"

"You're blushing, dear." She winks and walks away before I can dispute her suspicion.

Because that's all it is, right? There's no way she has evidence that Atticus and I are seeing each other. We've been nothing but professional in the office. Well, at least when others are around. I can't say we keep things completely professional when his door is closed.

My phone buzzes before I can dwell too much on Mrs. Romano's words. I pick it up and smile when my best friend's name scrolls across the screen.

ELON
Are we still on for tonight?

INDIGO
Yep. I'm really nervous. Mr. Whittington's message was vague and concerning. He's going to bail.

ELON
He's not going to bail. He would have said as much if that were the case. He just has questions.

INDIGO
You don't know that. What if I can't answer his questions or he doesn't like my response? Plus, I'm behind on finalizing the business plan. I haven't had time to get it done with how busy I've been.

ELON
Darlin' relax. You're not behind. You're making sure you've covered all your bases before you hand it over. That's all you need to say.

INDIGO
Yeah, I guess. I just really need his donation. I've got a few small donors, but it's not enough to start up. I need his money or my trust.

ELON
You know I love you, but you are being way too stubborn about your dad. Tell him.

INDIGO
Never gonna happen. See you at seven.

Setting my phone down, I flip through my notebook until I find today's to-do list. Quickly scanning through it, I curse when my eyes land on the upcoming charity gala. I completely forgot I have to swing by the office to finalize the catering details with Lisa today. I promised her I'd be there no later than 4:30 pm to discuss the options with her.

"Shit," I mumble under my breath. Closing my notebook, I push to my feet. I need to tell Atticus I have to leave early.

But that's not my biggest problem. Lisa's office is in the opposite direction of the restaurant where I'm meeting Elon and Mr. Whittington. I'm going to be lucky if I make it on time, especially if I go home to freshen up first.

I knock on Atticus's door, and he looks up at me and smiles. "Hey, Princess."

The tension in my body relaxes at the smooth sound of his voice. It does not go unnoticed by me how much I now like it when he calls me princess. A few weeks ago, I would have been seething at the nickname. Now hearing it gets me excited.

"Hi." The response comes out breathy and weak. I clear my throat and step closer to his desk. "I know this is last minute, and I'm sorry, but I have to leave early today. I have to be at my second job's office no later than 4:30."

He sits back in his chair, looking calm and every bit the sexy god he is. "Is this for the charity event company?"

I nod. "There's a gala coming up and I need to finalize the catering details with my boss. If I miss this meeting with her, she'll fire me for sure."

He waves off my unspoken plea. "It's fine. Do what you need to do. I don't have any pressing work-related needs this afternoon."

I quirk a brow. "Work related?"

He smirks and shrugs. "Baby, surely you've figured out by now that I have *other* needs I ache for you to fulfill."

I roll my eyes in an overly exaggerated motion. "Sorry to disappoint you, Mr. Rosi. Those needs are going to have to wait until another time."

He lets out a low growl that makes me chuckle. He always gets worked up when I call him Mr. Rosi.

"Later? Your place?" he asks.

"Can't. I have a dinner date with Elon and a potential investor. I don't know how long it's going to last."

His frown deepens. "Come over to my place when you're done. I'll wait up for you."

"Atticus." I sigh. "You can go one night without me."

"I'm not sure that I can."

"You don't have a choice tonight. But tomorrow, dinner at my place. Will that work?"

"Fine." He growls and looks anything but fine. "But only if you shut the door, come over here, and sit on my lap."

I'm shaking my head before he even finishes talking. "Not today, Mr. Rosi," I say his name in a teasing tone that I know gets him all worked up. "We both have too much work to do."

"You're mean." He pouts. I slowly step backward so I can easily make my escape. A part of me would love to shut his door and spend some quality time on his lap, but I wasn't wrong when I said we both have too much work to do.

I rest my hand on his door frame and glance around to make sure no one is in earshot. "I guess you'll have to find a way to punish me for it later."

Just as I reach my chair, he calls out my name.

"Yes?" I glance over my shoulder.

"Do you need a date?"

"A date?" I furrow my brow.

"For your charity event." He clarifies.

"Oh, a date." A slow smile tugs at my lips. "If only I knew where to find one of those."

~

My phone dings in my purse, but I don't stop long enough to check it. I'm already fifteen minutes late and the restaurant is still a block away.

I shouldn't have stopped by my apartment to change.

Lisa kept me at her office later than I'd hoped. I can't blame her.

I've barely been in these past two weeks. Between working on my business plan and all the extra work I've done for Atticus, I've been a little MIA.

In my defense, Lisa gave me permission to work remotely. I've done more than my fair share of work preparing for the upcoming gala. She has nothing to complain about. But that didn't stop her from wanting a face-to-face debrief on everything I've been working on. Everything that I'd already communicated with her via email.

As a result, I'm very late, and I suspect I just received a text from Elon asking me where I'm at.

The door to the restaurant comes into view and I increase from a fast walk to a slow run. The sudden change in pace has me tripping over my feet, and I almost dive headfirst into the sidewalk. Thankfully, I'm close enough to the already opened door that I'm able to brace myself against it and keep from falling.

The maître d' peeks around the corner with a shocked expression on his face. "I'm so sorry, ma'am. Are you okay?"

"I'm fine." I wave off his concern and smile. "It was my fault for practically running toward the door."

"Regardless, I still apologize." He gives me a slight bow of the head, then waves his arm through the open door. "Are you dining with us this evening?"

"I am. My dinner party should already be here."

He gives me a friendly smile and shows me to the hostess stand. "Then let's get you seated with them."

Moments later, a pretty young hostess is leading me through the sea of tables and toward a worried-looking Elon. When his eyes meet mine, they go wide with a mix of relief and fear. That fear has me stopping just short of the table.

"Indigo, you made it." Elon pushes to his feet and forces a smile. "So sorry to hear about your brother's episode. I hope he's doing better."

I furrow my brow as he pulls me into a hug. He leans close to my ear and whispers. "Darlin', I've been lying through my teeth for you. Go with it."

"Um ... He's fine." I stumble through the words. It takes a minute for my exhausted brain to pick up on what Elon is saying. "Much better now. I managed to calm him down."

"Glad to hear that," he says as he releases me.

I turn toward the table where Mr. Whittington is now standing. I reach my hand out and offer a shake. "So sorry to keep you waiting. Sometimes I'm the only one that can calm Jay after he has an episode."

He nods and takes my hand. "My son is the same way with my wife. When he gets worked up, no one else will do."

He's saying all the right words, but he doesn't look happy. My stomach drops and I have a bad feeling about this meeting. I'm ninety-nine percent positive that me being late has no bearing on the news he's about to deliver.

"Yeah, it can be tough on my schedule," I say, hoping my honesty wins me some points. "But I'll do anything for my brother. He deserves the best."

"Indie, why don't you have a seat?" Elon says as he pulls a chair out for me. "I'll wave down our server and get you a drink. Then we can order dinner."

Mr. Whittington is quiet while I study the menu to decide on my dinner choice. Once he and Elon place their orders, I do the same. The server isn't even gone for three seconds when Mr. Whittington speaks.

"Listen, Indie." He clears his throat and takes a sip of his whiskey. "I love the concept of your foundation, and I still want to see that business plan of yours, but I have some reservations."

I grab the water glass in front of me and take a large gulp. "I know I promised you the business plan by now, but I am working on it. I don't want to give you something that I haven't completely vetted. It's almost done. I just have to—"

He holds his hand up to stop me. "This isn't about delays. I appreciate the time you're taking to make sure you get this right. My reservations have nothing to do with the business model you've proposed or the time you're taking. Despite those things, I still have some reservations about you specifically."

"Me?" I gasp and have to snap my mouth shut from my surprise.

He gives me a sympathetic look and nods. "You have a great idea here, but I'm concerned about you being able to execute it successfully."

"Mr. Whittington, I assure you I am more than capable of running this foundation. I've spent my entire adult life preparing for it. My degree from Yale alone taught me most of what I needed to know to be successful, but I still fought to earn a position from the best charity event planning organization on the East Coast. I assure you, I am prepared to run this business."

He nods but doesn't look convinced. "You know our circle is small. I ran into your father the other day and he had no knowledge of your business plans."

I close my eyes and sigh. I should have anticipated this. I should have expected him to speak to my father at some point, and I didn't. A mistake I will not make a second time.

When I meet Mr. Whittington's concerned gaze, any hope I had that his donation was a sure thing vanishes. "I have left my father out of this for two reasons. One, he's very busy with his own company. They're expanding into new markets, and I don't want to distract him. Two, I want to do this on my own. Prove my worth to both myself and my father. I don't want my success to hinge on his contacts or financial support. This is my passion, not his."

"I appreciate and respect that. More than you know. But what I don't understand is why you are keeping your father in the dark about it. He was completely unaware that you even wanted to start a business. It's made me question your trustworthiness, especially since you're working for him."

"I can assure you, you can trust me. My father's lack of knowledge of my plans is not a reflection of my character. If he knew what I wanted to do, he'd try to control it. It's in his nature. I'm trying to protect the integrity of my business. Nothing more."

He opens his mouth to speak, and my stomach drops. He's going to bail without giving me a chance to prove myself. Once again, my father has crushed my dreams without even knowing what they are.

"If I may offer a suggestion?" Elon says. "There's a charity gala coming up that Indie single-handedly organized. Harold, why don't you attend? See Indie in action. I think you'll be more than impressed."

I reach across the table and squeeze Elon's hand. "That's a great idea. We still have a couple of seats open if you want to bring a guest as well. Just let me know, and I'll take care of everything."

He eyes me carefully. His expression is unreadable, and that makes me nervous. I can't afford to lose his support.

"Well, Miss Simons." He clears his throat before drinking the rest of his whiskey. "You've bought yourself some time. I'd love to see you in action. Send me the specifics, and I'll be there. I want to see this business plan of yours before the event. Then I'll decide."

CHAPTER NINETEEN

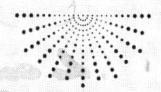

ATTICUS

DEMETRIUS

It's been a shit day. Drinks before dinner tonight?

ADONIS

Just turned in my dissertation. Drinks sound like a great idea.

EROS

Yes! Where are we going?

DEMETRIUS

Don't care. Somewhere with hot and willing chicks.

ADONIS

Always thinking with your dick.

DEMETRIUS

Did you miss the part about it being a shit day?

EROS

What are you going to do if you pick one up? Bring her to dinner tonight and introduce her to your family?

DEMETRIUS

{middle finger emoji}

ATTICUS

Working late. Not sure when I'll get out of here.

> **EROS**
> Seriously? The one time I can join you, you're not coming?

> **ATTICUS**
> Deadlines. I can't miss them. See you at dinner.

Sighing, I push my keyboard aside and rest my elbows on my desk. I've hit a roadblock in the development of the forecasting tool I've been working on, and I can't seem to see a solution. I know it's there, but it's hiding from me. Just out of sight.

I scrub my hands down my face and stare at my computer screen. I'm missing something and it's bugging me. I know it's got to be something in the code that the program is interpreting incorrectly, but what?

I can't afford to hit a wall right now. Time to complete this is slowly dwindling, and if I miss this deadline, everything I've worked for will be for nothing. Without this forecasting tool, I've got nothing more than another information summary software program that's no different from the dozens of others already in existence.

"You look deep in thought." James's voice booms through my open door. I look up to see him push off the door frame and walk in. "Am I interrupting?"

"Of course not." I adjust my tie, then run my fingers through my hair. A nervous habit that I always do when things aren't going my way. "Just finalizing the report."

Not a total lie. I need this code done before I can write the report. It's something I should have done at least two weeks ago, but James doesn't need to know just how far behind I am.

"Good, I can't wait to see the results." He unbuttons his jacket and takes a seat in the chair opposite my desk. "If you want to go over the presentation before the meeting, let me know. Maybe a mock run through would be helpful."

"Yeah, that'd be great." I say the words, but it's anything but great. I haven't even started on the presentation and the meeting is scheduled for the end of next week. I have so much to do and no time to talk about it.

"Anyway," he says as he looks over his shoulder. "I really stopped by to see my daughter, but she's not here."

I look past him to Indigo's empty desk chair. She told me she wouldn't be in until late this morning. Something to do with her volunteer work. She's canceled on them a lot lately and didn't want to again. From the look on James's face, I don't think knowing that will make him happy.

"Yeah, sorry. She's running some errands for me. Should be back soon." The lie slips right out like the most natural thing I've ever said. It makes me feel like shit. I don't lie. Not even simple white lies like this one. "I can have her call you when she gets back."

He waves off my suggestion like it's unnecessary. "She's avoiding me. I don't like it when she does that."

"I've kept her busy the past few weeks preparing for this meeting. I'm sure it's not intentional."

"Everything my daughter does is intentional. Especially where I'm concerned." He slaps his leg in frustration, and for a moment, I think he's going to stand. But then he turns his gaze back to me and says, "Is she taking the new roles I asked you both to fill seriously? I want her to understand how a successful business functions."

I struggle to keep my expression neutral and shift nervously in my seat. This isn't something Indie and I have talked much about since the day he asked me to mentor her. "To be honest, sir, we haven't had a lot of spare time these past few weeks to go over much beyond project related tasks. Once this meeting is off my plate, working with her will be a priority."

What I don't tell him is that Indie has no interest in this new role and never wants to talk about the business beyond normal and expected admin tasks. I'm not about to force this on her if it's not what she wants.

He pins me with a serious stare, something I now know he only does when he's truly unhappy. "This is important to me. Just as important as this project. Don't let me down."

"Yes, sir. I'll do my best."

Neither of us speak or move for several beats. I can't help but think I'm the source of his current unhappiness. I don't like it.

I've worked hard for James since joining the company, and I don't want to let him down now. Looks like Indie and I need to have another talk about this new role.

He slaps his leg again, and this time, he stands. "I know you will, Atticus. I can always count on you. I look forward to seeing the final report."

"I'll get you a copy as soon as it's done."

He strolls out my door without another glance back. My stress level was already high before he stopped by. Now it's practically unmanageable.

Having that conversation with him was the worst thing he could have done for my psyche. I'll be lucky if I'm able to clear my mind enough to read this code, let alone find errors in it.

∼

I DON'T KNOW HOW LONG I SIT THERE STARING AT MY COMPUTER screen after James left without making progress. It feels like it's been hours when it's probably only been minutes.

But the person standing in my doorway is a welcomed sight.

"You're back." My eyes roam down Indie's body in appreciation. She looks so fucking beautiful it makes my chest hurt. Today she's wearing a pale purple, sleeveless dress that hugs all her curves. My hands itch to grab hold of her hips and drag her close to me.

She nods, steps inside my office, then closes the door. I hear the faint click of the lock. "You look stressed."

I lean on my elbows and run my hands through my hair without breaking eye contact. "I am. But seeing you is already making me feel better."

"Anything I can help you with?" Her voice is low and seductive as she pushes off the door and saunters toward me.

"Not unless you suddenly became an expert in code writing and machine learning."

Her smile turns feline as her hips sway side-to-side as she steps around my desk. "Don't talk nerd to me, Mr. Rosi. I can't be held responsible for my actions when you do."

A low growl escapes me as she steps between my legs. When she shoves her hands into my hair and scrapes her nails against my scalp, I lean into her. "I love it when you call me that."

"And I love it when you growl at me like that, *Mr. Rosi*." She says my name in a slow, drawn-out tone that has my dick standing at attention.

My hands find her hips, and my fingers dig into her as I pull her closer. "How was your volunteer work?"

"Good." Her hands work their way around my neck, and she clasps her fingers together. "You're tense. Everything going okay?"

"Better now." I rest my head against her stomach and breathe in her sweet scent. Then I run my hands down her thighs and under the hem of her dress. I groan at the feel of her soft, warm skin under my touch. "I want to feel you."

She leans into me as my hands slide up her hips. My fingers reach the edge of her panties and pause. I want to yank them down and bury my face between her thighs until she's screaming my name.

Apparently, she has other ideas because she steps back, causing my hands to fall. I frown at her, and her smile grows.

"How about a little role reversal today? I'm in control until you're relaxed."

My first reaction is to object to her statement, but then I freeze. Her words stir something else in my mind. "What did you say?"

Her brow furrows, and she pulls her bottom lip between her teeth in a nervous gesture. "Um, I'm in control?"

"Before that."

She tilts her head to the side, studying me. "How about a little role reversal?"

A light bulb goes off in my brain, and I know what I need to do to fix the code. I grab her hips and tug her against me before I pull her lips to mine. "You're a fucking genius, Princess. I need to reverse the order of the variables to make this work."

"I'll pretend I know what that means." She chuckles and returns her hands to my hair. Before I can explain, she drops to her knees and reaches for my belt. "But I'll take it as a positive and get back to taking control for a change."

My dick jumps at the closeness of her hands to my groin. I run my finger along her jaw, then over her perfectly pink pouty bottom lip. "How exactly do you propose to do that?"

Heat flashes in her eyes as she opens her mouth and takes the tip of my finger between her teeth. Then she sucks it into her mouth up to the second knuckle. When I growl, she chuckles.

"How about I show you, Mr. Rosi?" She unzips my dress pants and fists my already hard cock.

I slide my hand around her neck and pull her mouth to mine. I dive in, parting her lips with my tongue and tasting her like it's the first time. She kisses me back, but it's brief. Her hand presses against my chest and pushes me back into my chair.

"Relax. You're stressed. Let me make you feel better."

Her mouth is around my tip before I can even wrap my brain around her words. My head falls back and I groan as her soft, warm mouth moves down my shaft.

"Fuck, Princess." I fist my hand in her hair and fight the urge to push her further down my cock. "That feels so good."

Her tongue darts out, and she flattens it along my length and licks up, dragging her soft pink lips across my silky skin. When she swirls her tongue around the tip, licking up my pre-cum, I almost lose it.

"Such a good girl," I whisper through ragged breaths.

I tighten my grip on her hair and thrust forward. It's not an action I meant to do, but my body is reacting to her in ways I can barely comprehend. To her credit, she's ready for my thrust. She opens her mouth wide and takes me all the way back into her throat.

"Baby," I moan.

When I look down at her, her eyes are locked on mine. The moisture building in the corners has me ready to pull my cock away and make her feel good. I love a good blow job, but not if it's hurting her.

"Don't," she says around my cock. "I want this."

She must see my concern in my expression because she sucks me deeper and harder. It feels so fucking good. All I can do is sit back and let her take the control she asked me for. I'm at her mercy.

Her hands grip my hips as she takes me deeper, sucking me hard. My tip hits the back of her throat again and I'm ready to explode.

"I'm going to come," I say in warning. I want to pull out and bury myself deep inside her, but if she wants this, I'll let her take it.

She doesn't back down or slow her attack on my cock. She sucks harder until my orgasm rips through me and shoots down her throat. She swallows every ounce and doesn't relent until my body stills.

Only then does she release me with a pop and lean back on her heels. It takes me a moment to catch my breath and come back down from the high she sent me on. Once I do, I pull her onto my lap and kiss her hard.

I taste my release on her and it causes the feral beast inside me to come to the surface. I want to claim her in ways that I don't fully understand. These feelings inside me are foreign and completely new. They're feelings I'm not quite ready to put into words.

"Feel better?" she asks, her words breathy and full of need.

"I do." I drop my forehead to hers and take a deep breath. "Join me for dinner tonight. With my family."

She jerks back, more surprised by my question than I am. I never bring girls around my siblings, but Indigo is different. This thing between us is real.

"You want me to meet your family?"

I shrug as if it's no big deal, even though I know it's a huge step in our relationship. "You've already met my sister. And you've sort of met my brothers."

"Dinner is a big deal, Atticus. Are you sure you're ready for that?"

I brush a strand of her hair out of her face and tuck it behind her ear. I don't hesitate with my response. "Yeah. I'd love it if you joined me for family dinner."

She stares at me for a moment, her expression unreadable. My nerves kick into overdrive, and I think that maybe I made a mistake. Maybe it's too soon for family dinners.

But then she gives me a gentle smile. "I'd like that."

The breath that leaves me must express my relief, because she chuckles and rests her head on my shoulder. I wrap my arms around her and hug her tightly.

The past few weeks with Indie have been a rollercoaster of emotions. Some of them I'd prefer to forget. Because I can only think of one word that truly captures how much she means to me.

Love.

~

I SQUEEZE INDIE'S HAND AS WE STEP OFF THE ELEVATOR AND START down the hallway toward Penny's apartment. She squeezes back and gives me a calming smile. I'm not sure if the squeeze is for my comfort or hers.

Probably mine.

I'm more nervous than I should be about introducing her to my siblings. It's not that I don't want them to meet her—because I do —it's more that I'm concerned about what they'll say to her about me.

My siblings can be relentless in their teasing and bringing her is opening myself up to them in ways I'd prefer to avoid.

Penny will be nice. She wants to see all of us find someone and settle down. But my brothers are wildcards. There's no telling what they'll say or do.

"Last chance to bail," I say just before we reach the apartment door.

A soft chuckle escapes her, and she rests her other hand on my forearm. It feels nice. Like something couples do. I like it.

"It'll be fine. I'm looking forward to this."

Tugging her closer, I tuck her into my side and give her a quick kiss. "Okay, but I warned you. My siblings can be intense."

"I can't wait." The way her eyes light up makes me smile and shoves those pesky nerves of mine to the side.

Then it hits me.

Indie probably hasn't ever experienced family dinners like mine. From what she's told me about her family dynamics, this will be new to her. This revelation relaxes me and changes my outlook on the entire evening.

"Just don't listen to anything my brothers say about me. It's all lies."

I knock on the door, and she laughs.

Within seconds, the door flies open. I groan when I see it's Demetrius that answers it. His grin turns positively evil.

"Well, well, well. What do we have here?" He crosses his arms and leans against the door frame. His eyes roam up and down Indie's body. I growl and punch him in the arm. He laughs, then he turns to everyone else. "Tattie brought the hottie!"

"D!" Penny slaps his arm, but he ducks around her, causing her to mostly miss. His laughter only grows. "I told you to be nice."

"How was that not nice?" He points at Indie with appreciation. "She's hot."

Penny and I both glare and this time Indie laughs. When I look down at her, she's giving my brother the biggest smile. "Thank you. That's very kind of you to say."

Demetrius's smile falters at her rather proper response, but then nods. "You're welcome. It's good to see you again."

I swallow a groan as the memory of her sneaking out of my bed in the middle of the night comes back to me. I forgot Demetrius caught her in the act.

"You're Demetrius, right?" Indie asks.

He nods. "But you can call me D or Dem or whatever." He holds his hand out for her, and she takes it. "And you're Indie."

"That's me. It's nice to officially meet you."

"You too," he says with nothing but politeness. Then he turns his gaze to me and it turns mischievous. "I hope you're ready for tonight, big brother."

"I'm here, aren't I?" I grin and move past him so I can introduce Indie to the rest of my family. "I know you've seen this guy," I point toward Adonis, who's sitting on the couch, "but I don't think I introduced you when he was at the office. This is Adonis, or Donnie."

Donnie waves, but the introduction is cut short when Indie sees the adorable little girl sitting on Toby's lap next to him.

"Oh, my goodness." She coos. "Who is this little beauty?"

I've heard Indie talk about the kids she's trying to help with her foundation, so I know she loves kids, but seeing her reaction to Tabitha is a different experience. She's a natural, winning over Tabitha without having to try. Tabitha jumps off Toby's lap and into Indie's waiting embrace.

"Are you going to tell her your name, sweetie?" Toby encourages her.

"Tabby!" she says with the clap of her hand before holding up three fingers. "I'm free."

Indie gasps with wide eyes and a huge smile. "Three! Wow, that's so grown."

Tabby nods. "Yep. I'm a big girl."

"You are." Indie adjusts the blue skirt of Tabby's dress so it's covering her bottom. "Is blue your favorite color?"

Tabby shakes her head. "I like wuh-wo."

"Yellow is a great color too." Indie points at the little yellow flowers on her pink shirt.

"Hi, I'm Owen and this is my husband Toby. I can't believe you understand our girl." Owen grins from where he's standing behind Toby. "No one ever does."

Tabby pushes against Indie and flies back to Toby's lap. Indie laughs. "I work with kids. Many of them struggle with communication."

Toby's brow furrows. "I thought you worked for Tat?"

"I do, but only temporarily. It's a long story." She waves it off like it's no big deal and turns to me before Toby can press her for more information and asks, "Tattie and Tat? What's with the nicknames?"

"It's because of all my tattoos. It's the most original name my brothers could come up with."

"Would you prefer asshole?" Eros asks as he steps up next to me. "That works too."

Indie's smile grows. "I've certainly called him that a time or two."

Eros holds his hand out to her. "I'm Eros, the best one in this crazy lot."

I snort. "Hardly. He's the baby, and we often call him that too."

Eros's brow furrows and grumbles. "One attempt at the Dirty Dancing lift, and you assholes won't let it die."

"Did you succeed?" Indie asks, her eyes twinkling with excitement.

"Not even close." His smile grows. "Fell flat on my back and bruised my ass. But the girl didn't get hurt, so there's that."

"Hmm." She furrows her brow and looks him up and down. "I would've thought a guy as big as you wouldn't fall."

"Baby has no coordination." I tease. "Can't dance to save his life."

I pat Eros on the back as I lead Indie past him. He glares at me and calls out. "The night's young, bro. I hope you're prepared to be roasted in front of your girl."

"Can't wait," I call over my shoulder before I turn my attention back to Indie. "And this guy in the kitchen is Trent, Penny Love's husband."

Trent turns from the stove and waves. "I'd shake your hand, but I'm elbow deep in sauce."

"No worries. It's nice to meet you." Indie waves. "Whatever you're cooking smells amazing."

"Thanks. Pasta Primavera with spicy sausage."

"Trent is a food critic," I add. "He's kind of a food snob, so he doesn't know how to make a bad meal."

"Maybe that's why you look so familiar," Indie says. "I feel like we've met before?"

"He goes to those charity events sometimes." I add. "Wouldn't surprise me if he's been to one you organized."

"You organize events?" Trent asks.

"Fundraisers and charity galas. I work as an event planner for Lisa McAllister."

Trent's smile grows. "No way. I know Lisa. She's a great person, but tough. I can't imagine working for her."

"She is, but she's also fair. I've learned so much from her."

"Indie has plans to start her own foundation," I say as I lift her hand to my lips. "One day, you're going to be attending one of her events."

"Is that so?" Trent's smile grows as he watches how I am with her. Trent can be just as bad with the teasing as my brothers. "What kind of foundation?"

"One focused on providing financial support to families that can't otherwise afford cognitive behavior screening, therapy, or treatment for their kids. There's a real need, and insurance coverage is often lacking."

I lean down and kiss her forehead as Trent asks her more questions about her plans. I decide to leave them to talk since I know Trent will be nice to her. I turn to find Penny staring at me with hearts in her eyes.

All three of my brothers are in a line with their arms crossed over their chests and playful expressions on their faces. They're here for battle, and I'm the target.

I stop next to Penny and say, "Am I going to survive?"

"Nope." She doesn't hesitate with her answer. "But I'll do my best to help you out. It's good seeing you in love."

I furrow my brow. "Who said anything about love?"

The question tastes sour and feels all kinds of wrong. I know my feelings for Indie run deep, but I'm not ready to say them out loud. Not yet.

"Don't worry, little brother." She loops her arm through mine and leads me toward our brothers. "I won't tell anyone."

That doesn't make me feel better. If Penny can see how deep my feelings for Indie are, chances are high my brothers can too. If they suspect I love her, they'll be ruthless.

But then Penny lets out a loud gasp and presses her hand to her belly. Everyone's attention shifts to her.

"You okay?" I ask.

She nods. "Just Braxton-Hicks. Perfectly normal at this stage in my pregnancy. Just means my body is preparing for this baby."

"Are you sure?" I ask. "Do we need to call your doctor?"

"No." She chuckles. "I'm fine."

Our brothers rush to her side, and they each do their part to annoy her with their doting and concerns.

Indie slides up beside me and slips her arm through mine. She looks up at me with a teasing glint in her eyes. "Saved by the pregnant sister."

"Thank fuck. Now they'll be too distracted to roast me in front of you."

"Bummer. I was looking forward to hearing some dirt on you."

I pull her around to my front and hug her close. "Stick around, and I'm sure there'll be more opportunities."

"Oh, don't you worry. I will." Her tone is teasing, but the words have an entirely different effect on me.

I hear her say she's mine. That she's not going anywhere, and that she'll be here again.

That causes my chest to tighten even more with feelings that I won't be able to contain much longer.

Indie *is* mine, and I don't plan on ever letting her go.

CHAPTER TWENTY

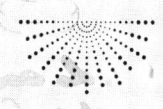

INDIGO

ATTICUS
You look so hot in that skirt. It's giving me bad thoughts.

INDIGO
Contain yourself.

ATTICUS
What if I don't want to?

INDIGO
We both have a busy day. Focus on work.

ATTICUS
Or you could sneak into my office for a quickie.

INDIGO
There is no such thing as a quickie with you.

ATTICUS
You say that like it's a bad thing.

INDIGO
Just stating a fact.

I check the time again like it's somehow going to magically move backward since the last time I checked. I need at least another eight hours to get all my shit done. Unfortunately, I don't have eight hours. I have ten minutes.

Only five minutes have passed. Still barely enough time to get both Atticus's report and my business plan ready for the courier.

I can't miss this deadline. If I do, we're both screwed.

I promised the business plan would be on Mr. Whittington's desk by five o'clock this afternoon. If I cannot meet this promise, he's going to walk away. I just know it.

I don't know what I was thinking when I agreed to this. I should have requested one more day. At least give myself time to get Atticus's report off my plate. Plus, the charity gala is tonight, and he wants it before the event.

I flip through the pages of my business plan one last time. Rather than send it to the printers like I'm doing with Atticus's report, I decided to print and bind it myself. It's not as nice as what the printer could do, but it looks professional.

Either way, it has to do.

I slip it into an envelope and set it aside.

Atticus's report requires a little more organization since he has so many sections and wants it printed with custom dividers. Plus, he needs ten copies.

I've already checked the USB drive files to make sure everything is there and labeled correctly. All that's left is double checking the mockup copy I printed this morning.

This would have been so much less stressful on both of us if he'd gotten me the final report yesterday like originally promised. Between me rushing to get everything in order and the last-minute rush service for the printers, it's going to be tight.

Setting his report on the counter, I flip through the pages one last time to make sure everything is correct. I'm about halfway through when a voice behind me causes me to jump.

"Indie, have you seen Trisha?" Mrs. Romano says.

When I jump, a small section of the report slides from my hands and onto the floor. "Oh, no."

"Oh, dear. Let me help you with that." Mrs. Romano kneels next to me and scoops up the paper. Thankfully, it's only about twenty pages, so it doesn't take long to get them back in order.

"Sorry, I startled you," she adds. "You look stressed. Anything I can help you with?"

I give her a tight smile. "I'm almost done here. In about," I check the time again, "six minutes, this will be out of my hands. I'll relax then."

"Is this the report for the big promotional presentation tomorrow?"

I nod. "Atticus, I mean, Mr. Rosi, got it to me a day late, so it's been a hectic morning getting this finalized and ready to send to the printers."

I silently scold myself for referring to him as Atticus. It's not that big of a deal. A lot of admins refer to the managers they work for by their first names. But I never have. I don't want anyone to get suspicious about our relationships. Things will be simpler if we keep it a secret.

"Alright. If you're sure." I nod again and this time she returns my smile. "Well, if you change your mind, I'm always here to help."

She turns to leave, but then stops like she's just now remembering something. "Oh, the reason I stopped in was to ask if you'd seen Trisha. I can't find that girl anywhere."

I shake my head. "Sorry. I've been buried in this all day. I've hardly seen anyone."

"Okay, well." I feel her eyes on me, but I don't turn to look at her. I've got to focus on getting this done. "Try to relax tonight. It looks like you've earned it."

I nod because what can I say? There will be no relaxing tonight. As soon as I get this out the door, I have about an hour's reprieve before I have to rush home to get ready for tonight's gala.

My stress level increases at the realization that I don't have enough time to get ready.

I'll relax when I can finally quit this job, and I'm no longer working for my dad.

I think for a moment about how much time I've got left. Maybe six months? Since Atticus and I got together, I've stopped counting the days, weeks, and months. Is that a good or bad sign?

My phone buzzes next to me on the counter. My two-minute warning. Clearing my mind of all distractions, I focus on flipping through the remaining pages, then slip it into a large envelope.

I reach the front desk at the same time the courier steps out of the elevator. I hand off both envelopes with detailed instructions and sign off on them. Once he's in the elevator, I lean against the counter and sigh.

"Are you okay?" Annie asks.

I glance over at her and smile. "Yeah, I'm great."

Then I push off the counter and head down the long hallway toward my desk. I've got one hour to relax. It's not much, but I'll take it.

Then my phone buzzes in my hand. When I look down, I frown when my stepmom's name flashes across the screen.

~

THIS IS THE LAST THING I HAVE TIME FOR TODAY, BUT I WILL NEVER turn my back on my brother.

Jay had a meltdown at school. He was doing fine with his recovery from it until Dad came home early. According to Frannie, Dad lost his temper, and it sent Jay into a downward spiral that she can't bring him out of.

I make it to my dad's penthouse in record time. As soon as I step inside the door, I hear yelling.

I cringe. Raised voices only agitate Jay more.

"Thank goodness you're here." Frannie's in tears as she steps up to me and pulls me into a tight hug. "He came home in a bad mood. Finding out about Jay's episode at school set him off. I can't get him to calm down."

"Is he yelling at Jay like that?" The words come out sounding every bit as angry as I feel.

She shakes her head. "He's in his office, but Jay can hear him."

"Jay in his room?" I ask.

She nods, and I rush past her. My heart breaks when I push open Jay's door and find him curled into a ball in the middle of his bed.

"Jay." I rush to his side and pull him into my arms. He willingly comes to me and wraps his shaking arms around my waist. "It's okay. I've got you. Take slow breaths for me. Can you do that?"

His breathing is hard and much too fast. He's going to hyperventilate if he doesn't calm down.

He doesn't respond right away, so I exaggerate my own slow breathing so he can feel the movement of my chest. "Come on, buddy. Feel me breathing. Match my movements."

We sit like that for several minutes—my breathing pronounced until he's breathing with me. His body finally stops shaking, but he doesn't loosen his hold on me. He's hugging me so tight it's as if he's afraid I'll vanish.

"Do you want to talk about it?" I ask once I'm confident he's calm enough to talk to me. He shakes his head and buries his face deeper into my side. "Okay. You don't have to. We can just sit here quietly until you're ready."

I have no clue how much time passes before he finally looks up at me. I'm trying really hard to not let my own anxiety take over. I don't even want to know how little time I have left to get ready for the gala tonight. I was already running behind schedule. Now I might as well toss that schedule out the window and forget about it.

But Jay's worth it. I'll sacrifice my life for him if I have to.

"Why does he hate me so much?" His voice sounds so small and weak. It causes my already broken heart to shatter even more.

"He doesn't hate you. He just doesn't understand."

A lone tear breaks free from his eye, and he quickly wipes it away. "But he always gets so angry with me. I didn't do anything wrong."

"People tend to get angry when they don't understand something. It's not your fault."

"Don't coddle him." As if we summoned him, Dad's angry voice booms through the door. I look up at him and glare.

"Dad. This is not the time." My words come out just as angry as his did. "If I want to hug my brother, there isn't anything you can do to stop me."

His eyes narrow, and I can tell from the way his jaw tenses that he wants to say more. Thankfully, he doesn't. Instead, he redirects his anger at me. "Shouldn't you still be working?"

"No, I shouldn't," I say in a tone that suggests my work schedule is none of his business. I look down at Jay and smile. "Are you okay if I go talk to Dad for a minute?"

He glances at Dad with a wary expression before he looks back at me and nods. I kiss his forehead and push to my feet. When I reach Dad, he's glaring at me. "Can we take this to your office?"

His jaw ticks and his hard eyes stare at me for so long I'm not sure if he heard me. Then he nods and disappears down the hallway.

I sigh and return to Jay. "Give me another hug before I go talk to Dad."

Jay doesn't hesitate to jump into my arms. This kid gives some of the best hugs for someone who suffers from social anxiety and sensory sensitivities. It's a shame Dad doesn't see just how great this kid really is.

"I'm gonna have to leave soon. I've got an event tonight. Will you be okay?"

He nods. "Thanks for coming over."

I pinch his chin and smile. "Anytime, kiddo. Anytime. If you need me to come back after my event, I will."

As much as I hate to leave him, I don't have a choice. I can't imagine this conversation with Dad going well, and I still have to run home and change before Atticus picks me up.

Reluctantly, I make my way down the hallway toward Dad's office. I find him pacing in front of his desk looking like a pissed off lion ready to defend his territory. He's so lost in his anger, he doesn't see me approach.

I lean against the door frame and knock. His body jerks in surprise, and he spins to face me.

"Why are you so mad?" I ask.

"Why am I mad?" He growls. "It's bad enough that I have to figure out how to manage an anxious child. I don't need my oldest keeping secrets from me. When were you going to tell me about your business plan?"

"I wasn't," I say with a remarkable amount of restraint. He's seething, and I can't seem to find two shits to give. Besides, I've had time to prepare for his confrontation ever since my last meeting with Harold.

He falters and clenches his hands to his side. "What do you mean, you weren't going to tell me?"

"It means exactly that. I had no intention of telling you about my business plans. Why should I? You've never taken an interest in my life. Why start now?"

"That's not fair." His hands relax and some of the anger in him seems to deflate. "I have a great deal of interest in your life."

I snort. "Could've fooled me. I've never been anything more than a tool for you and Mom to use against each other. Neither of you have ever taken the time to ask me what I want out of life. You just want me to be like you, and Mom wants me to be like her. Newsflash, I don't want to be like either of you."

I hold his confused gaze for several minutes, waiting for him to respond. But he doesn't. He looks too stunned by my reaction. I don't know what he thought I'd say or do, but apparently that wasn't it.

"I gotta go. Goodbye, Dad. Try to be nicer to your son. He's trying really hard to get better. And for some ungodly reason, he still wants to make *you* happy."

I don't wait for Dad to respond. I exit his office and head straight for the door. I have an hour and a half to improve my mood and get ready for this gala.

There's no way in hell I can be late. Not after the last time. Lisa will have my job and make sure I never work in this industry again if I screw up a second time.

∼

AFTER AN EMERGENCY PHONE CALL TO ELON, AND THE LONGEST CAB ride in my life, I finally step off the elevator to my floor. I take off down the hall in a sprint. I only slightly relax when I see Elon leaning against the wall next to my door.

It took me forty-five minutes to get home. Without help, I'll never be ready in time. Elon is my stylist in shining armor, ready to help make me stunning in less than forty-five minutes.

"Gawd, you suck," I say as I take in his appearance. He's wearing a perfectly tailored deep blue tux that looks sexy as hell on him. "Why do you look so good? You said you wouldn't have enough time to properly primp for tonight if you came over to help me and yet," I wave my hand up and down his form, "look at you. So not fair."

He shrugs and looks down at his attire. "I guess it didn't take me as long as I thought it would. Now let's get you inside so we can make you equally as stunning. What time is your Greek god picking you up?"

I told Elon that Atticus offered to attend as my date. He'll be the first date I've ever taken to one of these things. I hope he's not bored the entire night. I'm usually too busy working to enjoy myself. But Elon will be there to keep him company while I'm running around taking care of details, so that's something.

I dig my phone out and check the time. "Shit. I've got less than forty minutes now."

"Plenty of time," Elon says in an annoyingly relaxed tone. "Lead the way to the goods."

"And by goods, you mean my dress, right?" I ask as I unlock my door.

"Dress, shoes, makeup, hair products, all of it." He waves his hand in a flurry as he follows me inside and down the short hallway to my bedroom. "Your hair looks fabulous, so don't wash it. Make that a lightning-fast shower. Got it?"

"Got it." I rush into my bathroom, pulling my hair into a tight knot on the top of my head. Thankfully, my water gets hot fast and I'm in and out of the shower in five minutes. When I walk back into my bedroom with nothing but my robe on, Elon is standing at my vanity looking through my makeup.

He looks up at me and smiles. "That Coco Chanel dress is divine. No need to worry about your Greek god getting bored tonight. When he sees you in that dress, he's going to have plenty of fantasies running through his mind to keep him busy for hours."

A little more of the tension releases in my shoulders as I look over at the dress for tonight. It's a gorgeous shade of blue with an iridescent shimmer to it. The fabric is satin. It's strapless, formfitting, and floor-length, with a high slit on one side, revealing my leg and thigh when I walk. I've been looking forward to wearing it ever since I saw it in the store.

"Well, then." I put my hands on my hips and smile. "Make the rest of me gorgeous and worthy of this dress. We're running out of time."

"Easy peasy." He gives me a dramatic eye roll. "Darlin' you're already gorgeous."

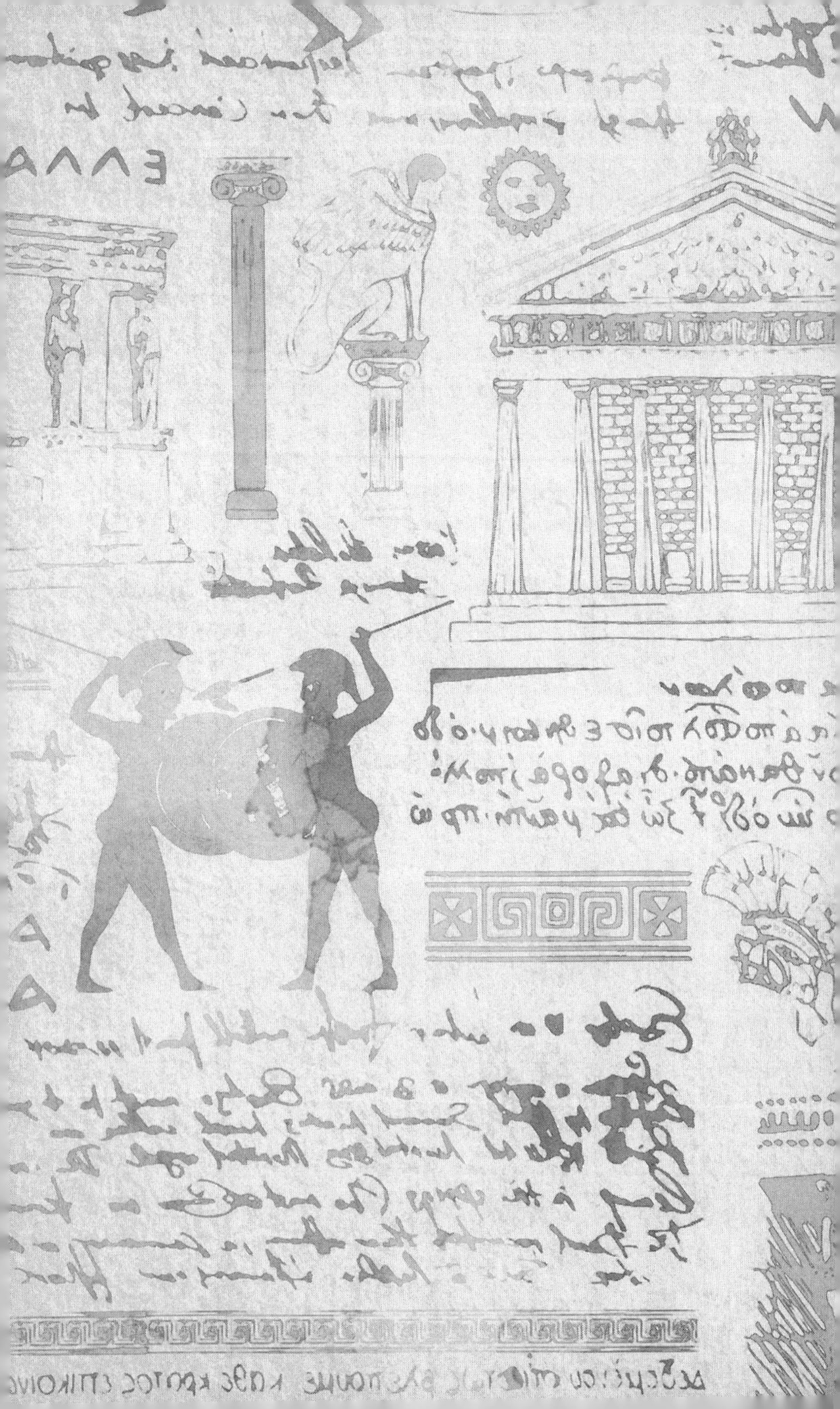

CHAPTER TWENTY-ONE

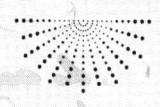

ATTICUS

DEMETRIUS

You are so pussy whipped.

ATTICUS

Grow up.

EROS

Gotta say, I never thought I'd see the day when my big brother settled down.

ADONIS

What's wrong with settling down? You didn't give me shit when I moved in with Lulu. Though considering how that turned out, you should have.

DEMETRIUS

You've always been a one girl kind of guy. The rest of us haven't.

ADONIS

Having one girl to come home to every night isn't so bad. Just make sure she's the right girl.

EROS

Sounds boring.

DEMETRIUS

> For once, I agree with Baby. Why settle for one when I can have all the available and willing women in the city?

PENNY LOVE

> I'm with Atticus. Grow up. And when did you become such a pig?

DEMETRIUS

> I take offense to that. There's nothing wrong with enjoying the single life.

The town car I hired pulls up outside of Indie's building at exactly 5:59 pm. One minute before I said I'd pick her up.

The event doesn't start until eight, but she has to arrive early since she's in charge of the organization. She tried to convince me to meet her there instead of picking her up, but I refused. This is technically our first date, and I'm not even sure it classifies as that, considering she's working.

That's something I plan on rectifying soon. Knowing Indie, she'll probably argue that all those dinners at her place are dates, but I don't count those. She deserves to be taken out. Pampered with a nice dinner. Maybe some dancing afterward. And definitely a long night tangled together under the sheets.

For now, I'm going to make the best of tonight and romance her as much as I can, despite her having to work.

"I'll be down shortly," I say to the driver as he opens my door.

He nods. "I'll be waiting right here, sir."

I step inside her building and make my way to the elevator. Before I even press the call button, the doors slide open. Standing alone on the other side is Indie's best friend and the man I am irrationally jealous of, Elon Ruppert.

His eyes immediately roam down my body, and his smile widens. "Damn. Indie is a lucky woman."

I fight the urge to roll my eyes as we switch places. "Thanks, I think."

"Oh, my praise is definitely a compliment." With his hands in his pants pockets, he leans against the edge of the door so it can't slide shut. For someone in such a fancy tux, he looks casual and relaxed. I'm never relaxed in a tux. "Any chance one of those handsome Greek brothers of yours bat for my team? Or a cousin that's just as hot as you?"

A slow chuckle escapes me, and I shake my head. "Um, 'fraid not."

Being jealous of this man is ridiculous. He's not interested in Indie like that. They're friends. *Good friends*. The best of friends. Would I be jealous if he were a woman? I don't think so, but it's hard to say. All I know is I want to be as close to Indie as him. I want her secrets, her fears, her struggles. And she still keeps those from me.

He's still smiling and there's a twinkle in his eyes that I hate myself for noticing. Then his lips shift, and he almost looks like he's pouting. "That's too bad. I rather think I'd enjoy having some fun with a Greek god."

I groan and look at the ceiling, causing him to laugh even harder.

"I'm just teasing. Sort of." He shrugs. He leans around the edge of the door and pushes the button for Indie's floor. It snaps me out of my thoughts and back to the reason I'm here. I didn't even realize I hadn't pushed it. "Your girl is waiting for you, and she looks fabulous. Try to keep it in your pants until *after* the gala."

There are so many things I want to say to him for those comments, but all I can focus on are two words. *Your girl. My girl.* Because he's right. Indie may not have fully accepted it yet, and our relationship is still very new and in a delicate place considering our working conditions. But she is still *my* girl.

"Thanks," I say before the doors close. He nods with that same mischievous grin he always wears and slowly backs away.

If I'm not mistaken, I've earned Indie's best friend's approval. That's something I should celebrate, not be jealous over. If Elon is rooting for Indie and me, then that means we have a stronger chance at making this work.

The elevator doors open, and I make my way down the hallway to her door. Beatrix barks at my knock, and I hear her shuffling around inside. Moments later, the door flies open and I stop breathing.

Words escape me, as do all rational thoughts. I surge forward, cup her cheeks between my hands, and pull her mouth to mine. I kiss her like it's the last time she's ever going to let me get this close to her.

She moans and doesn't resist opening up to me. I lick and nip at her bottom lip before I dive my tongue into her mouth and taste her sweetness. I instantly turn hard as steel. What I wouldn't do to drag her back to her bedroom instead and show her just how much she turns me on.

Her hands slide up the lapels of my jacket and around my neck. When her fingers dig into my hair, the groan that escapes is feral and needy and about to set me off. If this kiss goes on any longer, I'm going to ruin this dress she's wearing. Some small, intelligent part of my brain screams at me that this is not a good idea.

I break the kiss and drop my forehead to hers. We're both breathing heavily and struggling to regain control of our hormones.

Once I can formulate words again, I say, "You're stunning. That's what I meant to say instead of messing you up with a kiss."

She chuckles. "I liked the kiss."

I look down at her mouth, and my smile grows. I wipe my thumb under her bottom lip before I place a light kiss against her mouth again. "You might want to go fix your lipstick before we leave."

She nods and steps out of my embrace.

"You might want to clean up your face too." She waves her finger in the air in a swirling motion close to my face. "You've got something right there."

While she heads back to her bathroom, I step into her kitchen and grab a paper towel. Sure enough, I wipe a good bit of her red lipstick off my face. I pull my phone from my pocket and use my camera app as a mirror to make sure I got it all.

Moments later, Indie rejoins me by the front door. She's perfectly put back together, and no longer looks like she'd been kissed to the edge of her existence. I desperately want to change that. I like seeing her all messed up and lusting over me.

But she's working tonight.

Instead, I take her hand and tug her to my side. "You ready? Our car is waiting downstairs."

"Yeah." She still sounds breathless, and that makes me smile. "I need to grab my purse off the counter."

I bring her hand to my mouth and kiss her knuckles before I release her. The shy smile she gives me causes my dick to twitch. Indie is always so assertive and confident. Seeing this vulnerable side of her is nice. It makes her that much more attractive and endearing to me.

I love her strength, but there's something about this shyness that makes me love her even more.

My face freezes mid-smile, and I stare at her as she walks away again. I'm surprised by how easy thoughts of love and her come to me. Is it even possible to love her like that at this point in our relationship?

I think about all the ways we've gotten under each other's skin these past several months. Not to mention all the heated looks and arguments. We certainly know how to push the other's buttons. But in the best way possible.

Then I think about all the stolen kisses and smiles. The secret glances that are only for each other when no one else is looking. The way she makes me laugh and feel better about myself and my position.

Indie may infuriate me sometimes, but I still like it. So yeah, I am in love for the first time in my life.

I just hope she loves me too.

∼

I'M IN COMPLETE AWE OF INDIE.

She's in her element and killing it like a pro. She's working hard and has barely taken a break since we arrived, and her smile is still holding strong. She loves this.

Her passion for this is evident in every smile she gives and every action she makes. She's checked every single table, place setting, arrangement, auction item, food and drink option, and music selection. Nothing will happen tonight that Indie hasn't put her personal touch on.

It's also clear the people working alongside her respect her. She's damn good at this job. She's firm when she needs to be, but always kind in her delivery.

She laughs often—a laugh unlike anything I've seen at the office.

I already knew she had no business working as my assistant. But that fact is more clear now than ever before.

This is what she's meant to do, and it's a shame her father doesn't see this side of her. If he did, he never would have forced her into working for his company for one month, let alone a full year.

"She's amazing, isn't she?" Elon says from his seat next to me.

I glance over at him and smile. He's watching me watch her. I didn't know he was attending tonight's gala until he slid into the seat next to mine. It's something I should have picked up on when I saw him exiting Indie's building in his tux, but my mind was singularly focused on Indie.

I'm not sure if he's here to keep an eye on me or as moral support for her. Either way, he's not such a bad guy. He cares a lot about Indie, and that alone makes me like the guy.

I nod, shifting my eyes back to her. She's giving instructions to some of the staff. "She's in her element. This is where she belongs. Not sitting at a desk working as my assistant."

"Agreed." He raises his glass in the air before taking a sip. When he doesn't say more, I glance over at him to find him watching me with narrowed eyes.

"What?" I ask.

He clears his throat before he looks at his glass and twirls in on one end on the table. "Indie is a very special person. She's tough and can handle just about anything life throws at her, but that doesn't mean she's incapable of hurting or being hurt."

I can't help but smile at how he's trying to warn me not to hurt his friend. "Just spit it out. Tell me what you want to tell me so I can tell you it won't happen."

His eyes shoot to mine and his lips lift in the corners. He's trying to fight his smile, but he can't. "I like you, and I think you're good for Indie. Just don't be the reason she comes to me crying. Ever."

"Making her cry or hurting her in any way is the last thing I want to do."

"Good. As long as it stays that way, then you have nothing to worry about. But if that ever changes, be ready to hide. Because I will hunt you down and bury you."

My smile grows, and I squeeze his shoulder. "She's lucky to have a friend like you."

"That she is." He nods and shifts his eyes past me. "Keep that smile on your face. Our girl is heading our way."

Our girl. I can't help but chuckle at how just a few hours ago I would have growled and internally grumble at hearing him refer to Indie as his. But now it doesn't bother me. Elon is not a threat to my relationship with Indie. The only person who can screw that up is me.

"You two look like you're getting along." Indie's cheerful voice hits me right in the chest. Seeing her happy is one thing but hearing it in her voice elevates my excitement for her.

Elon slips his arm around my shoulder and leans into my side. "Yes, Atticus and I are becoming best buds. If he keeps acting all charming and sweet, he might replace you in my life."

"Ha!" Indie chuckles. "Now I know you're lying, because no one will ever replace me in your life." Her eyes hold mine and I swear they're fucking twinkling. "Has he threatened you yet?"

"Nah," I lie. "Like he said, we're becoming best buds."

Elon chuckles, and her eyes shift between us. "I don't believe you for one second."

I hold my smile and push to my feet. Kissing her cheek, I ask, "Can you sit with us for a while, or do you have more work to do?"

"I can sit." She runs her finger along the lapel of my jacket, her heated gaze lingering on the movement. It's a look I love seeing in her eyes. "Dinner is about to be served, which means the work portion of my evening is mostly done."

"Good." I pull her close to me and press a kiss to her red lips, not even caring if her lipstick transfers to me. I want to feel her lips on mine. "Then you can sit with us and tell me why you haven't told your father about all this."

She grunts, and Elon snorts. "My father doesn't care about what I do or want. All he cares about is his business."

I cup her cheek, fighting the urge to argue with her about this. I'm pretty sure she's wrong about her dad, but their tumultuous history makes it impossible for either of them to truly see the other.

"Well, you're truly amazing and should be proud of what you do. Your dad is missing out on who you really are."

Her eyes soften and she shakes her head. "He doesn't see me. He only sees what he wants to see."

"He would if you showed him." I insist.

"Preach it," Elon says under his breath.

Indie rolls her eyes. "No ganging up on me. Dad has made up his mind about me and there's nothing I can do to change that."

I kiss her forehead. "I think you're wrong. Hopefully, one day soon, I'll prove it to you."

CHAPTER TWENTY-TWO

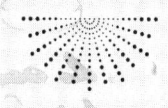

INDIGO

ELON

I really, really LIKE him.

INDIGO

Yeah, he's not so bad once you get to know him, is he?

ELON

Not so bad? Those aren't the words I'd choose. Add in the dreamy way he keeps looking at you with his sexy Greek god attitude and SWOON.

INDIGO

{eye roll emoji} You're probably swooning at the hot bartender as well, so your swoonworthiness isn't exactly on par with mine.

ELON

GASP! Are you suggesting the sexy Greek god isn't swoonworthy?

INDIGO

Oh no, I'm swooning. But I am suggesting that your swoon level is overly exaggerated.

ELON

I am offended by that.

> **INDIGO**
> {kissing face emoji} You still love me.

> **ELON**
> That I do!

This night has been perfect, and it's all because of Atticus.

One reason I never bring dates to work-related events is because they complain that I'm too busy working and not paying enough attention to them. *Um, yeah. Because I'm working.*

But not Atticus.

He sat on the sidelines and let me do what I needed to do without a single word of complaint. In fact, he's praised me for how hard I work at my job. That's a new experience for me, and it's causing my heart to do this weird fluttering thing it's never done before.

Even Elon loves him, and that's no easy feat. Elon has always been overly protective of me *and* my heart. He knows my family history and the exact number of times a man has used me to get close to my father.

His trust in Atticus is *everything*. It means Atticus can be trusted with my heart. That's not something I've done in a really long time.

As much as I've tried to keep Atticus at arm's length, it's useless. I like him. Like *really* like him. The like I feel for this man is bordering on the edge of something more—something deeper—that I'm not ready to fully acknowledge. But it's there, constantly nagging at my heart.

The last of the plates are currently being cleared from the dinner that was served, and the music is shifting to something more appropriate for dancing. A few couples have already gotten up and taken the dance floor, and a few others are lingering at the bar.

The speaker we brought in to discuss inner city youth community centers did a fabulous job. This event already brought in a nice chunk of change to support the organization, but I think her talk opened up those pockets even more. Everyone loves supporting a good cause, but when kids are involved, they always do better.

Overall, I'd call tonight's gala a huge success.

Glancing behind me, I notice Harold Whittington's seat and the one saved for his guest are still empty. I sigh, hoping his absence isn't a bad sign. I've worked countless hours on my business plan over the past couple of months. If he hates it, I'm screwed.

"Indie, relax." Elon reaches across Atticus and nudges my arm. "He's just late. You know he's a very busy man. Give him more time."

"Who's late?" Atticus asks.

I didn't tell Atticus this investor was coming tonight. Or how important it was that tonight went great. "The investor I told you I'm trying to secure was supposed to be here to see me in action. He's a no show, which is sad because tonight has been perfect."

Atticus takes my hand and lifts it to his lips. "You're perfect. Anyone with eyes can see that."

I snort and Elon sighs. When I look over at Elon, he has his hand pressed against his heart and the goofiest smile on his face as he stares at Atticus.

Yeah, I'm screwed in more ways than one. Atticus is proving to be a much more complex man than the one I thought he was when I first met him. He's still cocky, with a very dominant personality, but he's also kind, generous, and caring in ways I never let myself see before.

I am officially head over heels in deep like for this man.

"Thank you," I smile and try to mask my growing feelings, so he doesn't see them written all over my face. The way he smiles back at me suggests I failed.

"Dance with me?" he asks.

His deep chocolate-brown eyes hold my gaze. He may be asking me to dance, but there's so much more behind this look. Emotions I can't quite put words to because I've never felt this way before. It's not just lust or need or even want. He cares about me. He just might be head over heels in deep like for me too.

Once again, words fail me with this man, and all I can manage is a quick nod.

He squeezes my hand and pulls me to my feet. Even in my high-heeled shoes, he towers over me. He exudes power and strength that leaves me feeling weak in the knees and needy for so much more than a dance.

He must read my mind because a slow smile lifts his lips. Cupping my cheek, he leans in close to my ear and whispers, "Later, Princess."

With his hand on my lower back and his side pressed close to mine, he leads me to the dance floor. We join the other couples, but I don't really see any of them. All I see is Atticus. All I feel is this crackle of need and attraction and seriously deep like between us.

He takes one of my hands and places it around his neck while he clasps the other in his hand and holds it close to his chest. Then his arm snakes around my waist and tugs me close until our bodies are flush.

My hips press against his thighs while his semi-hard erection presses into my belly. I gasp at the feel of him, and he chuckles.

"I've been fighting a hard-on all night, Princess. Watching you work—doing something you truly love—is a huge turn on. Very dirty thoughts have been running through my mind all evening."

I glance up at him and flutter my lashes. His eyes darken.

"Oh, yeah?" I twirl my fingers in his hair at the base of his neck. "What kind of dirty thoughts?"

A low growl escapes him, and my smile grows. I love seeing him get all worked up over me.

Leaning close to my ear, his tongue darts out and flicks the lobe, sending a shiver throughout my entire body. "An image of this dress, despite how stunning you are in it, crumpled on the floor next to your bed, and you're sprawled out like an offering in nothing but these high-heeled shoes."

His hand on my back slowly moves up and his fingers tease the edge of my dress right where the skin of my back is exposed.

"You're restrained with your hands secured to your headboard with my tie. You're blindfolded so you can't see what's coming next. The anticipation. The need. Builds."

"Oh God." I moan softly against his chest, burying my face so no one can see the effect his words are having on me.

"My hands and tongue claim every inch of you painfully slow until both of us are ready to explode. I make you beg for every *touch*, every *kiss*, every *lick*."

My hand tightens around his neck, as does his around my waist. His fingers splay out across my back in a possessive hold that presses his thick erection, that is now fully hard, into my belly.

He takes a deep breath and groans like I'm the best thing he's ever smelled. "I make you come on my hand first with my fingers deep inside you," he whispers in my ear. "I revel in the feel of your body squeezing around them like a vise grip. I don't give you a chance to come down from that release before I put my mouth on you. Replace my fingers with my tongue, fucking and licking you until you scream my name so loud your voice is hoarse. I suck that tight little clit of yours between my teeth until you beg me to stop. But I don't. I couldn't even if I wanted to. When you beg, it only makes me want to give you *more*."

"Atticus." My hand clenches around his neck. "Stop talking."

His answering chuckle is deep and gravelly and intensifies the arousal building between my thighs.

Still gripping my hand in his, he places his finger under my chin and forces me to look at him. "No, baby. I'll never stop talking dirty to you."

In what feels like slow motion, he lowers his mouth to mine. It's a light kiss. Just a slow peck. But he doesn't pull away. He lingers—our lips just barely touching as our breath mingles and becomes one.

I want to deepen the kiss, feel his tongue in my mouth, taste him, devour him. But this isn't the right place for that. I'm technically still working, and no one needs to see me jump this man like the crazed, horny woman that I currently am.

"Indie," he whispers my name, and there's so much feeling behind the way the syllables roll off his tongue. "Fuck, baby. Do you have any idea what you do to me?"

"Yeah," I breathe. "I feel it poking me in the stomach."

A deep rumbling laugh escapes him before he presses another kiss to my lips. Then he straightens and spins me around the dance floor as if he didn't just say all those dirty things to me in a crowd of some of the wealthiest socialites in the city.

When we spin around toward the main entrance, I freeze. Everything good about tonight vanishes, and I'm filled with dread.

Standing just inside the ballroom, glaring right at us, is my dad, with Harold Whittington by his side.

∼

SEEING MY DAD'S ANGRY FACE STARING AT ME FROM ACROSS THE ROOM is like an ice bucket dumped over my head. Gone is the need and want I felt mere moments ago toward Atticus. His presence effectively snuffed out the fire feeding the chemistry between us.

I extract myself from Atticus's embrace, but he pulls me back to his side before I make it more than two steps.

"We'll face him together," he whispers.

I shake my head. "This doesn't involve you."

My dad's anger is with me, and only me. There's no reason to make things worse for Atticus if it can be avoided. At this point in Atticus's career, I'm not sure he could do anything to lose my dad's respect. He's the golden child, the chosen one, the person Dad sees as his next executive-level employee.

I don't hold this against Atticus. Not anymore, at least. He's earned his place in my dad's company. Whereas I'm nothing more than an interloper biding my time until Dad releases me from this hell.

I'm the one that's always been on Dad's shit list, and it looks like I've solidified my place in the top position for the foreseeable future.

Yep. Those angry dagger eyes are for me.

Atticus grabs my hand and tugs me back. "How can you say that? My lips were on yours the same as yours were on mine. This is *our* relationship. We're in this together."

I cup his cheek and force a smile, even though nothing inside me feels happy anymore. Dad is going to ruin this. He'll make sure of it.

He always does. "That's where you're wrong. Where my dad is concerned, it's only ever about me."

I pull away from him and make my way across the room. Out of the corner of my eye, I see Elon stand and walk toward Atticus. But I don't look back. I keep my eyes focused on Dad and Harold.

I stop a few feet short of where they're standing. With my arms clenched close to my sides, I focus my attention on Harold. "Mr. Whittington. Based on your present company, I can only assume this means you've chosen to not support my business venture."

He clears his throat and glances nervously at my dad. He seems surprised by my directness. At this point, I don't see any reason to tiptoe around the issue.

"Considering the business plan you promised me today never arrived, you've given me no choice but to pull out. I love all your ideas, but I'm not confident you're the right person for the job."

Those words hurt far worse than they should, and I fight back the tears that sting my eyes. I refuse to let my dad see me fall apart. "It should have been delivered to your office no later than five, as promised. I handed it over to a courier myself."

He shakes his head. "Never made it. I have to be honest here, Indie. Between your lack of professionalism and your father's concerns about your competence, I'm afraid I'm going to have to bow out. I hope you understand."

I glare at my father. Considering he has no problem telling me how much of a failure I am to my face, I can only imagine what he's said about me behind my back. "I've no doubt my father has said many horrible things about me. I can assure you they're all lies." I turn my gaze back to Harold. "But I know that doesn't matter to you. It's never mattered to the people my father owns. Thank you for your consideration."

I turn to leave, but Harold stops me with his angry reply. "No one *owns* me, Miss Simons. I made this decision based on your merit."

I chuckle. "Keep telling yourself that lie. If you based it on my merit, the outcome would be very different."

"Indigo!" Dad's voice booms. "That's no way to talk to a friend of mine. No wonder your little venture is a failure."

"*Little* venture?" I bark out. "There is nothing *little* about my plans. Just because you're too narrow minded to see what's right in front of you doesn't mean it's *little*. I've worked hard for this, *Dad*. All of this," I wave my arms around the room in exasperation, "happened tonight because of my hard work. Over the past three years, I've been responsible for raising over seven million dollars for countless charities by organizing and managing events and galas just like this one. All of which you'd know if you bothered to take the time to get to know *me*. But no. It's easier for you to pretend I'm just like Mom."

"That's enough." He grinds out through gritted teeth. "We'll talk about this at home."

"No, we won't, because there's nothing more to discuss."

I sense his closeness before I feel Atticus's hands rest on my arms. He steps close to me and says, "Sir, this isn't what it looks like."

"I don't need you to come to my defense," I say and pull away. When I look back at him, I see the hurt in his expression.

"Atticus, I know this isn't your fault," my dad says. "My daughter has a tendency to use people to get what she wants. I'm sorry she's dragged you into this."

Atticus snorts and shakes his head. "She didn't use me. If anyone did the using, it's me."

The way he says that rubs me the wrong way and my defenses immediately rise. All rational and logical thought gets pushed to the back of my mind and every moment of betrayal from my past claws its way to the top.

Every man I've ever dated has used me to get to my dad, and Atticus's tone suggests that's exactly what he did as well. A part of me knows that's wrong—that he meant that in a very different way—but my anger and insecurities are stronger.

Before I can voice my frustrations, my dad speaks. "Atticus, we'll talk tomorrow. If you don't mind, I'd like to speak to my daughter *alone*."

"With all due respect, sir, this—"

Dad holds up his hand as he pulls me to his side. "Tomorrow," he says with so much authority and anger that he leaves no room for debate.

Atticus looks between me and my father, his expression still pained. I sense he wants to argue otherwise, but when he meets my gaze, I nod. I want him to leave. He doesn't need to see any more of this interaction. He's already seen too much.

Elon steps up next to Atticus and wraps his arm around his shoulder. Atticus jumps in surprise. "Come on, man. Let me get you a drink."

He shakes his head. "Not like this. Not while this is unsettled."

"Seriously, Indie," my dad says with nothing but disgust in his tone. I look to his side and see that Harold is gone. At least he left before this shit show took a turn for the worse. "Did you really have to mess around with my best employee? I hired you in the hopes it would help you become a better person, not to use your boss as a plaything."

"Dad!" I yell.

"James," Atticus mumbles.

Our voices mingle together in shock.

My dad shakes his head before he turns to me. "I'll be in the car. Don't make me wait."

Then he barges out of the room, signaling that this conversation is paused until we're behind closed doors.

Without looking at Atticus, I follow Dad. I can't handle the rejection that I'm sure is coming. Dad will not stand for a relationship between Atticus and me. I know this game all too well. If I don't walk away, he'll threaten Atticus's position. He's done it before.

Atticus will choose his job. Why wouldn't he? Lord knows I'd run from this drama if I could.

"Indie, wait!" Atticus calls after me, but I don't look back. I can't. It'll hurt too much.

"Let her go," Elon says. "Just give her some space."

Atticus says something else, but I don't hear the words. My head is too overwhelmed by these emotions. My chest hurts and it's a struggle to breathe.

Once again, my dad ruined the few good things I had in my life. In one night, he destroyed my chances of starting my foundation and took Atticus away from me.

Why does my life always suck?

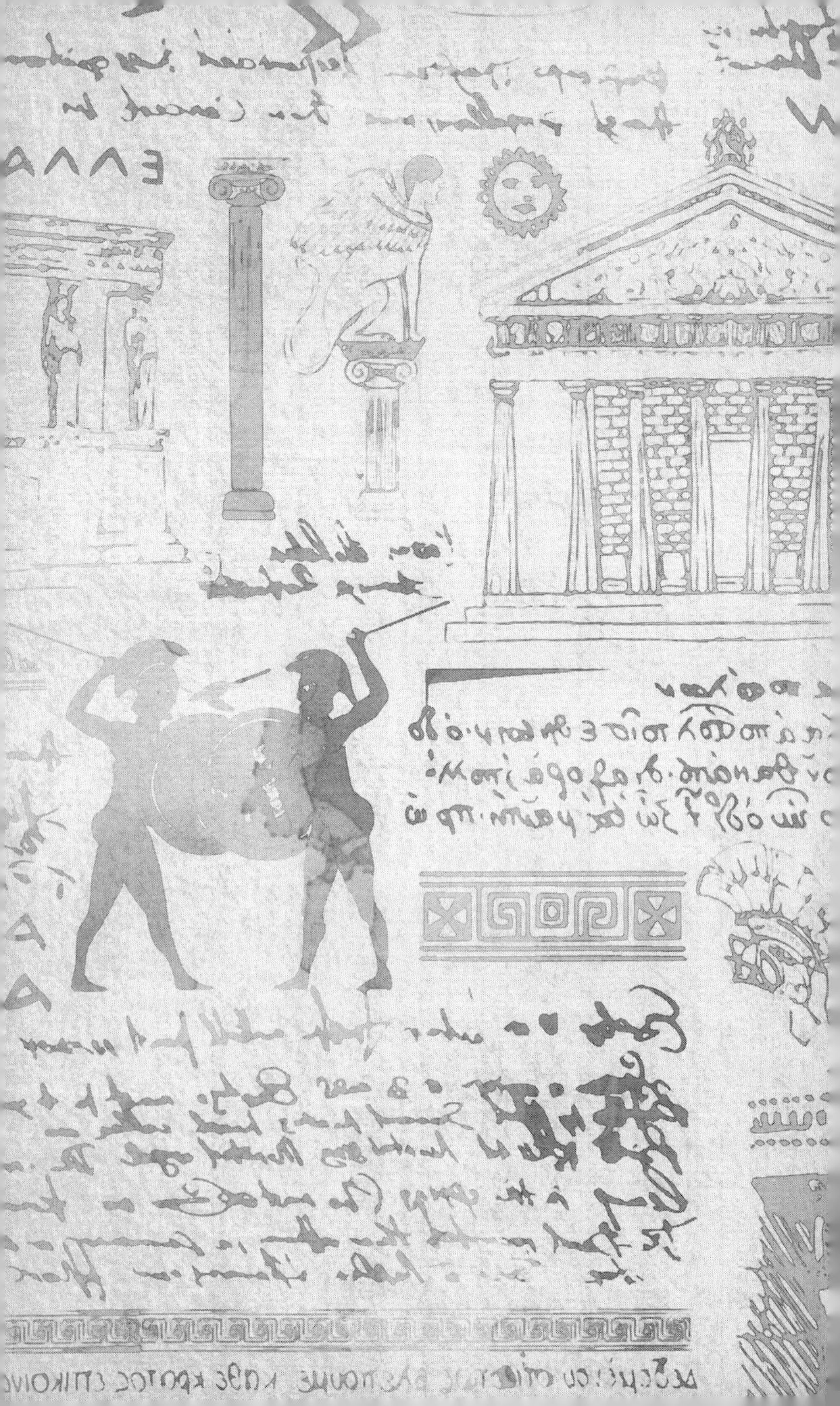

CHAPTER TWENTY-THREE

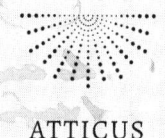

ATTICUS

> **ATTICUS**
> Where are you?
>
> Indie, please answer me.
>
> If I have to sit outside your apartment all night long, I will.
>
> Baby, you're worrying me. Please answer me.
>
> There isn't anything your dad can say to keep me away.
>
> Let me fix this. Once I talk to your dad, it'll be fine. Trust me.
>
> Please.

My entire body aches, especially my back and neck. I hardly slept a wink, though I dozed off a few times. But never for more than ten minutes at a time. I waited for her all night, and she never came home.

Camping outside my girlfriend's door in a wrinkled tux is not something I've ever done before. Based on the troubled looks I got from a few of her neighbors, it's not something they've seen or done either.

Thankfully, no one called the cops or building security. Unfortunately, waiting here all night didn't do me any good. She must have stayed with her father or Elon, and she never responded to any of my messages and ignored all my calls.

I hurt all over. I'm tired. I think it's safe to say that today is going to be a crap day. Which is outstandingly inconvenient since I have what might be the biggest meeting of my career scheduled in less than five hours.

Pushing to my feet, I reluctantly make my way to the elevator. I need to run home, shower, and get ready for this meeting. It's not something I can miss if I want to keep my job.

Assuming I still have a job after last night.

James was definitely pissed, and I couldn't tell if it was at me, Indie, or both of us. I guess I'll find out soon enough.

When I step out onto the sidewalk, I stuff my hands in my pocket and head toward the subway. As much as I hate it, salvaging my relationship with Indie is going to have to wait.

~

The office is bustling by the time I make it in. It's a little after nine, and I can't recall the last time I showed up this late in the morning.

Based on all the confused faces I keep running into, I'd say everyone else is surprised to see me coming in this late as well. Especially considering the meeting I have in a little under two hours.

I pause when I reach my office. Indie's not at her desk. A part of me had hoped she'd be here, even though I knew otherwise. She's hiding, and I've no clue where or how to find her.

James might know where she is, but I'm not convinced he'd tell me.

He hasn't called my cell phone yet this morning, which is unusual considering how late I am. If I don't answer my office phone, he always calls my cell. This leads me to believe he hasn't tried to contact me this morning at all. I hope this isn't a bad sign regarding my future with the company.

However, my office isn't empty. Leon is pacing in front of my desk, looking just as stressed and nervous as I feel. When he sees me approach, he stops and his shoulders sag.

"Finally. Where in the hell have you been?"

Unlike James and Indie, Leon has tried to call me at least ten times since seven this morning.

"Sorry," I say as I round my desk. "It's been a bad morning."

"Yeah, well, it's about to get worse." Leon huffs. He places his hands on his hips, and the look on his face says it all. "The report arrived from the printer about twenty minutes ago, and it's all fucked up."

I freeze mid-step and jerk my eyes to his. "What do you mean, it's all fucked up?"

"The sections are out of order and the cost benefits analysis section is completely missing."

"No. No, no, no." I scrub my hands over my face. "That's the section the investors care the most about."

"I know." Leon drops into the chair opposite my desk. "I have a couple of admins working on fixing it. It won't be pretty, but it'll be done. By the way, where's Indie? Shouldn't she be here fixing this mess?"

I groan and take my seat. "I'm not sure she's coming in today."

"Why not?" His frown deepens. "Kind of a bad time for her to decide not to work, isn't it?"

Rubbing my hands down my face, I sigh. He's going to kill me when I tell him what happened. I hold his gaze and just spit it out. "Indie and I have been seeing each other."

His eyes widen. "Say that again."

"Indie and I are dating. Well, we were. After last night, I don't know where we stand."

"Okay. Hold up." He lifts his hand in the air with a confused look on his face. "You've been dating the woman who's been making your life hell for the past several months? How in the hell did that happen?"

"I don't know. But it did and now I'm in deep."

"How deep?" he asks.

I hold his gaze but don't answer him. I don't have to. He can read my feelings all over my face.

"Dammit, Atticus. You fell for the boss's daughter? Are you insane?"

"Yeah," I huff. "And the best part is, he knows. Found out last night when I accompanied Indie to a gala as her date. Her dad showed up unexpectedly."

"Shit." He rubs his hands down his face and groans. "Was he pissed?"

I nod. "Though I'm not sure if he's pissed at me or her or both of us. Well, he's definitely pissed at her. I'm just not sure how pissed he is at me. For all I know, I won't have a job after today. Add in a fucked up report, and things aren't looking so great for me."

"And you haven't heard from James this morning?" he asks.

"Nope. Which isn't like him. Not on days when we have important meetings. He should be here in my office discussing last-minute details. I don't know what his absence means."

"Well, there isn't anything we can do about it now. Let's just focus on preparation. You go over the presentation while I oversee the correction of the report."

"Okay." I nod absently. "This meeting is going to suck. I expected to go through the presentation several times by now."

"It'll be fine." He gives me a reassuring smile, but I don't buy it. He knows I'm fucked the same as I do. "You know this. Aside from me, no one knows this project or code better than you."

"Thanks for the vote of confidence. I need it today."

He pushes to his feet and starts for the door. When he reaches it, he stops and turns to me. "One more question."

"Yeah?"

"Who sent off the report yesterday? You or Indie?"

I furrow my brow. "Indie did. Why?"

"You don't think she'd sabotage you, do you?"

"No way." I answer without hesitation. I don't care what our history includes. She wouldn't do something like this on purpose. At least, I don't think she would.

I hold his gaze, and he must see the hint of doubt creeping in. "I hope you're right, man."

With a forced smile, he turns and leaves. I close my eyes and think about the past few months with Indie. Sure, we've had some rough patches. Especially with all the prank gifts I sent to her. But I don't think she's this malicious. She wouldn't jeopardize my career. Not after everything that's happened between us.

But doubt is a bitch, and it's nagging at the back of my mind like a virus. I'm not going to be able to get this thought out of my head until I talk to her.

∼

I PLOP DOWN IN THE CHAIR AT THE HEAD OF THE CONFERENCE TABLE and sigh.

It's over.

It didn't go horribly, but the meeting was mediocre at best. Mediocre is not okay. Mediocre will not cut it. Mediocre won't earn me the large, posh office upstairs.

James showed up at exactly eleven. He never waits until the last minute to show up for big meetings like this. He's always early. Oftentimes, he'll show up an hour ahead of time to help staff prepare or take on the responsibility of seeing to all the last-minute admin tasks so the presenter doesn't have to stress about it.

Not today. It was as if he didn't care if I failed or succeeded. With my mediocre performance, I call it a failure.

"Well, that went better than expected," Leon says as he takes the seat next to me.

"It was horrible. I'm screwed and probably out of a job." I fall back in the chair and groan. "I'm definitely not getting that promotion now."

"It wasn't *that* bad." Leon continues. His voice is a little too cheery, so I know he's faking it just to make me feel better. It's not going to work. "They loved it. The report looked fine in the end. Sure, it could have been better, but we made it work."

"Making it work doesn't cut it for me," I say a little too harshly. It's not Leon's fault I'm in this position. I have no one to blame but myself. "I excel. I strive for the best at all times. Simply making it work won't help me achieve my career goals."

"This was just one meeting, man." Leon sounds dejected, making me feel like an even bigger asshole. "I know it sucks. Especially since we spent so many hours making this perfect. But it's just one meeting. One out of countless more to come. The issue with the report wasn't even your fault. You can't control the printer staff. Don't be so hard on yourself."

I drop my head back on the chair and let out a deep breath. "No, but I can control my actions. I should have let others help me with the report. I failed as a manager, and that's on me."

"What are you talking about? You're the best manager I could ask for."

I glance over at him, and the look of sincerity on his face makes me feel marginally better. "Thanks, man. I appreciate that. We make a great team, but if I want to make it upstairs, I need to learn to trust more than one person. I need to learn to lean on all my staff, not just you. Hell, I could've had you help with more of the report preparation, but I didn't."

He opens his mouth like he's going to argue differently, then stops. Because he doesn't have a point to argue. I'm right. I don't let enough of my team help with my personal projects. I let my previous work history dictate my current work habits, and I screwed myself.

"Well, that was ... Not your best," James says from the conference room doorway. He'd left to show the investors out while I stayed behind to lick my wounds. I hope he was able to salvage whatever damage I caused from my lack of preparedness.

"I'll leave you two alone." Leon goes to stand, but James puts his hand up to stop him.

"No need. This will only take a moment," James says. Leon slowly sits back down. He glances between James and me with an expression of worry and discomfort. Welcome to my club. "Despite the lack of preparedness, the investors are pleased with the work you presented. Address the questions we got and fix the damn report before the end of next week. I promised it to them by next Friday. Don't fail me."

"Yes, sir. I'll get it done."

"Good. Now, go home and get some sleep. You look like shit."

"Sir, can we talk about last night?" I go to stand but freeze midway.

He shakes his head, a deep frown marring his face. "We'll talk about everything else later."

Without another word, he turns and disappears around the corner. I let out a deep sigh and gather my things.

"Are you leaving?" Leon asks.

I nod. "I have to find Indie. I can't get my head on straight until I fix things between us."

"Tell me what I can do to help in the meantime." Leon follows me down the hallway toward my office.

"You can start on those code-related questions. Maybe take a stab at fixing the damn report."

"You sure about that?" He sounds unsure, and not because he can't do the task. But because I'm a shitty boss for not letting him help me more until now.

"Yeah, I'm positive. I need—" I stop, causing Leon to run into me. He stumbles backward but catches himself before he falls.

Indie is standing at her desk, looking like a goddess—my goddess—in her tight pencil skirt and pale pink silk blouse. She's a sight for sore eyes, and all I want to do is pull her into my arms and hold her close.

"You're here," I say. The words come out a little louder than I intended. My surprise is evident in my tone.

Her gaze snaps up to meet mine. The regret and sadness in her eyes has me barging toward her. I take her by the hand and drag her into my office.

"Atticus!" She pulls away from me, but I don't let her go. I can't let her go. We have to talk this through because losing her is not an option.

I shut the door behind us and lock it. Then I spin her around and pin her against the door. Just having her this close to me again eases the tension I've carried in my body since she left me last night. Even the ache in my back and neck feels better.

"Where the hell have you been?" The tension may have eased, but my words are still harsh and demanding. "I've been worried sick."

"Atticus, let me go." She pushes against my chest, but I don't budge.

"Not until you talk to me. I need to know we're okay."

She shakes her head, her eyes welling up with tears. "I can't do this. *We* can't do this. Don't you get it? My father wins. He always wins."

Seeing her upset softens me even more. The last thing I can handle right now is seeing her cry. I cup her cheek and brush away a tear that falls down her cheek. "What are you talking about? Is it really that big of an issue that he found out about us before we were ready to tell him? We'll talk to him. Get him to understand."

"No, we won't. He won't understand. He never does. This is over, Atticus." She pushes against my chest again, but with less force and strength.

"No." I lift her up, wrap my hands under her ass, and press my body against hers. My cock thickens at the closeness. "This is far from over, baby. We're just getting started."

I crush my lips to hers. She resists me for about two seconds before she melts into me and kisses me back. Her hands slide around my neck, and she shoves her fingers into my hair. It's an action I've grown to love from her. Her fingers fisting my hair and her nails scraping against my scalp make my body come alive with arousal.

The groan that escapes me is carnal. I press my aching cock into her center, and she tightens her legs around my waist. She may have said this is over, but her body's response to me says something else entirely.

With equal fervor, we deepen the kiss. My teeth nip at her bottom lip before I swipe my tongue across it, soothing the bite. Her moans push me to take it deeper, to claim her, to show her exactly how much she means to me.

Her skirt is bunched at her waist, making it easy for me to pull her panties aside and run my finger along her center.

"Fuck, Princess." I growl. "You're so wet."

I tease her entrance with the tip of my finger. She thrusts forward, forcing me deeper inside her, and it makes me smile. Slowly and methodically, I slide my finger in and out of her while she kisses me like she's been starved for me.

"Atticus, please," she moans.

"Tell me what you need, baby."

"You. Inside me." Her hand glides down my chest and between our bodies until she's cupping my cock. When she squeezes me, my head spins with need.

She fumbles with my belt and zipper and has me gripped in her warm hand before I can even wrap my head around what she's doing. She squeezes and pulls on me until my tip is rubbing against her clit. We both moan at how fucking good it feels.

I want to slam inside her so badly it hurts, and it takes all the strength I possess to resist. "Baby, I don't have a condom."

"I'm on the pill," she breathes as she repositions me at her entrance.

I freeze and pull back to look her in the eyes. "What are you saying?"

"Fuck me. Please. I want to feel you." There's a mix of desperation and sadness in her words that niggles at my mind, but I'm too hard and needy to dissect it.

I press my tip inside her, intending to take this slow, but it feels so fucking good that slow is an impossibility. Her walls clamp down around me, sucking me deeper inside her until she's completely full. Of me. And only me.

"Fuck," I grind out. She feels so good—too good—and if I'm not careful, I'm going to come before her. And that will not do.

I pull out until only my tip remains inside her, then I slam back in, burying myself deep until my balls slap against her. That one action was almost too much, and I still.

We're both breathing heavily. Our breath mingles as our lips hover close to each other. She swirls her hips, creating the slightest bit of friction between us, and that's enough to almost send me over the edge.

"Baby," I growl. "I need you to hold still for a moment."

"Can't." She pants. "Need you. To. Move."

"If I do that, this is over way too fast. With no barrier between us, this is intense."

She lets out a low whine, and I chuckle.

"Are you laughing at me?" She playfully slaps my chest, but there's hardly any energy behind it.

"I am," I say honestly, right before I press my lips to hers.

I like her like this. She's completely at my mercy. Lost to this connection we share. If only this were enough to convince her that what we have is real, and that no one—not even her father—can get between us.

I move, pulling myself out of her and back inside in agonizingly slow strokes. It doesn't take much for her body to reach that edge that I so desperately want to push her over. She tightens around me, her walls clenching around my cock like it's her favorite thing in the world.

Feeling her get closer and closer, I increase my speed. The second her body tumbles over that edge and crashes into a sea of bliss, I fuck her hard and fast.

She cries out my name, and it's a little too loud for office sex. I kiss her, swallowing her cries and making them my own. She's still coming around my cock when my release finally takes me.

My movements become erratic, but I don't stop. I want every ounce of my release deep inside her. I want to fill her so full of my seed and mark her as mine.

Because she is mine.

Fuck James Simons if he tries to get between us.

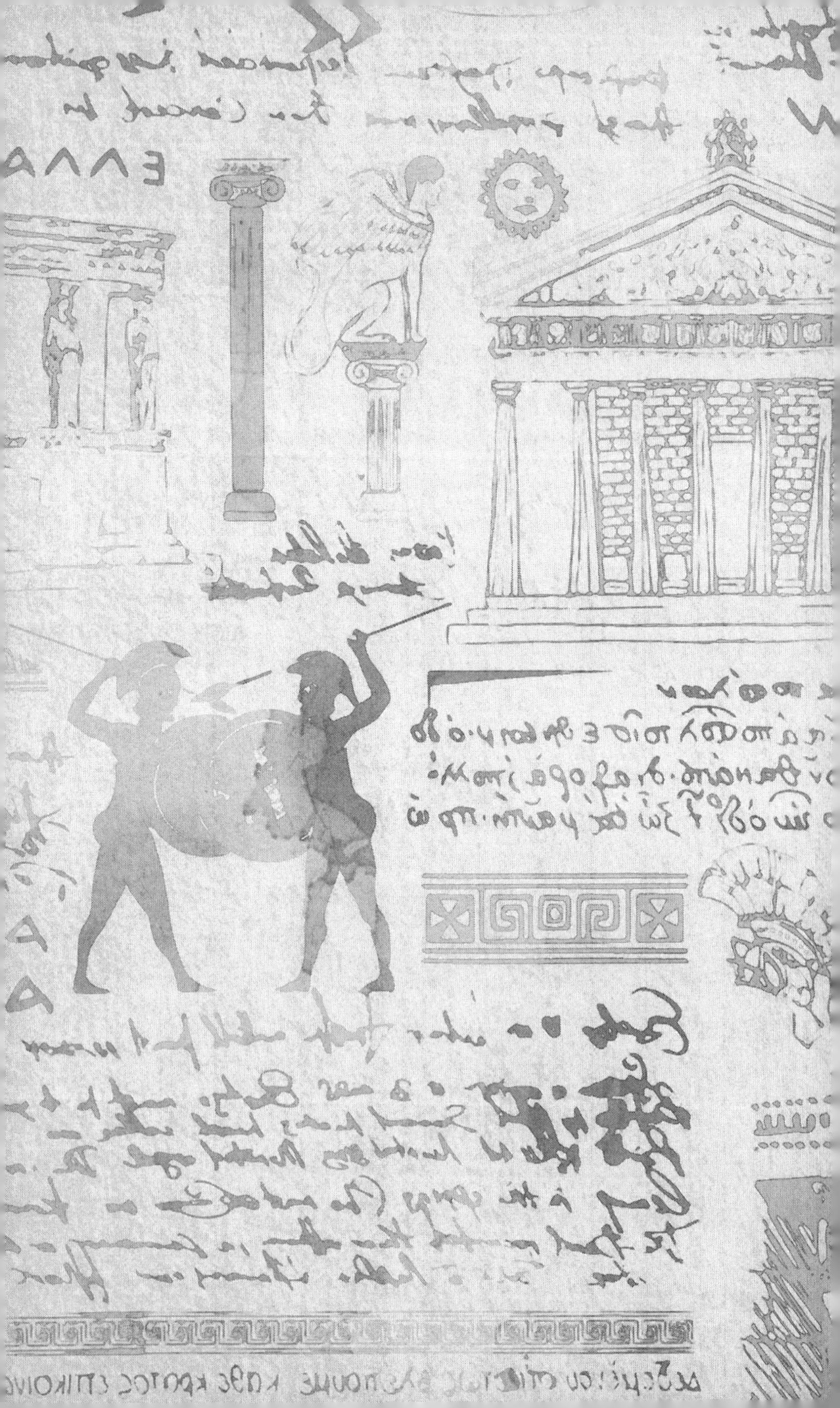

CHAPTER TWENTY-FOUR

INDIGO

ELON
You okay?

INDIGO
Never better.

ELON
Darlin' I was there. No need to lie.

INDIGO
Then why are you asking me such a dumb question?

ELON
Hey. I thought there was no such thing as a dumb question.

INDIGO
There is when you witness the downfall of my relationship and follow it up with 'You okay?'

ELON
Okay, fine. Let me rephrase. How much tequila do you need me to bring?

INDIGO
That's more like it. Enough to put me out of my misery. And I'm coming over to your place. Mine's not safe.

> **ELON**
> And why are we avoiding your apartment?
>
> **INDIGO**
> Atticus knows where I live.
>
> **ELON**
> I'll stock up on limes too.

"Oh my God." I slap my hand against Atticus's shoulder, trying to push him away. "I can't believe I just did that."

He lifts his head and frowns. "Did what?"

I squeeze my eyes closed and fight back the tears. This is so much harder than I thought it'd be. The plan was to come in, clean out my desk, and leave before his meeting ended. I didn't expect it to end so soon.

"Baby." He kisses my forehead, then each cheek before he lightly brushes his lips across mine. He's still buried deep inside me, and his gentleness is making it hard to not clench my inner walls around his cock. "Talk to me."

I open my eyes and meet his loving gaze. *Yes, loving.* There's so much emotion and need behind his dark brown eyes. This man wants me, and I have to let him go.

"Hey," he brushes a strand of hair away from my face. "What can't you believe you did?"

"Had sex with you against your office door," I say in a whispered rush.

A faint smile lifts his lips. "You were a little loud. Don't be surprised if someone heard us."

"This isn't funny." I push harder against his chest, and this time, he pulls his cock out of me and lowers my feet to the ground. I instantly miss the feel of him, and tears prick at the corner of my eyes.

"Let me grab some tissues to clean you up."

He quickly stuffs his cock into his pants and turns to his desk. I clench my thighs together as I feel his release trickle down my leg. I drop my face into my hands to hide the tears that break free. I lose all control of my emotions as reality really sinks in.

I just let Atticus fuck me bare, knowing it would be the last time we're together.

Moments later, he's pulling my hands away from my face and replacing them with his. "Baby, why are you crying? Did I hurt you?"

I shake my head. "It's not you."

I grab the tissues in his hand, but he pulls them from my reach. "Let me."

My skirt is still bunched at my waist, making it easy for him to slide the tissues between my legs and wipe me clean of his release. It's such a sweet yet domineering action. One that says he'll take care of me. That I'm *his* to take care of. It's enough to drag a sob out of me.

He repositions my skirt so it's covering me and then pulls me into a tight embrace. "Indie, baby. You're killing me right now. Tell me what's wrong."

I take a deep breath and extract myself from his embrace. Cupping his cheek, I press a quick kiss to his lips. "I've got to go."

He grabs at me, but I pull away. "Indie! What do you mean, you have to go?"

I shake my head and rush to open his door. I no longer care if anyone sees me crying. I have to get out of here before I completely lose my mind.

I grab my purse from where I sat it on my chair, forgetting about everything else I came to pack up. I don't really need any of it anyway.

"Will you stop?" Atticus reaches for me again, but I rush down the hallway toward the elevator. I hear his footsteps following me, and cringe at the impending scene this is creating. It's going to make my father even more pissed at me than he already is.

The doors slide open just as he reaches me. I hold my hand up to stop him. Thankfully, he listens. "Don't. Let *me* go. You'll forget all about me soon enough anyway."

His shoulders slump and the pain on his face tugs at my heart. I step inside the elevator and press the button for the lobby. He steps up and rests his hand on either side of the door frame, but not so it'll stop it from closing.

I meet his gaze and it nearly knocks the wind out of me. There's so much pain and anguish clouding his expression. Before the doors close, he whispers. "Forgetting about you is impossible. I love you, Indie."

The doors click shut just as the last syllable of my name rolls off his tongue. Another sob escapes me, and I crumble to the floor in a heap of tears.

∼

AFTER LEAVING THE OFFICE, I RUSHED HOME. I PACKED ENOUGH clothes and necessities to get myself through a few days and grabbed Beatrix.

Elon doesn't get off work for a few more hours, so instead of waiting outside his apartment, I decide to hang out on the back patio of a pet friendly coffee shop close to my place. It's far enough out of the way that, should Atticus decide to come looking for me, he won't find me.

Just thinking his name brings tears to my eyes.

I squeeze my eyes shut and drop my head back so the warm summer sun can heat my face. Maybe if I sit like this long enough, the sun will ease the pain from what my father made me do. It's doubtful, but one can hope.

He loves me. I can't believe he loves me. I didn't expect that.

The only reason I agreed to Dad's demands was because I assumed Atticus didn't care about me like that. We were just having fun, right? So what if it was exclusive fun? It was still just fun.

We weren't supposed to get serious about each other.

This is all my fault. I can try to blame Dad all I want, but the blame lies entirely with me. I never should have allowed anything to happen between us in the first place. I knew what my dad was capable of, and he didn't disappoint.

True to his usual MO, he forced me into a different position with the company—one where I have to work more closely with him on the top floor—and then he demanded I end things with Atticus. I reluctantly agreed to his terms because he threatened to fire Atticus if I didn't comply.

Dad's always been good at figuring out exactly how to get me to do what he wants.

"Are you alright, dear?" a gentle, yet raspy voice says from beside me. My eyes snap open and I meet the worried gaze of an elderly woman. She's petite, with her silver hair pulled back in a low bun. She has kind eyes and a warm smile. She looks like the grandmother I've always wished I'd had.

I wipe my cheeks, suddenly aware that I'm crying. I was so lost in my thoughts, I hadn't even realized I lost control.

I nod vigorously. "I'm fine. Sorry if I disturbed you."

"Oh, nonsense." She waves me off. "You weren't disturbing me at all. But you do look sad. I hate seeing such a pretty girl like you so upset. I'm a good listener if you need me to lend an ear."

"I couldn't impose on you. My past two days have been terrible. You don't want to hear about my sad, pathetic life."

"Is it a man?" she asks.

I find myself nodding despite my insistence that she doesn't want to hear about my life. "My father doesn't approve."

"Ah, yes. It's never easy when a parent doesn't like the man you bring home."

I chuckle, although there's no humor behind it. "Actually, it's the other way around. My dad doesn't think I'm good enough for the man."

She frowns. "What kind of father would think his own daughter wasn't good enough? He sounds like a shit."

This time when I laugh, it's genuine. "He is. He's never bothered to really get to know me. He makes assumptions about me based on my mother's behavior. I can't say I blame him where she's concerned, but I've tried to show him who I really am, and he refuses to listen."

"Parents are fickle creatures. Raising kids is the hardest job a person is ever given. We try to do right by them, but we often fail, thinking we know best. Admitting that we're wrong is the worst part."

I snort. "I don't think my dad has ever admitted he's wrong a day in his life."

"No one ever wants to be wrong, dear. But there are ways to get them to see the light. It takes patience and determination. Heart and kindness. Do you love this man?"

My eyes widen at her question. I haven't let myself think about how deep my feelings for Atticus run for fear the truth will completely break me. But hearing her ask me that question has my eyes clouding over with tears.

"Yes," I mumble. "Very much."

She nods in approval. "And does this man love you?"

"He said he does."

The woman stands and gathers her things. She stops right next to me and leans down to pet Beatrix. Beatrix lets her like she's a long-lost friend.

She straightens and meets my watery gaze. Then she cups my cheek and smiles. "Don't lose hope, dear. Hope is the one thing that will get you through any ordeal. Trust me on that. Hang onto hope like a lifeline. It will get you far. I see a strength in you that I'm not sure you can see yourself. Let your father see that strength along with all the parts of you that you hide from him."

My mouth falls open, and I start to object, but she chuckles. "Don't deny it, my dear. I can see it written all over your face. You hide your true self from those who need to see it most. Show him, and all will be well."

Before I can say another word, she leaves through the back gate and disappears around the building. Beatrix nuzzles my leg. I lean down, pick her up, and hold her close to my chest.

"Is she right? Do I need to let my dad see the real me?"

Beatrix lets out a single bark, and I laugh. "So that's a yes."

She lets out another bark and looks up at me like I'm an idiot.

Maybe that's because I am.

Elon hands me the largest margarita I've ever held, and I couldn't be more grateful. I take a big gulp before I sink back onto his couch and sigh. "This is so good. Thank you."

"Anything for you." He takes a seat next to me with his own glass and holds it out to me. We clink our glasses together and drink.

Unlike my modest apartment, Elon lives like the wealthy heir that he is. He has a top floor penthouse with stunning views of Central Park and a large, open floor plan with a kitchen fit for a gourmet chef. He even has a gourmet chef that comes three days a week to prepare all his meals.

There are three bedrooms on one side, each with their own bathrooms. The other side contains a large office and his bedroom suite that shares the same Central Park views as the living room.

Unlike my father's penthouse, Elon's has personality. It looks like a real person with feelings lives here.

"What are we drinking to?" I ask.

"To getting your life back." He holds his drink up to me again. "And that sexy Greek god of a man. We can't let that one get away."

I hold Elon's gaze for a moment too long, and my tears return. His smile fades and he reaches for my hand. "It'll be okay. I'll help you figure this out."

I nod, even though I'm not sure I believe him. "He said he loves me," I whisper as Elon is mid-sip of his margarita.

He coughs and spits it all down his front. "Warn a guy before you drop a bomb like that on him."

"Sorry," I give him a weak smile.

"Seriously? That man told you he loves you?"

"Yeah."

"And what did you say?"

I take another large gulp of my drink and drop my eyes to my lap. "Nothing. I was in the elevator, leaving. He said it right as the doors were closing."

"And you didn't go back up?" he says a little too loudly.

"No! How could I after everything my dad said? He threatened to fire Atticus if I didn't end it with him."

"That man is not going to fire one of his best employees. He just said that to control you."

"Well, it worked." I down the rest of my drink and hand Elon the empty glass. "Another one."

He rolls his eyes like he's annoyed by my request, but I know it's just for show. Elon loves playing host.

He pushes to his feet and pauses to look down at me before he heads to the kitchen. "When are you going to woman up and let your dad see the real you?"

"Arg." I let out a deep groan. "You're the second person to say that to me today."

"Who else is giving you such amazing words of wisdom?" He calls out from the center island in his kitchen.

"This little old lady who caught me crying on the patio at the coffee shop. She went on and on about not losing hope and said that if I wanted my man back, I had to let my dad see the real me."

"Darlin' she's not wrong."

"But how do I do that? Dad and I have shared this dynamic for so long, I don't think either of us knows how to interact differently."

"The same as you do with any relationship," he says as he hands me a fresh drink. "Communication."

I glare at him, and he raises his brow. "Fight me on it. You know I'm right."

I groan and guzzle more of my drink instead of answering him. I know he's right but it's not what I want to hear. I stare into my glass like I'm searching for something.

"You're not going to find the answers at the bottom of that glass," Elon says.

I look over at him feeling a lot dejected. "Maybe not, but shouldn't we at least check?"

He shakes his head and chuckles. "You know what you need to do."

I let out a long growl in frustration. "But communication with my dad is hard."

He nods. "It probably will be for quite some time, but you have to start somewhere."

"Yeah, I suppose you're right."

"Let me ask you this." He sits down on the couch so he's facing me. "Do you love Atticus?"

I drop my head back and let out another loud groan. "Were you at the coffee shop disguised as a stylish grandma, handing out free words of wisdom?"

He laughs. "No, but I take it she asked you the same question."

"She did."

"And?"

I hold his gaze and sigh. "Yes, I love him."

He smiles and takes my hand. "Then let's devise a plan where you get to keep him, and he gets to keep his job."

"You make it sound so easy."

"It's anything but." His smile turns playful. "But I'm convinced we'll figure it out."

"I hope you're right." I lift my glass and clink it to his again, then down it in one long drink.

Normally, I'd say I needed a clear head when strategizing against my dad. But after the day I had, I need alcohol more.

ΕΛΛΑ

CHAPTER TWENTY-FIVE

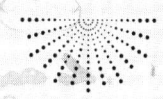

ATTICUS

DEMETRIUS

You done sulking yet?

ADONIS

Don't be a dick. He's hurting.

EROS

Who's hurting? Did I miss something?

DEMETRIUS

Tat lost the girl.

EROS

Dammit. Why does all the good stuff happen when I work all weekend?

ADONIS

This is hardly 'the good stuff' asshole.

EROS

{eye roll emoji} You know what I mean.

ADONIS

No I don't. Be kind and sensitive to your older brother's feelings.

PENNY LOVE

WHAT??? Indie broke it off with Tat? NOOOOOOO……..

ATTICUS

> Leave me alone, assholes. This isn't over, and I didn't lose anyone. I AM GOING TO FIX THIS.

It's been days—*DAYS*—since I last saw Indie, and I can hardly breathe. I went from seeing her almost every day for weeks to a complete absence of her in my life. Even when she drove me crazy, refusing to do her job, I think I unconsciously desired to see and be near her.

All my pranks and morning interactions—or fights—were all about getting closer to her. To break down the barrier she's put up between us. I just didn't recognize it before now.

Going cold turkey on Indigo Simons is the unhealthiest thing I've ever been forced to do. I need her, crave her, long for her in ways I never knew existed.

I've called and texted her more times than is socially acceptable. I've showed up at her apartment, but she never answers the door. She's been radio silent and I hate it.

Even James has been annoyingly silent. He's said nothing to me about the meeting last week or my relationship with his daughter. I tried to schedule a meeting with him yesterday, and his assistant told me he was out of the office until further notice.

I've never felt so fucked in all my life.

I've got no assistant, no girlfriend, a boss that's ignoring me, and an office full of gossips.

The whispers and hushed conversations every time I pass two or more staff members huddled together drive me insane. Apparently, the downfall of my life is far more important than actual work.

Now I know how Indie felt all those months when everyone talked about her behind her back. The rumors about what happened are wild and extremely imaginative.

They range from James catching us in very compromising positions, to Indie being pregnant, to some ridiculous weird relationship that included her best friend Elon and me together while Indie watched. I've no clue where these people get their information, but whoever starts this shit has quite the imagination.

I fucking hate gossips.

Almost as much as I hate not seeing Indie every day.

I stare at her empty desk and my chest aches. I have to fix this. But I need to find her first.

Needing to stretch my legs, I push to my feet and head to the break room. I've drunk more coffee in the past week than I ever have. My sleep schedule is shit, and I'm too tired to think straight most days.

The break room isn't empty when I arrive. I almost rush back out without paying attention to who it is just because I don't want to talk to anyone, but they see me before I can make an escape.

"Mr. Rosi," Mrs. Romano's gentle voice says. "Here for some coffee?" She holds the pot up like an offering. "Made a fresh pot."

I nod and head to the cabinet for a clean mug.

"Thank you," I say as I hold it out and she fills it for me.

"You're very welcome." Her smile is kind and somehow manages to make me feel a little more at ease. She's unlike all the other admins. I never catch her gossiping or stirring shit up just for the fun of it.

"There are some cookies on the counter, if you'd like one." She points behind us toward the counter on the opposite wall. "Double chocolate chip. Made them myself."

"Thank you, but I'll stick with the coffee." I hold my mug up and turn to leave, eyeing the cookies as I do.

She must see my expression of longing because she stops me. "Let me wrap a few of those up for you. You can eat them later if you like."

Rather than arguing with her or turning her down, I wait. She grabs a small plastic bag from one of the drawers and places three of the best-looking dark chocolate chip cookies I've ever seen in it.

I take the bag from her with a smile and quickly turn to leave. I'm not in the mood for polite conversation right now.

When I leave the break room, I take the long way around the

building. Trisha was at the front desk talking to Annie, and I'd like to avoid those two as much as possible.

But my detour takes me past Stefon's office and I freeze when I see James is standing in his doorway. They're shaking hands, and they're both smiling.

Fuck. If I lost this damn promotion to the likes of Stefon, I might as well hang up the towel. That man is a tool and a horrible manager.

Stefon catches me staring, and his smile grows. He says something else to James that makes him laugh, and my grip tightens on my mug.

James must sense someone watching because he slowly turns his head in my direction. His smile fades to a deep frown. From the smirk Stefon tries to hide, he's clearly enjoying my demise.

James says something else to Stefon, then heads my way. He stops right in front of me with a look of disappointment on his face.

"Atticus." He nods with a deep sigh. "Meet me in my office in ten minutes. I'd like to discuss last week's meeting with you."

Without giving me a chance to reply, he pushes past me and disappears down the hallway.

I let out a puff of air and continue down the long hall to my office. Today is already a shit day. Might as well make it worse.

∼

JAMES DOESN'T LOOK UP FROM HIS DESK WHEN I ENTER HIS OFFICE. There are no warm greetings, no words of praise, and no signs that he considers me a valuable employee. It's safe to say I have fallen from my boss's good graces.

"Shut the door behind you and have a seat," he says without looking up. He's typing on his computer like he's too busy to be bothered with the likes of me. He's never treated me this way before.

Is it my job performance that's pissed him off or that I've been seeing his daughter outside of company time?

Or should I say, *was* seeing his daughter? Since she won't return any of my calls, I can only assume she's done with me. I plan to change that as soon as I get the chance. I just need five minutes of her time.

I stare at James, willing him to stop what he's doing and look at me. I know I screwed up, but I didn't cause any permanent or long-term damage to the company. Sure, the meeting could have gone better. Yes, the report had errors that needed correcting. But the investors were happy. They're still on board and giving us their full support for the product launch.

Overall, I am still a success. He has to see that.

After a few minutes, he finally pushes his keyboard aside, laces his fingers together on his desk, and stares at me. I've never seen him so unhappy in all the years I've worked for him.

"I'm at a loss of where to begin," he finally says. His voice is low and gruff.

I cross my legs, resting my foot on my knee. "Why don't you start with whatever seems to have upset you the most?"

His nostrils flare as he huffs out a breath. "Do you know why I hired you?"

I shrug, not really sure where he's going with this. "Because I'm good at what I do?"

"No," he barks back in reply. "I hired you because you're the *best* at what you do. I don't tolerate anything less than the best. That was not your best performance last week."

"I know I made some mistakes. Mistakes I plan to rectify. Mistakes that I can assure you will not happen again."

"Good." He nods and his expression softens. He seems to like that last statement, but I'm not convinced he truly understands my meaning. "That's what I like to hear. In the meantime, I decided to hold off on making a decision regarding the promotion. Vic will remain on for a few more months. Stefon will begin a mentoring program under him, effective immediately. And I'm giving you another chance to prove to me that you really want an executive position. If you can do that in the next two weeks, you'll join Stefon in the mentoring program."

"Two weeks?" I ask. My brow furrows as I process this. What

could I possibly prove to him in two weeks that I haven't already proven?

"Yes. That should be enough time to move past this scandal with my daughter. In the meantime, I expect you to lie low and focus on your career. I'll deal with her."

"Scandal?" I frown.

He sighs and sits back in his chair. "I apologize for my daughter's actions. I should have known better than to assign her to work with you. She's always been a bit of a rebellious wildcard. You're not the first man she's used to get to me. She's just like her mother in that regard. Irresponsible and greedy. Which is why I thought holding her trust fund hostage would be enough of a motivator, but I was wrong. She still used you to try to take me down."

"Sir, you have this all wrong. Indie did not use me."

"You don't have to come to her defense. I know my daughter well. I'd hoped that by making her work here, she'd learn to value money. With you as a mentor, she'd also learn a good work ethic. But that didn't happen. Instead, she went right back to her old tricks. Some people are a lost cause. No amount of love or hard work can change them."

I push to my feet, my frown deeper than it's ever been. My sudden movement causes James to flinch. "Forgive me for being frank, sir, but I don't think you know Indie at all. She's none of those things. She's kind, generous, and selfless with her time and money. She's intelligent and cares more about making the world a better place than she does about the size of her bank account."

His expression falls into something resembling pain. "It's worse than I feared. She's really gotten to you, hasn't she?"

"I'm not sure what you mean by that, but the only thing that I fear is working for you. I'm not sure I can work for a man that's so blind to his own daughter's character and heart. His *amazing* daughter."

"You are not resigning!" His hand slams down on his desk to punctuate his point.

"If I want to quit, you can't stop me."

"Atticus. This is ridiculous. You can't throw away your career for someone like Indie. I love my daughter, but she's not worth it."

I huff out an incredulous laugh. "That's where you're wrong. She's worth *everything*. I thought I was the only one that could screw up my chances with her, but I was wrong. You said something to her, I just don't know what. Fix it, or I resign."

I don't wait for him to respond. I turn around and barge out of his office. He calls out my name, but I don't stop. Thankfully, the elevator opens immediately, and I'm able to make my escape without further confrontation.

Rather than going back to my office, I hit the button for the lobby. Then I open my message thread with my siblings and fire off an emergency family meeting request. I'm going to need some advice and support if I hope to win Indie back.

~

By the time I arrive at Penny's apartment, everyone is already there, including Trent's brother and his husband. The fridge is stocked with beer and there are several opened bottles of wine on the kitchen island.

"Pick your poison," Trent says with his typical charming smile. No wonder my sister fell for this guy. He's always so happy. Not to mention he can cook better than most trained chefs.

"Beer." I nod toward the stove. "What's cooking?"

"Stir fry. Should be ready soon."

"Smells delicious, and I'm starving." I take my beer and head to the dining table, taking the last open chair for myself. My stomach grumbles and I press a hand over it. I haven't eaten a good meal since the gala with Indie. Food has been the last thing on my mind.

Penny is sitting in the chair opposite me with her hands resting on her very pregnant belly. I nod in her direction. "You ready to pop that thing out yet?"

She narrows her gaze with a frown. "First off, don't refer to my baby as a thing, and second, we're here to discuss your screw up."

"I didn't screw up," I say, surprised at how calm my voice sounds.

"Then what seems to be the problem?" she asks.

"I threatened to quit my job today." The room falls eerily silent at my announcement. I look around to find everyone staring at me. "What?"

"Say what?" Demetrius asks.

"My boss—Indie's father—interfered with my relationship with her. I don't know what he said or did, but she's pulled away from me because of him. I told him to fix it or else I quit."

"But you love your job!" Penny cries. When I look up at her, there are tears welling up in her eyes.

"I do. But I love Indie more."

There are several gasps and lots of shocked faces staring at me. Penny's tears spill down her cheeks. Eros and Demetrius stare at me like I grew two heads. Adonis, Trent, Toby, and Owen are grinning like I just told them the best news ever. At least someone is happy for me.

"What did he say?" Dem asks.

I shrug. "I didn't give him a chance to respond. I left."

"You just up and left?" Donnie asks. I nod.

"That's ballsy, I'll give you that." Dem holds his beer up to me and shakes his head.

"He didn't really give me a choice. He has the wrong impression of his daughter, and I can't work for him if he's going to continue to treat her the way he does."

A sob escapes Penny, and she waves her hands in front of her face. Trent rushes to her side and squeezes her shoulders.

"Hey, you okay?" he whispers in her ear.

She nods. "I can't believe one of my brothers is in love."

"Yeah." Trent tosses me a huge grin. "It happens to the best of us."

"Can we not dwell on that fact and focus on my dilemma? I may be out of a job before the end of this week. If that happens, I'd like to make sure I still get the girl. Any advice?"

"Dude! You just threatened her dad for her," Eros says, his voice laced with amazement. "If that doesn't win her over, then I don't know what will."

"He's right," Toby adds. "Standing up to an unsupportive parent screams true love. If she doesn't see that, then she's not the one."

"But she has to be the one. I've never felt like this before."

Toby's smile grows. "Then everything will be just fine."

Everyone nods and mumbles their agreement. It should make me feel better—calmer—but it doesn't. I can't fight off the little voice of doubt that's still whispering in my ear.

The only thing that will calm my nerves and soothe this ache in my chest is Indie in my arms. Hopefully, that will happen before the week's end.

CHAPTER TWENTY-SIX

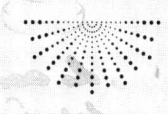

INDIGO

INDIGO

Wish me luck.

ELON

Darlin' you don't need luck. You've got brains on your side.

INDIGO

I also have a blind father that refuses to see those brains.

ELON

I guess someone will just have to work extra hard to make him see.

INDIGO

I'm not sure that's even possible. But I'll try.

ELON

You've got this! I'll be waiting with a celebratory drink in hand. Now stop procrastinating and go kick ass.

INDIGO

What if Atticus refuses to talk to me?

ELON

He won't.

> **INDIGO**
> But the last time I saw him was not exactly my best moment.

> **ELON**
> You mean when you tried to break up with the man you love? Then had sex with him against his office door. Very hot BTW. And then ran. Is that the moment you're referring to?

> **INDIGO**
> I can do without the sarcasm, thank you very much.

> **ELON**
> You're welcome.

> **INDIGO**
> Asshole.

> **ELON**
> You love me. Now go get your man back.

My belly flutters with nerves the moment I step inside the elevator. Instead of hitting the button for the top floor, I chose the one just below it.

At a minimum, I owe Atticus an apology. With any luck, after today I'll get a shot at repairing the damage I've done to my relationship with him. Assuming he still wants me after the way I left the last time I saw him.

I ignored all his calls or text messages for days. He eventually stopped. At first, I took that as a good sign. But that's just stupid. It's never good when the man you love stops talking to you.

Hell, I wouldn't blame him if he never wanted to speak to me again. Fingers crossed, I can fix this.

Apology first. If Atticus agrees to talk, then I know there's hope. Then I'll deal with my dad.

The elevator doors slide open, and I am immediately greeted by Annie's smiling face. As soon as her eyes lock with mine, her smile fades.

"What are you doing here? I heard you were fired. By your own father."

I force a smile. "Nope. Not fired. In fact, he moved me upstairs."

I don't bother telling her I have no intention of taking the job Dad is trying to force me into. I also don't bother to tell her why I'm here. Instead, I continue down the long hallway to my old desk.

My steps falter when I see my desk is not vacant. None other than Trisha, the one person who despises me the most and desperately wants to nail Atticus, is sitting in my chair. *Of course they'd promote her to Atticus's assistant.*

Glancing past her, I see Atticus's door is closed. Either he's in a meeting, or he's avoiding her. I hope it's the latter.

I don't bother to ask her if he's free. I move around the desk to open the door, but she steps into my path.

"You can't go in there." She insists.

"I can and I will."

"He's in a meeting with Leon. He asked to not be disturbed."

I roll my eyes and bite back a smile. He never shuts his door when he meets with Leon. He's avoiding her.

"I'll take my chances." I push past her and open the door. She rushes to pass me and steps between me and Atticus's desk.

"I said he can't be disturbed." She spins to face Atticus, who is now standing with his hands in his pockets and his eyes trained on me. "I'm so sorry. I tried to stop her, but she refused to listen."

"It's okay, Trisha. You can go."

"Um." She stumbles and shifts her eyes between us. "Do you want me to call security?"

He flinches and then shifts his gaze to her. "Why would you do that? Her father owns this company."

"But you said you didn't want to see her."

His eyes slowly fall closed and his jaw tenses. "I said that *you* were not to disturb me. I didn't say anything about Indie."

I pinch my lips between my teeth to keep from smiling.

"But—"

"That'll be all, Trisha," he says. His tone is professional, but it's clear what he means. He wants nothing to do with her.

If I know her, she's made daily advances on him since I left. She made it perfectly clear to whomever would listen that she intended on snagging Atticus. And she didn't care what she had to do to get him in bed.

With a huff and a glare in my direction, she leaves, shutting the door behind her with a little too much force.

"You're here," he says, dragging my gaze back to him.

He's still standing behind his desk. I take a moment to really look at him. His suit jacket is off and slung over his chair. He's rolled his shirtsleeves up in that delicious way I love that shows off his tattoos. His beard is a little scruffy. It looks like he hasn't trimmed it since I last saw him. His hair is disheveled like he was just running his fingers through it, and his tie is askew.

Overall, he looks sexy and sad. I don't like seeing him sad. Especially since I'm the one responsible for it.

"Um, yeah." I shift my gaze to Leon to find he's smiling. He looks like he's enjoying our discomfort. "I just came to apologize." I look back at Atticus, and his shoulders slump. I guess that's not what he was hoping for. "I mean, I have a meeting with my dad in like," I check the time on my phone, "wow, less than five minutes. Looks like I'm going to be late."

"Indigo, can we talk?" Atticus asks.

I nod without looking up at him. My eyes sting with tears. The last thing I want to do right now is cry. I clear my throat before I continue. "I'd like that. I have to talk with my dad right now, but if you want to call me later, we can arrange a time."

"Okay. As long as you promise to answer." One side of his mouth ticks up and it makes me smile.

"I will. Promise." I point toward the door behind me. "Well, I better go before Dad blows a gasket without me. I'd rather be present for that event."

This earns me a chuckle. "I can only imagine."

"Let's just say it's about to get fun upstairs. Hold onto your seats."

"Good. We could use a little shake up."

We stare at each other for a moment, neither of us looking away. It's as if we're locked in place with so many unspoken words between us. Our connection is still as strong as ever.

I want to rush to him and hug him close, but I can't. Not until I settle things with Dad. Besides, Leon doesn't need a show.

I turn and open the door to leave when he calls out my name. I look over my shoulder and meet his heated gaze. It sucks all the air out of my chest.

"Yes," I breathe.

"Thank you for coming. It's really good to see you."

I smile. "It's good to see you too." I give him a small wave and then add, "Oh, and I'm sorry you're stuck with Trisha. That was never part of my plan."

He chuckles. "Don't worry. It's only temporary. My new assistant starts on Monday."

"Good to know." I give him one last wave before I walk out the door, shutting it behind me.

For the first time in days, I smile. Everything is going to be okay.

∼

I STARE AT DAD'S CLOSED DOOR FOR SEVERAL MINUTES, UNABLE TO GET myself to open it and walk in. I'm not looking forward to this conversation. Not because I don't know what to say—believe me, *I do* —but because I have no clue how he's going to react.

The last time we talked, he forced me to end things with Atticus and made me promise to never enter into an intimate relationship with him again or else he'd fire Atticus. Then he informed me I'd be working closely with him until I fully understood his business.

I'm here today to tell him no. To all of it.

He can keep his damn trust fund and all the demands he makes on me just because I had the misfortune of being born to a gold-digging mom and a forever blind dad.

After today, he will no longer control my life. Either he opens his eyes and sees the real me or he'll never see me again. Period.

I take one last deep breath and open the door.

Dad isn't sitting at his desk like I expected. Instead, he's facing the large window that overlooks Central Park with his hands in his pockets. His shoulders are slumped, and even though I can't see his face, his body language suggests he's just as sad as Atticus was when I entered his office a few minutes earlier.

"I was afraid you weren't going to come," he says without turning around to face me.

"I'm only a few minutes late." I fight the urge to apologize like I usually do with Dad, but I bite back the words. I'm not sorry. I've rarely been sorry where he's concerned, and I can't continue to lie about my feelings. We're going to get it all out today, no matter the consequences.

I think he lets out a low huff, or maybe it's a snort. I can't tell. He turns to me and leans against the window. "You're never late. I was worried."

I shrug. I can't argue with him there. He's right. I may not have taken this job seriously, but I'm never late when it counts. Like ever. I'm the person that always arrives five minutes early. I can't help it. Even when I'm right on time, I feel like I'm late.

"I had to make a quick stop downstairs first," I say, more as a way to keep the conversation going than to provide an excuse. I'm done giving Dad excuses for my decisions.

"To see Atticus?"

I cross my arms over my chest and prepare myself for battle. He's not wasting any time starting in on me.

"Yes." I respond sharply, leaving no question that I'm ready for his fight.

But then the fight doesn't come. There are no words of anger. No accusations of poor behavior. No declarations of epic failures. He looks... Sad.

Are all the men in my life sad right now?

"Atticus is a good man," he says after several beats of openly staring at each other like we're seeing the other person for the first time. "He's by far the best man you've ever dated."

"We're not dating." My voice cracks and I fight the tears that threaten to form. Dad doesn't get my tears. Ever.

He pushes off the window and walks toward me. "Something tells me that's going to change very soon."

"Listen." I rub at my face to relieve the tension building in my eyes. "I didn't come here today to talk about Atticus."

"Then why did you come?" His voice is calm. There's no accusation or hints of threats behind his words. It confuses me.

"I ... Well ..." I let out a deep exhale and rest my hands on my hips. He's not saying any of the things I prepared myself for, and it's throwing me off my game.

He was supposed to tell me how much of a failure I am. Or that I screwed up a simple job in the most epic way. That I need to grow up and start taking life seriously.

"I don't want to fight with you anymore, Princess. I want my daughter back. The one who used to hang out with me at the office and joke around and goof off with her dad like she thought he was cool. Even though we both know I'm not."

When I look up, my breath hitches as I meet his glassy stare. My dad looks like he's about to cry, and I can't breathe.

"There aren't enough ways to say I'm sorry to you for my behavior over the past, oh I don't know, twenty years." He turns away from me and goes back to the window. "I was such a fool over your mother. You can't tell it now, but there was a time when I loved her deeply. So much so, I was blind to who she really was. I think it was love at first sight for me. Not for her though. All she saw when she looked at me was a payday. It's all she still sees. The day I figured that out changed me forever."

He drops his head like he's looking at something on the street. I move to stand next to him and follow his gaze. The distance is too great to make out anything specific. It's just dots of people walking on the sidewalk and cars creeping down the road.

"She used you against me so much that I turned cold to both of you."

"I know," I whisper.

"When you told me that you never wanted to come to the office with me again, I assumed that was her influence. I didn't once consider it was because you had no interest in my business. I assumed it was just another way your mother turned you against me. That somehow, she was going to figure out how to extract even more money from me through you."

I shake my head. "It wasn't either of those things. I just wanted to be a young girl. I was almost a teenager, and let's just say, teenage girls are not interested in running multi-million-dollar companies."

He lets out a low chuckle, and it makes me smile. I look up at him, and despite the smile playing on his lips, he still looks sad.

"Dad." He looks down at me. "Is it possible that we've both spent years making the wrong assumptions about the other?"

"Yeah." His voice cracks, and he clears his throat. "I think there's a strong possibility that's exactly what we've done. Especially me."

He turns to his desk and grabs a large envelope. When he turns back to me, he looks nervous. "You will no longer be required to work at my company. Your trust has been reinstated with no strings attached. You're free to live your life as you see fit, without interference from me."

"Seriously?" I stare at him with raised brows. "Who are you and what have you done with my father?"

He chuckles, and this time it reaches his eyes. He holds the envelope up and his smile grows. "This is good. Really good. If you'll let me, I'd love to invest."

I stare at it, my heart pounding in my chest so fiercely that my ears start ringing. "Is that—"

"Your business proposal?" I meet his gaze again. "It is. And it's really good. Why didn't you show this to me? I had no idea this is what you've been working on all these years. I would have helped you, Princess."

I nod vigorously, fighting back the tears. "I wanted to do it myself."

"Always so damn independent." He huffs and pulls my proposal from the envelope and flips through it. His eyes focus on something on one of the pages and an emotion crosses his face that I don't recognize. "Do you really think something like this can help Jay?"

"Yes," I say without hesitation. "He can live a normal, fulfilled life. He just needs the right support. I so wish you could see that."

He's silent for several minutes as he stares at the page. I wish I could read his mind. I've never seen him look like this before. It's ... *Vulnerability.*

"You know," he finally says. "I never planned on getting remarried or having more kids. Frannie was a surprise I wasn't prepared to handle. She's so unlike your mother. I know that, but even after all these years, my guard is still up. I don't deserve her or Jay."

"No arguments there." I laugh.

A smile slowly lifts his lips. "But I love her." He pinches the bridge of his nose and squeezes his eyes closed. "And Jay. I need to do better. I want to do better." When he looks at me, my heart stops. He's completely letting his guard down with me. That's something he's never done. "Will you help me understand? With him? With all of this?"

"Of course," I whisper. "I'll do anything for Jay."

"Even spending time with your good for nothing father?" He gives me a weak smile.

I nudge his arm. "You're not all bad. Just a little blind to the things you don't understand."

He nods and slides my proposal back into the envelope and hands it to me. "There's a letter of support and my pledge to help get you started. I also included a list of other potential donors that I think will be interested in what you're doing."

"Are you serious?" I look up at him with wide eyes. He holds his smile and gives me a single nod. "What changed your mind about me?"

He chuckles and heads to his desk. "Let's just say a certain someone from downstairs set me straight."

My smile grows. *Atticus.*

"I know I can't take back all the things I've done or change my past actions. And I don't expect your forgiveness. At least not right away. But do you think we can work toward repairing our relationship?"

Tears well in my eyes. "I'd like that, Dad."

After a somewhat awkward hug, I head for his office door. Just before I open it, he calls out.

"Indie."

I glance over my shoulder. "Yeah?"

"For what it's worth, I am sorry."

"Me too, Dad. Me too."

I give him a wave and head for the elevator. For the first time since I was a little girl, I'm leaving my dad's presence with a smile on my face.

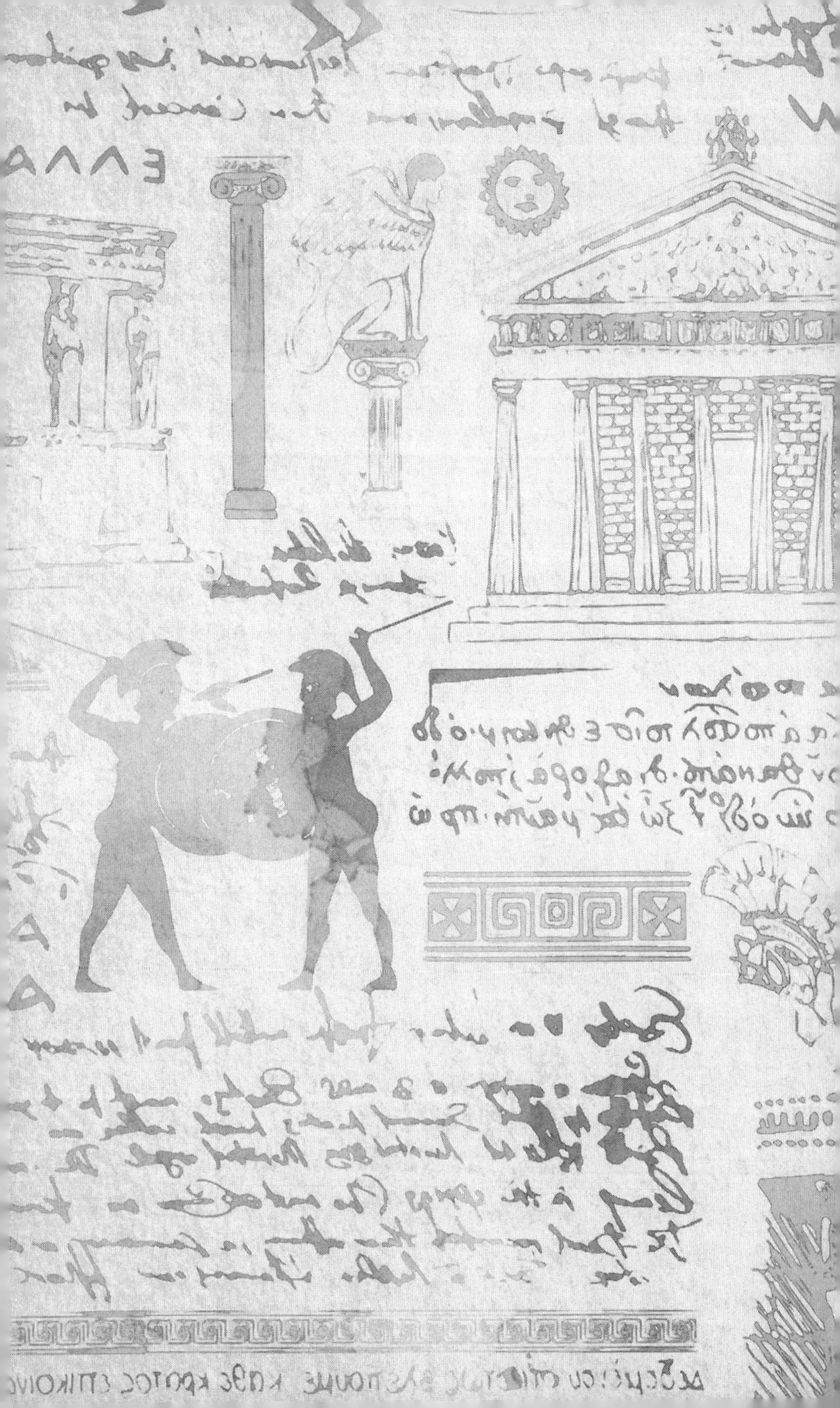

CHAPTER TWENTY-SEVEN

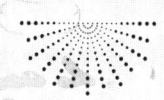

ATTICUS

ADONIS

Drinks tonight? My committee and the university accepted my dissertation. I am officially done and set to graduate.

DEMETRIUS

Hell yes! First round is on me.

EROS

Dammit, I have to work.

ADONIS

Chill out, baby brother. We'll come to you tonight.

EROS

Seriously! You'd do that for me?

ADONIS

I'm feeling generous. I don't care where we go as long as there are plenty of drinks. I am also officially done with Lulu.

ATTICUS

That's awesome, Donnie. Congratulations. But I can't tonight. I gotta go see about a girl.

DEMETRIUS

WTF

> **EROS**
> Since when do we choose hoes over bros?
>
> **ATTICUS**
> Watch it ...
>
> **DEMETRIUS**
> Isn't that a line from a movie?
>
> **ADONIS**
> Yep. Good Will Hunting. Bro can't even come up with his own material.
>
> **ATTICUS**
> Fuck off.

I stare at the door for several minutes after Indie shut it behind her. A warm, tingling feeling works its way up my body and settles over my heart. *She came back.*

After ignoring my messages and calls all week, I wasn't sure if I'd ever see her again. That hope I've been desperately hanging onto blooms into something so much more. Something bigger.

I'm going to get Indigo Simons back.

"You should see the goofy grin on your face." Leon laughs.

His laughter is enough to snap me back to reality. I shake my head and turn my focus to him. I'd forgotten he was here.

"Sorry. Back to our meeting." I sit back in my chair and look at my notes to remind me what we were discussing. "Right. I was about to discuss giving you more responsibility. Assuming you want it."

Leon stares at me, blinking like he can't decide what it is he's looking at. "Are you fucking kidding me right now?"

"What?" I ask, a little taken aback. "I thought you'd be happy about this. Did I read you wrong?"

He shakes his head. "No, man. You didn't read *me* wrong, but I think maybe *you* read Indie wrong."

I furrow my brows. "What do you mean?"

He rolls his eyes so hard I swear they're going to pop out of his head. "You're an idiot, you know that? Why the fuck are you sitting here with me when she's upstairs? She came back. For you."

I shake my head. "She came to talk to her father. You heard her."

He reaches across my desk and pops me upside the head.

"Hey, what the fuck!" I frown.

"That's for being an idiot." He points at me. I don't think I've ever seen Leon this emotional about something before. "Who cares why she said she was here? She came to see *you*. This is your chance."

"My chance for what?" I really have no clue why I asked that question out loud. I know exactly what he means. I should have followed Indie, dragged her to a private corner somewhere, and kissed her senseless. Or at least until she agreed she loved me just as much as I love her.

"Dude, you've been moping around here all week. You're miserable without her. If you don't get your ass upstairs and fix this ... Whatever it is ... Relationship? Were you two in a relationship?" He waves off his question. "Doesn't matter. Just go fix it."

"But we're in the middle of a meeting." I insist. "And she's in a meeting with her dad."

"Well, then." He pushes to his feet. "I'll make this easy on you. Our meeting is over."

"But I'm not done discussing the new role I'd like you to fill. I'm trying to give you a promotion, you dumbass."

"Great, I'll take it. But for the record, you're the dumbass."

I narrow my gaze. My frustration is rising with how dismissive he's being about this promotion. I thought he'd be excited. "You don't even know what I'm asking of you."

"Yeah, yeah. You finally realized how awesome I am, and you're ready to give me more responsibility. I finally earned your trust. Thank you. I'm flattered. With my help, we'll never miss a deadline or have to deal with a screwed up report again. I'll make sure of it. Now go get the girl before she slips away."

He walks over to the door, opens it, then waves his arms as if to signal for me to leave. I straighten my tie and walk toward him.

I pat his upper arm. "Thank you."

He smiles and nods toward the hallway. "You're welcome. Now go before you miss her."

With a final nod, I rush down the hallway. I reach the elevator just as someone is getting off. Thankfully, it's not going down. With any luck, she's still upstairs.

~

Stepping into the elevator, I hit the button for the top floor and wait. And wait. And wait. Why is it when I'm in a hurry, it feels like these damn doors never close?

If she passes me going down on one of the other elevators, I'm going to be pissed at myself. Leon's right. I never should have let her walk away until we settled things between us.

When the doors open, I rush past the receptionist's desk—ignoring her calling my name—and head straight for James's closed door. I hope that means she's still inside.

I sling the door open to find James sitting at his desk. Alone.

My shoulders slump.

"How long has it been since she left?" I ask, not bothering to announce why I'm here.

"Hi Atticus." He smiles up at me. "Shut the door and have a seat."

I shut the door behind me, but I don't take a seat. Instead, I stand in front of his desk with my arms crossed over my chest. "When did she leave?"

"We'll get to that in a moment. I need to talk to you first about your position."

I shake my head. "I don't care about that. I only care about her."

He raises a single brow. "What are you saying?"

I huff, getting frustrated that he won't answer my question. All I can think about is chasing down Indie and making her mine forever, and this asshole wants to talk about my job.

"I'm saying that Indie is more important to me than this job. I choose her. Now, will you please tell me when she left or where I can find her?"

"She left about five minutes ago. I think she was going home, but

I can't be sure." I turn to leave, but he calls out. "Wait. We're not done here."

"Sir, can this wait?" I ask. "Please."

"No, it can't." He says in his typical authoritative tone. "I want you on this top floor—with me—working beside me to make this company a better place. You've proven that you've got what it takes."

"But the meeting last week was ..." My voice trails off. I can't bring myself to say just how bad it really was.

He waves off my concern like it doesn't matter. "We already established that wasn't your best performance. And we both know why. I'm more concerned about how you've handled yourself these past few days. A lesser man—and lesser employee—would have let that get him down. You didn't. You've already corrected all the issues and the investors are happy. I'd like you to step in as Vic's replacement."

I'm shaking my head before he even finishes that last statement. A deep frown covers his face.

"You don't want it anymore?" he asks.

"I do." I drop my head and rub my hands over my face. I can't believe I'm about to say this to my boss. "But I'm not ready. I've made some critical mistakes in managing my staff. I need to fix those mistakes, show them I trust them, before I leave them. I've already put a new plan into action to make sure the right people are ready and prepared to lead if I move up."

"When." He corrects. "When you move up."

I huff out a small smile. "When I move up."

"How long do you expect this *correction* process to take?"

"Give me three months to pull together a new project management platform for my team. One that better highlights the tasks at hand and not only the skills required to meet the demands but also my team's skills. I've held my projects too close, not trusting others to help, when I could've pulled in staff that compliment my weaknesses."

The smile on James's face returns. "The plan of a true leader. I accept your request for three months on the condition that you make time to work with Vic at least one day a week. He's getting irritated that I keep asking him to delay his retirement."

"I can do that."

"Good. Now that we have that out of the way." His gaze is serious as he pushes to his feet and steps around his desk. James isn't nearly as tall as me, so when we're standing side-by-side, he has to crane his neck to look up. He loses all power of intimidation, but he still tries to maintain it. "My daughter."

"What about her?"

"What are your intentions with her?"

My brow furrows. I wasn't expecting that question from him. Based on what I've observed and the stories Indie has told me, I didn't think he cared who she dated.

Deciding to be completely honest, I say, "Well, sir. I love her. I plan to do whatever it takes to make her mine. I'd like your blessing."

"And what if I say no? I can't have your relationship with my daughter interfering with your work anymore. Look what it almost cost you already."

"No. My relationship with her wasn't the issue. My lack of reliance and trust in my team was the problem. I'm more than capable of keeping my personal and professional life separate. I'll be disappointed if you don't support my relationship with Indie, but that's not going to stop me. I'll pursue her anyway. Like I said, I love her."

He nods and squeezes my shoulder. "You're a good man, Atticus. I like you. I'm lucky to have you on my team, and my daughter is damn lucky to have earned your affection. Treat her right, and you and I will never have a problem."

"Thank you, sir."

He nods toward the door as he steps around his desk and sits. "Take the rest of the day off. I believe Indie was going home."

I don't reply. I don't even bother saying goodbye. I head out of his office and straight for the elevator.

I'm going to go get my girl back.

∽

I SHOULD HAVE TAKEN THE SUBWAY. TRAFFIC IN THE CITY IS unpredictable and never ending. I'm trapped in a sea of yellow and black cars as the cab I flagged down slowly makes its way across town.

I hope she's still home when I get there. If I miss her again, I've no clue where to look next.

After what feels like a lifetime, the cab turns onto her street. I sigh in relief when the road is clear. Finally, a break in what has felt like obstacle after obstacle determined to keep me away from Indie.

In a matter of minutes, we park outside her building. I quickly pay the driver and rush toward her door, but the sway of long, dark hair catches my attention in my peripheral vision.

I look down the sidewalk and catch a glimpse of Indie walking Beatrix just before she disappears around the corner. *The dog park.*

I take off in a sprint. She's about a block ahead of me, so she shouldn't get away, but panic still sets in. The past week without her has been hell, and I can't go another day living like this. She's it for me, and I have to tell her.

I just hope she feels the same way.

When she reaches the gate to the park, I slow my pace. I watch as she kneels next to Beatrix and pets her little head before she lets her off her leash. Beatrix licks her hand happily before she jumps from side to side, and then takes off in a run toward the doggy playground.

Indie watches her for a moment with a look of longing on her face. She doesn't see me standing nearby, so I take this moment to study her. She's so goddamn beautiful it makes my chest hurt. But that beauty is so much more than skin deep. It's her heart and personality that I find so attractive.

She also looks happy, and that makes me a little nervous. Is she happy because her life is perfect without me in it? Or is it because she felt the same hope I did when she stopped by my office?

She makes her way toward the bench behind her, but she doesn't sit. As she watches Beatrix, her expression changes. She's deep in thought.

I can't wait a minute longer to be near her, so I rush through the gate and sprint toward her. It crashes shut behind me, making a loud clanging noise. Indie's head snaps toward the sound, and when she sees me, she presses her hand to her chest.

"Atticus," she says once I'm in ear shot. "What are you—"

I don't let her finish. Without a word, I cup her cheeks and crash my lips to hers. She doesn't hesitate. She opens up for me and kisses me back. We kiss with such fervor and need. It's as if we've been deprived of oxygen for far too long, and if we don't meld together to become one, we won't survive.

Her tongue darts out first, dragging a deep groan out of me. The way she kisses me back instantly makes my cock hard. Having her in my arms again and feeling her lips against mine like this has me struggling for control. My body is begging to strip her down and fuck her right here and now. But I can't. We're not alone in this park.

My hands move from her cheeks to the back of her head. I grip her hair and tug her head to the side so I can dive deeper into her.

We're all lips and tongue and teeth as we fight for dominance. We taste each other, taking turns savoring the feel of our connection. This woman is it for me, and I can't believe it's taken us this long to get here.

We've had four months of the most intense and anger-driven foreplay. Those months feel like a massive loss in this game we played, but it didn't stop us from finding our way to each other.

She sucks my bottom lip between her teeth and bites down, causing my cock to swell to the point of pain. That one small action is enough to cause my control to snap, so I quickly pull away before I get us arrested for public indecency.

"Fuck, Princess." I drop my forehead to hers. We're both breathing heavily, and it takes us a few minutes to calm down before one of us can speak.

She slides her arms around my neck and holds me close. "You're here."

I nod. "Always."

"Atticus." There's pain in the way she says my name, and I don't like it. "I'm really sorry. I didn't—"

"Shh." I press a finger to her lips. "No more apologies. Just new beginnings. We both made mistakes. A lot of them. I'm far from perfect, and I'm sure I'll make more mistakes, but if you'll have me, I'd like a chance to prove to you that we belong together."

She stares at me with conflict and doubt in her eyes. "But what about your job? My dad? Can we really make this work?"

I cup her cheek and press a light kiss to her lips. "Of course we can make this work. Your dad loves me."

This earns me a laugh. "Good to see your confidence and cockiness are still intact."

I shrug. "Why shouldn't I be? He gave me his blessing. Not that I needed it, and I told him that too. You're mine and I'm not going to let anything get in the way of us."

Tears well up in her eyes as she looks up at me. "You talked to my dad?"

"Yeah. Told him I love you, and that I'm going to pursue you no matter what he says or does. He can't stop me from being with the woman who owns my heart."

Her tears break free, and I wipe them away with my thumb. "No one has ever stood up to my dad for me."

"Baby, I'll stand up to anything that gets in my way of being with you. You're mine, and I'll go to war with anyone or anything that tries to take you away from me."

"Oh my God, I love you." She kisses me hard and with so much force and love and ownership. Like she's afraid she'll lose me if she doesn't stake her claim on me right now.

As if that could ever happen.

"Baby," I whisper against her lips. "Do you think we could collect Beatrix and head back to your apartment? My dick can't handle much more of this. I need to fuck you senseless."

She chuckles. "Yes, please."

CHAPTER TWENTY-EIGHT

INDIGO

INDIGO

Is this what heaven is like?

ELON

I wouldn't know. I've never been invited. Not sure I'd make it past the pearly gates even if I begged.

INDIGO

Yes, you would. You're one of the best people I know.

ELON

Meh, tell me why you think you're in heaven.

INDIGO

Gawd, he takes such good care of me. I know it's only been two weeks. But he cooks and cleans. HE CLEANS!!! I didn't know men like him existed.

ELON

So he's still staying at your apartment every night?

INDIGO

Yeah. He kind of just came over with a bag and never left. In fact, he now has a place in my closet.

ELON

Are you okay with that?

> **INDIGO**
> Yes! I am more than okay with it. I think I want to make it official. Is it too soon to talk about him moving in?

> **ELON**
> Sounds like he already has.

> **INDIGO**
> Elon! Tell me if this is too soon?

> **ELON**
> Darlin' relax. Stop thinking you have to play by a set of rules. This is love. There are no rules. All that matters is you're both happy and on the same page.

> **INDIGO**
> I think we are.

> **ELON**
> Then there you go.

A shiver runs through me from the cool morning air. All that covers my naked body is a thin sheet. I roll over, seeking Atticus's body heat, but his side of the bed is empty.

I groan as my eyes slowly blink open. The morning sun is filtering around the blinds, which means Atticus is probably getting ready for work. I listen intently to pinpoint where he is. The light is shining from the crack below the bathroom door, and I think I hear the shower running.

I debate on grabbing the covers that are bunched up at the foot of the bed and curling under them to get a little more sleep. I don't have to be anywhere until ten.

But then I picture his hard body under the spray of the shower head and a smile lifts my lips. Slipping into the shower with him sounds like a lot more fun than sleeping.

I crawl out of bed and make my way across the room. As soon as I open the bathroom door, his eyes find mine. A huge smile spreads across his face. He opens the shower door and crooks his finger to call me over.

"I need to brush my teeth first," I say as I step inside.

"I don't give a shit about that. Get over here."

His demand instantly excites me, and my body fully wakes up and is aroused. Then again, it doesn't take much for this man to arouse me. We've both been insatiable since we officially got together.

I step toward him, and as soon as I'm within his reach, he grabs hold of me and pulls me toward him. Before I can even catch my breath, I'm flush against his chest and his mouth is on mine.

He lifts me into his arms, and I wrap my legs around his waist. His hard cock finds my center like a heat missile. And dammit if I'm not on fire for this man. Then he spins me around, presses me against the shower wall, and enters me in one hard thrust.

My head falls back, and his mouth finds my neck. He licks and sucks and kisses me with every hard pump he makes inside my body. He fits me so perfectly that his hard length finds that spot deep inside me without fail every single time. Before I even catch my breath, my release builds.

He adjusts his hips so his cock rubs my clit as he thrusts. The added friction with his deep penetration sends me over the edge. This man can make me come faster than my toys.

Magical fucking penis.

"Fuck, Princess. You suck me so hard." He groans and his movements become more erratic as his orgasm peaks.

His crude words drag my orgasm out until we're both coming together. He's such a dirty talker in bed and demands so much from my body that he often leaves me feeling like a limp noodle. I absolutely love it.

As his body stills, he kisses me tenderly and lovingly. It's in complete contrast to the way he just fucked me. It means now he's going to make love to me. Slow and easy and intimate.

This is when our connection becomes so much deeper than just the physical way our bodies fit together.

This is when our souls come together, and we truly become one.

∽

By the time I'm dressed and walk into the kitchen, Atticus already has breakfast served and is pouring me a cup of coffee. His shirt sleeves are still rolled up, showing off his delicious arm porn, and he hasn't put on his tie. He's so sexy when he's half put together.

He must hear me approach because he turns around with a smile and hands me my coffee. I take it from him and press up on my tiptoes to give him a kiss. "Thank you."

"I made you an egg, cheese, and bacon bagel too."

He slaps me on the ass as I head to the table. "You're too good to me, you know that?"

He chuckles. "So I shouldn't tell you I packed you a lunch too?"

I turn to him and my jaw drops. "You didn't."

His smile is so wide and big I swear my heart flips over in my chest.

"I did." He nods toward the purple lunch bag sitting on the counter. "You said you were too busy for lunch today. I can't have you skipping meals."

"Okay, that's it. You have to marry me." The words tumble out of me before I have a chance to rethink them and filter my brain. I slap my free hand over my mouth and gasp. His smile fades slightly, but his eyes darken. "I mean, not marry me, marry me. I'm just saying if you keep spoiling me like this, I'm liable to lock you up and never let you go."

He steps close to me, takes my coffee from my hand, and sets it on the counter. Then he places his hands on my hips and tugs me close to him. "Someday, when the timing is right, I will ask you to marry me. Glad to know that's something you're open to."

I nod like a dumbstruck fool trapped in a trance. *Did he just say what I think he said?*

As if he can read my mind, he says, "Yes, you heard me correctly, Princess. One of these days, I'm going to make you my wife."

"Oh, okay," I whisper. He chuckles and presses a kiss to my lips.

"Let's eat. I have to leave soon, and I'd like to have breakfast with my girl before I do."

A little lightheaded and woozy from that admission, I fumble toward the table.

We sit beside each other like we always do. Neither of us ever sits at the head of it. We prefer being close.

I glance around the table and take a deep breath. The smell of eggs and bacon causes my mouth to water. He even poured us each a glass of orange juice. The entire scene is so domestic and unfamiliar. My family never ate meals like this. Not even before my parents divorced.

I look over at Atticus just as he takes a bite of his own sandwich. Looking at him now, I can't believe there was a time I thought I hated him. I was so blinded by Dad's interference in my life, I couldn't see the wonderful man in front of me.

"Don't forget, we're having dinner with my dad tonight."

"I remember," he says around a bite of food. After he swallows, he downs half his juice. "I can't wait to meet Jay. I hope he's not too nervous."

"Oh, he's nervous. I've never brought a boy over before—his words—and he's afraid his protective skills will suck. Also his words."

This drags a laugh out of Atticus. "I'll be sure to act scared."

"That will probably make his entire month. He's been working hard on using his words to speak his mind. He plans on practicing on you."

He raises a brow. "Why me?"

I shrug. "I'm his only sister. He thinks it's his responsibility to make sure you're deserving of me."

He leans over and kisses my cheek. "I can't wait to prove myself to him."

∽

As soon as I open the door to Dad's penthouse, Jay comes running toward me with a huge smile on his face. When he spots Atticus behind me, he falters, slows his steps, and schools his expression. It's as if he just remembered he's supposed to play the role of the protective little brother.

I chuckle and rush toward him. "Give me a hug first, then you can interrogate Atticus."

He wraps his arms around my waist and hugs me tight. I love hugs from this kid.

"You ready to meet my boyfriend?" I whisper so only he can hear me. He nods and extracts himself from our embrace. "Jay, this is Atticus. Atticus, this is my brother Jay. Short for James, after our dad."

Atticus holds his hand out for a shake. Jay stares at it for a moment before he tentatively lifts his hand and takes it in a firm grip. It's faint, but I see Atticus's brows tick up slightly in surprise. My brother's grip must be stronger than he expected.

"It's very nice to meet you. Indie has told me a lot about you."

"Huh," Jay says. "She hasn't told me anything about you."

"Is that so?" Atticus looks at me. This time there's no denying the lift in his brows.

I chuckle. "Yeah, well. You haven't come up during any of my visits."

"Is it true you work for our dad?" Jay asks.

Atticus turns his attention back to my brother. "Yes. I'm one of his senior managers."

"Hmm." Jay crosses his arms over his chest and glares up at him. "Are you in this relationship for my sister or to get closer to our dad?"

Atticus matches his stance, but his expression is softer. "For your sister. She's my priority."

I can't help but smile at that. I lean closer to him and rub my hand on his back.

"What if Dad tries to make you quit seeing her?"

"Jay!" I say in shock. "What kind of question is that?"

They both ignore me.

"He already tried that." Atticus answers him. "I told him not a chance. She's more important to me than a job."

My eyes snap up to his, but his focus is solely on Jay. Tears sting my eyes, but I fight them off. I didn't know Dad tried to stop him from seeing me the same way he tried to get me to break up with him. Only I did as Dad requested.

I thought I was protecting him and his job. In the end, it didn't matter. Atticus did what he wanted to do, regardless of my efforts.

I'm grateful for that. It means I get to keep him.

Jay narrows his eyes, but he's fighting back a smile. He likes Atticus. I can tell.

"What are your intentions?" Jay asks. "Are you going to marry my sister?"

"Jay!" I yell.

Atticus laughs, and for the first time since we arrived, he looks at me. He slides his arm around my waist and tucks me into his side before he kisses my forehead.

"Yes," he says simply. Then he turns back to Jay. "Any more questions?"

"Are you going to ask our dad for permission first?"

Atticus snorts. "No. Why would I? The only person I need a yes from is your sister. She's all that matters to me."

Jay stares at him for a moment longer before he looks at me and shrugs. "He can stay. I like him."

Atticus chuckles, and I roll my eyes. "Thanks. So glad you approve."

My tone is sarcastic, but I'm really happy to hear Jay say that. He's important to me, and I want him and Atticus to get along.

I look up at Atticus to find him smiling down at me. He cups my cheek and gives me a chaste kiss. "That went well. Don't you think?"

I nod. "Why didn't you tell me Dad tried to stop you from seeing me?"

He shrugs. "Does it really matter anymore? I changed his mind, and now you're mine. Nothing is ever going to change that."

I turn into his embrace and cup both his cheeks. "I love you."

"Love you too, Princess." He kisses me again.

For the first time since I was a little girl, I feel like my life is on track. My relationship with my dad is not perfect, but we're both working hard to repair it. Jay is finally getting better now that Dad is taking his treatment seriously. I'm finally in the position to start my foundation. Mom is still Mom, but I don't think anything will ever change how she is.

But most importantly, I have a man I love who loves me back.

It's amazing how freeing the love of a good man can be.

As long as I have Atticus, everything else will always work itself out.

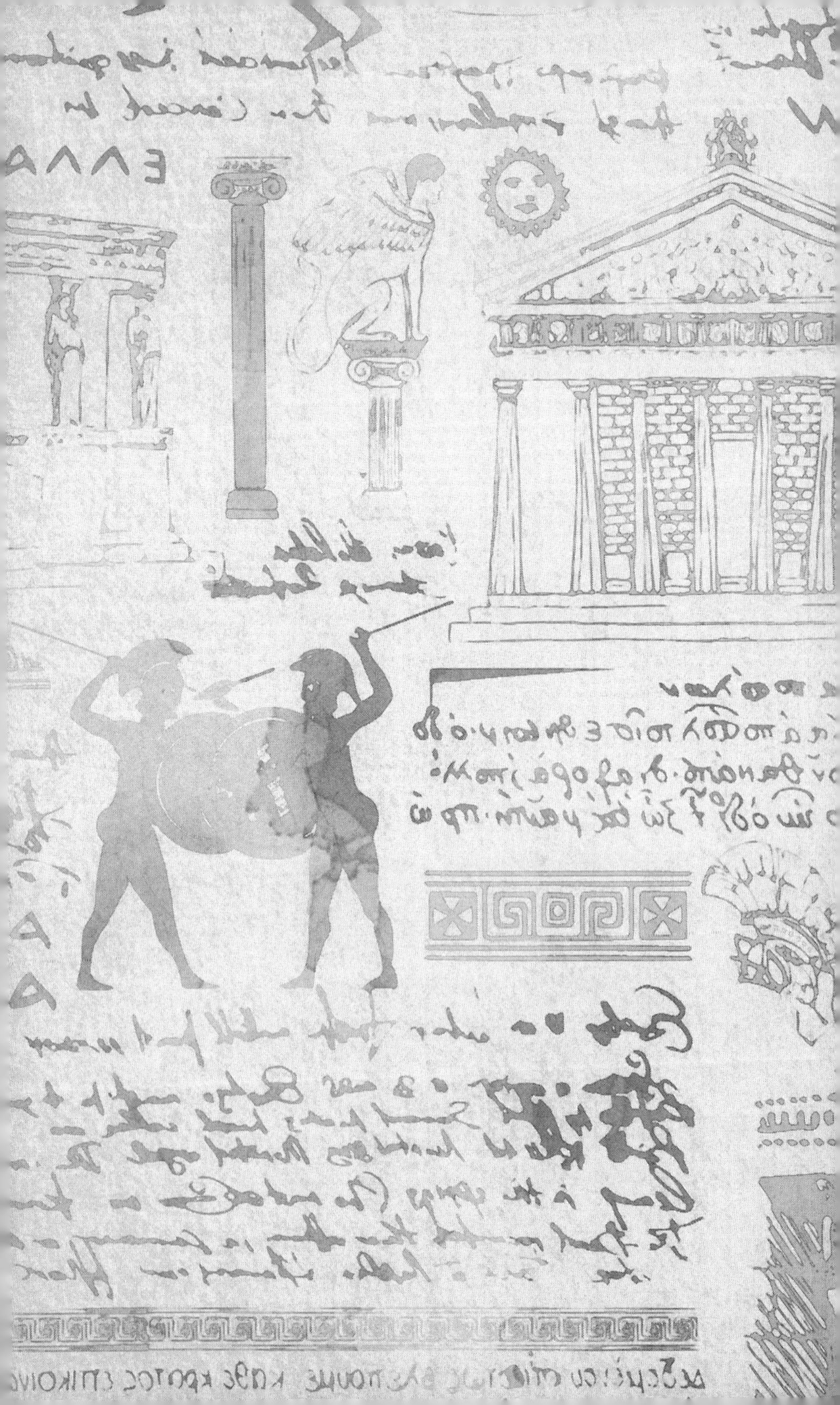

EPILOGUE

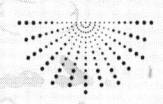

INDIGO

INDIGO
Where are you?

ATTICUS
Getting ready for our date.

INDIGO
But where? You're not at home and you said we'd leave in less than an hour.

ATTICUS
I am well aware of what we discussed. I will be there on time.

INDIGO
I am so confused right now.

ATTICUS
{laughing emoji} Don't worry, Princess. This is our first official date, and I'm picking you up like a good date should.

INDIGO
You don't have to do that. We already live together.

ATTICUS
So what? Prepare to be wooed.

INDIGO

> I already am, love.

I can't stop pacing the floor. I expected Atticus to be home when I got here, and his absence makes me nervous. Tonight will be the first time we've gone out on a private date, just the two of us.

I had it all planned out in my head how it would start. I'd come home and find him waiting for me sitting on the couch watching TV. We'd shower together, get dressed together, and leave together.

We can't do anything together if he's not here.

I check the time again, and I've got less than five minutes before he said he'd be here. I rush to the bathroom and check my hair and makeup one last time. I don't know why I keep checking it. It hasn't changed since the last time I checked it. Like, three minutes ago.

I'm nervous and anxious about what he has planned. He's been elusive about our date ever since we set it. He wouldn't even let me have a say in the restaurant. He just told me to be prepared for the best date of my life.

Newsflash, buddy. Any date with you automatically skyrockets to the top of the best date list. I don't need to be wooed. I just need his love.

I apply another layer of lipstick and dab the excess off just as there's a knock on the door. I squeal in excitement.

"He's here," I whisper to myself with a broad smile.

I take off in a sprint toward the front door. At first, I thought this charade he's playing was silly. He lives here. He has a key and can let himself in. But the excitement and anticipation building inside me has me changing my mind.

It's been a long time since a man picked me up for an actual date, and I can't wait to see what Atticus has planned.

When I reach the door, I pause, take a deep breath, and try to calm my excitement. It doesn't really work.

I run my hands down the skirt of my dress, put on what I hope is a sane smile, and then open the door. Whatever calm I'd managed to find vanishes as soon as I see him.

My smile covers my entire face and I clasp my hands together in excitement. He looks deliciously yummy in a nice dress shirt with his sleeves rolled up so I can see his tattoos just the way I like it. He's wearing nice dress pants with a matching vest. I let it slip once that this was my favorite look on him. Sexy professional looks good on him.

He's holding an embarrassingly large bouquet of blue, red, and white roses in one hand and a bag of gummies in the other. I swoon.

"Hi," I whisper.

His eyes rake down my body, leaving a trail of hot white flames in his wake. I'm wearing one of his favorite dresses. It's a pale pink one shouldered number with an open back and flowy skirt. I paired it with my favorite high-heeled shoes that add three inches to my height.

He steps forward and slides his arm around my waist. "Hi beautiful."

He presses a light kiss to my lips. I run my hands up his chest and let my fingers curl around his vest. I want to pull him closer and deepen the kiss, but he pulls back before I can.

"I want to mess you up so badly, but if I do that, we'll miss our reservation."

"I'm not opposed to staying in."

He shakes his head and frowns. "No way. I'm taking you out tonight. We've got plenty of time for …" his eyes roam down my body again, "other things later."

He steps back and holds the bouquet out for me. "These are for you."

I smile and hold them close to my face to breathe in their scent. I love fresh flowers—any kind—but these are particularly beautiful. "I love them. Thank you." I turn toward the kitchen to dig out a vase. "I don't think I've ever seen blue roses like this before."

I turn to look at him and he's rubbing his hand around his neck like he's nervous. "The florist told me blue roses signified trust and commitment. Something I promise to always give you." He steps up next to me and takes my hand. "White is loyalty. I will always put you first, Princess. And red, well that should be obvious. Love."

My heart flutters in my chest and I swoon so hard I fall against him. This man is my everything.

I sling my arms around his neck and press up on my tiptoes so I can kiss him. "I love them, but not nearly as much as I love you."

"Good." He gives my ass a playful slap and kisses me back. "Now let's go before we miss our reservation. I have a car waiting, and he's double parked."

I grab my clutch from the counter and meet him by the door. "Where are you taking me?"

He takes my hand and locks the door behind me. As he leads me down the hallway toward the elevator, he lifts my hand to his lips and smiles. "It's a surprise, baby. Patience."

I give him a goofy smile as my excitement rises. I've been bouncing around all day in anticipation, and I've no clue how I can get any more excited than I already am.

"I love surprises," I say as I lean into him.

"I know." He chuckles. "Hopefully, this one lives up to all the hype."

"I'm sure it will be amazing."

Shortly after I'd introduced him to Jay, he surprised us with a trip to Luna Park in Coney Island. He had coordinated the day with Jay in advance and surprised me with it. That was the day he learned how much I love surprises.

Ever since, he's tried to find little ways to surprise me. Sometimes it's with a nice home cooked dinner or a small gift or in the little things he does for me like clean. I still can't get over the fact that he cleans.

When we step out on the sidewalk, there's a man standing by a black town car with the door opened. "Good evening, Miss Simons."

"Hello," I say a little breathless as Atticus helps me inside. Once we're both seated, our driver shuts the door and gets in behind the wheel. My eyes widen when I see the bottle of champagne in the bucket of ice affixed to the center dash. "What's this?"

I look up at Atticus as he leans forward and fills two glasses. He hands one to me then wraps his arm around me and tucks me into his side. "I thought it would be nice to share a drink on our way to the restaurant. This is Veuve Clicquot. I heard it was your favorite."

I stare at him in awe. "You heard correctly."

We clink our glasses together and drink. In addition to the champagne, there are more roses in the car. He plucks one of the red roses from the bouquet and hands it to me.

"For you, my love."

"Thank you." I bring it to my nose and sniff. "I love the smell of roses."

He leans in close to my neck and breathes me in. "I love the smell of you."

I cup his cheek and press my lips to his. "You smell pretty good yourself."

We mostly drink in silence as we make our way to the restaurant. He keeps his arm around me, and I lean against him. It's sweet and loving, and while it causes my body to stir with arousal, there isn't anything sexual about our interaction. That's not what this date is about. At least not yet.

About thirty minutes and almost two glasses of champagne later, the car comes to a stop. A moment later, the driver opens the door to let Atticus out. He reaches in for my hand to help me out next. When I see where we are, I gasp.

"Oh my God. This is my favorite restaurant."

"I know." He smiles, looking very proud of himself.

"How did you know?"

"I have my ways." He gives me a quick kiss then leads me to the door of L' Atelier.

L' Atelier is a picturesque French style restaurant with an atmosphere perfect for a quiet romantic dinner. It has a large center circular bar built upon racks of wine. One side of the restaurant is arranged with larger tables and booths to accommodate parties of four or more, while the other side is filled with tables and booths for two. The overhead lights are dim and each table flickers with the flame of a single candle.

The far wall is lined with wine racks and there are several support posts throughout the restaurant that also contain geometric shelves designed to stack wine bottles in an artistic display.

L'Atelier is as much a high-end wine cellar as it is a restaurant, which is one of the reasons I love it so much.

"I can't believe you brought me here," I whisper to him as the hostess shows us to a quiet table near the back. It's set apart from the others, giving us added privacy.

L'Atelier is not cheap. A dinner here for two will set him back at least five hundred dollars. A separate table like this will cost extra.

He pulls out my chair and waits for me to sit before he leans down and kisses my neck just below my ear. "Only the best for our first date."

That drags a laugh out of me. "I still can't believe we've been living together for weeks now, and this is our first official date. How crazy is that?"

"Pretty crazy. Which is why I pulled out all the stops. I want tonight to be perfect."

I reach across the table and squeeze his hand. "I'm with you. It's already perfect."

Then a loud shrill fills the room, and I gasp. "Shit. I forgot to silence my phone."

I dig it out of my purse and immediately silence it. Then I frown when I see who it's from.

"What's wrong?" Atticus asks.

"It's your sister." I say as I swipe to answer. "Hello?"

"Thank fuck," a male voice says. "Where's Atticus?"

I furrow my brows. "Who is this?"

"Oh, sorry. It's Demetrius. I've been trying to call Atticus for the past forty-five minutes and he's not answering his phone. Do you know where he is?"

"He's with me. We're out for dinner."

"I'm sorry to ruin it for you, but Penny Love is in labor."

"In labor!" I say way too loudly. I meet Atticus's wide eyes and he's on his feet with his phone in his hand before I can even ask my next question. "Where are you?"

Demetrius gives me the name of the hospital while Atticus reads through all his missed messages.

"Shit. I have over thirty missed texts and ten phone calls," he says.

"Come on. Let's go." I take his hand and lead him through the restaurant toward the front door.

"Indie, wait." He stops causing me to stumble back. "We can eat dinner first. I doubt the baby will come that fast."

I look up at this amazing man and cup his cheek. "Your family is important to you. I wouldn't dream of asking you to stay. You need to be there for her. For all of them."

He pulls me flush against him and kisses me hard. His tongue parts my lips and he tastes me before he pulls away. "Have I told you how much I love you?"

"You have. But you can tell me as often as you like. I love hearing it."

"I promise. One of these days, I'll treat you to a nice date."

"I know, and I'm sure it'll be the best date of my life when it happens. Now let's go meet your niece or nephew."

∼

Twenty minutes later, our car pulls up outside the hospital. Atticus spent most of the drive on the phone with his brother while clenching my hand tight. He's nervous for his sister, and I think it's cute. She's in great hands and her pregnancy has been ideal. There's no reason for concern.

Once inside, we get directions to the waiting room for maternity on the third floor. The elevator ride is quick and opens up to a large room. We see his brothers immediately.

Atticus takes two steps and freezes. "Mom? Dad?"

My eyes widen as I look past his brothers to an older couple behind them. The man is tall, with dark hair with a dusting of gray.

He shares the same chocolate-brown eyes as Atticus. The woman is also tall, with long blond hair that is mostly gray, in a single braid tossed over her shoulder. They're both wearing matching wide smiles.

"Surprise," his mom says with open arms.

"What are you doing here?" Atticus asks with nothing but admiration in his tone. "Why didn't you tell me you were coming?"

"We wanted to surprise you kids. Timing works out perfectly with Penny Love, doesn't it?" She pats Atticus's cheeks like he's a little boy then her eyes fall to me. Her smile broadens. "And who is this beauty?"

"Um, Mom." Atticus rubs the back of his neck the same as he always does when he's nervous. "This is Indie. My girlfriend."

"Girlfriend!" She gasps. "No one told me you had a girlfriend."

Her eyes shift between us as tears well up in them.

"Mom, don't get all emotional on us," Atticus says. "This isn't a reason to cry."

"Don't tell me not to get emotional. One of my sons has a girlfriend that I'm meeting at a very important family event. That means this is serious."

Atticus's eyes find mine and he gives me a loving smile that says it all. "Yeah, Mom. It's serious."

He moves to my side and takes my hand. "Mom. Dad. Meet Indie. Indie, these are my parents, Jane and Basil Rosi."

I hold out my hand for a shake, but Jane ignores it. She pulls me in for a tight hug. "It's so nice to meet you."

Before I can get a word in, I'm passed off to Basil and he's hugging me tight. "It's about time my oldest boy found a woman to keep him straight. Welcome to the family."

"Um, thanks," I say because I don't know what else to say. This is all so very different from my family.

Atticus pulls me back to his side as if he's trying to protect me from them. It makes me laugh. "Don't scare her off. I like this one and want to keep her."

His words cause my chest to flutter and my stomach to feel light.

If he only knew what he did to me, he'd never worry about losing me.

Before anyone else gets a chance to speak, Trent enters the room in scrubs, a huge goofy grin, and tears in his eyes. "Mom and baby are perfect. It's a girl."

Cheers fill the room and countless hugs get passed around. Trent takes his mom and Penny's parents back first to meet the new addition. After what feels like an eternity, Trent leads Atticus and me back to the room.

Penny is sitting up in the bed, looking unfairly beautiful for someone who just gave birth. She's holding her new daughter, wrapped in a pink blanket, in her arms.

"Come meet your niece," she says to Atticus. She holds the baby out for him. "Her name is Athena."

Tears well up in Atticus's eyes as he takes her in his arms. It takes my breath away. Seeing the man I love cry just might be the sexiest thing I've ever seen. Not to mention, he looks so good holding a baby.

He looks over at me, and waves me over. "Isn't she perfect?"

"Yeah, she is." I rub his back and peer down at her. She's got the cutest little button nose and a head full of long dark hair. Her little mouth opens in a yawn and then she snuggles her face closer to Atticus's chest. Talk about swoon.

"Do you want to hold her?" he asks.

"Yes," I don't hesitate to take her from him.

I cradle her in my arms. Her little hand pokes out from the blanket and I take it mine. She wraps her tiny fist around my finger and squeezes. Her skin is so soft and delicate. Everything about her is precious and pure and wonderful.

Atticus rests his chin on my shoulder and kisses my cheek. "You look good with her in your arms," he whispers. "It's giving me all sorts of visions of our future."

I glance over at him and meet his heated gaze. "You think about having kids with me?"

"Princess, I think about having everything with you." He presses a kiss to my lips, and then walks over to Trent to shake his hand.

He's so calm and collected. It's like he's completely unaffected by the fact that he just told me he thinks about having kids with me.

My heart is pounding so hard that I'm amazed Athena is still asleep in my arms. I look back down at her and let my imagination run.

I can see it all. A happy life with him and at least three kids running around raising havoc. Knowing my luck, they'd all be boys just like him. Cocky, demanding, and a little rebellious.

It sounds like the perfect life, and I can't wait to start living it.

∽

WANT MORE **ATTICUS AND INDIGO**? CLICK HERE (https://ariabliss.com/bonus-content-sign-up/) to get your **FREE** *Never Trust the Boss* bonus scene for a sneak peek into their future.

∽

DON'T STOP NOW. CHECK OUT ARIA'S OTHER SERIES, THE MUTTER Brother's family saga in *Truck Off*: An Enemies to Lovers, Mistaken Identity Small Town Romance with **Chase and Lina**. CLICK HERE (https://www.amazon.com/dp/ B0BZ2VF2JH) to grab it today. Chase Mutter is everyone's favorite Mutter brother, and everything I don't want in a man. He's a charmer, a jester, a prankster to the core. And he just played his cruelest trick on me. I should hate him for it. But I still want him, and that makes me the fool.

∽

OR DIVE INTO THE A DRUNK LOVE CONTEMPORARY ROMANCE SERIES where the Rosi brothers were first introduced! In this sweeping family saga, you'll meet the four siblings, a few of their closest friends, and their sexy, irresistible counterparts. Start at the beginning with Aria's reader favorite.

Heath and Alicia fight for love in *Not for Me*: A Fake Dating Romance

A Drunk Love Contemporary Romance, Book 1.

CLICK HERE (https://www.amazon.com/dp/ B09FJ3GSWS) to grab your copy.

BOOKS BY ARIA BLISS

The Mutter Brothers
Truck You: A Hate to Love Small Town Romance
Truck Me: A Grumpy-Sunshine Small Town Romance
Truck Off: An Enemies to Lovers, Mistaken Identity Small Town Romance

The Rosi Brothers
Never Trust the Boss: An Enemies to Lovers Romance

A Drunk Love Contemporary Romance
Not for Me: A Fake Dating Romance
Let Me Stay: A Friends to Lovers, Best Friend's Sister Romance
Lead Me Here: A Grumpy-Sunshine Romance
Aside From Me: A Roommate to Lovers Romance
Make Me Go: An Age Gap Romance

Hearts of Watercress Falls
Healing Hearts: A Second Chance at Love Small Town Romance
Trusting Hearts: A Single Dad Small Town Romance
Falling Hearts: A Secret Marriage Small Town Romance
Laughing Hearts: A Best Friend's Sister Small Town Romance
Forgiving Hearts: A Hate to Love Small Town Romance

Standalone
Good Wine & Bad Decisions: A Sexy Romance

An After-Hours Affair
In Charge: Book 1
One Drink: Book 2

You're Mine: Book 3

Charm Me: Book 4

Stuck Together: Book 5 (A Holiday Romance)

CONNECT WITH ME

Website: http://ariabliss.com
Subscribe to my Newsletter: https://ariabliss.com/sign-up/
Follow me on Amazon Author Central: http://www.amazon.com/author/ariabliss.author
Follow me on Instagram: http://www.instagram.com/ariabliss.author
Follow me on goodreads: http://www.goodreads.com/ariablissauthor
Follow me on Bookbub: https://www.bookbub.com/authors/aria-bliss
Join my Facebook Street Team: https://www.facebook.com/groups/SassySuperFans/
Follow me on Facebook: http://www.facebook.com/ariabliss.author/
Follow me on Twitter: http://www.twitter.com/ariablissauthor

AUTHOR BIO

Steamy Emotional Contemporary Romance

Aria Bliss writes steamy, emotionally charged contemporary romance with humor, drama, and big feels. She has a soft spot for single dads, second chances, forbidden romance, and grumpy bad boys with sweet centers that are impossible not to love.

Made in the USA
Columbia, SC
20 July 2023